# PRAISE FOR LINNY MACK

"Linny Mack's debut novel, *Changing Tides*, is a **captivating tale** that explores the intricate dance between love, loss, and rebirth. With a narrative that will keep you on the **edge of your seat**, and an ending you won't see coming, this **story will break your heart** and piece it back together, one beautiful shard at a time."

–Buck Turner, bestselling author of *The Keeper of Stars*

"Mack's **striking debut shatters your heart** in fourteen different ways before masterfully piecing it all back together by the end. Cape May, Sophie, and Liam, will have a place in my heart forever."

–Lily Parker, author of *The Best Wrong Move*

"A **breathtaking debut**, *Changing Tides* is a masterclass in slow-burn romance, brimming with depth, heart, and hard-won healing. Featuring **beautifully drawn characters** in their 40s, it celebrates love not as a reckless leap but as a **courageous journey**—one where finding each other begins with first finding ourselves.

–Shaylin Gandhi, author of *When We Had Forever*

"This story of two broken people struggling to heal themselves grabbed hold of my heart and refused to let go. **An ode to fate and found families,** *Changing Tides* is a satisfying, slow-burn romance that will make you believe in second chances."

–Lindsay Hameroff, author of *Never Planned on You*

"Every page of Mack's debut was filled with the warmth and comfort of found family, the **bittersweet nostalgia** of childhood summers, and the yearning excitement of new love. Her characters have found a forever home in my heart!"

-Christy Schillig, author of *Wish You Weren't Here*

# Choosing You

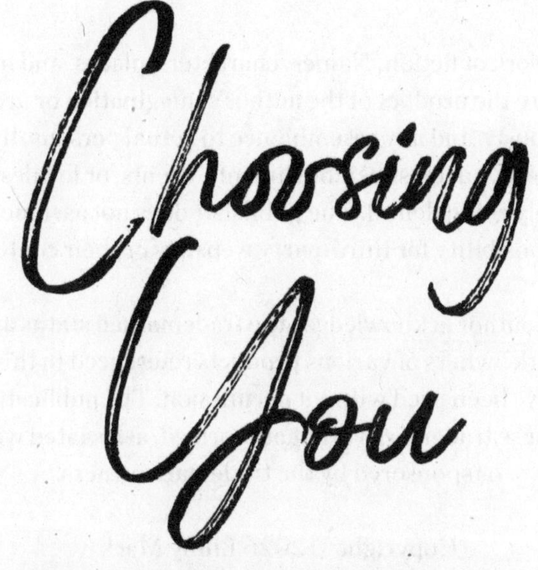

LINNY MACK

Page & Vine
An Imprint of Meredith Wild LLC



Paperback ISBN: 978-1-964264-30-1

For every author, artist, and dreamer out there just waiting to be chosen.
You are seen. You are worthy. This one's for you.

# Prologue

## Melanie

### THEN

I try the gray two-story colonial's front door first. Of course, it's locked. I knew it would be. I thought if Cara wasn't home, someone might be, and I could just hang out in her room and wait. No such luck.

"Ugh," I groan, wiping sweat from my brow. It's exceptionally warm for late spring.

I should've known nobody would be here—Cara's got practice, her parents are always working. But today my own house feels so empty, I'm actually debating whether to befriend the spider hanging out in the dusty corner of the Cotes' porch. Or worse, join the soccer team even though I can't stand sports, just so I'd have more people to hang with than my one best friend who somehow knows everyone. It's that same old ache in my chest, like I'm on the outside looking in.

I'm content each day when I pick Cara up for school. I'm fine at school, the two of us moving through our classes together, eating lunch in the courtyard with her boyfriend, Liam. It's after school when Cara and Liam have sports or activities, and I don't, that the loneliness settles in. That's when the isolation burns through me, making me feel as if I'm the last person on earth.

I plop down on Cara's front steps to wait for her to get back from spring soccer practice. She won't be back for another hour, but I have nowhere else to be. My parents are home, but they're constantly at each other's throats. I don't feel like listening to it. Cara's parents won't be home for hours, and her house feels like a vacation compared to my own. I'm an only child, a junior in high school, and I swear my parents are waiting until the day I graduate to announce their divorce. There's not an ounce of love left between them. I mean, not that *I've* ever been in love to know, but I can just tell. They can barely stand to be in the same room together.

This is usually my favorite time of year in my hometown of Cape May, New Jersey. The weather is perfect: not too hot, not too chilly. When it feels too warm in the sun, there's a salty ocean breeze to cool you down.

The hiss of a school bus stopping in front of me startles me out of my pity party, and then Cara's younger brother Josh sprints down the steps. I look up at him and smile.

"Hey," he says with a grin. "Cara's at soccer." He stops in front of the stairs where I'm sitting and leans on the railing, gazing down at me. For a sophomore, Josh has some height to him. He's taller than me by at least four inches. Sparse facial hair peppers his cheeks, and two dimples bookend his mouth. When he smiles at me, his blue eyes glisten. *Why have I never noticed this before?*

I rush to a stand. "Oh, I know." I wipe my sweaty palms on my jeans. "I just figured I'd wait for her. I didn't want to go home... I'll go." I swallow the knot in my throat and start gathering up my things.

"Mel, you don't have to go," Josh says, catching my elbow.

I sigh, meeting his gaze. "I *should* go. It's weird—me waiting for her like this." I nod like it's just now occurring to me that sitting on my friend's front porch until she gets home is odd behavior. I pick up my book bag and sling it over my shoulder, wincing with embarrassment. "Don't tell Cara I was waiting for her, okay?"

Josh smirks and gestures to my emotional support guitar leaning against the side of the porch—it comes everywhere with me. "Do you want to jam? I don't have any homework so..."

At this, I crack a smile at my friend's formerly goofy little brother. I've known Josh since I was a toddler—basically since I was born. Our moms met at Library Story Time and the rest is history. He and Cara have always treated me like one of their own.

*This isn't weird.*

I take in his relaxed fit jeans, slate blue Quicksilver T-shirt, and mussed up vans. He looks like he's always looked, but now I notice he's wearing a white puka shell necklace. A woven leather bracelet sits on his wrist, drawing my eyes up his toned forearm. An iPod sits clipped to his jeans pocket, headphones around his neck. He's changing for sure. He's growing from a boy to a *guy.*

"Mel?" Josh interrupts my assessment of him, shaking his shaggy hair out of his eyes with a flick of his head. "I said, 'Do you want to jam?' You spaced."

Josh took up guitar in seventh grade and even though I play too, we've never played together. I always keep my music just for me. I don't share it with anyone. I have a notebook I carry around with me with lyrics I jot down and when I'm feeling inspired, sometimes I turn them into songs. I have no idea if they're any good, but I do know singing and writing music makes me *feel* good and with all the other crappy things happening in my life, that counts for *everything.*

"Sorry." Heat creeps to my cheeks but I shake it off. "Sure, let's see what you've got." Pushing my wavy strawberry blonde hair behind my ear, I pick up my guitar case.

"Well, come on then." He jogs up the steps and unlocks the front door while I wait behind him. This feels a little strange, hanging out with Josh without Cara, but I think it's only because today, I am noticing Josh in a more-than-my-best-friend's-little-brother way. And Cara likes music, but she's an athlete. She doesn't get it and teases me sometimes for carrying my guitar and my notebooks around. It *would* be nice to collaborate with another musician. Plus, I'm *desperate* for some meaningful connection.

Josh leads me through the house I've been inside a thousand

times. The family's two Bernese mountain dogs, Bear and Teddy, immediately greet us with boisterous barking. "Okay, okay, hi, pups." Josh stops to ruffle the dogs' ears. They sniff us both and lick our hands and then immediately go back to lying by the back door.

I've been here often but without Cara, it feels unfamiliar. Like I shouldn't hang out with Josh without her. Like it's some kind of awkward first date. Even though this is *so not a date*. We're friends. We share a study hall. He's my best friend's brother. That's all this is.

"Do...you want to go get your guitar?" I ask, jutting my thumb toward the stairs.

Josh's cheeks turn pink. "Oh, yeah, duh. I guess you wouldn't come up to my room. That would be weird."

I giggle. "Just a little." I pace around the kitchen, looking anywhere but directly at Josh. *I will not make this more than what it is. This is* Josh.

"I'll be right back." He jogs up the steps and is back in less than a minute with a deep blue Ibanez acoustic-electric guitar in his hands and a shit-eating grin across his face. "Check this baby out."

"Wow," I breathe, reaching out to pluck a string. "She's beautiful."

I move into the living room and set my case on the carpeted floor, opening it to reveal my surf green Fender Newporter, my most prized possession.

"Yours is nice too."

I pull my guitar out of the case and sit on the edge of the couch, tuning it and plucking the strings as I go.

Josh watches me, shifting back and forth, silence hanging between us.

I look up from my guitar. "You can sit down, you know. It's your house," I tease, a gentle smirk playing on my lips.

"Right, yeah." Josh slings the guitar strap over his shoulder and perches on the edge of the armchair. "So, what songs do you know?"

I laugh. "I know a lot of songs. What songs do *you* know?"

"'Wonderwall'?" Josh suggests with a quirk of his eyebrow.

I nod. "Yeah, okay. I know 'Wonderwall.'"

My fingers find the chords, a little stiff at first, and when I open my mouth to sing, my voice wavers. I can feel Josh's eyes on me as he starts to sing along, his voice warm with a rough edge to it. The way he looks at me, the way he sings like it's no big deal. Not perfect, but real. It's like he's giving me permission. And it makes me brave. Something in me loosens, and the words tumble out before I can stop them. For the first time in my life, I let my voice pour out, unguarded.

I watch Josh's strumming fingers through my long lashes but don't look up to meet his eyes.

He beams, slipping into the riff like it's second nature and adding in a punchy rhythmic tap on his guitar between chords. The sound fills the space between us, steady and sure, and it makes me want to keep going.

Our eyes meet, and I have to ignore the unexpected tingle sparking up through my ribcage when our voices come together. We finish out the entire song in unison, taking turns grinning at each other. Something blossoms inside my chest, and I recognize it as happiness. I haven't had fun playing music in a long time. It's usually me writing sad lyrics or singing sad songs. This isn't sad. This is collaborative. This is fun. This makes me *really* happy.

"What else do you know?" Josh asks when we finish the song.

I push my lips together thoughtfully. I'm kind of an emo girl, and not many people know it. "Do you know any Saves the Day?" I bite my lip, waiting for Josh to tell me they suck, but instead he grins.

"'Through Being Cool'?" He doesn't wait for me. Instead, he jumps right into the song, strumming and singing like it's second nature.

It takes me a moment to get over my shock but then I join in, matching his melody with harmony on the chorus. His fingers expertly pluck the strings without a guitar pick, and I am more impressed than I care to admit. I stop singing, finding myself overwhelmed by Josh, no longer the little brother type he has been to me for most of my life. My fingers move instinctively, but I can't find my voice, so I let Josh's smooth melody seep into my soul while he finishes out the song.

Before I can react, we're interrupted by clapping. "Well, look at you two." Cara's cheerful voice startles us. "You sound great together." She plops next to me on the couch, still in her soccer uniform, blue eyes glimmering. Cara cracks open a water bottle, taking a long gulp before letting out an *ahh* sound. Her blonde hair is piled in a knot on the top of her head, a few stray pieces escaping. A streak of dirt runs across one knee, and her cheeks are flushed like she just ran a mile, but her signature wild energy is still buzzing off her.

"You're home early." Josh leans his guitar against the chair and scratches his chin.

"Coach wasn't feeling well so she let us go early," Cara says with a shrug. "Sorry to break up your little music date."

I feel my cheeks heat and scoff, embarrassed. "It's not a date."

"Yeah, we were just jamming." Josh's voice cracks, and I realize he may be just as mortified as I am at his sister's insinuation.

Cara barks out a laugh. "Right, okay." She rolls her eyes, her mouth twisting into a half-smirk as she treks into the kitchen, retrieving a bag of chips from the pantry. "Well, Mel, do you want to work on this project or stay here with Josh?" She drags out his name in a taunting way that only makes me more self-conscious.

I stand abruptly and move to put my guitar in its case. "Definitely the project." I shoot Josh an apologetic look, but he's avoiding eye contact with me. I close my case and walk into the kitchen with Cara before turning back to him. I pause, turning back to him. "This was fun, Josh."

"It was," Josh agrees, planted in his spot. "Maybe we can do it again."

I grin. "I'd like that," I say, because it's true. I turn to go. "See you later," I say over my shoulder.

I follow Cara upstairs, trying my best to put Josh out of my mind. It's probably just because no guy has given me attention in a *really* long time. I'm sure that's all it is.

I almost convince myself of that when Cara whirls on me, wagging a finger and frowning. "What the hell is up with you and my brother?"

# Chapter One

## Melanie

### NOW

"Same shit, different day," I mutter to myself, swiping a bar towel across the sticky counter, still tacky from the happy hour rush. Soon it will be the dinner rush and the open mic night rush.

I sigh, dreading the evening ahead of me. There was a time when I loved this job. Being a bartender means you get to talk to people, hear their stories, sometimes be their therapist. The same people come back to me, again and again, and I have come to look forward to my regulars. Except for today. Today, I am drained. I'm tired of it. Life is monotonous and boring. I am forty-one years old, single, living in an apartment above a storefront, and managing a bar. I used to think I was going places and now the only place I'm going to is the kitchen walk-in for more maraschino cherries.

"Mel, earth to Mel." My boss and friend Andrew is waving his hand in front of my face. "You good here? Chelsea has a track meet, and I missed the last one."

"Yeah." I let out a breath and give him a tight smile. "I'm good. Wish her luck for me."

"Open mic night. Should be a good one." Andrew arches his eyebrows.

"My favorite," I say sarcastically.

I've been working at The Ugly Mug for longer than I care to

admit. After high school, my life went a little off track. I thought I'd work here for a couple of months and then figure out my future. Maybe even go to college. But months turned into years. Waitressing turned into bartending, which turned into managing.

Andrew treats me well and quite frankly, I don't know what else I *would* do. I don't know what another life looks like for me. But I *am* sick of it. I just don't have the courage to find out—to pick up and try something or somewhere new.

"Why don't you sing a little tonight?" Andrew gestures to my guitar case, leaning against the stage area. "You bring that thing with you everywhere, but you never sing."

I shake my head. "It's always a full night," I say, not meeting his assessing gaze. "The bar is always packed, and the list of performers is always too long to squeeze me in."

"Then put your name on there now," Andrew urges, handing me the sign-up clipboard.

I let my gaze linger on the empty spaces, mulling it over for a moment before shoving the clipboard back at him. "Don't you have a track meet to go to?" I roll my eyes.

Andrew laughs softly, holding up his hands. "Okay, okay." Then softer, "I'm just worried about you, Melanie. You seem...sad."

The truth is, he's not wrong. Up until a year ago, some of my friends were still single so I had people to do things with. I had plans every weekend. It didn't feel like I was on my own. Gradually though, everyone started to pair off, each finding their person.

I wanted to find mine too. I tried fix ups and dating apps. And it's always the same—awkward small talk that fizzles out, or someone who's only looking for a hookup. After a while, it just didn't seem worth it to keep swiping. I'll admit, I'm lonely. When I come to work or on the rare occasion go out with friends, I put on a happy face. But continually going home to an empty apartment wears on a person.

I turn away from Andrew and tap the computer screen, distracting myself from uncomfortable emotions. "Well, I'm *not*," I retort.

Andrew is about ten years older than I am, but he's known me a long time. He knows when I'm not okay.

"Okay, I'll leave it alone." He starts for the door but turns back. "Mel? I'm always here, you know."

I soften at this and offer him a tight smile. "I know."

"Have a good night," he says. Then he's gone.

A Friday night in the beginning of June picks up fast. The dining room and outdoor seating are packed and on a wait. I'm tending bar faster than I have in weeks. Our open-mic night attracts bands and singers from all over the area since there aren't too many places offering this opportunity. Every performer gets a twenty-minute time slot, serving as the perfect background noise for a busy shift.

When things get underway, I am finally able to get out of my own head. There's no time for anything else when there are customers to be served and lines out the door. Finally, around nine thirty, things calm down enough that I can take a break.

"I'll be back in a bit. I'm going to see who can be cut," I tell Kasey, the twenty-something girl tending bar with me tonight.

"Sounds good." Her eyes light up.

I know she's hoping to get cut early because she wouldn't shut up about going to Atlantic City with her friends after this. My body aches just thinking about going to a club after working a bartending shift. *Oh, to be young again.*

"Start rolling some silverware," I say, gesturing to the quiet corner of the bar. "I'll try to get you out of here."

"Thanks, Mel," Kasey chirps.

I push through the double doors to the kitchen and duck straight into the closet-sized office. The spinny chair creaks as I drop into it, and I kick the door shut behind me. *Finally, some silence.* Just me, the hum of the ancient mini fridge, and the stack of shift schedules I don't want to look at. I check my phone like someone might've called me in the last couple of hours. Spoiler: nope. No texts, no missed calls, no nothing. Most of my friends are posting pictures of their kids' soccer games or anniversary dinners. Meanwhile, I'm sitting in a bar office that smells like fryer oil, muttering to myself.

"A fucking lonely loner," I say out loud, because apparently, I'm also my own best company. "How did I get here?"

Once upon a time, I thought I'd be somewhere else entirely. A singer-songwriter under the neon lights of Broadway in Nashville, playing sets until someone offered me a record deal. I had notebooks full of lyrics, the guitar, the voice people said could take me places. Instead, I'm here—scrubbing spilled beer off sticky counters and cutting servers early like it matters. The worst part is, I don't even know when I stopped believing Nashville was still a possibility. I still carry my guitar everywhere, but now I only play music for myself. The clock on the wall ticks slowly, a stark reminder of life passing me by.

If my parents cared, I'd imagine they'd be disappointed in me. They split up just after I graduated high school as predicted, and my mom doesn't even live here anymore. She and her new husband live on a lake in the Pocono Mountains, and I'm lucky if I see her for Christmas. I sigh, swiping a stray water bottle cap into the trash, imagining her with her new husband in their beautiful lake house. If I think about it too hard, it makes me bitter.

My dad worries about me, though. He lives locally and I see him regularly. Every time I see him, he asks if I'm okay. I think he hoped I'd eventually find someone to settle down with but...it's complicated. Now, I can't help but think it's too late for me.

A knock at the door interrupts my pity party. "Melanie?" It's Tyler, one of my best servers.

"There's a table out here asking for a manager." His voice sounds pained.

I paste a smile on my face. "Be right there."

It's another hour before I'm back behind the bar. The restaurant has quieted down, and most of the patrons are sitting around the bar, listening to various singers and bands. I'm refilling a Cape May IPA for one of my regulars when the door swings open, bringing with it a gust of air and a face so familiar to me, I think I might be hallucinating. The man is tall, easily six-foot-two, with a five-o'clock shadow and sunglasses propped on his head, despite it being dark out. He wears a tight gray T-shirt and has a soft black guitar case slung over his shoulder.

*It can't be.* I squeeze my eyes shut and then open them again. *Just someone else showing up to try to sing tonight.* I shake my head in disbelief and turn away, allowing the man to sit down and settle in before I approach him.

"Mel, can I have a refill?" my good friend Miles calls from the corner. He and his fiancée, Jenna, are open-mic night regulars.

My neck tingles and my cheeks flush. "Yeah, sure." I zoom over to Miles and take his empty pint glass, replacing it with another full one.

He side-eyes me. "You okay, Melanie?" Miles's brow furrows.

"Yeah, you look pale." Jenna reaches for my hand.

I suck in a steady breath. "Yeah. Yes. I just saw a ghost, is all." I force a smile. But when I turn around, he's still there, perched on a stool on the opposite corner, out of Miles and Jenna's sightline. *The furthest thing from a ghost.* He's perusing the menu, and since I cut Kasey, I'm the only bartender left. I have no choice but to go over and take his order.

I watch him carefully for a moment or two from behind the post in the middle of the bar. If he's noticed me already, he hasn't let on. He looks the same, just older. His hair is still that dirty blonde color with traces of honey. His body is lean but muscular, his forearms sinewy, probably from always holding and strumming a guitar. He glances up at the young girl singing a Taylor Swift song and smiles, showing his twin dimples that I never could get over. *Josh.*

It's him all right. He has aged gracefully; he's got to be forty now. Close to forty-one. I am suddenly extremely self-conscious. The makeup on my face is hours old by now, probably settled in the crow's feet around my eyes. *What does my hair look like?* I try to catch a glimpse of my reflection in the computer screen. I pull my lip gloss out of the apron tied around my waist and smear some on, then pressing my lips together, I walk over to him. *Maybe he won't remember me.*

"Hi," I say tentatively, placing a bar napkin in front of him.

"Hey." His voice comes out husky, but he doesn't look up, still scanning the menu. "Is your kitchen still open?"

"Yep," I squeak. "What can I get you to drink?" I'm desperate for a reason to turn around.

"Just a Coke, please." Finally, he tears his eyes away from the greasy laminated menu and offers me a tight smile.

"Coke, got it," I breathe nervously. "Coming right up."

I whirl around to safety. My heart is hammering in my chest like it might just break through it. My palms are sweating, and the back of my neck is tingling. But he didn't immediately react to my face so maybe I'm in the clear. I'm scooping ice into his glass when his voice catches me off guard.

"Melanie, is that you?"

## THEN

MEL,

~~I HAD FUN PLAYING GUITAR WITH YOU THE OTHER DAY.~~ WANT TO JAM AGAIN SOON?

JOSH

Josh,

I'd like that. But let's keep it between us for now.

Melanie

# Chapter Two

## Josh

### NOW

I watch the blush creep up her neck to the tips of her ears before she finally turns back to me, Coke in hand. She offers me a guarded smile. I'm sure she's angry at me. *I'm* angry at me. For so many things in my life, but suddenly, ditching Melanie twenty-five years ago without a word is at the top of my list.

"I thought that was you," she says cautiously. She moves toward me and sets the Coke down.

"I wasn't sure," I admit, "until I saw your wrist tattoo."

Melanie bites her lip and looks down at her left wrist, studying it. My sister's name, forever etched on Melanie's skin: Cara. Warmth blossoms in my chest.

"Oh," she says, looking back up to meet my eyes. "I got it as soon as I was old enough. It's her handwriting."

I smile wistfully, raking a hand through my hair. "I know," I breathe. "I'd recognize it anywhere." Then I roll up my sleeve and turn my forearm over to show her my own tattoo in my sister's honor: "Love you, bro – Cara" from my sixteenth birthday card.

Melanie is speechless but she reaches out and grazes the ink on my arm, her eyes glassy. A jolt of energy sizzles up my arm from her barely-there touch. It's been far too long since I've laid eyes on Melanie.

"You haven't changed a bit," I tell her, offering a half-hearted smile. Her strawberry blonde hair, the color of a new penny, piled on top of her head, has streaks of rose gold in it, and her blue eyes look tired, but they still glimmer when she smiles. She's wearing a short-sleeve black polo shirt with the name of the bar on it, but I'm able to see a hot pink Hawaiian flower tattoo cascading down her upper arm. Shamefully, I find myself wondering if she has any more. I shake the image from my mind. We were just kids, and unlike me, I'm sure Melanie has her life together. She's probably married now with children of her own.

Melanie offers me a grin. "Neither have you." She takes a step closer to me and leans on the bar. "Did you want something to eat?"

"Uh, yeah. I'll just do the crab cake sandwich." I push the menu toward her and take a sip of my Coke.

"Coming right up." Melanie turns and swiftly walks toward the computer, entering the order and then turning her attention to the other patrons.

I let myself watch her for a while. She is as beautiful as she ever was, her cute teenage figure filled out with the curves of a woman. She talks happily with customers at the other end of the bar, bouncing from party to party, ensuring that they have whatever it is they need. She leans against the center post, arms folded across her chest, watching the various singers taking their turn on stage. From here I can see there is no wedding ring on her left hand. Of course, that doesn't mean anything. If being in Nashville all these years has taught me anything, it's that the tips are better when you're single.

*Why am I hoping she's single?* We were so close back then. She was my first girlfriend, but it felt like so much more than that. Melanie was my first love. I feel terrible about the way I left town, but I was just a kid, mourning the loss of my sister, and doing what I was told.

Melanie doesn't look my way again until my dinner comes out. She takes it from a food runner and brings it to me herself, smiling at me. She looks less hesitant now, and I can't help but wonder why. I'm sure she has questions. I was hoping to run into her while I'm here. I assumed she'd have moved away the first chance she got, but there was a part of me that really longed for the chance to see her again. Now that I'm here, I have to say *something.* I can't let this regret linger in the air between us.

"Here you go," she says, lips curving as she puts the plate in front of me. "Be careful, the plate is super hot."

"Thanks," I murmur, plucking a fry from the plate and shoving it in my mouth to buy myself a minute to think.

Melanie doesn't immediately turn away, which gives me hope that maybe she'd like to talk too.

I finish chewing, and we speak at the same time.

"So, how are—"

"It's been so lo—"

We laugh, and it feels like yesterday, sitting side-by-side in Mr. Herman's study hall, laughing at inside jokes no one else got.

"You first," she says, gesturing to me. She moves to lean in the corner of the bar adjacent to me and I can smell her perfume. Suddenly, I'm back in high school. Her scent—cinnamon and vanilla maybe?—is so familiar to me, I could pick it out anywhere.

"I was just going to ask how you are." I flick my gaze to hers.

Melanie plasters a smile on her face that looks forced, guarded somehow. Like maybe this is the smile she gives everyone who comes in here, that doesn't really know her. "I'm well," she says quietly with a convincing nod.

"You look great," I say, but my words fall flat. Small talk has never been something I was good at, and it feels especially strained, given our history.

"What brings you back to town?" Melanie asks, knowing my entire family left the state shortly after Cara's death. My parents couldn't take the pitying looks that small-town life offered everywhere they went. They moved us south, to Tidehaven, South Carolina, where the towns are equally small, but no one knew us—traces of Cara nowhere to be found.

I sigh and run my fingers along my jaw. "You want the publicity version or the truth?" I smirk so she knows I'm not going off the deep end.

Melanie lets out a little snort of laughter. "You can tell me whatever version you want, Josh." She smiles, but it doesn't meet her eyes.

I push my lips together in a tight line. "I got dumped. By my band and by my girlfriend." I let out a huff of air. When Melanie doesn't immediately react, I keep rambling to fill the silence. "The truth is, I'm stuck. I'm supposed to be writing an acoustic album, and I can't come up with a damn thing," I admit, scraping a hand down my face.

"So, you came back *here* for inspiration?" Melanie raises her eyebrows. She doesn't acknowledge my music career, though I'm sure she knows it took off. I also know it's something she used to want for herself.

I let out a grunt, scratching the stubble on my jaw. "I came back here because it's one of the last places I remember feeling happy, despite losing Cara." I pick up my sandwich, no longer too hot, and take a bite.

"I see," Melanie murmurs. "Well, I hope you find what you're looking for." She turns away, scouring the bar for anyone who may want her attention. There's a lull in the music. Then her eyes find mine again, and just as hope blooms in my chest, it disappears when she says, "I'll let you eat before it gets cold."

And then she's gone.

## THEN

***Josh,***

***I have been having such a great time making music with you. I've never been able to collaborate with someone else. It feels really good.***

*The thing is, Cara is asking me questions, and I think she thinks it's weird. Has she said anything to you? I don't know why it matters. It's not like we're dating. And she spends all her free time with Liam and then I'm all alone. I'm tired of feeling alone. *sigh**

*So listen, this can be our notebook. Let's pass it back and forth and we can put lyrics in it or just chat, ok? If she sees me with notes, she's going to want to know who they're for. This is much less obvious. And if you don't mind, let's just downplay this for now. Maybe instead of practicing at your house, we should go to the park or somewhere else? Just a thought. Let me know what you think.*

*Mel*

MEL,

I LIKE IT. YOU KNOW HOW DRAMATIC MY SISTER CAN BE. I'M REALLY NOT IN THE MOOD TO DEAL WITH IT. THE NOTEBOOK IS A GOOD IDEA. LET ME THINK WHERE WE CAN PLAY BESIDES MY HOUSE. WHAT ABOUT THE PARK ON LAFAYETTE WITH THE GAZEBO? MEET THERE AFTER SCHOOL? 3:30? LET ME KNOW.

JOSH

PS – THIS HAS BEEN REALLY AWESOME FOR ME TOO.

# Chapter Three

## Melanie

### NOW

As the night wears on, I keep waiting for Josh to wave me over and ask for his check, but he never does. He settles in, picking at his food and nursing his soda. I can't help wondering why he didn't order a drink, but that's hardly the only thing I'm curious about. Every time I sneak a look at him, something catches me—how his hand drums the counter, how he seems settled here, like doesn't want to be anywhere else. He looks older, sharper around the edges, but somehow still the boy who used to sit on his porch with a guitar and make me laugh until my stomach hurt.

Around midnight, the crowd in here thins, and I find myself able to breathe a bit. I hover, debating whether I want the solitude of the office closet or the chance to talk to Josh. He's been here for hours, and even with my check-ins, he doesn't look like he's in any rush to leave.

I duck behind the center of the bar where he can't see me and reapply my lip gloss, sticking a piece of gum in my mouth while I'm at it. I don't usually mind these late-night shifts, but I always end up leaving here smelling like food and beer. I smooth my hair, like that'll undo hours of grease and fryer smoke clinging to it. I never cared what anyone thought before—not really—but with Josh, it feels different. It feels like being seventeen again, waiting for him to notice me.

I can't help thinking about the way he said goodbye. Or, rather, *didn't* say goodbye. He left me a stupid note in my mailbox. Didn't even have the courage to give it to me himself. I thought we were close and that he'd at least respect me enough to come by and tell me to my face that he was moving. I was stuck at home with a broken leg. I *should* be mad at him. Part of me still is. But watching him now, it's hard to hold onto it. He's here. After all these years, he's here, and something in me can't stop wanting to know why. I let out a sigh. I saunter over to him, hands in my back pockets.

"I thought you'd be heading out by now," I say, fighting the twitch of my lips.

Josh lifts a brow. "I could say the same for you." He nods toward the other patrons at the bar. "You've been hustling."

I laugh. "I've still got two more hours till we close." I duck under the bar and pull out the stool next to Josh. Surely, I can sit for a minute. "Ugh, my feet ache."

"I bet they do," he says, glancing down and then slowly raking his eyes up the rest of my tired body. "Do you always close?"

"Andrew and I take turns," I say, resting my head on my hand and peering up at him sideways. "His kid had a track meet tonight, but usually I'm off on Fridays."

Josh nods in understanding. "Got it."

"So how long are you in town for?" I ask, hoping my voice doesn't give away my desire to see him again.

"Indefinitely." His lips quirk and he gives me an easy shrug.

"Indefinitely?" I repeat, curiously. "Well, where are you staying?"

He laughs sheepishly, scratching the back of his neck. "That...I haven't figured out yet."

"Josh, it's midnight. Don't you think getting a place to stay should've been one of the first things you did?" I cross my arms over my chest, but I'm smiling.

He nods, pushing his lips together. "Yeah, probably. I didn't plan on staying here this long and now it's late."

I shake my head, fighting a smile. I can't believe what I'm about to say next.

"You could stay with me," I offer, eyeing him cautiously. "As long as you didn't turn into a predator in the past twenty-five years."

Josh barks out a laugh. "Who, me? You've known me since I was in diapers. I should've known we'd pick up right where we left off."

I laugh with him, both of us eyeing each other, years of bottled-up feelings threatening to spill over. I wait for him to speak first. Where we left off was a lot more than...this. At least it was to me.

"Okay," he says, shaking his head. "If you insist."

"Well, I'm not going to beg you or anything." I roll my eyes. "But I also don't want you sleeping in your car."

"Oh, I brought my tour bus," Josh deadpans.

We stare evenly at each other for a beat before I let out a peal of laughter. Then we're both cackling and wiping tears from our eyes.

After a moment, Josh quiets and holds out an open palm to me. A gesture of unspoken apology. Maybe even an invitation. I slip mine into his, and the shock of his skin against mine is like static—unexpected and electric. I don't let go, and neither does he.

"Are you still playing music?" he asks.

I push my lips together and shrug. "Sometimes. Just for myself though." I look down at our locked hands.

"You were supposed to go to Nashville," Josh says, his voice husky.

"That didn't work out," I mutter. "Clearly."

My chest constricts when I think of all the reasons why it couldn't have worked out between us.

He chews on his lip. "But you still play." He says it more like a statement than a question.

I gesture to my ax, leaning against the wall in the corner. "I do. I always bring my guitar to open mic nights, thinking maybe if it's slow enough, I'll get up there and play a cover song." I let out a short laugh, shaking my head. "It's stupid."

"It's not stupid," Josh scoffs. "It's slow right now. Get up there and play," he urges. "I'll man the bar."

I shake my head. "I can't. I have to go check on those guys." I gesture to three older men who come in weekly.

Josh quirks his eyebrows, a smile playing on the corners of his mouth. "They look fine to me," he says, nudging me with his foot.

My ankle sizzles. Josh is so much like Cara. Both always had the power to make me do anything they wanted. I'm not sure what that says about me, but his encouragement brings me right back to our youth. Memories flood through me and I have to fight back the sting of tears. Tears for the past and everything we both lost. And tears for the present.

"Come on, no one else is coming in here tonight." Josh glances toward the door. He's probably right. There are only about ten patrons left in the whole place and most of them are at tables, being taken care of by our closing server Lexi.

Before I can answer, Josh hops off his barstool and heads for the now-empty stage. He takes the mic, and at first, I'm sure he's going to sit down and play one of his songs. After all, he's *Josh Cote* now—rising country music star. No longer the boy I once fell in love with. Instead, I'm flabbergasted when he speaks.

"Hey everybody, we have a special guest here at The Ugly Mug tonight. She's *your* favorite bartender and mine—your own, Melanie Glick!"

It feels like everyone in the entire restaurant has their eyes on me, and the three older gentlemen in the corner of the bar start clapping and hollering my name. I have no choice but to go up on the tiny platform stage.

I look at my feet the whole walk to my guitar I left leaning in the corner. My palms are slick on the guitar neck, and I'm shaky, like I just downed three espressos. I glare at Josh as I pass, though really it's myself I'm mad at—for being terrified and yet still wanting to impress him. Josh steps off to the side, leaning against the wall with his arms crossed, amusement dancing in his eyes.

I lick my lips, my cheeks burning, and adjust the mic. Then I clear my throat. "I, uh, I haven't played anything for anyone in a *really* long time. But Josh wouldn't let this go," I murmur into the mic. A chuckle from the small crowd. *Okay, I can do this.*

My pulse is racing with stage fright but for the first time, I look up and there isn't a face in the bar that isn't turned toward me, smiling. "Let's see if I remember this one."

My hand is shaking as I strum the first chords to an old Dashboard Confessional song Josh has never heard me sing. It comes back to me, and I remember how to play it in the same way that I remember to breathe. Second nature. Suddenly, I'm right back there in the Cote's living room, playing with Josh for the first time. Halfway through the song, I look toward him. He's in the same position, but his blue eyes are piercing straight through me, and I wonder if he's remembering the first time too. I force myself to look away. I can't sing the song *to* Josh. That would be weird.

When I finish, everyone left in the bar claps and cheers. The men in the corner start shouting "Encore, encore!" to which I roll my eyes and shake my head.

I pull the mic to my mouth murmuring, "This was a one-time gig." I grin and lean my guitar back against the wall, brushing past Josh with a teasing glance. "I hope you're happy."

He follows me back to the bar, perching again on his stool. "Happy doesn't even begin to cover it."

I duck back behind the bar and pick up his glass, refilling it with Coke. I set it in front of him and turn to check on my three regulars.

"I can't believe you're still here," I tease them.

"Yeah, well, we can't believe you can sing and have never gotten up there before," Carl, the older man in the middle says with a finger wag in my direction.

"I just don't sing too much anymore," I say, waving him off and diverting my attention to their empty glasses.

"Didn't look like that to me," Bob, the balding grandfather type says.

I decide a change of subject is needed. "You boys ready to go home and go to bed?" I give them a pointed look.

They all laugh. Carl groans with a stretch. "Yeah, let's cash out boys."

"I'll be right back," I smile and turn toward my kiosk.

It's nearly one a.m. before the rest of the patrons leave, and Josh and I are the only ones left. "You don't have to wait for me, I'm going to be at least an hour," I say cautiously. "Maybe I could give you my key."

Josh waves his hand. "Naw, I'll help you. I've worked in my fair share of bars. Just tell me what to do."

I hesitate, bite back a grin, and finally hand him my sticky, laminated closing task checklist and a wet rag. "You can start by wiping down the counters and the bottles back behind the bar."

Josh cocks his head at me. "You'll let me back there with you?" There's a sultriness to his voice that sounds vaguely flirtatious. I force myself to ignore it. Josh couldn't possibly be interested in me, and I don't dare let myself hope otherwise.

I roll my eyes, stepping around him. "*I'm* going to dry storage to get some more bottles for tomorrow."

Lexi is in the back, perched on a stool, rolling the last of the silverware. Her eyes flick to me and she grins when I push through the door. "Who's your friend?"

I frown. "I'd hardly call us friends now. We were a long time ago, in high school... He moved away. I haven't seen him in years."

"Doesn't look that way to me—he's hanging on your every word," Lexi says with a smirk. Leave it to the young twenty-something to pick up on everything I don't. The truth is, I thought Josh seemed interested, but I don't want to let myself go there. All it will do is give me false hope for something that died a long time ago.

"Pshh, he is not. We're just catching up."

"What's his name?" Lexi asks, and it sounds like a challenge.

I whirl on her just as she's putting her last roll of silverware in the bin and standing.

"Josh Cote," I say, silently wondering if the name will ring a bell. I head for the walk-in.

Lexi follows me. "Josh Cote?" Her jaw falls slack in disbelief.

I spin around and narrow my eyes at her.

"The country singer?" Lexi asks, her eyes bulging out of her head.

"Maybe?" I push my lips together. Is Josh really that recognizable now? I mean, I know all about him, but for Lexi to know who he is? That's...unexpected.

"Maybe? Melanie. He's like...a celebrity. Maybe like a C-lister, but still. Tell me you knew this." Lexi puts her hands on her hips.

I fumble for words. The truth is, I paid attention to Josh's career for a long time when he first moved to Nashville. Then I stopped because seeing him follow his dream when I *so* lacked the courage to follow mine was just too painful. I guess I hadn't realized just how famous he is.

"I might've heard something like that," I admit, throwing my hands up.

"Jesus, Melanie. You live under a rock." Lexi spins around to go. "Have a good night," she calls over her shoulder.

When I walk through the door to the bar a few minutes later, Lexi is getting Josh's autograph and asking him for a selfie. He happily obliges her, eyeing me from across the bar with a slight upturn of his lips.

It's another forty-five minutes before Josh and I leave. He follows me two streets over to my apartment above an antique store. The building is sky blue and old. The creaky wooden steps that were once painted white are now chipped and splintering, but it's home. It's been home for the past five years. I unlock the front door to the shared foyer space and place my finger to my lips, signaling for Josh to be quiet so as not to disturb my neighbor. Then I push open the front door to my apartment. It's cozy enough with a gray sofa and navy-blue armchair. A TV sits on a small catty-corner entertainment center. Beyond that is a dining area and a kitchen to our left.

I head right to the linen closet and pull out a pillow and blanket for Josh. He drops his duffel bag at his feet and kicks off his shoes.

"I'm sorry. This *is* a two-bedroom, but the second room is now my closet." I wince as I say it, assuming Josh will think I'm ridiculous.

He chuckles. "All good, I'm fine with the couch." He sits down on it and hugs the pillow to his chest, inhaling. I have to stop myself from wondering if it's my scent he's looking for.

"Okay, well, wake me up if you need anything." I chew on my lip and fumble with my hands instead of meeting his earnest expression.

"I'll be just fine. Night, Mel." He shoots me a reassuring smile.

I return it and turn to go. "Good night, Josh."

"Sleep well." I hear him say just as I close my door.

## THEN

**Josh,**

**Cara was grilling me on the way to school. She keeps asking what is going on with us and no matter how many times I say NOTHING!!!! She doesn't believe me. I don't know what else to do. She's acting kind of mad but saying she's not, you know her typical huffy passive aggressive way. Maybe I should just mess with her and tell her we're banging and see what she says.**

**Mel**

MEL,

BANGING...

NO, DON'T DO THAT. I'LL HANDLE CARA. SHE'S JUST BEING NOSY. I DOUBT SHE EVEN REALLY CARES. I DON'T WANT TO STOP HANGING OUT.

JOSH

PS – THANKS FOR THE VISUAL.

# Chapter Four

## Josh

### NOW

Melanie's apartment stays dark for hours in the morning, so I don't wake up until eleven a.m. I haven't heard her moving around yet either, so I take my time getting up. I still can't believe I'm in her apartment, on her couch, after spending the night reconnecting with her. I admittedly don't want to say goodbye to her today, but I probably should find my own place to crash while I'm here.

I rub sleep out of my eyes and swing my feet around to the floor. The couch wasn't uncomfortable, but my back hurts this morning. I guess that's what happens when you're over forty. I pad into Melanie's kitchen in search of the coffee pot. The kitchen is tidy and smells like disinfectant. There are no dirty dishes in the sink, and the counters are clear. There's a small café table with a vase of white carnations on it. In the corner, a tiny five-cup coffee pot with a canister of coffee next to it. Perfect for just one person. I find myself wondering about Melanie's life. I fully expected her to be married with a couple of kids. It seems to be just her here.

I fix the coffee and while it brews, look around the kitchen and living area. She has various photos on the fridge. One catches my eye. It's Liam, with his arm around a brunette woman and two little girls on their laps. There's a photo of Melanie and her dad, and one of Melanie and Cara at junior prom.

A loud yawn interrupts my snooping as Melanie pads into the kitchen. "I thought I smelled coffee," she murmurs, glancing at me shyly.

"I can't wake up without it." I shrug. "I hope you don't mind."

"Not at all," Melanie steps closer to me so we're face to face. "No one ever makes me coffee in the morning." She puts her hands on my chest, smoothing out my rumpled T-shirt, a gesture that feels too familiar and yet, I wish she'd do it again. A chill shoots down my spine at the contact.

My breath catches but she doesn't drop her hands. "Happy to be of service," I murmur. Our eyes lock and for a moment, neither of us speaks.

Melanie shakes her head as if coming back to reality. She clears her throat. "So, what are your plans today?"

"Well, I haven't been here since I was sixteen," I say, walking over to the beeping coffee pot.

"Mugs are up there," Melanie interrupts, gesturing to the cabinet in front of me.

I reach up and grab two mugs, pouring us each some coffee. She gets cream from the fridge and pours some in hers, then silently offers it to me.

I shake my head, slurping a small sip of my black coffee. "I was thinking about exploring a little. I've got to write this album, and I need to find the inspiration." I pull out a chair at the table and sit down.

Melanie nods, taking the seat across from me. She nurses her coffee, sipping quietly.

"Do you have work today?" I ask, raising my eyebrows.

"Not until tonight," Melanie says. "I'm hoping Andrew will close though. I've been there late too many times this week."

I nod, understanding. "Would you—would you want to go out with me today? We can explore and catch up a little."

Melanie looks up at me for the first time since sitting down. When our eyes meet, my chest tightens. *What is this? Nostalgia. That's all it is.* She licks her lips.

"Sure," she murmurs. "I'd like that."

An hour later, we're at the old railroad, gearing up for a pedal train tour. It's one of those things you don't do when you're a local. I'll admit though, I'm kind of excited. The train is smack dab in the middle of nature, and I'm hoping it brings me some clarity. Things haven't been easy lately. First, Kiera dumps me, then my band. I honestly don't blame any of them. Kiera told me I'm never focused on her, only my music and myself. I'll admit, I am introspective, but I always try to be a good boyfriend. She was ready for things to be more serious, and I didn't see that for us. I had to keep pumping the brakes. I wasn't crushed when she walked away, just a little bummed out. I thought we were having fun. The sex was great; we always had things to talk about too. But I keep things bottled up inside, it's my armor, and she didn't like that I always kept her at arm's length.

My band breakup came out of left field though. I had no idea they were so frustrated with me. I always set out to be a solo artist, but I probably wasn't clear about that when we started taking off. They wanted a big tour, but I didn't. I need a break from the limelight to do some soul searching. I'm feeling lost and looking for my purpose. It's not their problem, but I thought they'd be understanding about no tour. I apologized for the confusion, but they were still pretty pissed at me. It's my face the label wants though, and I can't apologize for that. I will, however, be groveling to *said label* when I can't write this album. That's seeming more and more likely by the day.

Melanie and I step up to the check-in booth, and I dig out my wallet.

"Hello, folks," the elderly man behind the window greets us. "Would you be interested in a double or a quad bike today?"

"Double, please." I glance sideways at Melanie and offer her a hopeful smile. I hope she doesn't mind that I'd prefer to hang with just her and not strangers on a weekend getaway.

She doesn't flinch. Instead, she leans against the side of the booth, watching the swarms of tourists.

"That'll be ninety dollars," the man says. "Cash or card?"

I hand him my card, and Melanie grabs my forearm, her jaw falling open.

"Josh, we can split it." She makes an attempt to tug my arm away, but the man already has my card.

"This is my adventure, Melanie, so if you don't mind, I'd like to pay for it, okay?" I grin at her. She rolls her eyes but the corners of her mouth turn upward anyway, betraying her.

"Fine, but I'm buying lunch." She juts out her lower lip, and the sight of it does something to my insides. I'm warm all over, despite the early summer breeze.

"Whatever."

The man directs us to the old train platform where there are a couple of families and one other couple milling about. I'm surprised to find there is an empty bench.

Melanie sits first and I probably sit too close to her, but the feeling of her thigh grazing mine is too enticing for me to scoot over. She doesn't seem to notice or hear the hammering that my heart is doing in my chest, so I don't move and silently will myself to calm down.

"Are you nervous?" Melanie asks, jarring me out of my internal pep talk.

I laugh self-consciously. "No. I'm not nervous about the pedal train..." I hesitate, swallowing a knot in my throat before meeting her eyes. "It's just...really great to see you."

We're interrupted before Melanie can reply.

"Okay, folks, if you're in a two-person train, you can climb into one of these." The attendant gestures to her right. "Quad trains, you can climb into these behind me."

We walk over to the first two-seater, and I offer a hand to help Melanie off the platform and into her seat. Once everyone is sitting, the attendant explains that the train tracks loop around through the marshes, the nature preserve, and over some water before coming back to this very spot. "Now, you won't move if you stop peddling, so make sure you keep your feet on the pedals. On your cards, there is a list of animals, birds, and insects to spot on your journey. Be sure to take in the sights. They are one of a kind! Have fun and good luck!" she says, pacing the platform.

Before I have a chance to say anything else, Melanie starts pedaling, propelling us forward slowly. I join in, and we move in silence for a moment or two, both of us working hard to find a pace ahead of the others.

"I'm really happy to see you too, Josh," Melanie says it so quietly, I almost don't hear her.

When I glance her way, she's smiling wistfully at me.

"It's been too long," I murmur in agreement. "You feel like home."

Melanie smiles softly and shakes her head. "No, it's not me that feels like home. It's this place." She opens her arms and gestures around us.

"I'm not so sure about that," I say, shaking my head.

Melanie looks uncomfortable for just a second before pushing her sunglasses that are resting on top of her head down over her eyes. "So, what are your plans while you're here?"

"You're looking at them." I laugh, scratching the back of my head. "Though I guess maybe after this, I should find somewhere to stay. You don't want me all up in your space for another night."

"I don't know... If you don't mind the couch, I kind of like the company." A corner of her mouth tips upward, like she's trying not to look so hopeful.

I'm not sure why but my chest tightens. I nod, looking at her. It's a good thing we don't have to steer this thing too much because neither one of us has looked at the track in front of us. "I guess, maybe for a couple of nights. We can see how things go."

"Well, I have work tonight anyway so you won't be in my way." Melanie elbows me with a teasing grin.

"You don't have a boyfriend that's going to come knock me

out when he realizes I'm staying with you, do you?" I tease.

Melanie shakes her head. "Sadly, no. It's just me." She looks like she wants to say something else but holds back.

"Okay." I nod, convinced. "If you're sure, Strawberry Girl." I use my old nickname for her. It rolls off my tongue like no time has passed at all.

Her eyes light up and she smiles again, "I'm sure."

## THEN

*Josh,*

*I was thinking about how Cara keeps asking what's going on with us. It's nagging at me, so I started writing lyrics about it. I have never written my own songs but... I've been playing around with these words in my head. It needs a melody. I'm not sure how I'm hearing it. What do you think?*

*You're a song I shouldn't write,*

*A spark I shouldn't light.*

*But every melody pulls me in,*

*Like the way you smile when you begin.*

*It's wrong, it's right, it's something new,*

*I don't know the notes, but I know you.*

*We keep it quiet, keep it cool,*

*But every note bends the rules.*

*If you knew what I felt inside,*

*Would you stay, or would you hide?*

*It needs more though. Want to work on it with me? Also...don't show anyone!!*

*-Melanie*

MEL,

THIS IS SO GOOD. ARE YOU IN MY HEAD? FOR REAL, I FEEL THAT SO HARD. I LOVE IT. LET'S DEFINITELY WORK ON A TUNE TODAY. I'LL TRY TO THINK OF SOME MORE WORDS IN THE MEANTIME. BY THE WAY, LOVE THE HIGHLIGHTS YOU GOT. I'M GOING TO START CALLING YOU STRAWBERRY GIRL.

J

# Chapter Five

## *Melanie*

### NOW

The pedal train outing with Josh feels like a first date. I guess in many ways, it is. I haven't seen him in years and before Cara's death, I was so fixated on Josh. I stupidly thought we'd end up together back then. I thought maybe I'd graduate, wait a year for him to graduate, and we'd head off to Nashville together. But unfortunately, it didn't turn out that way. I was left reeling and alone after Cara died. I know Josh struggled too. He never came back to school after her death, and I was recovering from my broken leg, among other things I've never shared with anyone. I wanted so badly to see him, but I was literally a prisoner in my house. I couldn't force him to come see me. So, we just didn't see each other, except for the funeral, when I couldn't get close enough to him to have a real conversation.

Now I desperately want to ask why he left without a word. I want to spill everything I went through in his absence, how lonely it all felt. The urge presses at me, but I bite it back. We're only just reconnecting, and the last thing I want is to push him away—especially when I've missed him more than I can admit out loud.

"So," we say at the same time. We laugh, our gazes locked. My chest flutters, and I have to look away. I fix my gaze on the marsh in front of me.

"You never settled down?" he asks, looking sideways at me.

"Nope." I shrug. "It's just me."

"Never met the one?" he probes further, cocking his head. I can't tell if he's interested in me or just being nosy.

I sigh. I'm not prepared for the emotions that his question brings up. I shake my head. "I've dated off and on but it always seems to fizzle out. People drop off. I've been ghosted more times than I can count. I'm just...everyone's second choice."

Josh's brows push together in a frown, his lips forming a tight line. He shakes his head. "No, no way. I refuse to believe that." He reaches across my lap and pulls my clasped hands apart, taking one in his. "If I never left here, you would have been my *first* choice." His voice comes out husky.

Before I can say anything, someone shouts from the car behind us. "Wow! Look at that!"

Josh and I stop pedaling and turn in our seats, looking for the owner of the voice. We find a teenage boy, pointing up to the tall wooden perch anchored in the middle of the marsh. Sitting on the top of it is a single bald eagle.

"Wow," I breathe.

"I know. I've never seen one up close like this." Josh drops my hand, reaching into his pocket for his phone before snapping a couple of pictures. I should do the same, but I'm entranced, watching him, and wondering what things might have been like if he'd never left.

To make up for Josh buying my train ticket, I insist on taking him to lunch. The problem is, it's already two p.m., I'm due at work at four thirty, and there is a wait everywhere. That's an early summer Saturday for you. We're moseying around the mall when I get an idea. "Do you like poke bowls?" I ask Josh, grabbing his hand so he stops walking.

"What's a poke bowl?" He squints at me. *He's been in*

*Tennessee too long.*

"You know, it's a rice bowl with ahi tuna, avocado, vegetables—there's usually a dressing." I frown. "You really haven't had one?"

Josh chuckles, scratching his chin. "I haven't, but I'll try it."

"Then I know just the place," I tug his hand and lead him back up to Jackson Street. "There's a little beach hut. We can get a bowl and eat it on the beach. Then I have to get ready for work," I say, pushing down the sadness about leaving him alone for the evening. Twenty minutes later, we're walking up the path to the beach across from the fish hut that doesn't have a name. We settle in the high sand, and I pass Josh his takeout container and a plastic fork. He opens it and pokes his fork around for a minute or two, eliciting a laugh out of me.

"You can mix it up," I tell him teasingly. "Or, you can take a single bite of each ingredient. There is no wrong way."

"Why do I feel like you think there is a wrong way though?" Josh eyes me skeptically, a fork full of poke bowl hovering in front of his mouth.

"Just eat it! You like tuna, don't you?" I furrow my brow, suddenly wondering if he actually does like fish. There are so many things I don't know about him anymore.

"I do," he says, nodding. "Okay. Here goes." He shoves the bite in his mouth and makes an approving sound that I find oddly sexy before going back in for more.

"See?" I ask, giggling. "I told you." I dig into my own bowl, and we eat in comfortable silence, perhaps because this is the first thing we've eaten today, or perhaps because neither of us knows how to start talking about all of the things left unfinished.

When Josh is done, he sets his container aside and leans back on his elbows, spreading his legs out in front of him.

I do the same but turn on my side to look at him. The sun is warm up here on the high sand, and I have a delicious urge to curl into Josh and take a nap. I let myself wonder again what might've happened if Cara had never died. If Josh had never left. We planned on telling her about us after the football game, the night of the accident. But I also had things to say, and I never got the chance.

I drove with Liam and Cara to the game because that's what we always did. It would've been weird if I told her I was going with Josh, and I'd meet them there. After the accident, I wished I'd gone with Josh. I wished I'd have told her before the game and maybe she would've gotten so mad, we'd have been late and missed that drunk driver. There are so many should-haves and what-ifs attached to that night.

Josh and I were so excited to tell Cara. We actually thought she'd be happy for us. I'm sure she would have been. A dull ache settles in my chest at the memories flooding my brain. We never got the chance.

"You okay?" Josh asks, shading his eyes and squinting at me. "You're awfully quiet." "I was just thinking..."

Josh furrows his brow in question.

"About the night of the accident. How we'd planned to tell Cara about us," I continue.

Josh's face falls and he sucks in a breath. "Oh, yeah, that." He sits up, turning to face me. I do the same. When Josh looks at me, his eyes are tender. He tucks a stray hair behind my ear and lets his hand linger on my cheek for a split second. It's a gesture that feels natural and foreign all at the same time. "I'd like to think she would've been happy for us," he murmurs.

"Yeah?" I ask, biting back a hopeful smile.

"Yeah. In fact, I know it." Josh nods.

"I miss her," I say sadly, looking down at my hands.

He offers me his hand and rubs tiny circles on my palm. "Me too," he rasps. "Every day." Josh keeps my hand in his and pushes to a stand, pulling me with him. We brush sand from our legs and pick up our trash. "We better get back so you can go to work." He takes my trash from me and trudges ahead to the trash can as if he can't escape the memories fast enough.

The last place I want to be tonight is work, but I can't call out on Andrew. Saturday nights in the summer get really busy. We really need two managers on. Thankfully, he did text me that he's closing. After lunch on the beach with Josh, we raced back to my place, where I took a quick shower and put on my super attractive work clothes. Honestly, they've never bothered me before but with Josh watching my every move, suddenly I'm wildly self-conscious of the food smell ingrained in the fibers of the clothing, no matter how many times they're washed. I made my best effort though, with a tight-fitting pair of jeans and enough body spray to fool my brain into forgetting about it.

I come out of my bedroom and find Josh sitting on the couch, idly strumming his guitar, a blank notebook open in front of him.

"Wow." I beam when he looks up at me. "You wasted no time getting to work."

Josh huffs. "If only I could actually write something," he mutters. "So far, all I've got is this chord progression." He starts strumming the chords G, D, E minor, and C.

I frown, a smirk twitching on my lips. "Are you playing 'Wagon Wheel'?"

"Damnit, I am!" Josh taps his hand on the top of the guitar. "I thought I made that up." He lets out an easy laugh, shaking his head.

"Stuck, are you?" I offer him a commiserative smile.

"I could really use a collaborative jam sesh," he admits, pushing his lips together.

"I wish I could but, duty calls." I walk toward my front door. When I turn back to say goodbye, I find his eyes fixed on me.

"Mel, think about it, okay? I'd love to play with you again." His chin lifts, a hopeful expression dancing on his face.

I smile, turning to go. "Okay. Bye, Josh."

I pull the door shut behind me.

Hours later, there are too many of us behind the bar. Ashley, Maura, our barback Chris, and I don't all fit. I'm getting frustrated, tripping over everyone, so I duck out. I run into Andrew as he's coming out of the kitchen. "We can cut someone behind the bar, I think, if both of us are here," I holler, pitching my voice over the noise of the bar.

"I'll take a look," Andrew calls back, already glancing toward the bar.

I push past him, heading for the office when he catches my elbow. "You okay?"

"I'm just burnt out." I sigh. "Too many late nights this week."

Andrew makes a *tsk* sound, like he's thinking. "I'm sorry," he says. "I'll be around more next week."

I give him a smile that doesn't quite reach my eyes. "I'm good. I just need a few minutes." The words taste automatic—the kind of thing I've said to him a hundred times before. I walk away before he can answer, the weight of my own honesty pressing in as I close the office door and relish the solitude.

I plop down in the chair and check my phone. No messages. I open Instagram, searching for Josh's profile. I haven't looked at it in ages. I'm not even following him. The first photo on his feed is a picture of him and a girl with a familiar face. She's some celebrity, but I can't place her. The post is two months old and there are no other recent ones. I tap the follow button and swipe out of Instagram. I open Google and type "Josh Cote's girlfriend."

The headlines that come up surprise me:

Josh Cote and Keira Muller Split

Josh Cote Single After a Year with Keira Muller

Keira Muller Crushed Over Split with Country Star Josh Cote

Rising Music Sensation Josh Cote: Alone After Split with Girlfriend and Band

I don't bother to click on any of them. Looks like he's single. The thought of a very single Josh Cote sleeping on my couch while I'm just behind a wall makes something bubble in my belly. Desire? Curiosity for sure. I force myself to push it aside. Josh clearly doesn't want to talk about these things, or he would have told me.

There's a knock on the office door and Andrew pokes his head in.

"Mel, how about instead of cutting one of the bartenders, you just call it a night? I got it from here." He offers me a reassuring smile.

It's only ten thirty and I'm off tomorrow. Freedom is so close I can taste it.

I chew on my lip. "Are you sure?"

"I'm sure," he says emphatically. "You have been covering for me a lot lately."

I nod in agreement, a rush of relief loosening my shoulders.

Andrew cocks his head toward the front of the restaurant. "Get outta here."

He doesn't have to tell me twice.

## THEN

*Josh,*

*What do you think of this?*

*Your fingers strum in the summer breeze, I wonder if you ever think of me.*

*Harmony's easy, but love's out of tune, ← is this lame???*

*Still, I'd play forever if it's next to you.*

*-M*

STRAWBERRY GIRL,

ARE THESE LYRICS FOR ME? :) JK JK. I LIKE IT. I DON'T KNOW ABOUT THAT LINE THOUGH. HERE'S WHAT I GOT:

IF THE WORLD SAYS NO, THEN LET 'EM TALK,

WE'LL FIND OUR SONG IN THE QUIET SPOTS.

GIRL, JUST SAY THE WORD,

AND I'LL REWRITE EVERY LINE YOU'VE HEARD.

WHAT DO YOU THINK?

PS – THIS STUDY HALL IS SOOOOO LAME. MR. HERMAN IS SNORING.

*J-*

*LOL! He always falls asleep.*

*Your third line is missing a syllable so you need to make it longer somehow to fit.*

*I wonder if we could put these together.*

OKAY. GOT IT. HOW'S THIS:

YOUR FINGERS STRUM IN THE SUMMER BREEZE,

I WONDER IF YOU EVER THINK OF ME.

HARMONY'S EASY, AND WE'RE OUT OF TUNE,

BUT, I'D PLAY FOREVER IF IT'S NEXT TO YOU.

IF THE WORLD SAYS NO, THEN LET 'EM TALK,

WE'LL FIND OUR SONG IN THE QUIET SPOTS.

<u>STRAWBERRY</u> GIRL, JUST SAY THE WORD,

AND I'LL REWRITE EVERY LINE YOU'VE HEARD.

JUST A FEW LITTLE TWEAKS. I THINK THE CHORD PROGRESSION WE WORKED ON THE OTHER DAY MIGHT FIT. WANT TO TRY IT TOMORROW? CARA HAS A SOCCER GAME.

ARE YOU GOING TO ALEX'S PARTY?

-J

*I don't know... those parties aren't really my scene. Everyone gets so drunk, and we're always in a field in the middle of nowhere. I have to squat in the woods to pee. I'm on the fence, but your sister will probably make me go with her and Liam. Plus Memorial Day Weekend? I don't know.*

COME ON – IT'S THE FIRST PARTY OF THE SUMMER. YOU HAVE TO CELEBRATE. AND I'LL BE THERE.

*Probably the only thing I'm excited about.*

I MAKE YOU FEEL EXCITED? OOOH LA LA.

*You make me feel safe. I'll think about it.*

# Chapter Six

## Josh

### NOW

Before Melanie has even left for work, I am perched on her couch, trying to write. I came here looking for inspiration, and being with Melanie has been so nice. But every time I think about writing, painful memories are all I see. Memories that I haven't had to face until now. I'm worried that coming back here was a mistake. Not that I regret seeing Mel again, but being here is forcing me to face my demons, and I wasn't prepared for that.

After an hour of strumming a chord progression that sounds an awful lot like "Country Roads," I lean my guitar against the chair and pace the apartment. While nice, it's largely devoid of personal things that might tell me who Melanie is today. I don't dare open the door to her room. I know that would be an invasion of privacy. If only I could channel some of the creativity she and I once shared together.

I pad down the narrow hallway and duck into the bathroom. The fluorescent light flickers once before humming to life. I wash my hands before opening the medicine cabinet to find band aids and over-the-counter medications. On the shelf behind the toilet is a bunch of hair products and perfumes. One bottle sits at the edge, the glass cool in my palm when I pick it up. I uncap it and breathe in. The scent is unmistakably her... Melanie. It's sweet with a sharp edge, bergamot and vanilla maybe? It hits me in the chest, stirs something low in my gut.

For a second, all I can picture is her tangled up in sheets beside me. My stomach flips, heat curling under my skin. I carefully set the bottle back and remind myself I have to keep my head on straight. It would be so easy to fall into bed with Melanie. But there is so much left unsaid between us, apologies that get stuck in my throat every time I look her way. I move and yank open the fridge, pulling out a bottle of water and ignoring the beers tucked way in the back.

I don't drink anymore. It's new. I've only been sober for a year, but I'm already better than I've been the past two years. The music industry is hard, and I've made mistakes. There is a ton of professional pressure, peer pressure, late-night partying, and questionable decisions. I felt myself spiraling the past few years, and even though I didn't abuse alcohol or drugs every day, when I did, it was always in excess. My creative energy was stifled by it. I'd lose days at a time from going on a bender and then needing to recover from it. And then one major mistake snapped me out of it all and back to reality.

Since giving up alcohol, the people close to me, who I thought I could always depend on, have decided I'm no longer fun. My band didn't respect the boundaries I put in place for myself. Keira left me, saying some bullshit about wanting different things. But I have held strong. I *want* my creativity back. I want my *ambition* back. Nothing seems worthwhile anymore. Did I make it? Sure. Did I achieve a lifelong goal of making music and going on tour? Yes. But at what cost? Now I'm washed up and alone.

I plop on the couch and rake a hand down my face with a loud groan. Then I see it, under the cushioned ottoman is a shelf, holding our high school yearbooks, and—I can't believe it—several composition books, stacked on top of each other, much like the blank one sitting in front of me. I pull the stack out.

There are three. The first one has an inconspicuous cover, but our initials are on the front in the bottom right corner of the white frame. I flip it open. This is the first notebook we started passing back and forth in Mr. Herman's study hall. I chuckle to myself as I read through it. The way we questioned if we should keep our jam sessions secret. The first lyrics we started brainstorming together. Meeting places. Random conversations and flirty innuendos. My chest constricts. What I wouldn't give to go back and do it again. The right way. Make things better.

I can't help myself as I read every page, drinking in these teenage memories like they were yesterday. I find a section about a party I wanted Melanie to go to and as I read, my mind goes back to that night.

*"Josh, I can't find Cara. Do you know where she is?" Melanie stumbles over to me. We're at a party in a dark field in the middle of nowhere. There was a bonfire at one point, but I think Alex let it go out so as not to attract the cops. I'm talking to a few guys from school about summer plans.*

*"I don't, I'm sorry." I step closer to her—she looks wobbly on her feet. I place a hand on her shoulder. "Are you okay?"*

*Melanie's eyes glaze over. She's had too much to drink. I thought she said this wasn't her scene. Maybe this is why. Her lip trembles. "I'm just ready to go," she hugs herself, rubbing her upper arms.*

*I turn back to the guys I'm talking to. "Uh, guys, I'm gonna jet." I tell them, cocking my head toward Melanie. I turn back to her, draping my arm over her shoulders. "Let's get you home."*

*"But I drove," Melanie wails. "And I can't drive now. I was hoping Liam or Cara could drive my car home."*

*"I'll drive your car home," I tell her calmly, shifting her toward the dirt lot where everyone's cars are parked.*

*"You don't have a license!" Melanie snaps, looking angrier than she did a second ago. "God, they're probably off having sex somewhere. I hate parties."*

*I swallow the bile that rises at the image of my sister having sex right now. I clear my throat. "I have a learner's permit, and I finished my behind-the-wheel classes," I say when we reach her car.*

*"And you have your license, so you can supervise me."*

*Melanie snorts out a laugh. "I'm pretty sure there are laws against that, Josh. And clearly I'm in no shape to supervise* anyone.*" She frowns, and I can't help but think she's the cutest girl here, even drunk. I don't ever drink more than one beer at these parties. When it gets warm, I top off the top so people think it's a new one. It works like a charm, and I always have my wits about me. Call me a nerd if you want. I guess I kind of am.*

*Melanie sighs. "I really want to go home, so I guess you'll have to do." She reaches into her wristlet for the keys to her old white Buick that she calls White Lightning. She tosses them to me and with a scowl and a point of the index finger says, "*Don't *crash my car."*

*I grin. "No promises."*

*But we make it back to her place in exactly twelve minutes, unscathed. "How will you get home?" she asks, turning in her seat to face me.*

*"I can walk. It's not that far." I shrug. "Do you need me to walk you up?" I ask.*

*But Melanie doesn't answer me. Before I can react, she puts her clammy palm on the back of my neck, yanking me closer to her, her lips hover over mine.*

*Ordinarily, I'd be psyched, but she's drunk and I'm not. And this...thing between us has become so important to me.*

*"Josh," her voice comes out as a whisper. Then her lips graze mine.*

*I pull back abruptly. "Mel, I can't."*

*She recoils as if I slapped her. "And just why the fuck not?" She frowns, crossing her arms over her chest, angrily.*

*"Melanie, you're drunk. That would make me a complete asshole." I growl, tugging at the collar of my T-shirt. It's hot as fuck in her car.*

*"News flash, Josh.* You are *an asshole." Melanie scoffs. She holds out her open palm. "Give me my keys and get out of my car."*

I flip past the note of my groveling for forgiveness, the

memory still fresh in my mind. I knew I had feelings for her that night. I went home and jerked off and then tried calling her private phone line at least three times. She ignored me.

The next entry in our notebook was our first completed song. The lyrics are so juvenile, but they make me smile. Under each line of lyrics, one of us wrote the chords. I pick up my guitar and start strumming it, quietly singing the lyrics. My heart swells from the memory. I can't believe we wrote this when we were sixteen and seventeen, and it sits unappreciated in this notebook twenty-five years later. It's *good*. For teenagers anyway. I'd say it rivals a young Taylor Swift.

I'm so into the music, I don't even hear the front door open and close.

"What are you doing?" Melanie's voice jolts me out of my musical reverie.

I set the guitar down, caught off guard. "I...uh, was playing our old song." I bite back a smile.

"You were invading my privacy is what you were doing." She frowns, folding her arms across her chest.

I flinch. "Your privacy? What? I wrote this music with you. It's just as much mine as it is yours."

"Yeah, well, the notebooks are mine now." Hurt clouds Melanie's expression, and I can't tell what she's madder about: everything we've yet to discuss, or the fact that I was strumming a memory that sparked feelings she wasn't ready for. "And no one said you could look at them."

Anger starts to bubble in my chest, and I force it down. "Melanie, you had it under the ottoman. Just out for anyone to see." I fight to keep my voice level.

"Well, no one ever comes over here. It's just *me*, so there was never a risk of that before." She turns and hangs her purse on the coat rack by the door. "I'm going to bed."

Melanie starts toward her room without giving me a second look.

"Melanie, come on," I call after her.

She slams her door.

## THEN

MELANIE – ARE YOU OKAY? I TRIED CALLING YOU SO MANY TIMES YESTERDAY. PLEASE DON'T IGNORE ME.

*I'm fine, Josh.*

YOU'RE NOT FINE, MEL. I'VE KNOWN YOU LONG ENOUGH TO KNOW.

*I'm good. Look Mr. Herman is drooling.*

I DON'T WANT TO TALK ABOUT MR. HERMAN, MEL. I WANT TO TALK ABOUT WHAT HAPPENED ON FRIDAY.

*You mean how I tried to kiss you and you pushed me away? What's there to say?*

YOU WERE DRUNK, MELANIE. JESUS. I WASN'T GOING TO TAKE ADVANTAGE OF YOU.

*Well I wasn't so drunk that I don't remember how shitty you made me feel. Why didn't you want to kiss me, Josh? Don't you like me? I thought I felt something happening here but I guess I was wrong.*

OH MY GOD, MELANIE. THAT'S EXACTLY WHY I DIDN'T KISS YOU.

*What?*

BECAUSE I LIKE YOU, MELANIE. OKAY? I LIKE YOU. AS MORE THAN A FRIEND. I LIKE YOU SO MUCH THAT YOU'RE THE FIRST PERSON I THINK OF EVERY MORNING AND THE LAST PERSON I THINK OF BEFORE I GO TO SLEEP. I LIKE YOU. AND I DIDN'T KISS YOU BECAUSE I DIDN'T WANT TO FUCK THINGS UP. BUT I GUESS I ALREADY HAVE.

*That's the nicest thing anyone has ever told me.*

IT IS?

*I like you too, Josh.*

# Chapter Seven

## NOW

I wait until there are no noises coming from the living room before creeping out of my room to use the bathroom. Josh is asleep on the couch, a soft snore coming from his chest. He's got his left forearm over his eyes and the blanket twisted around his legs. I tiptoe over to the couch and study him while he sleeps. The rise and fall of his chest is so steady, it makes my own chest ache. The creases of his face are relaxed and smooth, no lines of worry, no defenses in his expression, just the boy I used to love.

I remember the way my heart used to race around him, late-night jam sessions, and whispered promises that never made it past September. Back then it felt so simple, until it wasn't. Now watching him sleep, his quiet vulnerability and his achingly familiar features, I want to reach out and touch him. But I don't. Because the knot of everything left unsaid tightens in my chest, like a memory I'm not sure I want to keep. Even still, I feel tenderness toward Josh, buried under the weight of old wounds and unanswered questions.

I probably overreacted tonight. But when I heard him playing that song—the first one we ever wrote together—I was overcome first with sadness, then with anger. How could he have let me go so easily back then? I needed him. We *both* lost Cara. I know she was his sister, but she was my best friend.

Even though his parents made him move, he could have called me. We could have helped each other through it. The truth of the matter is, I'm not sure I *ever* really got through it. Here I am, nearly forty-two years old, single and desperately lonely, with walls built up so high, I can never get a guy to stick around. I push everyone I meet away because breaking down my walls is too much work.

Josh shifts in his sleep, and I worry he senses my presence. For a second longer, I let myself wonder what he's dreaming about. Am I there? Was I ever?

I sneak into the kitchen for some water and quietly hurry back to my room before I wake him.

I awake the next morning to the smell of bacon. It takes me a minute to remember that I'm supposed to be mad at Josh, and this is probably an apology effort on his part. I rub my eyes, sit up, and search for clothes. I throw on a loose pair of gray pajama pants and a black T-shirt with no bra. I check my reflection in the mirror on my dresser, fluffing my bedhead. I put on some deodorant and body spray and swing open my door.

I find Josh standing over the stove, cooking scrambled eggs. Two coffee mugs sit on the café table. His shirt stretches across his broad shoulders, sending a shiver straight between my thighs. Josh was never a small guy—even in high school he towered over me—but now he's a man, his body made up of sinewy lines and sharp angles. He takes up all the space in this tiny kitchen. *My tiny kitchen.* And somehow it feels right. Like he belongs here.

"Hi," I say, startling him.

He whirls around, spatula in hand, and flashes me a devastating smile. "Good morning, Strawberry Girl," he murmurs. He turns back to the eggs, stirring them slowly.

I walk over to the table and sit down. "Making breakfast?" I ask, even though it's obvious.

Josh lifts a shoulder, uncertainty written on his handsome face. "I thought we could talk." Then gesturing to the mug in front of me. "That's for you."

I smile, taking note of the fixed mug. "Thank you," I nearly whisper.

"Cream and two spoonfuls of sugar, right?" Josh confirms.

I don't even get to marvel at the fact that he remembers what I put in my coffee yesterday morning because he puts a plate of scrambled eggs and bacon in front of me. The toaster dings and up pops four slices of toast. Josh gets to work buttering them.

"Yes. Thanks," I say, my voice breathy. I'm unsure what to say next.

A moment later, he's across from me with his own plate and our toast. "Melanie, listen." His voice is husky. "I'm really sorry I invaded your privacy last night. I was looking for inspiration and feeling stuck. Reading our old lyrics sparked something in me that's been missing."

He pauses, and I'm not sure what to say.

"I'm so sorry, Mel, for everything." Josh offers a hand to me across the table, but I don't take it.

"Okay. But that doesn't make up for the fact that I don't have any answers to my questions." I can't look at him, so I look down at my plate, chewing on my bottom lip.

"I know that," Josh agrees.

Silence hangs between us for several moments, both of us eating quietly. Finally, I can't take it anymore.

"Why did you leave without saying goodbye?" I finally ask, my voice catching in my throat. I work hard to steady my wavering breath. "It's all well and good that you're back, and I'm even happy you're staying *here* with me. It feels like old times, but Josh... I *have* to know." I pause, finally meeting his eyes. "You broke my heart."

Josh nods, shame written on his face. His shoulders slump as he scrubs a palm down his face. "I know. I know I did. I'm sorry, Mel." He pauses and sucks in a breath. "I know it doesn't mean much now, but I broke my heart too. I loved you so much." Josh's expression turns pained, like talking about the past will somehow widen the gap between us.

"Then why didn't you come see me before you left?" I practically shout, slamming my hand on the table. "I had a fucking broken leg, Josh. Or I would have been banging on your door to see *you*."

Josh bats at his eye, and I wonder if this conversation is too much for him. He shakes his head, sniffling. "You have to understand, my *sister* was dead. I was reeling. My entire world was upside down."

"So was mine! I was with her, remember? My *best* friend. And my boyfriend didn't want to talk to me," I cry, gesturing with my hands so wildly that I nearly knock my coffee mug over. Our eggs are getting cold.

"Melanie, I couldn't support you and handle my own grief. Jesus, I was sixteen. What the fuck was I supposed to do?" Josh doesn't match my anger. Instead, his voice is thick with emotion, his eyes glistening. "If it helps, I have regretted it *every* day since."

At this, I soften. My Josh. It was *always* Josh. In my teenage mind, we were supposed to end up together. "You have?" My voice comes out as a whisper.

Josh gets out of his seat and moves closer to me, getting on his knees and taking my hands in his. "Yes. *Of course* I have, Melanie. You were the first girl I ever loved. Maybe the only girl," he murmurs. Before I can respond, he says, "Write this album with me. A tribute to Cara."

I'm caught off guard, shaking my head. "Uh, no. Josh, I told you. I don't play for anyone but myself anymore."

"Don't you remember how good it used to be?" he whispers, never letting his gaze fall. "Think about it Mel, please?"

I swallow the knot in my throat. "I'll think about it," I murmur. "But I can't make any promises."

Josh smiles then, showing his dimples under his honey blond stubble speckled with gray. Another reminder of how much time has passed between us. He brings my hand to his mouth and kisses it softly, his mouth warm. "That's all I ask."

Hours later, I'm alone and feeling emotionally drained. Josh left me to meet up with some old friends from high school and frankly, I'm thankful for the space to think. That doesn't stop me from laying on his pillow on the couch though. I push the side of it over my face and inhale. His scent is ingrained in the flowery pillowcase. Something musky, cedar wood maybe. Definitely not the same smell high school Josh had, but so much better.

I close my eyes and before I know it, I'm remembering.

*"I think it's ready," Josh says, putting down the open notebook and picking up his guitar. "Let's play through it."*

*I wince. "I don't know... The harmonies are rough." I chew on my lip. Over the past couple of weeks, working on this song has become more than just a song. It's everything I'm feeling inside for Josh...my best friend's little brother. Except he's hardly little. No, Josh is filling out—he's all lean muscle and patchy stubble.*

*"Come on, let's just try it in unison," Josh urges. He strums the first chord and wiggles his eyebrows at me. He grins and shows me both dimples.*

*"Okay, fine," I roll my eyes.*

*Then we're playing together, Josh taking the lead on guitar and singing backup to my melody.*

*Your fingers strum in the summer breeze,*
*I wonder if you ever think of me.*
*Harmony's easy, but we're out of tune,*
*But, I'd play forever if it's next to you.*
*We keep it quiet, keep it cool,*
*But every note bends the rules.*
*If you knew what I felt inside,*

*Would you stay, or would you hide?*
*Don't call it a summer fling*
*I'll give you my paper ring.*
*I scribbled your name on my notebook page.*
*It's wrong, it's right, it's something new,*
*I don't know chords, but I know you.*
*Midnight tides, moon on the sand,*
*Sneakin' out with guitars in hand.*
*Strawberry girl, sing me a tune,*
*I'll play forever if it's next to you.*

*When the song ends, Josh's eyes lock with mine. He sets his guitar down, and I do the same. Suddenly I'm hyper aware of how close we are. Goose bumps prick my arms and before I know it, only an inch separates us. Josh leans closer to me. "That was amazing," he murmurs, entangling his fingers with my own.*

*I nod and a sound similar to "Uh-huh" escapes me.*

*"I like that it's about us," Josh says quietly.*

*"It's not about us," I murmur. "It could be about anyone."*

*"It's about me and you, Mel." Josh swallows. "Do you remember what I told you after Alex's party?"*

*I meet his eyes and nod. "You told me you like me." My voice is a whisper.*

*"Right. I do." Josh takes my hands in his. "As more than a friend."*

*"I like you too," I murmur, my lips turning upward. "As more than a friend."*

*Josh licks his lips, pushing his forehead into mine, his mouth hovering over my own. "Is it okay if I kiss you now?"*

*I nod and then his lips are on mine, soft and tentative. I open my mouth for him, and the kiss deepens, still tentative and uncertain but full of something that has been building in the background of our music for months. When we pull apart, neither of us speaks for a moment. The air between us is charged and delicate, like a note hanging in the space between chords.*

*"Do friends kiss like that?" I ask, smiling.*

*Josh leans in to kiss me again and just before his lips graze mine, he says, "No, I don't think they do."*

My buzzing phone startles me out of the memory. I pick it up and it's a text from a number I don't yet have saved. It's Josh. He's going to be late tonight. He decided to stay and hang with the guys. At least he's letting me know. I tell him I'll leave a key under the mat in case I'm asleep. I have to force myself not to be disappointed.

I reach under the ottoman and find the notebook I caught Josh with, flipping open to our very first song. Then I grab my guitar, and everything comes rushing back. The notes are rooted in my soul.

## THEN

M – NOW THAT WE'RE KISSING, DOES THAT MEAN I CAN KISS YOU WHENEVER I WANT?

*LOL! Within reason. NOT in front of Cara or anyone at school.*

GOOD THING SCHOOL IS ALMOST OUT THEN.

*I just want to make sure she'll be okay with it. Let's just play it cool for now.*

AND SNEAK AROUND LIKE WE ALREADY DO?

*Something like that.*

# Chapter Eight

*Josh*

## NOW

I look down at my phone for probably the fortieth time tonight. My friend Chris notices and scowls.

"You have some important music business stuff to attend to, or do you have time for your old pals?" He smirks, gesturing to my phone I'm glancing at under the table.

"Sorry." I shake my head. "I texted Melanie our plans, but I haven't heard back from her."

"Melanie?" My old buddy Aaron's eyebrows quirk up. Aaron and Chris were my two best friends in high school. They got out of Cape May for college, but they don't live far outside of town these days. When I texted that I was back, they jumped at a chance to grab a bite and catch up. Now they're throwing back a couple of beers over burgers, and I'm nursing my Coke. They were psyched to have a DD.

"Yeah, I'm crashing with her." I shove my phone back in my pocket and force my attention on my friends.

"*The* Melanie?" Chris confirms. "The one you were obsessed with?"

I flinch at his candor. "Obsessed is a strong word."

"Dude, you *loved* her," Aaron reminds me. "Like epic crush."

I bark out a laugh. "It was more than a crush. We had a thing going on." I take a sip of my soda and look anywhere but their dropped jaws. I can't believe they really had no idea.

"Pshh, you wish." Chris laughs. "I remember how you ditched us at that party to go home with her drunk ass. Following her like a lost puppy." He's joking but he has no idea how right he is. I was crazy about Melanie back then. It took me years to move on from the loss of her. I know she wants to know why I never stayed in touch. I wish I had the answer, but honestly, it's as simple as I was insecure and stupid. I absolutely should have called and checked on her. I should have made sure she was okay.

I shake my head, plucking a fry from my plate and chewing it while they watch me closely. "No, really," I say when I swallow. "We were hooking up the whole summer before eleventh grade. No one knew."

"No shit." Aaron chuckles, scratching his chin. "Too bad it never worked out."

"I think Josh made out just fine bagging Kiera Muller." Chris winks at me. "She's hot."

I laugh, shaking my head. "That's over." I lean back in my chair, crossing my arms over my chest.

"Dude." Chris scowls, giving me a look that says he thinks I'm insane. "Why?"

"We want different things," I say, making air quotes when I say *different things*. I lift a shoulder, dismissing it. "Trust me, I'm better off."

Aaron holds up his hands. "All right, all right, hear me out." He pauses and points an index finger in my direction. "You are single now. Melanie is single now. You're staying in her house..."

"How do you know she's single?" I quirk an eyebrow.

"That's kind of her thing," Chris interrupts. "She's always single... I'm not really sure why. She's still hot with a great body."

I shove him in the shoulder in jest. "I'm sure your wife would love to hear that," I growl, but I grin, shaking my head. "I don't think she forgives me for taking off back then."

"What? Your parents moved. You were sixteen." Aaron balks.

"You had to."

I cock my head side to side. "Maybe. But I probably should have done more than just left her a note."

"Dude!" Chris gapes at me. "Seriously?"

My neck tingles in embarrassment for my sixteen-year-old self. "I was messed up. That's my only excuse." I shake my head, hoping to clear the painful memory away.

"Yeah, well, now is your chance to make it right," Aaron says. "Rachel says fate works in mysterious ways and you should listen to the universe when it's telling you something." Rachel is Aaron's girlfriend. She is *mystical,* as Aaron likes to say and believes in the healing power of energy and cleansing auras.

"I'll see, I guess," I say, still unsure how to prove myself to Melanie again. I'm also unsure of what I'd even hope to get out of repairing our relationship. Maybe the status quo is better since I'm not sure what I could really offer her or what my future looks like.

We call it a night after midnight, and once I drop the guys at their respective houses and creep quietly back into Melanie's apartment, she's already gone to bed. I figured she would have, but I can't push aside my disappointment. I was hoping we could talk. I fill a glass with water and head into the bathroom to brush my teeth, feeling defeated. When I come out, I notice her guitar leaning against the armchair, and the same notebook with our first song open on the ottoman. It's almost like she was playing our song. She never did text me back. I assumed she was still mad, but maybe she was distracted by the music instead. Something like hope fills my chest as I settle onto the couch to sleep. Maybe she wants to play with me after all.

By the time the sun is streaming through the kitchen the next morning, Melanie is already gone. I must have slept like the dead because I didn't even hear her leave. I pad into the kitchen and see fresh coffee in the pot with a note in handwriting I'd recognize anywhere:

> ***Josh -***
>
> ***Working day shift today. Come see me if you're bored.***

My chest pulls tight. I've only been here for a few days, but I already can't imagine leaving again. Actually, that's not true. A home can be anywhere. It's Melanie that I can't imagine leaving again. I can't believe how long I've gone without her in my life. We might've left things unsettled, we may even *need* to have it out, but I know one thing's for sure, I can't let years go by again without knowing her.

I quickly shower, shave, and get dressed. I take my guitar and notebook out to the small, shared sunroom between apartments and sit down. A melody started to take shape in my head last night as I drove through the back roads on my way home. *I mean, back to Melanie's.* I sang it into a voice memo on my phone while I was driving, but now I need to get it down on paper. I don't know what the words will be yet, but I can hear the tune. I'm humming it and strumming the chord progression—Am, C, G, F. Strum, jot it down, strum some more, jot it down. I reach a place where I should be writing a bridge, but my phone dings in my pocket.

> Melanie
>
> Did you get my note? Sorry I missed you, but you looked so peaceful, I didn't want to wake you.

I smile at her words. *Sorry I missed you.* "I guess she's not mad at me," I say to no one but myself.

I hammer out a reply.

Company for lunch?

Her reply comes rapid fire.

Melanie

Sure. I'd like that.

I stand to go back into the apartment, put my guitar away, and grab my phone and keys when I realize I've locked myself out. I let out a groan, dragging my hand down my face. I'm not getting enough sleep or something. My brain has up and left. I lean my guitar in the corner of the sunroom, with my notebook, and hope none of the neighbors disturb it.

I jog down the rickety steps and walk up two blocks to The Ugly Mug where Melanie works. It's a gorgeous summer day that would elicit optimism in even the grumpiest of washed-up musicians. I find myself whistling the melody I'm attempting to write as I walk.

It doesn't take me long and I swing open the door to the dark restaurant to find Melanie right at the host stand, waiting for me. She grins and warmth radiates my insides. *How did I go so long without seeing her smile?*

"Hey stranger," she says, tucking a strawberry blonde wave behind her ear.

"Hey, Strawberry Girl." I smile, leaning against the host stand.

Melanie's cheeks pinken and I feel desire rush through me. I used to make her blush all the time. Or at least teenager Josh thought so. "Lunch?" she asks, picking up her purse and slinging it over her shoulder.

"You don't want to eat here?" I ask, quirking an eyebrow.

"I need to see the sunshine," she says, stepping around me and pushing open the door. She looks back over her shoulder. "You coming?"

Fifteen minutes later, we're sitting outside a café called Tisha's, sipping lemonade and quietly reading our menus.

Melanie closes hers and looks up, clearing her throat. "Did you have fun last night?"

"I did. It was great seeing Chris and Aaron."

Melanie's expression is warm, nostalgia brimming in her blue eyes. "It's always nice to see old friends." Our hands are nearly touching on top of the small table, knuckles a mere centimeter from each other. It would take nothing for me to reach out and lace her fingers through mine. Instead, I pull my hand away and scratch at the nape of my neck, smiling in return.

"I told them about our secret relationship. I'm not sure they believed me." I laugh and Melanie does too, but her eyes are guarded.

Before she can say anything, the waitress comes to take our order. We order salads, and just as I'm about to once again plead with her to sing with me, we're interrupted again.

"Well look what the cat dragged all the way up the coast." The voice belongs to my sister's high school boyfriend, Liam Harper. I haven't seen him in nearly twenty-five years, and I'm surprised he recognizes me. He's pushing a double jogging stroller and stops at our table.

"It's more like *across the country* these days." I laugh, standing up and holding out my hand. He shakes it but then surprises me by pulling me into a hug. "What's going on, brother?" I ask, pulling back.

"Not much. You back in town?" Liam arches a brow.

"Just passing through," I murmur, glancing sideways at Melanie. "Are these two cuties yours?" I ask, crouching down to say hello to the little girls.

Liam looks down fondly at them. "These are my daughters,

Lucy and Leah."

"Hi there." I wave at them. "I'm Josh."

The littlest girl puts her hands over her face and turns into the side of the stroller, but she's grinning shyly. The older one waves at me. "Hi, Josh. I'm Lucy."

"Hi, Lucy." I smile. I sit back down and motion to the empty chair at the table next to us. "Join us, Liam," I say. "I'd love to catch up."

Liam grabs the chair and turns it, sitting backward on it. "I only have a few minutes. We're walking to a play date." He shakes his head with a crooked grin. "Just file that under things I never thought I'd say."

Melanie laughs, patting his forearm. "Honestly? Me neither."

"So, Josh, what brings you back to town?" Liam asks. I can't read his expression, and I wonder how much he knows about the past—Melanie and me.

Before I can answer, Melanie does for me. "Josh is writing a solo album," she says, eyeing me carefully. She doesn't realize that technically, all of my albums are solo albums, and if I have my way, it'll be a *duo* album with her. "He came back for inspiration."

I sigh and nod. "Yeah, it's coming up on Cara's anniversary"

"As if I could forget," Liam deadpans, but his expression softens, carrying quiet compassion.

"I thought maybe coming home would spark some creativity," I admit. The truth is, this is a Hail Mary for me. If I can't write this album, I'm afraid I'll be dropped—but I don't dare say that out loud.

"Can you believe it's been almost twenty-five years?" Liam asks, looking back and forth between Melanie and me. "We should do something for it. Since you're here, Josh."

I nod, and the wheels start turning. "Maybe... How big are you thinking?" The truth of the matter is, we had a quiet burial for Cara, and then we left town. Her life never felt fully celebrated to me, and if I think too hard about that my heart splits. She *deserved* a celebration.

Liam pushes his lips together in thought. "I always wished we could've done something in her name, you know? Pay tribute to her."

I shake my head in agreement. "Oh, yeah, like some kind of memorial. Scholarship fund maybe?"

"A memorial benefit concert!" Melanie shrieks, just as the waitress brings our salads over. "The money we raise could go to a scholarship or something."

Liam checks his watch before standing and putting his chair back. "That's a great idea, Mel." He holds his hand out to me again. "I should let you two eat. Let's get together and talk about it."

I stand up and shake his hand, patting him on the shoulder. "Yeah. Sounds good." I nod. "I'll give you a call."

"Great. See you guys later." Liam calls, pushing the stroller away.

I sit back down and narrow my eyes at Melanie. "A *benefit* concert? Way to put me on the spot," I retort.

"Come on, Josh. You know how amazing that would be? You are a *star*—a concert in your *sister's* honor in your hometown to raise scholarship money? It'll be amazing."

I chew on my lip, thinking for a minute while Melanie digs into her salad. I watch her thoughtfully, the way she picks through her salad to find the perfect bite. Melanie has never been anything but unapologetically herself. She wears her heart on her sleeve. Even all these years later, I never question where I stand with her. It's refreshing and disarming all at the same time.

I suck in a breath, and she expectantly raises her eyes to meet mine. "Fine, you know what? I'll do it," I say, digging into my own salad. I take a bite and look at her again.

Her eyes sparkle with excitement, a hopeful grin pulls at her lips. "Yeah?"

"On one condition," I add, wagging my empty fork in her direction.

"What's that?" Melanie shoots me an exaggerated eye roll. She knows me too well.

"You play it with me," I say, taking another bite.

Melanie drops her fork in her salad bowl. "Come on, Josh, be serious." Melanie frowns. "I can't do that. *You're* the performer, not me."

"Why not? You were once a performer too," I scoff, taking a sip of my lemonade.

She stares quietly at me, chewing.

"Come on, we have all summer till the anniversary. Let's write some music," I urge. I play footsies with her and offer her a teasing smile. "You know you want to."

Melanie eyes me cautiously but I can see that she's spinning these thoughts around in her mind.

"It'll be like old times," I tell her, my voice softening. "I don't know about you but... I've really missed those times." This time I offer her my open hand.

Melanie nods and takes a deep breath, clasping her hand in mine and meeting my eyes. "I have too," she says solemnly. "Okay, fine. You sold me. Let's do it."

My eyes widen in shock. I didn't think she'd agree so easily. "Really?"

Melanie lets a smile break through then. "Yeah. Let's do it. For Cara."

## THEN

WHAT ARE YOU DOING THIS WEEKEND?

*Ugh, Cara wants to look at prom dresses tomorrow. There's a store up the parkway that apparently records what dress you buy for your prom so no one else at your school can get the same dress as you. She's hell bent on going. I don't even want to go to the prom.*

WHY NOT? I'M SURE YOU COULD FIND SOMEONE TO GO WITH.

*Not the person I want to go with.*

HUH... I WONDER WHO THAT COULD BE. :)

*Cut the crap, Josh. You know we can't go to prom together.*

WHY NOT? TELL MY SISTER YOU DON'T WANT TO GO BECAUSE YOU HAVE NO ONE TO GO WITH. THEN I'LL OFFER TO TAKE YOU TO CARA SO SHE THINKS IT'S HER GREAT IDEA.

*That actually might work...*

IT WILL WORK. AND THEN I CAN HOLD YOU IN MY ARMS ALL NIGHT AND TWIRL YOU AROUND THE DANCE FLOOR.

*Just no kissing! She still thinks we're just friends. This is a big deal, Josh.*

FINE. WE'LL SAVE THE KISSING FOR THE AFTER PARTY.

# Chapter Nine

## NOW

Josh and I finish lunch, and he somehow convinces me to jam tonight. I guess if we're going to plan a benefit concert for Cara, we'd better get to it. I'm trying not to think about how playing with him again will make me feel. When we were playing together as kids, we'd look at each other the entire time we played. My stomach in knots, cheeks flushed. He always kept his cool on the surface, but it was as if the music stirred up emotions between us that neither of us knew what to do with.

"I'll see you tonight," Josh says, scribbling his signature on the receipt for the waitress.

I nod, standing and pushing my chair in. "Okay, it'll be about five thirty, by the time all is said and done at the restaurant."

We stare at each other for a beat, nodding, perhaps neither of us quite ready to say goodbye. "I'll see you," Josh finally says, turning to go.

"Bye," I call after him, doing the same.

"Oh, Mel," Josh calls, jogging back. He stops so close to me, I think he might kiss me.

My heart flutters in my chest. "Yeah?" I whisper.

"I locked myself out of your apartment. Can I borrow your key?" He grins like a schoolboy, and I force a laugh down at my ridiculousness. *Of course he's not running back to kiss me.*

"S-sure," I stammer, flustered and digging through my purse. I push the key into his open palm and his fingers grasp around mine. The only thing keeping us from lacing our fingers together is my janky keychain. Still, we let our hands linger a second longer than necessary, and I instantly feel reassured that this isn't one-sided. Josh must feel it too.

He gives me a sultry smile as he pulls his hand away. "Thanks. I'll see you tonight."

With Josh gone and a quiet lunch crowd, there's nothing else for me to do but hole up in the office and go over the schedule for next week that Andrew asked me to finish. I fill my water bottle up from the tap behind the bar and push open the kitchen door. Even the kitchen is quiet today, forcing me to be alone with my thoughts. I sit down at the desk in the office and start skimming the preliminary schedule that Andrew left, taking note that Lexi and Julie both requested off on Saturday night and Ryan is hoping to pick up any extra shifts. But I can't help myself, my focus is all over the place and my mind wanders.

*"Come on, Melanie," Cara whines after school on a warm Friday in April. "I can't be the only one trying on dresses." It's a rare day where she doesn't have a game or practice and she's trying to convince me to go prom dress shopping.*

*"I told you, Car, I don't really want to go to the prom." I shrug. "But I'll help you find a dress you love. I promise."*

*Cara won't drop the subject of prom. She's asked me no less than fifty times. I know it's* prom *but it's our* junior *prom. I won't skip next year. This year just feels a little pointless to me.*

*"You have to go. Who will I get ready with?" Cara juts out her lower lip.*

*I roll my eyes. "Oh, I don't know, one of your bajillion other friends maybe?" I joke but it's true. Cara has so many friends. Soccer team, drama club, Honor Society. I am a loner and most of the time I'm okay with that. "I promise I'll go to senior prom. I just don't see the point in going this year when I have no one to go with and you'll be dancing with Liam all night."*

*Cara scoffs. "Liam doesn't dance. He'll stand there and watch me dance."*

*"He'll slow dance with you," I point out, pushing my lips together. "Then you two will sneak off to fool around, and I'll be all alone sitting at the table eating the entire dessert buffet. Sorry. Not interested."*

*Cara's eyes light up, and I instantly know what she's going to suggest. I know because Josh and I rehearsed this exact scene a couple of days ago in hopes it would land us at prom together. "I know! Oh my god, I can't believe I didn't think of this before."*

*I wince, scrunching my nose. "I'm afraid to ask," I say, really leaning into my acting ability.*

*"My brother!" Cara squeals, jumping up and down.*

*I arch an eyebrow at her. "Your brother?"*

*"You can take Josh to prom." Cara gives my shoulder a playful shove.*

*I laugh, shaking my head. "No, no, no. Josh and I are just friends," I say, even though it's far from true. Josh sees me. He makes me feel as if nothing else matters in this world but me and him. My stomach fills with butterflies, my cheeks heat. I fear I'm blowing my cover, but Cara doesn't seem to notice.*

*"So?" Cara asks, putting her hands on her hips. "Take him as your* friend. *You two are always playing music together anyway." She leans against the chain-link fence.*

*I chew on my lip, pretending to mull her suggestion over. "You wouldn't mind?" I ask, my brow furrowing. There's a part of me that is afraid to hear her answer.*

*"Of* course *not! You're my best friend. I just want you there." Cara pulls me into a hug.*

*"Fine. I'll ask him," I say cautiously, patting her shoulder blade*

*and pulling back from the hug.*

*"Oh, you don't have to do that." A proud grin spreading across her face. "I already asked him for you, and he said yes." She bounces back and forth on her toes excitedly.*

*"You what?" I shriek. "What if I said no to this little scheme of yours?" I fold my arms across my chest.*

*"You wouldn't have."*

*She's right about that because as much as Cara thinks this little scheme is hers, she's wrong. It's* ours, *and I can't wait to have a magical evening with Josh.*

*"Fine." I roll my eyes. "Let's go find some prom dresses."*

The buzzing of my phone startles me from the memory. I glance down. *Josh.*

I can't swipe quickly enough to open it, and I let out a growl when my phone gets my face ID wrong. *What's wrong with me?*

Josh

Cooking for us tonight. Is your favorite still chicken parm?

Butterflies swarm my insides, spreading warmth through my lower region. I am smiling as I tap out a reply.

Yes. 100%.

Josh

Good. See you at dinner.

Goose bumps rise on my arms, and I rub them away. "You still know how to get me, don't you?" I say aloud to my phone. I hate that after all these years, he can waltz back in here and make me want him again. Like he didn't just leave me alone in New Jersey, grieving the loss of my best friend, of him, of all the things left unsaid. I hated my parents and missed him like a lost appendage. And at the same time, it's as if he never left. As if he always knew we'd be back here, together again. Or, maybe I'm making all of this up in my head.

I want him. I hate how much I want him because I'm sure it will lead to nowhere good. He's not just Josh anymore—he's Rockstar Josh. He'll have his fun with me and then go off and chase his dreams again. But I think maybe, he might want me too. For more than just the music. There's still something between us. I feel it in the quickening of my heart every time he grabs my hand. His face always wearing the same tentative expression, like he's holding something back. But he never lets go of my hand first.

I let out a defeated sigh before tossing my phone to the side, determined to finish this schedule and keep my mind *off* Josh.

My afternoon picks up and before I know it, Andrew is walking in for the evening shift. I give him a debrief on the day and sling my purse over my shoulder, anxious to get home to Josh. I'm off tomorrow and we can stay up all night making music if we want to. For the first time in a long time, I feel excited about life. I'm looking forward to whatever these summer months getting to know Josh again may hold. Even if it means I'm left with a broken heart.

# Chapter Ten

## Josh

### NOW

As soon as I hear Melanie's footsteps outside the door, my heart jumps to my throat. She has always made me nervous, but now that she's agreed to play music with me again, it's a whole new level of insecurity. I'd be lying if I said I haven't felt things this past week. Our relationship was special. Losing both her and Cara at the same time? It damn near broke me. I turn away from the front door and force myself to focus on filling our water glasses.

"It smells good in here." Melanie's voice singsongs behind me.

I whirl around and offer her a smile. "I hope it tastes as good as it smells." I chuckle.

"I hope you didn't go to any trouble. I eat take-out like five out of seven nights a week." She smirks, reaching down to pull off her sneakers. She leaves them by the front door.

"I like to cook," I say, holding out a water glass to her when she stands up.

She takes a long sip before setting it on the small dining table and heading for her room. "Just let me get out of these clothes real quick," she calls over her shoulder.

"Sure, take your time," I call after her. I can't help but notice, she doesn't close her bedroom door, and I can see the silhouette of her trim body. She pulls off her work polo shirt and rummages through the dresser drawer at the entrance to her room in only her bra. She's breathtaking. I have to force myself to turn and walk into the kitchen so I don't gawk at her when she removes her jeans. She probably doesn't even realize she left her door open. *You perv.*

I open the oven and pull out a glass dish with chicken parm, filling two plates. Then I retrieve the Caesar salad I made earlier from the fridge. By the time I get everything on the table, Melanie meets me there. She's changed into black leggings and an oversized pink T-shirt that falls off her left shoulder. Her hair is piled on top of her head, a few strawberry blonde curls falling out at the nape of her neck. I always loved Melanie's neck and shoulders. As a lovesick teen, I'd stare longingly at them, imagining the soft kisses I'd plant there. All the while, she strummed her guitar, clueless to how infatuated with her I really was.

"Wow, Josh." Melanie pulls out the chair next to mine and sits. "No one has ever made me dinner like this." She stares in awe at the meal before her.

My jaw slackens with shock. "No one has ever cooked for you?" I can't imagine Melanie spending the last twenty-five years alone.

Melanie pushes her full pink lips together and shakes her head. "Besides my dad? No. There's never really been anyone serious." She offers me a wistful smile and shrugs half-heartedly.

"I find that hard to believe," I say, fighting the urge to reach for her.

Melanie lets out a dry laugh. "Believe it." She clears her throat. "I was going to stop and get us some wine but then I realized I haven't seen you drinking." She furrows her brow at me. "Are you sober?" Melanie's voice is gentle as she places her warm hand on my forearm.

I stifle a cough and nod. "It's only been about a year but yeah." What I don't add is, I know exactly how long it's been.

Melanie's expression softens, but there's no pity in it, only understanding. "That couldn't have been easy. I get it, though.

More than you think."

I shake my head and smile at her, wanting desperately to lighten the mood. "It's not that serious. I just don't like the person I turn into when I'm under the influence, and it makes me feel like garbage, so I decided to cut it out." I pause and seriously debate telling her the whole story. Then I decide against it—it would ruin me for her. "Apparently, to *some people,* that makes me less fun."

"I'll always think you're fun," Melanie says, pulling her hand back. She picks up her fork and meets my eyes, her own baby blues a pool of emotion. "This really looks delicious." She doesn't drop her gaze, and I wonder if she feels what I feel—the desperate longing for the past, the way we clung to each other without a care in the world. The plans we made that didn't pan out.

My cheeks heat and I'm sure they're pink—thankfully, my three-day-old beard hides it. "Well, thanks." I grin.

We spend a few moments eating in silence, other than the cute, satisfied noises escaping Melanie that I imagine her making in the bedroom. Heat pricks the back of my neck every time she looks my way. I want her and I can't have her—it will lead nowhere good. The best-case scenario here is for the two of us to make some music, reminisce, and celebrate Cara. If I get some tracks for the album out of it, that's even better.

"So, why are you really back here, Josh?" Melanie's question jars me out of my thoughts.

I laugh, wiping my mouth with a paper napkin. "What do you mean? I told you, I need inspiration for my album."

Melanie leans back in her chair and takes me in for a moment before speaking. "You're a country music star... you could have gone anywhere else to find inspiration." It's a statement not a question.

"I know." I nod and take a sip of water, deflecting further. "I wanted to come home." I look away for a moment, but she doesn't take her eyes off me. I stifle a cough. There's more to it than I've let on, but I'm not ready to share what's on my heart.

"Okay," she finally says, clearly choosing not to press me

further. "Well, I'm glad you're back."

I give her a tight smile. "Me too. Shall we make some music?"

We settle in the cramped living room with our guitars, Melanie in the armchair and me on the couch. I've noticed she's upgraded hers from her high school guitar to a rose gold Ibanez acoustic electric. I've set my music books out on the table as well as some blank staff paper and my phone with wireless microphones to record.

Melanie is quiet as she picks up her guitar, balancing it on her knee. She appears to be waiting for me.

"Do you want to play some covers first to warm up?" I ask, picking up my own guitar that I left leaning against the end table.

Melanie tucks a stray curl that has fallen out of her bun behind her ear and meets my gaze. "Sure," she says, and she begins strumming the chords to my biggest hit, "Without You."

I am barely breathing as I lean closer to her, desperate to close the distance between us. If she expects me to pick up my guitar and join in, she doesn't say so. She continues strumming the intro, and then her melodic voice fills the room. I swallow hard, feeling my throat constrict. Twenty-five years have passed and still the sound of her voice sends goose bumps up my arms. It is both a balm and a blade, cutting clear through the years that had stretched between us. Maybe somewhere beneath her composure, she also feels the spark that never really faded. My fingers instinctually tighten around the neck of my guitar, aching to play the next chord—but I don't. I'm too captivated by her, playing my melody, singing my words. I hadn't realized how much I missed her until now. My chest aches with the bittersweet twist of regret and, at the same time, hope for the future.

Melanie finishes playing and looks at me, smiling. "Surprise," she says with a slight shrug.

"You know my music," I rasp, unable to keep the emotion out of my voice. The back of my throat burns.

Melanie's face softens. "Of course I do, Josh." She reaches for me, placing her hand on my kneecap. "I'm *so* proud of you." Her brows knit together, and her voice is quieter. "The first time I heard this song on the radio, I knew I had to learn it. It helped me feel close to you when we were so far apart." But what I think she means is, ***when we left so many words unspoken. That's the real reason I'm here.***

My heart lurches in my chest. "Play it again," I murmur.

This time I join her.

We play through the song together, never breaking eye contact. When we reach the bridge, Melanie takes the third harmony. My chest constricts, and I'm not even embarrassed when my eyes sting with unshed tears. Being here with Melanie, making music together again, really is coming home. Melanie is home for me.

"What next?" she asks when we finish.

I'm so overcome with emotion I have to take a pause. I lean my guitar against the couch and run a thumb under my lower lid to prevent a tear from escaping.

Melanie's face falls when she sees the emotion on my face. "Josh, are you okay?" she asks, alarmed, setting her own guitar aside. She rises and comes to sit next to me on the couch. Without hesitation, she puts her arms around me, and I quickly reciprocate. The moment our arms close around each other, it's as if time has folded in on itself, drawing the past and present together into one fragile, breathless moment. It's not just a hug—it's the quiet ache of things we left behind. I'm sure Melanie feels the tremor of my chest, my uneven heartbeat carrying too many unspoken words.

"I'm so sorry, Mel," I whisper into her shoulder, letting my lips linger on her skin. Her arms fit around me like they always had, as if no time had passed, as if there were no long silences or unspoken apologies for the pain I caused her.

"Josh." Melanie's voice wavers and she sniffles. And in the quiet space between us, she softens. Maybe she hasn't forgiven me completely, but there's hope.

"I should have come sooner," I murmur, pulling back slightly so I can look at her without breaking contact.

"You were busy..." Melanie lets her voice trail off. "You made something of yourself."

I pull back, guilt washing over me, sharp and unrelenting. "And at what cost?" I let go of Melanie and scrape my hand through my hair. "I lost you completely. And I've missed you more than I ever let myself admit...until now."

"I've missed you too, Josh," Melanie croaks. She falls back into my arms, and I let her, stroking her back.

I let myself memorize the way she feels against me, as if holding her now will make up for all the years I didn't. We stay like that for a long time, and for the first time, I let myself think maybe this doesn't have to end—maybe it can be the start of something new.

## THEN

*Josh,*

*I need you to know how much last night meant to me. I can't call you because I don't want Cara to be suspicious. And you won't get to read this until Study Hall on Monday, but if I don't get it out, I'll burst. Thank you. Thank you for taking me to my prom. For my corsage. For dancing with me and being silly with me. For making me feel beautiful. And seen. And thank you for everything after... for your patience and gentleness with me. For making our first time special. I will remember it forever. I hope you know how much you mean to me, not just because of last night, but because of everything.*

*Love, Mel*

MELANIE,

YOU HAVE NO <u>IDEA</u> HOW MUCH YOU MEAN TO ME. I HAVEN'T STOPPED THINKING ABOUT IT SINCE SATURDAY NIGHT. NOT JUST WHAT WE DID BUT HOW YOU LOOKED AT ME AFTER. YOU'RE THE ONLY GIRL I EVER WANT TO BE LIKE THAT WITH. I HAVE NO IDEA IF I DID EVERYTHING RIGHT, BUT I KNOW IT FELT LIKE THE REST OF THE WORLD FADED AWAY AND IT WAS JUST US. I HOPE YOU DON'T REGRET IT BECAUSE I DON'T. NOT FOR A SECOND. SO... WHEN IS ROUND TWO? ASKING FOR A FRIEND.

*LOL - you better only be asking for yourself! I still can't believe that actually happened...with you. Not to be dramatic but I'm pretty sure you ruined me for anyone else. Ever.*

FOR ME TOO. NOW ALL THE LOVE SONGS ON THE RADIO MAKE SENSE. CAN WE PLEASE HANG OUT AGAIN ASAP?

*Maybe somewhere a bit more private than the gazebo? My parents won't be home until 6 today.*

LINNY MACK

SCHOOL CAN'T END FAST ENOUGH.

# Chapter Eleven

**NOW**

"Hold on," Sophie says, holding up her hand. "Josh has been sleeping on your couch for two weeks already?" I haven't seen her in ages, so we grabbed a coffee and parked ourselves on a bench at the Washington Street Mall. I'm filling her in on all things Josh, and she's looking at me with heart eyes.

I nod, sheepishly biting my lip. "He has...and when I am off, we are writing new music every night. Or playing old music. It's just like old times but better." I close my eyes and sigh, trying not to swoon and failing miserably. "And when I work, he comes in and hangs out at the bar for half my shift."

Sophie lets out a breath, blowing away the hair falling in her eyes. "Damn, what does he do? Just drink and keep you company?"

"Nope," I say with a grin. "He doesn't even drink."

"Melanie, this guy is...into you," Sophie says, looking at me as if I'm blind.

I shake my head. "I don't think so. I think we're just old friends catching up. And even if he is, he's only passing through. If I think about it as more than that, I'll get my hopes up, and I don't want to do that. A lot was great between us back then, but we were just kids and so, a lot was broken between us too."

It's not just old friends catching up though. Josh feels like he's a part of me that was missing or broken all this time. Like we should have never been apart and now that we're back in each other's lives, it makes sense why no one else ever chose me. But I don't say that to Sophie.

"Oh, come on! I love a second chance romance," Sophie whines, jutting out her lip and cocking her head at me like one of her little daughters might do.

I suck in a breath and wince. "I just can't let myself go there yet... I know it was so long ago, but losing him hurt so badly. And there are things he doesn't know that I don't know if I can ever tell him." I take a sip of my coffee and look away, feeling the sting of tears prick the back of my eyes.

Sophie gets it because she nods and changes the subject, for which I am grateful. "I understand. You've been through so much." She hesitates then says, "Ellie is babysitting for us tonight and we're going to the distillery. They have the fire pits open and a summer drink menu. You guys should come," she urges, not bothering to hide the hopeful expression in her green eyes. That's what I love about Sophie. She's so genuine and kind—you never have to wonder where you stand with her.

I have a rare Saturday night off so it's not out of the question. Josh and I planned to order in Thai food and work on our new song for Cara though. "I don't know, we're supposed to be writing music." I scrunch my nose.

"So what? Take a night off. I need to meet this guy," Sophie chides. "Before he's gone already. Plus, Liam said that you guys want to plan some kind of concert? If that's true, you need to start planning."

Sophie isn't going to let this go until I relent, so I sigh. "Okay, fine. I'll text Josh."

"Yes!" Sophie hisses. "That's my girl."

A few hours later, I'm dressed in a pair of wide-leg jeans, and a fitted black tank top. I let my hair fall around my shoulders in its natural waves and spritz on some perfume. Josh is waiting for me when I come out of my room. He's wearing gray shorts, a fitted black T-shirt, and leather flip flops that look like the ones he wore back in high school. He smells like bergamot and sandalwood, and his dirty blonde hair is pushed back off his face, revealing clear blue eyes taking me in.

"We *look* like musicians." I laugh.

"You look great," Josh says, his voice catching. He rakes his hands through that tousled hair of his and gives me a shy smile.

"So do you." I grin. "Shall we?"

"Sure," Josh says. "I'll drive."

"Oh shit. A distillery," I facepalm myself. "I didn't even think of how insensitive this is with you being sober and all. We can totally bail and do something else." I wince, guilt burning hot across my cheeks.

Josh gives me a reassuring smile. "Mel, I sit at the bar with you nearly every day," he says cautiously. "I'm fine. Like I told you, it was never a problem. I just like myself better sober." He turns and grabs his soft guitar case leaning in the corner. "Think anyone would mind if we played around the fire?"

I can't hold back my smile. "No, definitely not."

"Good," Josh says, slinging the strap over his shoulder. "Do you want to bring yours?"

I hesitate, opening and closing my mouth. I am not sure I'm ready to play for other people yet. "Maybe I'll just sing along with you." I finally decide.

"Let's hit it, then." Josh moves for the door, gesturing for me to go first.

We arrive at the distillery and find Sophie and Liam waiting for us around the bar. They're both drinking cocktails. Liam is holding an Old Fashioned, and Sophie has a drink I recognize as a Krabby

Patty.

"Yay! You're here!" Sophie cheers, hopping off her barstool and leaning in to hug me, careful not to spill her drink.

I wrap my arms around her first while Liam and Josh shake hands, exchanging pleasantries, then we all switch places.

"Sophie, *this* is Josh," I say, gesturing to my partner in crime with his guitar bag slung over his broad shoulder.

"Josh! I've heard so much about you." Sophie has to stand on her tiptoes to hug him, but she reaches up and gives him a squeeze like he's a long-lost friend.

"Let's go claim a firepit before it gets too packed," Liam suggests, gesturing to the back doors.

"Sounds great," Josh agrees.

Sophie and I follow the men outside. Late June brings plenty of tourists to Cape May and tonight is no exception. We grab the last fire pit before the wildflower field behind us, each taking a seat in an Adirondack chair.

"Oh! You guys didn't get drinks," Sophie chirps.

"That's okay," I say, eyeing Josh cautiously. He has already taken out his guitar and begun idly strumming a tune. "We can wait."

"Suit yourself, missy." She leans back in her chair and takes a long sip from the black cocktail straw.

"So, Josh, have you written anything new since you've been here?" Liam asks, leaning back and propping a hand behind his head.

"Well," Josh drawls slowly. "Not yet. But Mel and I have been revisiting some of our old tunes trying to see if they could work." He tosses a smile in my direction, and my heart does a little flip-flop.

"Yeah? You are playing again, Mel?" Liam raises an eyebrow at me.

I roll my eyes. "I'm always playing, Liam. I just don't play for *people*."

At this Josh huffs a laugh. "Until now. I'm pretty sure I've convinced her to play at this memorial for Cara."

"Speaking of which," Liam says, scratching his chin, "I talked to Miles about it—his dad's a councilman. Miles suggested Rotary Park because of the stage. He warned it might be tough to get a date mid-summer, but Labor Day weekend was still open if we moved fast. And, well... Miles went ahead and called. Locked it in, actually. Will you be sticking around that long?"

I'm not mistaken when I feel Josh's gaze burning into me, his expression unreadable. "I can stick around for however long is necessary. Let's do it," Josh says to Liam, but he's still looking at me.

"Geez, that was fast," I mutter, glancing at Josh who hasn't taken his eyes off me. He looks excited though, and something familiar blossoms in my chest. When we were younger, Josh and Cara were excited about *everything*. Even if it was something that I might've been uneasy about, their excitement was contagious. *Maybe it's that. Maybe I'm excited because he's excited. Nothing more.*

Sophie rolls her eyes, shaking her head. "You know Miles. When he gets an idea in his mind, he runs with it."

"So, we'll just advertise it as a benefit concert?" I furrow my brow. "It's outside at a park so how will we stop people from just coming in without a ticket?"

"I was thinking about that," Liam says slowly. "I don't think we should charge for tickets. I think we should just collect donations." He pushes his lips together and glances at Sophie.

"Yeah," Sophie agrees with an enthusiastic nod. "We can create flyers with QR codes, and everyone can donate leading up to the event. The QR code can take them to a website that shares Cara's story and a place to donate." She looks back and forth between Josh and me.

"You have definitely thought about this," I tease.

Josh turns to meet my gaze. "I think it's a great idea," he says, his voice thick with emotion. "I just wish I could have helped you come up with it."

"You just worry about the music," Liam says, nodding at Josh's guitar.

Josh laughs. "That I can do."

# Chapter Twelve

## *Josh*

For the first time in the two weeks since I've been back, I've been able to breathe. When we left town all those years ago, I didn't say goodbye to anyone—not Liam, not Melanie, not my buddies. We had the funeral, and the day after, there was a For Sale sign in the yard. We moved out before it sold, renting a condo on the coast of South Carolina. I started at a new high school the following week—my old life left behind like footprints in the sand at the water's edge, washed away by the tide.

But tonight, sitting around the fire pit with Melanie, Liam, and Sophie, talking about a memorial for Cara, I finally feel like I am whole again. The only thing missing from this beautiful night is Cara herself. I'm ready to fix things—to make things right with the people I hurt when I was sixteen. Starting with Melanie.

"You okay?" she asks on our drive back to her condo.

I've been quiet, concentrating on the dark road ahead. "I'm okay," I say slowly. "I'm just lost in my memories."

"I know what you mean," Melanie murmurs. I glance over at her and she's gazing out the window. "Time is funny, isn't it? It feels like it was just yesterday that we were two kids in love." Her voice is thick with nostalgia, and when I glance at her again, she's giving me a wistful smile, head resting on the back of the seat.

*We were in love.* That crazy first love that makes you feel invincible. My chest tightens and my throat runs dry. I let out a breath and swallow. "It does," I say, my voice thick. I swallow the knot in my throat and turn onto her street.

"You can park in the back alley. My neighbor is away this weekend." Melanie gestures toward the narrow side street. I turn the corner and pull into the spot beside her car.

Killing the ignition, I turn and look at her. Her eyes are hooded and her cheeks rosy. She's looking at me like she wants me to reach for her, but I can't yet. Not until I say what I need to say.

Melanie hums and then lets out a sigh. "Shall we go in?" She turns to open her door.

Before I can stop myself, I put my hand on her forearm. "Mel, wait."

She turns back, raising her eyebrows uncertainly. "What is it?"

"I haven't been entirely honest with you." I rake my fingers through my hair. "I did come back to find inspiration for my music—that much is true. But I also came back for another reason." I fill my lungs with air and close my eyes.

"Which is?" Melanie all but whispers.

"I'm in a twelve-step program. I joined voluntarily, honest. I've never been in any sort of trouble—I just felt myself heading down a dangerous path." I scratch at my chin and look away.

"Okay," Melanie says slowly, pursing her lips. "We should probably stop going to bars."

I shake my head. "No, it's not that. I'm doing okay. The desire for a drink isn't there. I got a hold on it before it was too late."

Melanie's expression is unreadable. "I don't understand. Then what is it?"

I sigh, scrubbing my hand down my face. "I'm at the part where I need to make amends with anyone I've wronged. I've done that for most everyone in my life. Except you, Mel. I don't like how we left things."

"Josh, you already apologized. I said I forgive you," Melanie reminds me, brushing my forearm lightly. "I'm *so* happy you're back," she adds, but there's a distance in her voice.

"I know," I say. "But Melanie, leaving you like that... It ruined all my other relationships. I loved you *so much*. I've never even come close to that feeling again. And seeing you now, knowing you're still single too... I have so much guilt. Like maybe I ruined your life too." I don't realize it, but my eyes have filled with unshed tears. One escapes and I move to brush it away, but Melanie gets there first.

Our eyes meet as she lightly thumbs away the tear streaming down my cheek. "You didn't ruin my life, Josh," Melanie whispers, cupping my face.

I nod. "I'm just so sorry that I left without saying goodbye. I'm sorry it's taken me twenty-five years to make things right." I suck in a breath. I'm also sorry for other things that have nothing to do with her and everything to do with why I hate myself so much. I swallow them—if I tell her, she'll hate me too.

"I know you are," she murmurs, pulling back. If I'm not imagining it, her tone has shifted. She seems uncomfortable now. "You were just a kid, Josh. We both were." Melanie sighs. "I'm glad you're back. And I'm glad you're taking the steps to heal."

"Thank you for forgiving me," I say, looking her in the eye.

"How could I not?" Melanie's voice is barely above a whisper.

Despite my instincts telling me to back off, I grab her hand, pulling her into a hug. Her body is warm against mine, and whatever trepidation she had moments ago is gone as she softens against me. "Let's go inside," she breathes into my neck.

I follow Melanie slowly up the rickety wooden staircase, willing myself not to feel the desire simmering in my gut for her. That ship should have sailed. We're adults now, friends. One of us with a ton of baggage. She doesn't need to be mixed up with me. I have to keep this platonic, no matter how much I ache for more.

Melanie slowly unlocks the front door. The landing is small, and my body is flush against hers as she fumbles with the keys. The heat between us is palpable, and yet tiny little goose bumps appear on the back of Melanie's shoulder. She drops the keys, and we both reach to get them.

"Damn it," she mutters.

"I got it," I say at the same time.

We crouch down together, bumping heads, both of us laughing and breaking the tension before our gazes catch. Our hands clasp around the key ring together, her touch sending a jolt of electricity up my arm. Neither of us pull away, and we stay there on the landing, looking longingly at each other. Melanie's gaze drops from my eyes to my mouth to our hands clutching the keys.

She clears her throat. "I got it." Her voice is a whisper as she gently tugs the keys out of my grasp. She stands and unlocks the door, pushing inside. I follow silently, feeling ridiculous for thinking we were having a moment. I can't even blame my foolishness on alcohol.

We kick our shoes off at the door, and I have the distinct urge to escape her as quickly as possible before I do or say something stupid. I rake my hands through my hair and head toward the bathroom. "Well, good night," I murmur, brushing past her.

Catching me by surprise, Melanie reaches for my wrist. "Josh," she says, her voice breathless.

I slowly turn to face her and as soon as our eyes meet, Melanie closes the gap between us. She lunges for me, cupping my face and kissing me like she's been starving for the taste for the past two decades. Our lips crash together, teeth clashing, and the space between us breaks like a dam. Melanie isn't tentative, she kisses me urgently, like it might be the last time. I kiss her back, wrapping my palm around her neck, the years we spent apart colliding into this one aching moment. It's messy and hopeful, and it steals the breath from my lungs.

Melanie walks me backward, shoving me against a bare wall, deepening the kiss for a moment longer, before pulling back, letting her teeth drag on my lower lip. She pulls back, biting her swollen lip and eyeing me cautiously. "Good night, Josh," she whispers. She heads for her bedroom. I don't move until I hear her bedroom door click shut.

And then I take a cold shower.

# Chapter Thirteen

## Melanie

The morning sunlight is streaming through the one window in my room, but I toss and turn—I'm in the blissful place between sleep and wakefulness, and I don't want to move. Memories of Josh and me flood my mind. My heart constricts and warmth floods throughout my body. I tug a pillow close to my chest, close my eyes, and give in to the memory.

*"I don't want to go to the party," I whisper to Josh during the last slow song of the prom.*

*He tugs me closer and twirls me away from his sister and her boyfriend. He dips his head low and murmurs in my ear, "Where do you want to go?" His warm breath lingers on my neck.*

In my sleep, my hand finds the spot on my neck where his breath once brushed. A sleepy smile settles across my face as I move deeper into the memory.

*"I'm not sure. Not there. My parents are home," I say, biting my lip and looking up at Josh.*

*He smiles, dipping his forehead toward mine. "Mine are, too."*

*All night we've fought the urge to give in to these growing feelings between us. Josh is supposed to be my platonic date set up by Cara, but neither of us wants to ignore the deeper emotions building between us. We've kept it a secret for weeks.*

*"I have an idea," Josh whispers.*

*Forty-five minutes later, we've changed out of our prom attire and we're walking up the beach path at Cape May point. Josh has a blanket tucked under his arm with the idea of looking at the stars from the beach with the lighthouse. I'm nervous. The lighthouse has been under construction for the past year—there's no one around. But I can't escape the feeling that we're doing something wrong.*

*"Don't be worried. It won't be too dark. The lighthouse is lit but no one is around. We're safe out here." Josh assures me as we settle on the high sand by the dunes. He spreads the blanket out and we sit close together, our legs touching. Josh drapes an arm over my shoulder, and I lean into him. He smells good.*

*"I had the best time with you," I murmur, glancing up at him.*

*"Think we pulled it off? Or are people going to ask if we're dating?" Josh quirks an eyebrow with a grin.*

*"If they do, we'll just deny it." I shrug.*

*Josh's face falls.*

*"No, I mean—for Cara's sake. Of course we're dating." I say, cupping his face.*

*Josh kisses me then. It's tender at first but then he angles his body toward mine, cupping my face and deepening the kiss. He gently tips me back until I'm lying on the blanket and he's hovering over me. My prom hair is falling out and bobby pins are poking my head, but I don't care because I'm here with Josh and he's all I see.*

*"I'm crazy about you, Melanie," Josh rasps, gently stroking my cheek.*

*"I'm crazy about you, too," I breathe, my voice hitching in my throat.*

*"I want you," he murmurs, then quickly, "I mean...if you want to."*

*I bite my lip and nod with a shy smile.*

*"Have you ever..." he pauses, swallowing, "done it before?"*

*I shake my head earnestly. "No," I whisper.*

*"Me neither," Josh admits.*

*He moves to my side and lays facing me. I prop myself up on my elbows.*

*"So, we'd be each other's firsts," I say slowly.*

*"I guess so," Josh says, pulling my face toward his so our foreheads are touching. "If that's what you want."*

*"I do." I kiss him, pulling him closer.*

*"Here?" Josh asks.*

*"We're all alone," I say, smiling into his lips.*

*Clothes come off slowly then. It's the first time I've ever seen Josh this way, and I'm not disappointed. He carefully helps me pull my T-shirt over my head, so it doesn't get stuck on my updo. Then he tugs off his own. We kiss again, slowly this time, taking care with each moment.*

*It's not long after that that we're finished, lying in each other's arms and listening to the waves.*

*"I'll remember this forever," Josh breathes into my ear.*

*"Me too," I sigh.*

A knock sounds at my door, startling me from my blissful dream. I sit up, rubbing my eyes, trying to find reality.

"Mel, you awake?" Josh calls from the other side of the door.

"Just a sec!" I call back, throwing the blankets off me. I glance in the mirror above my dresser, fluffing my hair a bit and wiping the sleep out of my eyes. My cheeks are rosy, and I wonder if it's because of the dream.

I take note of my satin pajama tank and shorts and, remembering our kiss last night, decide to forgo the robe. I swing open my door, and there he is, leaning in my door frame.

"Hi," he says quietly, a smile tugging at his lips as he drinks me in.

"Hi." I bite back a grin, tucking hair behind my ear.

"Liam texted that Miles's dad wants to meet with us about the concert. Do you want to come?" Josh's eyes gleam, his expression hopeful, and I wonder if he's thinking about the kiss. My cheeks warm at the thought.

"Oh...what time?" I ask. "I have work tonight."

Josh huffs a laugh and looks away. "It's only ten a.m., Mel."

"Right," I say, smoothing a palm over my hair self-consciously.

"It's at noon. So, do you want to come?" He asks again.

"Sure," I chirp. "I can do that."

Josh's face gives way to a grin. "Good. I'm glad. I'm going to get us some breakfast."

"Okay." My lips curl into a swoony smile. *He's going to get us breakfast.*

He turns to go but thinks better of it, turning back. He moves with purpose toward me before tipping my chin and planting a soft, sensual kiss on my mouth. It's entirely too short-lived and when he pulls back, he presses his nose into mine. "If it's okay with you, I'd like to keep doing this." His voice is raspy, sexy.

My breath catches. *Josh wants to keep kissing me.* "Okay," I breathe.

And then he's gone, whistling on his way to the front door.

# Chapter Fourteen

## Josh

Melanie and I pull up to the municipal building at the same time as Liam, Sophie, and Miles. When Miles sees me, he goes right in for the hug.

"How are you, man? Getting famous?" Miles jokes, pulling back.

I scratch the nape of my neck and tilt my head sheepishly. "Not quite yet." I laugh.

"I don't know, I've heard some of your stuff on Spotify. I think you're on your way," Miles says.

"He's just being modest," Melanie chimes in, giving me a smirk.

"We'll see if I can write this album." I laugh.

"You will, man," Liam says, patting me on the back.

We start walking as a group, up the steps to the municipal building. It's warm for June, feeling more like August, but the sun is shining and I'm with friends I wasn't sure I'd ever see again. Gratitude swells in my chest—I don't take any of this for granted.

We enter the foyer, and Miles hits the buzzer to bring us back. The secretaries know him by name and buzz us right in.

"So, my dad loves the idea," Miles is saying as we walk to the back of the large building. "But he said if we want to raise funds for a scholarship, we need approval from the superintendent."

Melanie says. "How do we get that?"

"Well, he's here today so I assume he'll give us a verbal approval at least," Miles says, pulling open a large black door and holding it so we can all walk through. Inside is a waiting area with two doors. One reads Board of Education and the other says Town Council.

*That's convenient.*

We come to another large desk with another secretary. "Hey, Colleen." Miles grins, leaning over the desk. "Is my dad ready for us?"

"Hi, everyone. Let me give him a call," Colleen says with a smile.

While she does, I mosey around, looking at the plaques, frames, and awards on the wall. There are state trophies from high school basketball tournaments, music awards from band competitions. Various news articles of town successes hang in wooden frames. My breath catches in my throat when I see the article detailing Cara leading her high school soccer team to the state championship in her sophomore year. I didn't expect to see it here, and I don't think I've ever read it. I run my fingertips over the glass in the frame. There's a photo of Cara in the right corner of the article—she's on her teammate's shoulders, holding a large gold trophy. Her smile is bright, ecstatic. I don't get to skim the article because Councilman John Corbin opens his door, startling me.

"Hey guys," he says, his expression warm and open.

I move back to join the group, and he holds out his hand to me. "Josh. It's been a while," he says solemnly.

"It sure has," I agree, shaking his hand with a pat on the back.

"Let's chat, shall we?" He gestures for us to enter the conference room, and we all take our seats. Another gentleman, that I assume is the superintendent of schools, sits with a hot cup of coffee. He stands when we enter and shakes everyone's hands.

"Can I get you all anything?" Colleen asks. I hadn't realized she'd followed us in.

"We're good, Colleen, thank you," Miles answers for us,

dipping his head in appreciation.

We all settle into various conference table seats. I can't shake off the news article, and I struggle to focus. I desperately want to read it, but then again, I don't. *I'm here now, that's what matters.* The meeting passes by in a blur. We hammer down some details—Rotary Park, six p.m. on September sixth—and the superintendent loves the idea of a QR code for donations. Sophie agrees to take the lead on that. They will send flyers home for parents to donate. We won't charge the day of, but whatever we raise leading up to the concert, we'll donate back to the school for a soccer scholarship, since that's the sport Cara loved most. Everyone is chattering happily as we walk out, but for some reason, I'm feeling low.

"You okay?" Melanie asks, turning toward me.

I push my lips into a tight line and nod. "Yeah. I'll be okay. It's just a lot, you know? I haven't thought this much about the accident in years."

Melanie reaches out and touches my bicep, sending a shiver through me. "I get it," she says gently.

"I think—" I pause, I don't want her to take this the wrong way. "I'm going to go to the cemetery."

Melanie's expression softens, her voice gentle. "Oh, okay. Do you want some company?"

I shake my head. "I don't think so this time. I'm sorry." Guilt settles heavy in my chest—she's only trying to help. "I just need to visit Cara on my own, if that's okay."

Sure, in the past twenty-five years, I've thought about Cara often. I've missed her desperately. Losing a sibling is like losing a limb. Growing up, we were always together. We were Irish twins—super close in age and each other's most trusted companion. Losing her broke all of us, but my parents whipped me out of town so fast, I didn't have to face being here without her. The memories overwhelm me. For the first time since I've arrived, I feel like I need a drink, and that's not a good feeling.

"Okay." Hurt flashes across her features but she recovers, giving me a forced smile. "I have to work at four so..."

I nod, my jaw tight. "Okay. I'll see if I can make it, maybe I'll stop in." *If I can stop needing that drink.* I don't say that part out loud. I don't want Melanie to worry about me.

"Okay." Melanie turns to go.

I should stop her and kiss her goodbye but everyone else is still nearby. I know she's probably reading into the shift in my mood but right now, I just have to get out of here and clear my head.

My conscience gets the better of me. "You want a lift home?" I call after her.

She shakes her head, shielding her eyes from the bright sun. "I'll walk. I'll be okay," she says. She doesn't wait for me to reply before she starts walking.

I easily remember the way to Saint Mary's Cemetery because in middle school, Chris, Aaron, and I used to ride through here on our bikes. The tricky part will be remembering where we laid Cara to rest. I park my car on the shoulder of the main path and get out for a walk. I think it'll jog my memory, and maybe the fresh air will do me good. It's been a while since I've felt the urge to drink like this.

There is no rhyme or reason to the placement of graves, and I realize I'm probably looking for a needle in a haystack. I quickly read each name on each headstone I pass—no trees or landmarks look familiar.

*Gates*
*Caldwell*
*Seymour*
*Williams*
*Harper*

"Oh...wow. Leah," I murmur to myself. I hadn't realized Liam's sister had passed. Sadly, we have something in common. She was my age. A dull ache settles in my gut, and I debate turning back.

*Cocozza*

*Brown*

*Smith*

I come to the end of a path and then I see a beautiful pink dogwood tree. It's much taller now than it was twenty-five years ago. Most of the pink blooms have fallen off in the sea breeze to make way for the green leaves, but this is it. It was newly planted and so much smaller back then, but I remember it because my mom specifically loved that there would be a flowering tree near Cara's gravesite. I hang a right and walk slowly between the headstones, being careful not to walk on a grave. Then I find her.

CARA COTE

BELOVED DAUGHTER SISTER AND FRIEND.

GONE BUT NOT FORGOTTEN.

JUNE 14 1982 - SEPTEMBER 16 1999.

My throat tightens and the backs of my eyes burn. I haven't laid eyes on her gravesite since the funeral. Other headstones around us have flowers, American flags stuck in the ground. Cara's is bare. Guilt pricks my cheeks. It says, "Gone but not forgotten," but that doesn't feel true anymore.

I'm not the praying kind but I drop to my knees anyway, the hot sun on my back and dirt sticking to my knees. I fold my hands, pressing them to my lips and close my eyes.

"I'm sorry, sis," I whisper. "I never forgot you."

The words hang there, heavier than I thought. Then the tears find me, and I have no choice but to give in to them. The memories press in, jagged and relentless. I have no choice but to surrender to them.

*"Josh." My father knocks on my door.*

*"Hey, Dad," I say, grabbing a hoodie. "I'm just heading to the game. I'm super late."*

*My dad hesitates, his face crumbling. "No, son, you're not. Have a seat."*

*I frown in confusion, sitting on the bed. "Okay." That's when I hear it—my mother's wail from the other room. Like a rabid animal. It's a sound that would haunt me for the rest of my life. "What's wrong?" I ask, panic rising to my throat like bile.*

*My dad sighs and rubs his hand down his face. "There's been an accident." His voice cracks. "Your sister..." He can't get the words out.*

*Nausea rises. Goose bumps pebble my arms. "What? No. Where is Cara?"*

*My dad sits down next to me and pulls me into him. "She was in the car with Liam and Melanie. Someone ran a stop sign."*

*Melanie. Oh my god. My throat tightens. Melanie and I thought it would be best for her to go with them tonight—so as not to draw suspicion.*

*"Is she hurt?" I feel tears stinging the back of my eyes.*

*"Your mom and I have to go to the hospital. I need you to come with us." He stands then. "Your mother is a wreck. I need you to sit in the back with her while I drive."*

*"Okay, Dad. Whatever you need," I say.*

I sniffle and wipe my eyes, shaking my head to clear the memory of the worst day of my life. We didn't know it at the time, but Cara was pronounced dead at the scene. I think when my dad told me we had to go, he still had hope. I shudder and stand, wiping my eyes with the heel of my palm. I don't know how long I have been here—I left my phone in my car. As painful as this has been, I needed to do it.

"I'll be back, Cara," I say to her headstone. "I promise."

# Chapter Fifteen

## *Melanie*

I push aside the discomfort that Josh left me with after the meeting. I know it's very new, but I expected some mild affection from him after this morning's breathless encounter. He seemed distant and uncomfortable throughout the concert meeting, and that distance lingered as he told me he was visiting Cara's grave site. It's been years since I've been there myself. Perhaps we could have comforted each other. Rejection stings me like a snapped guitar string mid-song.

I try to go about the rest of my day as I normally would. I stop by the grocery store and grab some essentials. The silence is deafening when I return to my condo. Slowly and methodically, I unpack the groceries, glancing every few moments at my closed front door. I play through an old tune we wrote when we were teens a few times. We've been trying to rewrite it the past few days. Subconsciously, I wonder if it'll beckon him home. *Home.*

I don't need one, but I take a shower, taking my time, hoping that Josh will be there when I get out. He isn't. Three thirty rolls around quickly, and I'm fighting the nagging feeling that something is terribly wrong. He still isn't back by the time I have to leave for work, fifteen minutes later.

"Where is he?" I mutter to myself. I pick up my phone for what seems like the zillionth time since we parted—nothing. I tap out a text.

I'm heading into work...hope you're okay.

My message goes unanswered, and I decide to walk to work to clear my head. Realistically, nothing negative happened between us. I should remain calm. I have no reason to think Josh has second thoughts. Maybe he is missing Cara—lord knows he wouldn't be the only one.

I plaster a smile on my face as I walk through the outdoor seating area and through the front door. It's a busy Friday night in June. Summer tourism is in full swing and even though I should be used to it, the season catches me by surprise each year. *I sure could use a change.* I push the thought aside, knowing I'll never have the courage to make it.

"Hey, Mel!" Andrew comes around the bar, breaking me out of my self-deprecating, intrusive thoughts. "You didn't bring your guitar." He gestures to my empty hands.

I suppose I forgot, preoccupied by thoughts of a disappearing Josh. I almost always bring it on open mic nights though, and it feels strange not to have it with me. "Oh," I utter with a half-hearted shrug. "I guess I forgot."

"Not like you ever play anyway," Andrew teases, but when he realizes I'm not laughing, he fixes his face. "You okay?"

I take a breath and force my lips into a practiced, too-bright expression. "Yep. I'm good." I walk behind the bar and pull an apron out of the drawer under the kiosk. Andrew follows, leaning on the bar. He's still giving me that look—like he doesn't quite believe everything is fine.

"Should be busy tonight," I say, glancing around the restaurant. It is already filling up.

"Yeah. It will be. The open mic book is filling up already." Andrew grabs an empty glass from the patron in front of us. "Another?"

The man nods, and Andrew moves around me to the tap,

expertly filling a fresh pint glass with almost no foam.

"I'm going to hang around and help you until eight or nine," Andrew says, his lips pressing together. "I'm anticipating a big crowd tonight. The town is crowded with tourists. It took me almost twenty minutes to get here." He turns and faces me, leaning on the bar and examining me closely with narrowed eyes. "You sure you're all right?"

"I'm *fine*," I huff with exasperation. "I'm just a little tired."

Andrew looks like he wants to press me further, but he stops himself. "Okay, well, I will work the floor, you work the bar. Let me know if you need anything." Andrew ducks under the opening even though you can lift it up to walk through. I always wonder why he does that.

Time passes quickly after that. I'm too busy serving customers to worry about Josh or to check my phone, though every time I get a breather, I find myself glancing at the door. Nothing.

Around seven-thirty, Miles, Jenna, Liam, and Sophie come through the door. For a moment, I feel excited thinking maybe Josh met up with them, but there's no sign of him. I pull my phone out of my apron, but it's nothing but a blank screen.

"Mel!" Jenna squeals, startling me out of my pity party. "I haven't seen you in forever."

The guys pull two barstools out for Jenna and Sophie and stand behind them. "Are you going to sing tonight?" Jenna asks excitedly.

I shake my head. "That's not happening." I smirk, turning and grabbing a Miller Lite for Miles and a Corona for Liam. "What are you girls drinking?"

"Margs!" they say simultaneously, laughing. I wish I could whip off my apron and join them on the other side of the bar.

"Coming right up." I get to work making their drinks as Andrew moves to the stage to introduce the first singers for open mic night.

I put on a happy face for my friends, but I can't shake my sour mood, and I know it has everything to do with Josh. Well, him and the status of my life. My friends would never say this, but they must think, *poor Melanie, all alone, still working at the same bar. They* never make me feel this way, but I know I am an outsider looking in. They all went on to find their partners, their happily ever after. What do I get? The same shit on a different day. When Josh kissed me, I saw a glimpse of the other side—it's so close I can taste it. But who am I kidding? Josh is going to write his album and leave again, and I'll still be here. My throat tightens as a knot forms. I swallow, forcing away my internal negativity before I turn around and face my friends.

"Hey! There he is," Liam's voice jars me from my thoughts. Hope blooms in my chest. *Could it be?*

I whirl around to see Josh strolling through the door, his guitar bag slung over his shoulder. Relief washes over me so fast it nearly knocks me off balance. I told myself I was just uptight from not hearing from him, but the truth is, I'd been carrying a knot of dread all day—wondering if he was okay, wondering if our kiss had sent him running. But he's here. *He's okay.* His shoulders are looser, his expression softer than the last time I saw him. He doesn't sit next to the group. Instead, he walks with purpose over to where I'm standing.

"Hi," he murmurs.

"Hi." I give him a weak smile. "You're here. I thought you were blowing me off."

"I'm sorry," Josh offers, reaching for my hand. "I just needed to clear my head."

I nod, letting out a breath. "Okay," I whisper. "I was just worried."

Josh catches his bottom lip and nods. "I didn't mean to worry you." He meets my eyes, and it takes everything in me not to grab his chin and kiss him.

I shake my head and wave him off instead. "It's fine. You're here now. Are you going to play?"

Josh's mouth slides into a slow, irresistible grin. "Play with me?"

I glance around the bar; it's crowded. "Oh, I don't know. It's busy in here. And I didn't bring my guitar."

Josh lets out an easy chuckle. "Excuses, excuses. I'll wait till it slows down then."

I nod, my lips curving into a smile. "Ha! Okay. Want something to drink? Coke?"

"Sure," he replies. "I'll go sit with your friends."

The dinner crowd thins out around eight thirty, and it's mostly people sitting around the bar listening to the various performers. I have been busy, but I can't help noticing how easily Josh fits with the group. I lean against the center of the bar, watching him. He's regaling Sophie and Jenna with tales of living in Nashville. They are hanging on his every word, and Josh is lapping it up, his grin growing wider with each laugh they give him. The conversation is flowing, he's grinning, and it feels right—easy. My heart swells just looking at him. I wish I could be nearer—that I wasn't stuck behind this bar. I want to be in the chair next to him, close enough to smell his cologne, to feel his breath on my neck.

"Mel, I'm heading out." Andrew startles me.

"Okay." I smile. "I can take it from here."

"Wait, Andrew!" Sophie grips his arm as he passes. "Can you stay long enough for Melanie to sing a song with Josh?"

Andrew points an index finger at her. "That, I can do." He glances over his shoulder at me, a mischievous twinkle in his eye.

"No." I hold up my hands, shaking my head. "I didn't even bring my guitar."

"So, you'll sing, and I'll play. It'll be great. Come on." Josh cocks his head at me, arching a brow.

"I don't know." I hesitate, chewing on my lip, cementing my feet to the sticky floor.

"It'll be good exposure for the memorial concert," Liam points out with a knowing nod.

I glare at him.

"Great idea! Andrew, you can introduce them and mention it," Jenna chimes in.

"Ugh, fine." I drop my arms in defeat. "But only because of the concert."

"Atta girl!" Josh says as I come around to his side of the bar.

Andrew is already on his way up to the mic. He takes the clipboard and skims it, finding who was supposed to be next. "Hello, everyone. If I could just have your attention for a moment. Shane? Are you here? You're supposed to be next but if you don't mind, we've got a very special guest here—well, *two* very special guests—that would like to sing you all a song." He pauses, looking around. I do the same, and the guy I presume to be Shane gives an easy *no problem* wave.

"These two are performing a Labor Day weekend memorial concert in Rotary Park in memory of a beloved Cape May resident who passed away twenty-five years ago. Lucky you, you're getting a preview tonight! So, without further ado, please welcome your own favorite bartender, Melanie Glick, and her old friend—you *may* know him, too—" He gestures to Josh and me in the wings with a wink. "Josh Cote."

Josh beams and immediately he's in his element. I eye him cautiously because I am *so not* in my element. As we fall in step together, he whispers, "'Wonderwall'?" It was the first one we played together—the first one we picked back up again recently.

I suck in a breath. "Okay...sure," I whisper, uncertainly.

Josh doesn't reply; he slings his guitar over his shoulder and steps up onto the stage. He grabs an extra stool that's off to the side and positions both stools on either side of the mic, taking a seat. I hesitate for just a moment before taking my own seat. Josh adjusts the mic, pulling it down to his mouth.

"Hey, everyone." He flirts with the crowd, giving them an easy smile that does funny things to my insides.

There are murmurs of hellos throughout the audience and suddenly, I'm keenly aware of just how many eyes are on me. Goose bumps rise on my arms, and a nervous shiver runs through me. I try to focus my eyes on Liam and Sophie, their amiable faces bringing me comfort.

"Melanie and I first played this song twenty-five years ago, when we were just kids. Recently, we've started jamming again." Josh glances sideways at me, offering a reassuring smile and a pat on the knee. All that does is cause butterflies to swarm my stomach.

I shudder, taking a shaky breath. *This is fine.*

"You ready?" Josh asks, strumming his guitar.

"As I'll ever be," I mutter and the crowd laughs.

Josh balances his guitar on his knee and starts the opening chords. The first verse instinctively belongs to me. He doesn't miss a beat when he joins in, alternating verses and coming together in harmony on the chorus.

We don't take our eyes off one another for the entire song. When he strums his last chord, Josh leans in and plants a soft kiss on my lips. I'm too stunned to even kiss him back. He pulls back smiling when the crowd erupts into cheers. Regulars are calling my name, women are screaming for Josh. Someone shouts, "Encore!" but Josh waves them off. I might've gone for it, but he pulls the mic low to his mouth.

"I believe it's Shane's turn." He winks and turns to me with a sultry grin. I'm a goner.

"Who could follow that act?" Shane shouts from the crowd.

We're making our way back to our friends when a gangly man with salt and pepper hair steps in front of us with a business card in one hand and his other held out to Josh.

"Josh Cote, what a pleasure. My name is Jim Jones. I'm the morning show host on Lite Rock 94.1. I'd love to talk to you and Melanie about your concert sometime." He's beaming.

Josh shakes his hand, and I am just about to open my mouth to say I don't think so when he says, "We'd love to! Isn't that right, Mel?" When he looks at me, his whole face lights up. This is his thing.

I give both of them a weak smile. "Right. Sure, that would be great," I mutter, forcing enthusiasm into my voice. "I'm sorry, you'll have to excuse me. I've got to get back to work." I duck around them, moving toward the bar.

"No problem at all—Josh and I will sort out the details here," Jim Jones calls after me.

I turn back, giving him a wave. Just what did I get myself into?

# Chapter Sixteen

## Josh

The next week goes by in a blur. Melanie and I only manage to spend two days together. Andrew is on vacation, so Melanie picked up extra shifts. Every time I see her, she looks exhausted, so I don't even push her to play with me. I make us some food each night, and she comes in and eats it on the couch while I play through the song I'm working on for Cara. Melanie eats and then curls up on the couch, listening and smiling at me before falling asleep.

Eventually, as the hours wear on, I have to wake her up so I can go to sleep. It would be too weird if I slept in her bed. Still, these moments with her are precious to me. I've kissed her again, but I haven't had the courage to take things any further. If we're getting a second chance, the last thing I want to do is mess it up. There are so many things we don't know about each other anymore. I worry that when Melanie finds out more about me, she won't like who I have become. So, I let myself enjoy these moments with her, but I don't take things too far.

It's Saturday afternoon, and I am fumbling with a tricky chord progression when she comes in the front door, surprising me. She worked the day shift today, but I didn't realize that the day had passed. I have been playing guitar for way too long. She kicks her shoes off by the door and makes her way to me.

"Hey," she says, plopping down next to me and tucking her legs under her.

I set my guitar down next to me and turn to her. "Hi. How was work?"

Melanie spreads her legs across my lap and lays back. It's intimate but feels strangely natural. I pick up one of her feet and start rubbing, working the soles of her feet with my own sore fingers from a day of playing guitar.

"Ohhh, that's amazing." Melanie moans, closing her eyes.

Something stirs in my chest. "You're amazing," I murmur.

Melanie nudges me with her other foot. "Now this one." She gives me a sleepy smile.

"Okay, okay." I laugh, going to work on her other foot.

"So, what do you have going on tonight?" Melanie asks, eyes still closed.

"Nothing really," I admit, cracking her toes.

She peeks an eye open. "Ow," she says, but she's smiling.

"Sorry." I laugh. "I have been inside all day working on Cara's song. I could use some sunlight, I think. I was waiting to see what you were up to."

"What did you have in mind?" Melanie asks, sitting up and pulling her feet back. I immediately miss the physical contact.

"You want to go down to our beach?" I tilt my head at her.

"Our beach..." She lets her voice drop.

"You know, by the lighthouse," I say, scooting closer to her and gripping her ankle so I can start rubbing her foot again.

Melanie's lips spread into a slow smile. "I know where our beach is," she says, her voice practically a whisper. "I just never thought of it as *our* beach."

I lick my lips. "And I've never thought of it as anything but."

Fifteen minutes later, we're trudging up the sandy path, Melanie with a blanket in her arms and a bag with sandwiches, and me with two guitar bags. We find our spot easily, a quiet nook between the dunes, the red and white lighthouse to our rear. It's the same spot we've always come to. It's the place where I first knew that my heart would always be tethered to Melanie's.

It's a late June Saturday, so there are still beachgoers parked along the shoreline, kids playing at the water's edge. The sun sits lower in the sky, and the air is comfortable. "Right here?" Melanie turns with a smile. I wonder if she is remembering prom night—the first night we claimed this place as our own.

"This looks like our spot." I grin. I wait for her to spread the blanket out before setting our precious instruments toward the back of it. Then we sit near the front, kicking off our sandals. The sand is cooler at this time of day. Melanie hands me a sandwich and we sit, eating in comfortable silence. I've never been so comfortable with anyone before. There is no pressure to fill the silence with Melanie—it's just us.

She picks up the trash from the sandwich wrapping and shoves it in the bag. Then she passes me a lemonade, and we both take a sip.

"This place has so many memories," she says quietly. When I look over at her, she isn't looking at me; she's watching grains of sand sift through her fingers.

"It does," I agree.

"Do you remember when we came here with Cara and Liam?" Melanie giggles as she says it, and our eyes meet. I laugh too, knowing exactly what memory she is referring to.

"Yeah, I do. And she all but suggested we move to Nashville together." I pause. "She really had no idea we already planned to do that." I huff out a nostalgic laugh.

For a moment, my words hang in the air. We sit still, looking at each other—perhaps both of us reflecting on everything we missed out on together. I cannot believe I missed out on knowing Melanie all this time. My chest constricts thinking about it. I'm about to tell her as much when she breaks the silence.

"Plans change, I guess," Melanie says, offering me a half-hearted smile.

"I didn't want them to," I say, my voice gravelly.

Melanie doesn't reply. She keeps her gaze focused on something down by the water. I get the sense she is holding back.

"I should have come back for you," I say, angry with myself.

At this, Melanie turns and shakes her head. "Josh, it's okay. I wouldn't have had the courage to go anyway."

"I don't believe that for a second," I say, and it comes out harsher than I mean it to. "You wanted it as bad as I did. To go there—to be a star."

Melanie catches my gaze before quickly averting her glistening eyes. She sniffles. "All that's in the past," she mutters. She shifts, turning to face me. "Let's hear this song."

It's clear Melanie doesn't want to talk about what could have been. I can understand that to some degree. Being back here has made painful memories resurface for me, too. But it has also made me realize that I missed out on a whole life with the first girl I ever loved. Maybe we wouldn't have ended up together, but maybe we would have. Now, I am struggling with letting things be or grabbing hold of them before I lose her again.

I pick up my guitar and begin to play. Melanie picks up the chord progression quickly and before long, we're building on the melody with beautiful harmony. Everything inside me is warm and tingly. *This* is where I should be.

After an hour of playing together on the beach, my phone interrupts us. It's a local number so I answer it on speaker.

"Hello?" I say.

"Is this Josh? Jim Jones here from Lite Rock 94.1." The booming voice comes through the speaker. I glance at Melanie, who gives me an eyebrow raise.

"It is. Great to hear from you, Jim," I say. Truthfully, I'd forgotten that I'd given Jim my number, but talking to him can't hurt. "Melanie is here with me."

"Great! That's great! Hi, Melanie." Jim's enthusiasm carries through the speaker, and this time when I look at Melanie, she's got her hand over her mouth, muffling a giggle. "Listen, I'd love to have you two on the morning show next week. You can talk about your story, how you met, and the concert in September. What do you say?"

I meet Mel's gaze and she casually lifts a shoulder, which I take as approval.

"Sure, sure, we can do that," I agree.

"And, do you think you could play an original song? Live? On the show," Jim asks.

This time Melanie holds up her hands and shakes her head, mouthing the word *no* at me.

"Oh, well...I'm not sure we'll have one ready," I muster.

"Just a small taste of something. What do you say?" Jim Jones is persistent.

I hold a hand up to Melanie and arch my eyebrows. *What do you think?* I mouth.

"I guess," she says quietly but out loud. Jim hears.

"Great!" Jim booms. "How is Wednesday?"

"Wednesday is good," Melanie chimes in for the first time.

"Let's do eight a.m. at the studio. I'll send you the address," Jim says, suddenly speaking quickly. He's probably afraid we'll change our minds.

"Sounds great, Jim. Talk to you soon," I say. We end the call.

"This should be fun, right?" I give Melanie my most optimistic grin.

"Super."

❧

By the time we head back to the condo, Melanie and I are both exhausted. We're trudging up the creaky wooden steps when my phone rings. This time it's my manager.

"Hey, Gary," I say, cradling the phone as I unlock the door. "What's going on?"

"I was just checking in to see how the acoustic album is going," Gary starts slowly. "Have you written anything yet?"

I glance over my shoulder at Melanie as we walk inside. I

can't help but notice her listening with interest.

"I have actually. Well, revisiting an old song I've never produced. And writing a new one for my sister." I sit down in the armchair.

"Great. That's good stuff. How long are you staying?" Gary doesn't pressure me outright, but there's an underlying urgency to his question.

I huff a laugh. "I don't know, Gary, I just got here."

"I'm just asking," Gary says, and I can imagine the way he's holding up his hands defensively.

"I know, Gar. I think it's...good for me to be out of Nashville for a while," I admit. I look at Melanie who is now sitting across from me on the couch, watching.

"Well, don't stay away too long. Keep me posted on your progress," Gary says.

"I will. Promise. We'll talk soon." I hang up with a sigh.

"Who was that?" Melanie asks, narrowing her eyes.

I groan. "My manager, Gary. Wants to know when I'm coming back."

"Weren't you supposed to be gone until you write this whole album?" Melanie frowns.

I might be imagining it, but there's a little pink to her cheeks.

"Yes. I am." I stand up and move to sit by her, tugging her close. "I'm not going anywhere soon, trust me," I murmur, tugging her closer and planting a soft kiss on her mouth.

Melanie pulls back, running her fingers through my messy hair and gazing at me with a lazy half smile. "Okay. But why did you say you have to stay away from Nashville for a while?" she probes.

I hesitate. I'm not sure I'm ready to talk about what went on down there yet. But the closer Mel and I get, the more it feels like I'm keeping things from her. "I just... There are influences." I let my words hang in the air. "Just trust me. Here is where I need to be for now."

"Okay." Melanie seems satisfied with this when she grabs the collar of my T-shirt and pulls me to her again, kissing me softly. "Can I ask a favor?" she asks without pulling away from our kiss.

I grin into her mouth. "Anything."

"How do you feel about ditching the couch?" Melanie pulls back, dragging her lower lip between her teeth.

"I'm not sure what you mean?" I furrow my brow. "I don't mind this couch."

Melanie giggles. "I meant...would you sleep in my bed with me tonight?"

I fight back the grin threatening to betray my poker face. "Oh," I say, licking my lips.

"I just...could use a warm body." A smile tugs at her mouth. "Just to cuddle."

"Cuddle," I repeat with a nod. "I think I can handle that."

# Chapter Seventeen

I'm warm and content as the sun streams through the small window in my bedroom. The air conditioner is blasting, but I'm not cold because I'm wrapped in Josh's embrace, our legs intertwined, his feet on mine, keeping them warm. It's been three nights of us sleeping together like this, and despite the feeling of his hard body against mine each morning, neither of us has made a move. I desperately want to, but I can't help but think if he wanted more than this, he'd go after it.

His cellphone alarm beeps and buzzes from the nightstand, startling him awake. I'm already awake, but I keep my eyes closed anyway. Josh reaches to turn it off and then his arm finds my hip again.

"Time to get up," he murmurs into my neck. His hot breath sends a jolt straight between my thighs. He kisses my neck, and his light stubble dragging across my skin has desire pooling in my belly.

I turn over to face him, letting my fingers trace his jawline. "I hate waking up early," I whisper. "But I love waking up with you."

Josh kisses me then, pulling me close enough that I can feel his desire. It's a relief to know I'm not the only one feeling these things. I never thought I'd see Josh again, let alone have a second chance. He deepens the kiss, tangling his fingers in my hair, his teeth clicking against mine. Hungry. That's the best way to describe it. I let out a soft moan, and he echoes it with his own.

"I want you," I say softly into his mouth. Relief at having admitted it flows through me.

Josh pulls back, meeting my gaze. He brushes hair off my forehead. "I want you too," he admits. "But we're due at the radio station in an hour and...I'd like to take my time with you." His voice is thick with yearning.

I groan. "Okay. That's fair," I say, moving away from him.

He tugs me right back. "Hey," he says, tracing his calloused thumb over my lower lip. "I *do* want you. Waking up with you the past few days has meant more to me than..." Silence hangs in the air for a moment as he struggles to find words. "I just—never thought we'd get a second chance. I don't want to screw this up."

"Me neither," I say, placing my hands on his face and pulling him to me. "And it's meant so much to me too."

"Good." Josh pushes up, throwing the covers off him. "Let's get this show on the road."

We take turns showering—seeing Josh walking around my condo in a towel, his broad shoulders still glistening with water, does something to me. It's not only that I want him—I do—but it's also that I want him *here*, with me. He fits. We move around each other naturally, getting ready for our day together. While I blow-dry my hair, he fixes my coffee and sets it on my dresser. He packs up our guitars, fills up my water bottle, and he's waiting patiently for me when I come out ready to go.

I drive us to the Lite Rock studio and Josh holds my hand the entire time. I keep stealing glances at him, but he appears lost in thought and I'm too jittery to make conversation.

"Are you okay?" His voice catches me off guard. "Nervous?"

"A little," I admit. "I'm sure this is nothing for you, but it's not every day I go on a radio show." I smile in spite of myself.

"Admittedly, I haven't done any interviews in a long time." Josh pauses. "I've been trying to lay low."

I give him a sideways glance, arching a brow. "Any particular reason why?"

Josh hesitates, his lips pushed into a line, his brow furrowed as if he's deciding how to answer. "Things in Nashville weren't great when I left. I felt like all eyes were on me and not in a good way."

I pull into a parking spot before I answer him. Unbuckling my seatbelt, I turn to him, tilting my head. "Care to elaborate?"

Josh's shoulders stiffen, and he crosses his arms, as if closing himself off. "Not really, to be honest." My face must betray me because he adds, "Not yet anyway."

His response feels callous and out of character, but I don't have time to push him. We're due inside in three minutes.

"We have to go in," I say, gathering my things. I don't meet his eyes.

"Mel, I'll fill you in, someday," Josh says, grasping my forearm to stop me from frantically walking away. "Before we go on a radio show is not the time though."

"Fine." I sigh. "You don't owe me anything, Josh." I open my car door and climb out, opening the rear door to grab my guitar.

Josh doesn't respond, and it's clear to me that it's because he doesn't want to get into whatever he's got going on before we walk into this interview. But I can't help but want to press him. Unfortunately, after the interview, I have to work the day shift. Josh and I will have to talk tonight.

Jim's assistant, Andrea, greets us as we walk in. The morning show is already underway—it starts at six a.m.—so Andrea leads us to a small waiting area where we'll wait to be introduced. She brings us both a bottle of Fiji water and a hot cup of coffee. Josh and I sit side-by-side on a small loveseat. His thigh grazes mine, and it's taking everything in me not to put my hand on his leg. I must be jittery because a moment later, *his hand* finds my leg. His warm palm cups my kneecap, and he traces circles around it with his thumb.

"It's going to be fine," Josh whispers, leaning close to me. I can feel the tickle of his breath on my neck. It's minty and I fight the urge to grab his face and devour it. Josh sets me at ease, even when he's not trying. "They even sprung for the good water." His lips twitch.

"Josh, Melanie! Thanks for coming." We're interrupted by Jim Jones himself, grinning at us from the doorway.

We stand and shake his hand, exchanging pleasantries.

"We're on a fifteen-minute music break, so let's bring you in and get you mic'd and ready." Jim gestures toward Andrea, who is holding the studio door open for us. "After you."

Ten minutes later, we're settled in the soundproof studio in comfortable chairs around the mixing board. We're wearing microphones and headsets, and Jim is just about to bring the show back from a commercial break. Despite Josh briefly prepping me on the ride over, my heart is racing, and my palms are sweating. How did I get here? What am I even doing? Who do I think I am? I'm nobody. At least Josh is someone—he's made something of himself. I have no business being here right now.

Josh glances over at me. "You okay?" His voice is barely audible. Then he leans closer. "You look a little green."

I swallow the knot in my tight throat and nod. My palms are already sweating, and he's grinning at Jim with maddening ease. Josh watches me carefully, but he's relaxed, drumming a lazy rhythm against his knee. *Typical man.* If I speak, I fear I may bail, and he's cool as a cucumber. I don't have time to say anything anyway because we're on in three...two...one.

"Welcome back to the Lite Rock morning show. This is Jim Jones! I'm here with the one and only country music sensation, Josh Cote! Welcome, Josh." I glance nervously at Josh who is grinning. If he's nervous at all, he doesn't show it. He's probably used to this.

"And Josh brought with him his friend and fellow musician, Melanie Glick. Melanie is a South Jersey local, and she's here because she and Josh are working on something very special. Isn't that right? Welcome, Melanie." My stomach twists as I adjust my headphones.

"Thanks for having us, Jim," Josh says, leaning into his mic.

"Yes, thank you," I echo, a blush creeping into my cheeks. "So happy to be here." *That couldn't be further from the truth.*

"Why don't we start by you two telling us a bit about how you met," Jim suggests.

I lock eyes with Josh and he chuckles. "Well, Jim, Melanie and I go way back. We've been friends since we were kids, but we were closest in high school."

"Wow. High school. Okay Josh, I didn't realize you were from around here," Jim admits. Then he turns to me. "I bet you loved this guy in high school, Melanie." His tone is teasing.

My neck tingles and my throat goes dry. Heat blooms across my chest like a sunburn. I can't meet Josh's eyes—not with Jim watching like he's just thrown a grenade between us. "Uh...yeah. He's hard not to love." I swallow the lump in my throat.

"So, are you two an item?" Jim asks. The way he looks at me gives me the creeps.

"Oh...no. We're just old friends," I mutter loosely crossing my arms. I glance at Josh whose face remains impassive.

"Gotcha, so how did you reconnect?" Jim asks, this time looking at Josh.

Josh stifles a cough, rubbing the back of his neck like the words got caught in his throat. "I came up here looking for inspiration. I haven't been here in nearly twenty-five years. I'm not sure if you know this, Jim, but my older sister Cara was killed in a car accident her senior year of high school. My family moved shortly after." Josh pauses, and it looks to me like he needs a minute. When he speaks again, his voice wavers. "I am sure you heard, I broke up with my band—or rather, they broke up with me, I guess. So, I set out to write a solo acoustic album. But I needed inspiration and a change of scenery, so I thought, what better to do than come home?" Josh glances my way and offers me a smile. The tips of his ears are pink.

"I did hear about the breakup, Josh. I'm sorry about that," Jim offers. "And about your recent split from Kiera Muller too."

When I look at Josh, he looks uncomfortable, but he leans

into his mic and says, "Hey, everything happens for a reason, Jim, am I right?"

"You are." Jim nods. "So, tell us how you reconnected with Melanie."

"She was working at The Ugly Mug when I walked in," Josh says. "I knew it was her immediately." This time, Josh looks directly at me, and my heart lurches into my throat.

"Melanie, did you know it was Josh?" Jim asks.

I clear my throat. "I did." I meet Josh's gaze. "We reconnected like no time had passed."

"When I was at The Ugly Mug, I had the pleasure of hearing you two play a cover song together. Have you always played music together?" Jim directs the question at me, but Josh answers.

"Not in twenty-five years." He huffs a laugh. "But we did, yeah. We started writing music together when we were just teenagers."

"Teenagers, wow." He quirks his eyebrows at us. My stomach twists, and feelings of unease rumble in my gut.

Josh laughs easily. "You know, crazy teens and their love songs."

Jim's eyes light up at this, his curiosity piqued. "And were you in love when you wrote songs together?"

The question comes point-blank. Before I can stop myself, I'm answering at the same time as Josh.

"Oh, I don't know. No. Jim, like we said, we were teenagers." I give a casual wave of my hand.

"I've always loved Melanie."

Josh's words overpower mine.

Suddenly, the air is too thick. I'm uncomfortable. Josh's words hit me like a dropped chord reverberating long after the sound is gone.

Jim thinks this is hilarious, and Josh and I look at each other, having no choice but to laugh with him. What else can we do? But something inside me clenches, and I'm unsure if it's from shock or something deeper.

"Sounds like you two need to talk." Jim lets out another

nervous chuckle, but Josh and I only look at each other. Questions swirl in my mind—*he's always loved me?*

It feels like hours before anyone speaks again though I'm sure it's only a matter of seconds since we're live on the air.

"Would you play one of your own for us now?" Jim asks, perhaps sensing the awkwardness.

"Our own...Mel?" Josh looks to me for approval. "'Every Song'?"

"Uh, sure. Okay." I nod, swallowing hard. We've only played it in the safety of my

apartment. Now suddenly, we're going to play it live on the radio. Josh picks up his guitar and begins strumming the intro.

The first verse has always been mine, so I suck in a breath and will my heart to stop racing. My first notes are shaky but by the time I get to the third line, I've found my voice, the soft melody coming out stronger.

*We swore forever in the back of your car,*
*Snuck out to the beach, counting every star.*
*Didn't know then, but we had it all,*
*First love's a promise, you won't think you'll fall.*
*We were just kids, didn't know what love was,*
*Late-night talks and scribbled hearts on our books.*
*Laughed too loud, got on everybody's nerves,*
*Didn't need much, just the two of us.*

*You're my favorite line in every song,*
*You're the reason I go on.*
*Don't call it a summer fling,*
*Cause you gave me a paper ring.*
*Your name's still there on my old notebook page.*
*Fingers strum in the summer breeze*
*Wonder if you still think of me*
*Faded ink, but I still see your face.*

*They said we were young,*
*But our love lives on in every song.*

*We sang our hearts out in the back of your car,*
*Reckless teens, counting dreams like they'd take us far.*
*Didn't know then how fast things change,*
*But first love memories never really fade.*

*You're my favorite line in every song,*
*You're the reason I go on.*
*Don't call it a summer fling,*
*Cause you gave me a paper ring.*
*Your name's still there on my old notebook page.*
*Fingers strum in the summer breeze*
*Wonder if you still think of me*
*Faded ink, but I still see your face.*

*They said we were young,*
*But our love lives on in every song.*

I have no idea how I get through it. I play the chords with muscle memory, feeling the notes run through my veins, while my brain spins in a fog. The vibration of the guitar presses against my ribs, each note pulsing through me. Josh's voice weaves through mine like we never stopped making music together—safe and familiar, brand new and exciting all at once. It's as if the music can explain everything we can't. The interview ends with Jim plugging the Labor Day weekend concert, and we wrap things up with a commercial break.

"That was great, guys. Thank you," Jim says with an infectious grin once we're off air.

I want to be happy, but I am stunned. I rip my headset off and leave it on the table, unable to catch my breath. The back of my neck is sweating, and my breathing feels erratic.

I suck in a breath through my nose, and my chest tightens,

my lungs unable to fill completely.

"Thank you, Jim." I rise to shake his hand, picking up my guitar bag. "I'm really sorry but I have to get some air." I excuse myself and bolt from the studio, bursting through the doors like I've been underwater for too long. Behind me, I hear Jim telling Josh how hot it gets in there. But the only thing echoing in my brain is Josh's words: *I've always loved Melanie.*

# Chapter Eighteen

## *Josh*

I find Melanie just outside, leaning against the sun-warmed brick building. She's taking slow, deliberate breaths and her eyes are closed—like she's trying to hold herself together. The sunlight catches her red hair, gilding her face in gold.

"What the hell was that?" My voice comes out sharper than I mean it to, but I step in front of her anyway, blocking her escape. "You just ran out of there."

"I should be asking you the same thing," Melanie retorts.

"What do you mean?" I scoff, folding my arms across my chest.

"You've always loved me?" Her voice cracks, sharp and too loud—like her words burned coming out. Her eyes find mine and when they do, I see that they're glistening. "Why would you say that? Live *on the radio*." She looks away, like she is trying to force away the emotion on her face.

"Because it's true." My voice drops, low and rough, laced with pain. I step into her space, bracing my hand on the wall to stay steady. "I *have* always loved you." The words scrape my throat, and I tip her chin so her eyes find mine.

Melanie shakes her head. "You don't even know me anymore, Josh. I don't know you. I don't know anything about you. And every time I bring it up, you brush me off or change the subject."

"So? That doesn't change anything for me," I protest. "I never stopped thinking about you. About us."

Melanie sniffles then and I realize she really is on the verge of tears. "Josh, you can't say things like this to me. The bottom line is, that was then, this is now. We're grown adults with baggage and you're just passing through—you don't live here. You might be here now, but you're a *star.* You're going to go back to your life, and I'm going to go back to mine." She meets my gaze. "Don't say things you don't mean."

"I do mean them Melanie. I've always meant it when I say I love you." I tilt my forehead into hers.

"If that's true, then I want the whole truth," she says, her voice quieter this time. "Why are you *really* back here?" She folds her arms across her chest, looking at me as if trying to see through me.

I didn't want it to come out like this but she's leaving me no choice. If I don't tell her now, I risk her shutting me out for good.

"Fine," I bite out. "You want the truth? You want the whole fucking picture?" My heart is pounding in my ears. I rake a hand through my hair as if it will stop the avalanche from coming out of me.

"A little over a year ago, I wrapped my truck around a tree. I swerved to avoid hitting a *kid* on a bike. I wasn't wasted—but I was over the limit to drive. I could have killed him. My license was suspended for a year, but that wasn't the worst of it. People looked at me differently. The people I thought I could count on pulled away. I lost everything that mattered to me, everything that made sense."

I laugh, bitter and hollow.

"My sister lost her life because some asshole decided to drive drunk and I—*I became that asshole.*" My throat burns. I press my fingers to my eyes, but the tears break through anyway. "I hate myself for it. Some days, it weighs so heavily on me that I can't breathe. I thought, what the fuck am I doing with my life? And I'm here because I don't know who I am anymore—I feel *lost.* So, I came back to the last place I remember feeling whole. Because everything feels broken, and you're the only thing that's ever felt like *home*. Okay? Does that satisfy you?"

I'm mid-breakdown when Melanie's arms are around me, grounding me like a lifeline. I collapse into her, sobbing, giving into my grief and shame, completely forgetting that we're outside the radio station in broad daylight.

"Shhh," she whispers, stroking my back. "It's okay. I've got you. Let's get you home."

She leads me to her car and opens my door first. I'm wiping my eyes with the base of my palm and taking deep breaths when she slides into the driver's side.

"I'm sorry," I mutter, unable to look at her. "I was going to tell you all of that, but I just—didn't want you to see me differently. Do you...do you hate me?"

Melanie's face falls. "Josh," she breathes. "Hate you?" She cups my face with both hands, like she's afraid I'll disappear. "God no. I love you. I have *always* loved you." Her words knock the wind out of me.

But as she shifts the car into gear, her eyes fixed on the road, I can't shake the dull ache that has settled in my chest. It feels like my confession has built a wall instead of tearing one down—as if by admitting the truth, I've only pushed her further away. That despite everything we said, she's slipping through my fingers. I can't help but feel like I've already lost her.

Melanie goes to work, and I lay on her bed, drifting in and out of sleep. The ceiling fan hums quietly above me, stirring the warm air, but it does nothing to lull me to a deeper sleep. I should get up and rehearse. Time is wasting away. But I can't. I'm pinned here, my body heavy with the weight of an elephant on my chest.

To be honest, I never dealt with my shit properly and now it's haunting me—clawing its way back in. Being back here, thinking about Cara and the way she died, it's bringing up all the feelings of failure I had after my own accident. I keep thinking about the crash, the headlines—*Rising Country Music Star Josh Cote Gets a DUI*—ugh. My stomach clenches.

I'm internally berating myself when my phone rings, a shrill sound cutting through the silence. I squint at the screen. A Philadelphia area code.

"Hello," I grumble, my voice scratchy.

"Josh? It's Mark. From SoundShift Records." His voice floats through the line, too casual.

"Hey, Mark. How are you?" I sit up, the room tilting slightly, and force myself to concentrate. I haven't seen Mark since my DUI, though I'm sure he knows about it. I'm sure Gary told him. I try not to let my embarrassment claw its way to the surface.

"I'm good. Look, I'm in Philly for a few meetings this week. Thought I'd see if we could meet up, chat about what you're working on." Mark doesn't phrase it as a question.

Panic sets in. *What am I working on?*

I don't want to be dropped by my label, but I have no idea what I'm doing. All I have done so far is revisit old lyrics and fall back in love with my high school girlfriend. I have absolutely nothing to show for the few weeks that I've been here.

"I'm here until Saturday. You free?"

I blink hard, like that will make everything click.

"When were you thinking?" If I have a few days, I can gather myself and present *something* to him.

"Is it too late for you to get up here tonight? Otherwise, tomorrow I'm free after two." Mark's voice is distant, like he's scrolling through his calendar. Philadelphia is over an hour from here so that doesn't leave me much time.

"Tomorrow is probably better." I drag my hand down my face.

"Great. I'll touch base in the morning, and we'll pick a meeting point. And Josh? Bring something to show me," Mark says, and then he's gone.

I drop my phone onto the mattress beside me. It lands with a soft thud but the weight of it feels enormous.

*Fuck.*

When Melanie gets home from work, I'm still lying in her bed, curled up in the same position she left me in.

"Josh?" she calls from the entryway.

"In here," I say without moving.

A moment later, Melanie is leaning in the doorway. Her work shirt is rumpled and untucked, her cheeks flushed from the late June air, and her hair is piled on the top of her head. "Whatcha doing?" she asks gently, eying me carefully.

"Nothing at all. I've been here since you left," I mumble, shifting over. I pat the spot next to me. "Want to lie down with me?"

Melanie smiles. "Sure, let me change." And then she's lifting her shirt over her head, standing there in her jeans and her bra, completely uninhibited. The late-day sun shines through the window, streaking across her bare skin. Dust motes dance in the light around her.

My breath hitches and she looks my way, her lips twitching. "It's nothing you haven't seen before," she says softly. She throws a loose-fitting pale blue T-shirt over her head and unzips her jeans, stepping out of them. The T-shirt barely covers her ass, and I catch a glimpse of the bare curve of it. I watch her closely as she rummages through her drawer for a pair of gym shorts. When she slips them on, I'm disappointed.

She slides into bed next to me and we're spooning. I tug her closer, and my hand rests on her hip. She sighs long and low, settling into my embrace. I plant a kiss on the crown of her head. The scent of her shampoo—coconut and vanilla maybe—wraps itself around me.

Everything feels right. For a moment. Until she says, "So, do you want to talk about this morning?"

I swallow hard. "Not really. I have other things on my mind."

I tug her close and press a kiss to the side of her neck.

"Josh," Melanie drags out my name and rolls over to face me.

I roll on my back and drape a forearm over my eyes with a groan. The corner of the ceiling is cracked, and I focus on that instead of the way Melanie is looking at me.

"Don't you think we should talk about it?" Melanie presses, leaning over me.

"About me loving you?" I shift, stroking her cheek, letting my thumb trace the line of her lip. "What's there to talk about?"

"Not that—" Melanie says, biting her lip.

"No." I cut in. "I don't want to talk about that." I push up on my elbows. "A rep from my record company called. He's in Philly and wants me to meet him tomorrow," I add, my voice sharper than I mean. "I'm supposed to have something to show him."

"Wow," Melanie says, brows lifting. "I guess you have to go."

I nod solemnly. "I do. I don't know what I'm going to play for him."

"Play 'Every Song,'" Melanie suggests without hesitation. "It's a great song."

"I can't play that song without you." I sigh and run my hands through my hair. "Come with me? Maybe they'll like the idea of a duet."

Melanie scrunches her nose, uncertain. "This is your thing, Josh."

I shake my head, pushing up to my elbows. "No, come on. If this song makes it on the EP, it's *our* song. Your name will be on it as a composer." I take her hands, squeezing them gently. "Please, Mel. I need you there."

Melanie leans over and pushes me back on the bed. Then she tucks into the crook of my arm and sighs. "You're lucky I love you so much."

## THEN

**LAST DAY OF SCHOOL! I CAN'T WAIT FOR**

TONIGHT. BONFIRE ON THE BEACH. CAN I FINALLY TELL CARA YOU'RE MY GIRLFRIEND?

*I'm not sure... I don't know how she'll take it.*

COME ON, MEL. THERE'S ONLY ONE WAY TO FIND OUT. MY FEELINGS FOR YOU ARE GETTING STRONGER. I DON'T WANT TO HIDE THEM ALL SUMMER.

*I know. Me neither. Let me think about it.*

I DON'T THINK YOU UNDERSTAND WHAT I'M TRYING TO TELL YOU, MELANIE. I AM FALLING IN LOVE WITH YOU.

*Josh... Wow. I love you too.*

SO WHY CAN'T WE TELL THE WORLD? OR AT LEAST THE SCHOOL?

*We will. Soon.*

# Chapter Nineteen

## Melanie

### NOW

I don't know how I let Josh talk me into this, but somehow I'm in the car with him on our way to Philadelphia. We're meeting an executive from SoundShift Records, and Josh thought it would be awesome if we played "Every Song" for him—together. There is a little part of me that is excited. Playing music I wrote for a record producer is something I never imagined I'd have the opportunity to do. The other part of me is completely terrified—sweating palms, uneasy stomach, racing heart. Josh didn't even tell this guy, Mark, that I'd be coming. I never thought Josh would think a surprise is a great idea, but he seems more at ease than he's seemed in weeks. Every time I look his way from the passenger seat, he gives me an easy smile.

Last night we ordered dinner and rehearsed the song until my fingers burned. I think we've got it down—we added a bridge and harmony on the third verse. I am really happy with it. Josh seems to be too.

We're quiet as we merge onto the expressway that will take us right into Philadelphia. I'm lost in thought, remembering our last summer together. I can't stop thinking about that day. Josh just finished up his sophomore year, I'd finished up my junior. He was begging me to come clean to Cara about us. We'd been sneaking around for weeks under the guise of writing music. Josh had just told me he was falling in love with me, and I loved him too. That night, there was a party on our beach. The one where we'd lost our virginity together. There were so many people, and we sat around a blanket with Cara and Liam, stealing glances at each other when we thought they weren't looking.

I can still hear the conversation in my mind.

*"Oh, will you two stop making googly eyes at each other?" Cara scoffed. "Don't act like we can't all see you."*

*My cheeks and neck grew hot. I felt so self-conscious in that moment—why would Cara embarrass us like that?*

*Josh recovered before I did. He looked tenderly at me and just when I thought he was going to admit to our secret romance, he said, "Mel and I have been working on a song we're excited about. That's all."*

*"Oh, a song, huh?" Liam chimed in. "Are you going to play it for us?"*

*I knew that was going to happen. A flush spread across my chest as more people began paying attention to us.*

*"Not yet," Josh said, glancing at me again. "It's not ready yet."*

*"Whatever." Cara rolled her eyes. "Hey, maybe you two will be famous in Nashville together one day."*

I'm jarred from my memory at the sound of Josh clearing his throat. "You okay?" He glances quickly at me before turning his attention back to the road. Outside, cars blur by at a high rate of speed, but in here, my world is paused in 1999.

Goose bumps rise on my arms, and I offer him a soft, wistful smile. "Yeah. I was just lost in a memory." I shake my head.

"Oh yeah? About us?" Josh quirks an eyebrow at me as he looks over his shoulder to change lanes.

"Maybe," I murmur, wiggling my own eyebrows playfully, even though deeper feelings stir beneath the surface.

Josh laughs, the sound low and familiar, like an old love song.

"We have a lot of great ones." He lets his voice trail off, like he's reaching for a memory he can't say out loud.

I nod, my smile fading slightly. "We really do. I haven't let myself think about them in so long," I admit sadly. I look down at my hands just as Josh reaches across the center console and grips one. His palm is warm and steady.

"I was thinking..." Josh starts, squeezing my hand just like he used to. "After this meeting, maybe we can explore Philly? I haven't been there in so long. Figured we could get a bite to eat and walk around a bit?" Josh looks so hopeful, it tugs at my heartstrings.

I picture us walking around Old City, popping in and out of stores, eating ice cream and listening to street musicians.

I don't hesitate—I'd go anywhere with Josh.

It's been so long for us and yet, we seem to have picked up right where we left off. Maybe it's impulsive, but it's also easy. We've slipped right back into a steady rhythm. No masks, no hesitation.

No other relationship I've had in the last twenty-five years has been so easy. It's a breath of fresh air. I can be myself with him. There is no need to hide how I really feel or play it cool. There are no first impression nerves. It's just *us*.

I don't bother to bite back my grin. "Of course. That sounds great." I squeeze his hand back, anchoring this moment. "Are you ready for this?"

"With you," he says, his voice low, scraping, "I'm ready for anything."

Twenty minutes later, we're walking into the lobby of the Renaissance Hotel, cool air conditioning sweeping over us as we head toward the bar. Mark Matthews is already waiting for us, nursing a highball glass with a dark amber liquid in it. I immediately worry about Josh and the pressure of this meeting—but his expression remains calm, unreadable. As we approach, his posture straightens.

"Mark, my man," Josh holds out his hand, and they shake firmly before Josh leans in for a quick one-armed hug and a slap on the back.

Mark pulls away, a look of surprise flashing across his features. "Josh! It's been a while." He gestures to me. "And who is this?"

"This is Melanie." Josh grins, slinging an arm around my shoulder, his tone easy but possessive. "We're old friends, used to play together all the time and recently picked it back up."

"Great!" Mark holds his hand out to me. "Nice to meet you, Melanie. Let's sit, shall we?"

Josh pulls out the stool next to Mark for me and takes the one on my other side. Once we're settled, a bartender comes over, placing cocktail napkins in front of us. I wait for Josh to order.

"Hello, folks. What can I get you to drink today?" The bartender greets us, tipping her head to one side and giving Josh her full attention. She's pretty with blonde hair piled high on her head and kind brown eyes. He doesn't seem to notice that she's looking only at him.

"Just a water with lemon, please," Josh says, his voice even, his arm slipping around the back of my chair, subtle but seemingly deliberate.

"And for you?" She purses her lips expectantly.

"Oh, water is fine for me too." I wave my hand in an effort to be casual.

"Still on the wagon, I see," Mark says with a nod as the bartender walks away.

Josh sucks in a breath. "Yeah. It's not easy, but it's what's best."

"Good man," Mark says, taking a sip of his own drink. "So, I'd love to know what you've been working on these past couple of weeks."

Josh chuckles, sipping his water as soon as the bartender sets it down. "Cutting right to the chase, I see." The men lock eyes, and it's only now that I realize they may not be as friendly as I originally thought.

"Well, Mark, as you know, I've been trying to write an acoustic EP. Something totally different from what I've done before." Josh runs a hand along his jaw.

Josh begins to tell him all about Cara, and Mark visibly softens. Josh fills him in on her death and scratches the surface of our history together. He talks about the old songs we wrote together. "I think I'm going back to my roots. Writing with nostalgia. The first song I've finished, I co-wrote with Melanie when we were teens. We've given it a refresh, and I'd love for it to be the first single."

Mark's smile is slow to form. Standing, he drains the last of his drink in one gulp. The way he is eyeing the two of us sends pins and needles straight up my spine. He nods and then taps the bar. "Tina," he calls, gesturing to the bartender. "Close my tab. Put it on my room charge." He rises to his feet, throwing a couple of bills on the bar and gestures to the lobby couches. "Let's hear it."

"O-okay." Josh nods and suddenly seems nervous.

We brought both guitars. They're leaning in their cases on the other side of Josh. He grabs mine first and passes it to me. We follow Mark out to the center of the lobby. I can feel the pulse in my neck as we settle in, guitars in hand. I'm used to singing alone in my apartment, not in hotel lobbies full of people. I look to Josh, and he offers me a reassuring smile.

There's a curved beige couch with a black armchair across from it in the center of the lobby. Mark takes the armchair and gestures for Josh and me to sit. We take out our guitars and Mark is eerily silent, watching us. Josh catches his bottom lip with his teeth. "You good?" he murmurs.

"Yeah," I breathe. "Let's do this."

We play through the song, and it's even more natural than the last time. Our voices melt together like butter. Several people stop to watch—something that would normally give me pause—but all I have to do is look at Josh and everything feels right. *This* feels right.

"Wow," Mark says before we've strummed the last chord.

"That's fabulous."

The look of relief that crosses Josh's features cracks open something inside me. *He was worried*, I realize.

"Thank you." Josh nods, flicking his gaze my way. "Mel is the one who had the old lyrics. We reworked them together."

I feel my face heat, and all I can do is smile.

"So, is this going to be a duet album?" Mark arches his eyebrows, looking between us.

"Oh, uh—we hadn't really discussed that," I mutter.

"But we are putting on a memorial concert on Labor Day Weekend, for my sister," Josh adds. "I figured I'd see where the wind takes me." He crosses his arms, his gaze flicking between me and Mark.

Mark chuckles and there's something intimidating behind it. "The wind better be taking you to Melanie. You two are fantastic together."

I blush, peering up at Mark through my lashes. "Thank you. But...I don't know. Josh is the star here."

"Tell you what, you two get this recorded and get it over to Gary and John. We're going to talk about this." Mark points at us. "This is good stuff."

Josh drops his arms and nods, relaxing. "Thanks, man."

"I'll be in touch." Mark stands, preparing to leave. Josh and I follow suit, shaking his hand.

As soon as Mark is gone, Josh throws his arms around me, peppering kisses all over my face and neck.

"Oh my god," he murmurs. "I thought he was going to hate it." He kisses my forehead and pulls back to look at me. "I'm so relieved."

"I'm relieved for you." I grin, fighting the urge to kiss him on the mouth in this lobby full of onlookers.

"I guess we're doing this?" Josh asks, his eyes lit with something electric.

One look at him, and I already know. My answer is yes.

# Chapter Twenty

## *Josh*

I don't know what I was thinking trying to be a solo artist. It doesn't make any sense. I've never been a solo artist. I've had my band and before that, it was Melanie. It was *always* Melanie. I have to pinch myself to believe she's actually going to do this with me. Our relationship is complicated and yet, she's still willing to do this with me. The way she took me in and gave me a place to crash, and now it's as if we were never apart. It doesn't feel real, and I will not let myself take her for granted.

Melanie sits back down on the beige couch and lets out a relaxed sigh. I sit next to her. "Are you sure you're okay with this?" My voice is earnest. "I can tell them no."

Melanie bites her lip, meeting my gaze. "I'm okay with it. Let's start with 'Every Song' and see how it goes," she says softly. "It's actually been fun for me. Playing with someone—you—again." She drops her shoulders. "I've been such a loner, I forgot what it feels like to collaborate. I kind of love it."

I can't resist now. I lean in and tip her chin toward mine, planting a soft kiss on her mouth. "Good," I murmur, smiling into her lips. I pull back and look at her seriously. "Melanie, the past three weeks with you have been some of the best times of my life."

Melanie doesn't hide the shock on her face, and a delighted smile crawls across her lips. "Mine too," she admits.

"So, what do you want to do? We're here. Let's do something

fun." I reach for her hand.

"I'm starving." Melanie stands, grabbing her guitar case and zipping her ax safely inside. "Can we start with that?"

"Definitely." I do the same and sling my case over my shoulder. "Let's go."

Twenty minutes later, we've stashed the guitars in the trunk of my car and we're walking up Chestnut Street to Franklin Social, a hip eatery in Old City. Melanie picked it, saying she came here on a Hinge date a while back—the only good thing about the date was the food.

A hostess greets us and leads us to a two-top table in the back of the restaurant. A busboy quickly comes and fills our two water glasses, letting us know our server will be with us shortly. I thank him and take a sip of water, clearing my throat. I watch Melanie, reading the menu. Even after all these years, her beauty alarms me. She has always had strawberry blonde hair, but in the sunlight, it looks like spun copper. She has a smattering of freckles over the bridge of her nose. I remember as a teen, she hated those freckles. I loved them, a tiny perfect map I could trace across her skin. Her startling blue eyes have tiny flecks of green in them, like sea glass, and a glint to them when she laughs.

Melanie looks like summer today, dressed in light denim shortalls and a white tank top. Her oversized black sunglasses are perched on her head, working as a headband. She wears a dainty gold cross at her collarbone that matches the tiny hoop earrings that move when she does. And that tattoo—so different from anything I ever imagined her getting—a garden of hibiscus flowers from her shoulder to elbow. I'm taken with her.

"So, what do you think you're going to get?" A blush rises to her freckled cheeks when she catches me staring.

I blink my eyes, shaking my head. "I haven't even looked yet."

Melanie huffs a laugh. "What have you been looking at all this time then?" Her brow knits together.

"You," I breathe, not bothering to hide my feelings.

Melanie swats my hand, amusement dancing in her eyes.

"Josh," she whines, "read your menu. I'm starving!"

Another ten minutes and we've settled on two appetizers and two entrees that we're going to share. Melanie forgoes an alcoholic drink, and I try to tell myself it's not because of me but I'm sure it is, and I love her that much more for it.

"I'd rather eat my calories," she tells me, reaching for a tostada as soon as the server sets it down.

"Well, I appreciate you," I murmur, trying to keep the emotion out of my voice.

The truth of the matter is, I've been feeling lost for some time now. I don't know what I was doing in Nashville, but somewhere along the way, I stopped waking up with purpose and started going through the motions. With my band, with Keira, with my health. I stopped thinking about what really mattered, and it got me into trouble. We're quietly eating, both of us seeming to be lost in thought. I realize it's now or never.

"Mel," I start, cautiously reaching for her hand. "About yesterday."

Melanie pauses mid chew and meets my gaze. She swallows and reaches for her water with her opposite hand, so she doesn't break our contact. She doesn't respond, but she doesn't take her eyes off mine.

"I'm sorry. To have unloaded all of that on you." I stifle a cough. "The thing is...for the past few years, I've only focused on one goal—make the music, get the record deal, do the tour, chase success. My world revolved around those things, and I shut out the people in my life who matter most to me. I hardly ever talk to my parents anymore, except when I go home for Christmas. I have no friends in Nashville anymore. I shut everyone out who could have pulled me out of the downward spiral I was on. Mistakes were made. People were hurt. My accident forced me to really look at who I am and what the hell I'm doing with my life. So even though I didn't need AA in the typical way, the twelve steps are helping me fix what was broken."

I lick my lips and pull my hand back. I pluck a French fry

from my plate and chew thoughtfully before continuing. "The thing is, while I was figuring it out, I was letting down everyone. I let my band down when I refused a tour. I let Keira down when I refused to take things to the next level. I quit drinking and quickly realized how many of my friendships revolved around making music and getting trashed afterward." I let out a breath.

"Josh..." My name falls from Melanie's lips in a whisper.

I shake my head, reaching for her hand again. "No, please let me finish."

Melanie nods, flicking her gaze from our joined hands to my eyes.

"I came back here with zero expectations. I just knew I needed to go back to my roots—to go home. I didn't know you'd still be here, let alone be single. I didn't have any idea we'd pick up where we left off...but I'm so glad we have. It feels right." I bring her hand to my lips and kiss her knuckles. "If you agree to do this with me...to make *our* music again, then everything else will have all been worth it. Because it led me back to you."

Melanie runs an index finger under her lash line, blinking rapidly. "I don't know what to say," she says softly. "I never thought I'd see you again. I didn't even know how to find you. I'm sure you have someone running your social media, so I never even tried to reach out."

"I do my own actually—I follow you on Instagram," I admit with a sheepish shrug, a slow smile crawling across my lips.

Melanie's eyes water then, and she swallows. "You do? I never post anything." A laugh bubbles out of her.

I shift in my seat, fixing my gaze on hers. "Mel, I don't think I've really been living all this time. I've felt more alive these past three weeks with you than I have playing sold out shows. I just needed you to know that." I swallow the knot in my throat.

"Thank you for telling me." Melanie sniffles. "Want to get out of here? There's a music store I want to show you."

We split the check—Melanie insists—and a few minutes later, we're strolling hand in hand up Chestnut Street toward Rustic

Music, a music store featuring vintage instruments and a vast collection of vinyl.

The store is quiet with only one employee and a few browsing customers, but I follow Melanie around as she excitedly points out vintage guitars to me. "This is where I got my new one." Her eyes crinkle when she smiles.

"Let's play." I gesture to a bench with several guitars on stands around it and an amp. We plug two electric guitars into the amp and put on the headphones. Immediately, Melanie starts playing our song, and we laugh at the way an electric guitar changes the sound. We play a verse and then carefully put the guitars back. Melanie grasps my hand and leads me to the back of the store where they keep the vinyl, and several old record players shoppers can test out. We laugh as we flip through, pulling out The Beatles, Pink Floyd, and Nirvana. The rich sound of the vinyl is warm and alive. I forgot how much I enjoy the textured layers of the imperfect recording. When Melanie replaces Nirvana's "About a Girl" with Fleetwood Mac's "Dreams," I hold out my hand—an invitation.

Melanie hesitates, just for a breath, before she laces her fingers with mine. Her cheek brushes my shoulder, and I think I feel her lean in. Suddenly, I remember the feel of her body like it was yesterday, and I can't help but spin her around the store. An audience of other shoppers pauses to watch us sway, but we pay them no mind. There is no one else in the world but the two of us.

By the time the last note fades, Melanie's eyes are glassy. Her breath is caught somewhere between a laugh and a sigh. Our gazes lock and she steps back, blinking a little too fast.

"Wow," Melanie says, smoothing down her hair, then letting her fingers flutter at her collarbone. "I wasn't expecting that."

"Me neither," I rasp.

I wasn't expecting any of this.

# Chapter Twenty-One

## *Melanie*

Before we head home, I take Josh for ice cream at the Franklin Fountain—an old-time ice cream parlor that only fits ten people comfortably, but there are tiny café tables inside and out and the homemade ice cream is to die for.

Josh and I each order a cone and join hands as we start the slow walk back to his car, licking the sticky ice cream as it drips own our hands. It's been ages since I've felt this content. Josh has been the missing puzzle piece in my life for decades now. I have always wondered what was wrong with me. Why couldn't I find the right one? Why did no one choose me? It's taken me forty-one years to be okay with not being someone's everything, but maybe I am meant to be Josh's.

We're quiet as we walk, and I let my mind wander. I let myself hope that there is more for us than just a summer thing. That this could be our second chance. I don't know what that would look like yet, but for the first time in my life, I'm not scared. I'm not afraid to make a change. I think that's saying something.

"How's the mint chocolate chip?" Josh asks, a mischievous smile on his lips.

"So good." I let my eyes roll back in my head. "How's your fudge brownie?"

Josh holds his cone out for me to have a lick and I lean in, taking a long, slow lick and eyeing him as he watches me. Then, before I can stop him, he smears the chocolate cone all over my lips and the outskirts of my mouth.

"Josh!" I squeal, laughing like my younger self.

Josh doesn't laugh. His eyes turn smoldering, and his hands wrap around my neck, tugging me to him. "You've got something on your mouth," he murmurs, his lips inches from mine. "I better get it." And then his mouth is on mine, kissing me deeply, like the other day outside my bedroom. Our tongues swirl together, and the mixed taste of mint and brownies on his cool tongue has me exploring every inch of his mouth. We are in the center of the sidewalk, pedestrians needing to step around us. I might hear a few wolf whistles, but I'm too caught up, too engrossed in our kiss to notice. Josh backs us off to the shoulder without breaking our kiss, threading his fingers through my hair with one hand and holding his ice cream with the other. His mouth claims mine with hunger that has been earned, like he's been aching for it.

Our teeth clash together as we part, Josh sucking gently on my lower lip before kissing the rest of the chocolate off the corners of my mouth. He leans his forehead into mine.

"People are staring," I whisper, biting back a giggle.

"I don't care." Josh straightens and brushes a hair off my face. "I was thinking—and you can say no if you want to—but it's getting late. Why don't we see if the Renaissance has any rooms left for the night?"

An involuntary grin spreads across my face and butterflies flood my insides. The thought of being alone with Josh in a swanky hotel room and not my tiny apartment sends a shiver through me. "I'd like that," I murmur.

Josh picks up my hand and licks away the melted ice cream that now coats it, a sultry look in his eyes. "Good."

Twenty minutes later, we're walking back into the hotel. The lobby is much quieter, and I am buzzing. I lean against the counter as Josh talks to the front desk, his flirtatious smile working to his advantage.

"Hey, aren't you that musician who sang out here earlier today?" the clerk asks. She's about our age with honey-colored curls and clear green eyes. I wait for Josh to check her out, but he doesn't. He reaches for my hand instead, giving it a familiar squeeze.

"We both did, yeah." Josh flicks his gaze to me, a smile grazing his lips.

"That's so cool," the clerk murmurs, clicking around on her screen. "It looks like the only thing I have left for tonight is a Parkview suite on the top floor."

"Saturday night in the summer, I guess." Josh says with a chuckle, lifting his hands, then turns back to the clerk. "We'll take it." He slaps his credit card on the counter, looking at me with mischievous eyes.

The elevator doors are barely closed before Josh's mouth and hands are on me. He backs me into the corner, raking his palms up my back, threading his fingers through my hair. His mouth crashes into mine, his stubble burning my chin—reckless, urgent, real. Soft and savage all at once. My breath catches, years of deprivation unraveling between our lips.

Josh drags his tongue along my neck and jaw, leaving tiny fires in his wake. Our mouths collide; our hands are everywhere. I feel him grow hard and time folds in on itself. It's messy and breathless, all teeth, tongue, and heat. But it's familiar—like coming home. And it makes me ache with want.

The elevator dings and the doors open. Josh tears his mouth away from mine, taking my hand and leading me quickly down the hallway—as if the floor is on fire.

We find our room quickly, and Josh fiddles with the keycard. I run my hands up and down his back, under his tight-fitting T-shirt. A low hum starts between my legs in anticipation. The key card doesn't work at first, blinking red.

Josh lets out a growl as I drag my fingernails down his back. "Come on," he says to the door. He pauses to kiss me again, softer this time, cupping the back of my head and pulling me to him. "I need you," he rasps.

Finally, as if the door itself understood his plea, it opens, and we're in the middle of a swanky hotel room overlooking the night skyline. There's a black accent wall and a red chaise lounge, but all we notice is the king-size bed.

Josh swallows, letting my hand drop. He takes a step closer to me, cupping my cheek. My pulse speeds up and my breath hitches as Josh plants a soft kiss on the corner of my mouth, slow and sensual, prompting me to open for him. Our tongues dance slowly, our breaths mixing, soft and steady.

Josh pulls back, his expression soft. "Mel," he says, and my name catches in his throat. I let myself believe he's been waiting for this too.

"I know," I whisper, pressing my forehead to his.

And then his mouth is on mine again, the feel of his hard body tangling excitement and caution together. My heart pounds, like it remembers every kiss that came before this one. All the sadness, the longing, the ache of what we used to share is poured into this moment. Josh's kiss turns hesitant as his fingers fiddle with the strap of my shortalls. "Do you want this as much as I do?" he growls through fervent kisses.

I nod because I don't want to pull away. "Uh-huh." It comes out like a breathless moan.

Josh unhooks the first strap of my shortalls, and it falls to the side. His mouth moves to my bare shoulder, and he kisses it softly, flicking his gaze up to mine. He cups my cheek, softly circling his thumb, and our eyes meet—the unspoken hope that maybe we're on the edge of rewriting everything.

He unhooks the other strap, and the shortalls fall to the ground. All at once I'm standing there in a lace purple thong and a tight white crop top, but I don't feel exposed; I feel cherished.

Josh's breath hitches as he drags his eyes up my body. His fingers graze my hip bone, the urgency from moments ago replaced with something savory. I tug at the hem of his T-shirt, and he helps me pull it off before returning his focus to me. Josh's mouth finds mine, his teeth nibbling at my lower lip before he drags his mouth across my jaw, down my neck and shoulder. He crouches as he kisses down my body to the hemline of my panties. His tongue grazes the purple lace and he sucks in a breath, cupping my ass.

"May I?" His voice is gravelly. He slips a finger under the lace band and looks up at me for approval.

"Yes," I breathe. It comes out like a sigh.

That's all Josh needs to hear because he yanks the purple lace to the floor, simultaneously kissing me from hip to hip. I tug him up off his knees and his mouth finds mine. He grips me tighter as I begin working at the button on his jeans, then the zipper. He steps out of them, never breaking the contact of our thirsty mouths. He pulls the hem of my crop top, and I let him yank it over my head. All that stands between us now is a bra and a pair of boxer briefs stretched with his desire.

We pull apart, assessing each other quietly. I swallow and reach behind me, unhooking my bra. I let it fall to the floor, revealing my breasts, the chill in the room instantly hardening my nipples. Josh lets out a gasp before enveloping one and then the other, sucking each one until soft moans escape me.

I slide my fingers into the waistband of his boxer briefs, wanting desperately to see the man he's grown into. His shoulders are broad, and his chest is hairless, save for a light blond happy trail. I tug them down, and my breath catches. Tattooed in black, just beneath the happy trail are our words:

*You're the reason I go on*

A gasp falls from my mouth. "That's...my handwriting." My voice is barely audible.

Josh clears his throat, looking down at the words etched in his skin. "It is. I took it from the copy of the lyrics you gave me." His voice is hoarse, thick with emotion.

I run my fingers over the ink and lick my lips. Josh cups the back of my head, pulling my gaze up to his. "You saved the lyrics?" I ask, tears welling in the back of my eyes.

"I saved it all, Mel. Every note we passed, every photo, every lyric." Josh's voice catches. He takes a shuddering breath and strokes my cheek with his thumb.

"When did you get it?" I ask, softly.

"My eighteenth birthday," Josh replies. "My memories of you—they kept me going all these years."

A stray tear escapes my eye, and my mouth crashes into his, all the hunger and urgency returned. We fall onto the end of the bed, Josh hovering over me.

"Let's see if we can make up for lost time," he rasps.

I don't argue.

# Chapter Twenty-Two

## Josh

Melanie slides backward until her head is resting on the pillow. I climb over her, raking my eyes over the length of her beautiful body. No one has ever even come close to Melanie for me. This moment is everything I've dreamed of for my entire adult life, and I intend to relish it—and her.

I brush my nose against hers and kiss her softly, hovering above her. She tugs me closer, her fingers gripping the nape of my neck as she kisses me deeply. I run a hand down her sides, feeling the warmth of her skin. She reaches between me, gripping my dick and pumping quickly.

I reach for her wrist. "Slow," I whisper. "Let me take care of you."

I slide my mouth away from hers, kissing and nibbling across her chest, taking each one of her perfect tits in my mouth and sucking until they pebble for me. She lets out a hiss that sends a jolt straight to my dick. The idea that I get to be with her like this again, after all these years, has me reeling. I can't wait to show her what I've learned.

I drag my tongue down the center of her flat stomach, swirling her navel before moving to her hips, forcing her legs apart. Dragging my hot breath across the lower region, I kiss her inner thighs until my name falls from her lips.

"Please," she whimpers, raking her hands through my hair in

an attempt to pull my face toward her center.

"You want it?" I breathe into her swollen pink lips.

"Very much." She lets out a soft cry.

I drag a finger up through her wet center, teasing her until I find the swollen nub that makes her gasp. Pulling her lips apart, I sink my tongue into her heat, sucking and nibbling, teasing her opening with a finger.

Melanie's arousal drips onto my hand as she squirms beneath me, her moans growing louder.

"Josh." Her legs tremble as she says my name. "Please. I need..."

I suck gently on her clit, and a loud moan escapes her. I pick my head up and look at her, a teasing grin spreading across my face.

"I need you." Melanie's voice cracks.

"I know, baby. You have me." I reach down and pump a finger inside her, then two. "You're almost there," I murmur, ducking down and devouring her again.

She cries out, writhing beneath me, and her legs tremble as she finds her release.

"I'm coming," she whimpers. "Don't stop. Don't stop."

I have no intention of stopping. I suck harder, tasting her sweetness as she climaxes.

She stills, and I hover over her, kissing her hipbone as she runs her fingers through my hair. I give her a moment to steady her breathing before I crawl back up the length of her body and find her mouth, kissing her softly.

"You taste so sweet," I say, swirling my tongue with hers. "Did you like that?"

"Uh-huh," she breathes. Her hand finds my cock, stroking lightly and then faster. I groan, deepening our kiss.

"It's your turn," she says, into my mouth.

I grab a hold of her hips and roll her on top so she's straddling me. She moves down my body, licking and nipping my sides, sending jolts of electricity through me. She glides her tongue across the ink just above my dick, and I'm dizzy with quiet desperation. She grips my cock, licking up the side of the shaft before taking me into her mouth. Her kiss is hungry and aching, like she's making up for lost time. She cups my balls and pumps my dick into her mouth. A guttural moan escapes me, and I tug at her hair. "Strawberry girl," I mumble, through erratic breaths.

Melanie picks her head up, a sultry grin crossing her face, and climbs back over me, my dick hovering at her entrance. "Hearing you say that—it's like it hasn't been..."

"Twenty-five years," I finish for her, my teeth catching my lip.

"You want more?" Melanie teases, licking her lips. She reaches down, rubbing the head of my cock over her warm entrance. Our eyes lock and I gasp.

"I don't have a condom," I mutter, annoyed at myself for not planning better.

"I'm on the pill," Melanie offers, angling a tit near my mouth, making it impossible to refuse.

I latch onto it, hungrily sucking and flicking her nipple with my tongue.

"Josh," Melanie cries.

I have no more willpower. I grab her hips and shift her, so she sinks right down onto my cock. We both cry out at the sensation. "You're so tight," I grind out as she seats herself, taking all of me.

"Oh my god, you feel amazing." Melanie moans, grinding her hips in slow rhythmic circles.

I circle her clit with my thumb, and she arches her back, crying out and giving me a show. I watch my cock slide in and out of her until I can't take the lack of control anymore. I flip her over like a rag doll and lift her legs onto my shoulders, driving deep inside. Our eyes are glued to each other, everything blocked out except our moans of pleasure and our synchronous breathing. My heartbeat is in my ears as I feel every sensation of Melanie's heat and slickness on my own skin. I feel her in every nerve ending on my body, the weight of the emotions of the last twenty-five years without her almost too much to bear.

Her legs drop, wrapping around my waist, pulling me closer until there's no space left between us. I rock into her, gliding my tongue across her neck and her jaw, finding her earlobe. "Mel," I whisper into her ear.

She moans in response.

"I meant it when I said I've always loved you," I murmur, driving into her.

Her mouth finds mine again in a feverish, urgent kiss. I drag my teeth across her lower lip, sucking until she begins to tremble underneath me.

"You were meant for me," I growl into the kiss, thrusting harder, feeling my release build. "Now come for me. Come hard."

A sharp cry escapes Melanie's lips as her legs tighten around me, her body going rigid as her legs convulse.

I pump into her until I see stars, my own legs trembling as I take the final plummet off the edge of the cliff that is Melanie Glick. I collapse on top of her, feeling the synchronicity of our heartbeats, our heaving breaths mingling together. Melanie drags her nails up my back, glistening with sweat. The sensation sends a shiver through me. How did I go this long without this girl?

Melanie lets out a satisfied laugh. "Well, you're not seventeen anymore."

"No, I'm not." I burrow my face in her neck with a laugh. Then, seriously, "There's more where that came from."

"I can't wait." Melanie tangles her fingers in my hair.

"What do you say we start with a shower?"

# Chapter Twenty-Three

## Melanie

It's been two weeks since Josh and I took things to the next level and I'm still pinching myself. I don't know how I got so lucky but suddenly it makes sense to me why no one else chose me before. It's not that I wasn't worth choosing—it's that on some level, I was waiting for this. For him. Every missed connection, every failed relationship, every empty swipe on an app feels less like rejection now and more like the universe biding its time. Because somehow, against every odd, I had to find Josh again.

We've fallen into an easy rhythm where I work, he writes music, and we come together in the evenings to rehearse until our eyes grow heavy and our fingers hurt. Then we fall into bed, making slow, passionate love before drifting to sleep in each other's arms.

Neither of us has dared to bring up what comes next. We're living each day as if the concert is the end goal, but I'd be lying if I said I don't want more, even if it means following Josh wherever he goes next. My whole life, I've never been a risk-taker. Content with the status quo and scared to make a move, somewhere along the line, I got stuck. Josh told me weeks ago he hasn't really been living all these years—neither have I. So, each night as I fall asleep in his arms, I send up a silent prayer that maybe this is our second chance. Maybe, we'll choose each other.

I'm daydreaming on the couch after a long day shift when

Josh walks in the front door with a bag of takeout from Fin's.

"Got dinner," he says, dropping it on the coffee table and plopping down next to me. He plants a kiss on the side of my head. "You toast?" He cocks his head at me. "You look really spent."

"It was a long, busy day shift. You know, July fourth weekend and all." I shrug and rest my head on his shoulder, and he slips an arm around me, tugging me close. "I'm thinking it might be time for a change."

"Oh yeah?" Josh quirks an eyebrow at me. "What kind of change?"

I chew on my lip, looking up at him from the crook of his arm. I'm trying to read his mind—if he'd like my change to include him. "I'm not sure. I am just tired of the restaurant business."

Josh lets out a low whistle but his face remains impassive. "I can't say I blame you there. I spent ten years in it in Nashville before I got my deal. It's grueling work."

"It is. And Andrew is good to me, but you got me thinking. I realize I haven't really been living either." I close my eyes, tucking further into his shoulder as Josh strokes my lower back.

He kisses the top of my head. "Well, let's figure out how we can start *living* together."

I sigh. "I don't even know where to start."

"Let's start with this dinner before our nachos get soggy." Josh grins, lifting out of my embrace and pushing up from the couch. He takes everything out of the bag, placing it in the center of my small table, while I fill us glasses of ice water.

Josh must've been extra hungry when he placed the order because he got coconut shrimp, loaded tater tots, nachos, calamari, and wings. We make our plates and start munching in silence. Josh seems energized, and I need some of his excitement to wear off on me.

"You too tired to rehearse tonight?" he asks, frowning at me.

I shake my head. "No, I'll manage. It's important. Besides, with the holiday, we'll probably miss practicing tomorrow."

"Yeah. And..." Josh hesitates. "I picked up a regular gig. Maybe on nights you're off you can join me, but the manager at Fin's asked if I'd consider playing there on Wednesday nights through the end of the summer. I don't have much else going on so I figured, why not?" He lifts a shoulder, tipping his head to the side.

I pause mid chew and meet his eyes. I can't imagine what it must be like to walk into a restaurant, be recognized, and immediately be gifted a regular gig. A twinge runs through me, sharp and unexpected. It isn't that I begrudge him the spotlight—he's earned it. Maybe it's that Josh and I have been making music together and now he's found some way to do it without me. I know it's not fair to feel that way. He's not working steady shifts like I am; of course he needs something that's his. Still, there's a quiet ache I can't shake, the uneasy sense of being left behind while he's already moving forward.

When I don't say anything, he adds, "I thought it would help promote the concert."

I offer him a tight smile. "You're right. It probably will." I take a long sip of my water before saying anything else.

Josh watches me carefully. "You're all right with it, aren't you?"

Guilt pricks the back of my neck, and I smile apologetically. "Yes. I'm sorry. I'm just tired."

"You sure that's all it is?" He reaches for my hand.

"I guess I'm just feeling a little lost in my own life, is all." I press my lips together. "It's not you."

"You'll figure it out, babe. I'll help you." He offers me a reassuring smile before plucking a piece of calamari off his plate, dunking it in the Thai chili sauce, closing his eyes, and moaning while he chews. "Man, I have missed good seafood."

This gets a snicker out of me. "It's pretty great," I agree.

"So, tomorrow, what's the plan?"

I get together with my group of friends for a barbecue on the Fourth, and we all catch the fireworks from the beach. I haven't even opened the group text to find out what the plans are yet, but I guess we'll go.

"Probably a party at someone's house and fireworks on the beach, like every year." I shrug.

"And...at the risk of sounding seventeen again, are we a couple at this public outing?" Josh's eyes have a teasing glint to them.

I huff a light laugh and reach for his hand. "Sure."

"Good." Josh seems satisfied by that answer, and it should make me happy. He wants to be with me. I need to stop feeling sorry for myself and appreciate the here and now.

"I am going to see my dad in the morning first," I tell him, getting up to throw my plate away.

"Do you want me to come?" Josh asks, and if I'm not mistaken, there's a twinge of hopefulness laced in there.

"Oh...uh, not this time," I say, wincing. "We haven't caught up in a while, and I really need to fill him in."

"All right," he says. "I'll just stay here and grind some more." He offers me a crooked smile, but I can't help feeling the weight of guilt pressing against my chest.

"You'll be okay?" I ask, hopefully.

"I'll manage." He leans in for a kiss and I almost change my mind, but I really do need to talk to my dad.

"Okay," I say, pulling back and brushing some hair off his forehead. "I won't be long."

July fourth falls on a Friday this year which means the town is abuzz with tourists. It takes me fifteen minutes to get over to my dad's house on the north side of town and by the time I get there, I'm mildly aggravated. I am so happy not to have to work tonight—Andrew is taking tonight, and I have tomorrow night.

My dad's house is away from downtown, and even though there are still tourists around, it's much quieter. I pull in his driveway and grab the library books I picked up for him before trekking up his front steps.

"Dad, I'm here," I call, pulling open his screen door.

"In here!" he calls back from the kitchen.

I move down the short hallway to find him standing at the peninsula, stirring a pitcher of lemonade. A plate of cheese and crackers sits in the center of the round kitchen table. I smile. My parents didn't get along for most of my life, but they didn't divorce until after I graduated high school. My dad is so much happier now and every time I see him, even though I never lived a day of my life in this house, he makes his little bungalow feel like coming home.

"Hi, Daddy," I say, walking around the counter and wrapping him in a backward hug. I plant a kiss on his cheek. "I picked up your library books for you, so you don't have to go downtown. It's a zoo." I plop down at the table.

"Thank you, love." My dad pours two glasses of lemonade over ice and sets one in front of me, taking the chair next to me. "So, tell me, what's new? You've been too busy for your dear old dad. You look tired." My dad pats my hand and my heart swells. My old man.

I sigh, twirling a finger around a lock of golden red hair. "I have been busy. I've been working like crazy..."

"*Just* work?" My dad arches his eyebrows, like he doesn't quite believe me. "Anyone new in your life?"

I bark out a laugh. Of course he's cutting right to the chase. "You got me." I hesitate for a moment. "Do you remember Josh? Cara's brother?"

"Of course," my dad smiles wistfully. "How could I forget? You two looked at each other like you thought the other hung the moon. Is he back in town?"

I sip my lemonade with a nod. "He is. He's a country artist now."

"No shit." My dad scratches his chin. "In Nashville?"

"I guess kind of all over? Anyway, he came back here to write an acoustic album. He's been staying with me." I grimace, afraid that even at forty-one years old, my dad will frown at my shacking up with someone. He doesn't bat an eye.

"Ah, I see." He reaches for the plate of cheese and crackers and carefully makes himself a stack. "And...you two are friends?"

My cheeks prickle with heat. "Not exactly." I let out a shaky breath. "There's a lot of history between us."

"I remember." My dad nods. Frank Glick has always been supportive of his little girl. I didn't make the best decisions when I was younger and I drove my mother crazy, but my father has never been anything but accepting of me. He knows everything that happened between Josh and me...before and after the accident. "And, have you talked to him about things?"

I push my lips together, knowing exactly what things my father is referring to. I shake my head. "No, that's ancient history. Telling him now wouldn't do anything except stir up emotions he doesn't need to deal with. I dealt with them for both of us."

My dad pats my hand and stares at me for a long time, his gaze making me squirm. Finally, he says, "I just wish you two had the chance to grieve together. You lost more than just Cara."

I blink back the sting of tears and sniffle. "I know, Dad. But it's just too painful."

My father nods. "Okay. Well, just think about it. If I were him, I'd want to know." He drains the last of his lemonade.

"You really guzzled that down," I quip as he pours himself another glass. "You need to watch your blood sugar."

My dad rolls his eyes, waving his hand. "Yeah, yeah."

"Dad, I'm serious." My father is a pre-diabetic and if I don't look out for him, no one will. Probably another reason I never got the courage to leave Cape May and go after my own dreams—my dad would be all alone.

"Okay, sweetheart." My dad drinks half of his glass and gets up to dump the rest in the sink. "Are you okay?" He squints at me from his position across the room.

"I told you yes," I say, growing irritated for no reason.

"Okay, well, I'm your dad. It's my job to check on you." My dad sits down again and scoots his chair closer to mine.

I sigh, knowing he isn't going to give this up. "I guess...

seeing Josh again makes me think I failed at life. I let my musical aspirations go. I work at a bar. I have no husband, no life, nothing going for me at all."

My dad scoffs. "Hey now, stop talking about my daughter that way." He cracks a grin, and I involuntarily match it. "Melanie Rose, you are so much more than your *job*. You are kind, loving, loyal. You're everybody's best friend. Don't be so critical of yourself. You're still young! It's never too late to go after a dream."

I smirk. "Of course, you can say that because it's not your dream."

"My dream is to see you happy." My dad's voice cracks. "If Josh inspires you to pursue your music again, you absolutely should."

At this, I cave and fill my dad in on the music Josh and I have been writing together. I tell him about the concert for Cara. I tell him how I have never felt so alive in my life. That Josh has awakened a dormant dream inside me that I had completely forgotten about. And that I've fallen completely in love with the man he's become. By the time I'm finished, I'm crying.

My dad reaches and swipes at the tear rolling down my cheek. "Melanie," he says slowly. "This all sounds wonderful. Why are you so upset?"

I sniffle, wiping my eyes with a napkin. "Because what happens next? This is fun and I'm having a great time, but at the end of the summer, Josh will leave, and I'll still be here. Doing what? Tending bar." It tastes bitter coming out of my mouth.

My dad's face falls. "Melanie, I'm not saying you shouldn't think about the future and what will make you happy, because eventually you should. But are you happy right now? Getting to know him again and making music?"

I nod, hugging myself for comfort. "Yes, of course I am."

"Then focus on the *now*. Enjoy it *now*. Or it will pass you by and you will miss it. Be where your feet are." My dad gets out of his chair and wraps his arms around me, offering comfort in the way only a parent can.

"Be where your feet are," I repeat.

"Yes."

I sigh, leaning into his embrace. "I'll try."

# Chapter Twenty-Four

## Josh

Melanie is at her dad's house for a while. At first, I think I'll wait for her but as time goes on, I give up waiting and focus on our evening plans. I prep the appetizer we're bringing over to Miles's and Jenna's place. I walk to the liquor store on the corner and pick up a bottle of wine that I think Jenna will like and a case of Miller Lite for Miles since I've never seen him drink anything else. Melanie is right—the town is packed. Luckily, we can park at their house and walk up to the beach to watch the fireworks later on.

When I get back from the store, Melanie still isn't back so I get out my guitar and play through "Every Song" a couple of times, adjusting the pre-hook the way we talked about. Then I open my notebook and make a list of the songs I've got so far for the EP.

EVERY SONG
THE SOUND OF HER NAME
...

I've got...two. To be fair, I don't even have that. I have a title for "The Sound of Her Name" and a few chord progressions I think could work. I haven't even shown it to Melanie yet. And if I don't get going, I'm not going to have enough for an EP. I'd like to present them with at least four songs by the end of the summer.

I pick up my guitar and start strumming the chords I've been tossing around in my mind. I hum it before I bring myself to sing the words. Once through, and I think maybe I've got something here.

"The sound of her name, soft in the air. Melody fading, but she's still there," I sing softly. I'm so lost in the music that I don't hear Melanie come in.

"What's that?" She startles me from behind and I jump.

"Geez," I hiss. "You scared me."

Melanie ignores me and picks up her guitar before plopping next to me. "I like it. What is it?"

"I was just fiddling with a song for Cara." I shrug. "It's nothing yet."

"Well, come on." Melanie nudges me with her knee. "Let's write it."

I grin. "Yeah? You really want to?" I thought Melanie was pulling back from collaborating on new stuff with me. Today she seems energized, and I find it irresistibly sexy.

"Yeah, I told you I want to." She locks her eyes on me. "Unless you have other ideas for how we could kill time before the party." She bites her lower lip, eyeing me teasingly.

I let out a chuckle. "I think we can make time for both of those things."

"Let's do it," Melanie chirps. She strums a G major.

I laugh, shaking my head. "I don't have any words yet. I was playing around with C-G-Am-F in the I-V-vi-IV progression."

Immediately, Mel starts strumming, before I've had the chance to show her. She picks it up right away, and my heart jumps to my throat watching her. I watch her play through it a few times before she glances up at me. "Like this?"

"Exactly," I say, finally strumming along. "The sound of her name, soft in the air. Melody fading, but she's still there," I sing. "I don't know what should come next," I admit, continuing to strum.

Melanie looks thoughtful as she repeats the chord progression. "How about this..." She licks her lips. "No answers come when you scream at the sky. Some get forever, some say goodbye." Her voice is melodic.

I'm unprepared for the lump that forms in my throat. I cough to clear it. Melanie's line is perfect, but it makes my heart crack open. Maybe I can't do this. Maybe I can't write a song for Cara. It might be too painful.

"I like that." I set my guitar aside, desperate to push away the sudden feeling of loss enveloping me. "You're sexy when you write songs," I murmur, crawling over to her. I pick up her guitar and set it on the armchair. "Let's pick this up later." I kiss her on the mouth.

Melanie giggles, kissing me back. "Josh," she whispers into the kiss. "I thought we were writing a song about your sister."

I deepen the kiss before pulling back slightly, resting my forehead on hers. "I can't think about my sister when you're so fucking sexy." I scoop her up, catching her by surprise and she shrieks. "We'll pick this up later."

I carry her straight to the bedroom, kicking the door closed behind me.

Hours later, we're hanging at Miles and Jenna's before the fireworks. The girls are inside cleaning up from the feast we just annihilated, and the guys are playing cornhole in the yard. I'm teamed up with Liam—Miles and Jack are the other team. The kids are running around with Pete and Maggie, the older ones tossing a Frisbee. I find myself smiling as I watch them between my turn throwing bags. This feels right, it feels like I should have never been anywhere else. The Josh I am here in Cape May is the closest I've come to the boy I used to be, before the weight of the world shaped me into someone else. For the first time in years, I'm not lost in the past or chasing after the future—I'm just me.

I toss my bag at the same time as my phone pings. I pull it out of my pocket in time to see a couple of text messages from Gary, my manager. The first message is a simple "Hey check this out." A link follows. I tap it—it's a link to People Magazine's Instagram post. It's a photo of Keira looking cozy on a daybed at some luxurious looking beach resort. The caption simply says, "Keira gets cozy with Damon Jennings." I must let out a growl because Liam calls my name from his side of the cornhole boards.

"Earth to Josh. You good, buddy?" He cups his hands around his mouth.

I shove my phone back in my pocket and pick up one of the bags that Jack has already gathered up for me. "Sorry," I mutter, preparing to take my throw. "What's the count?"

"Eighteen to twenty, us. Aim for just the board," Liam calls. The rules of cornhole are one point for the board, three points for the hole. Twenty-one wins.

I take a step and toss the bag underhand, landing squarely on the board.

"Woo!" Liam whoops, jumping in a circle. "Now just toss to me."

I toss the other two bags to him, and he catches them one-handed.

"Good game, suckers," Liam quips, slapping Miles on the back.

I shake Jack's hand, followed by Miles.

"This calls for one of Sophie's red, white, and blue Jello shots," Liam suggests. "It's America's birthday, baby."

I bark out a laugh and hold up my hands. "I'm good, I'm good. I'm not drinking tonight."

Liam's expression falters slightly, and he glances between me and the other guys, as if he just realized it now. "You sure? It's the fourth!"

"I'm okay." I give him a friendly nod, unsure about how much I want to divulge right now.

Before I can even decide, Jenna yells out the back door. "Boys! Let's start to head up to the beach."

I let out a breath through my mouth. "You heard the lady, boys," I murmur, grateful for the change in subject.

I bolt for the back door, finding Melanie in the kitchen sipping a glass of wine. She catches my eye and swallows before dumping the rest of her glass in the sink.

"Hey, alcohol abuse," Danny's wife Kristen scolds. "What's with you?"

Melanie eyes me in the doorway before flicking her gaze back to Kristen. "You said you were ready to go."

"You could've chugged it." Kristen rolls her eyes. "That's good wine."

"Sorry," Melanie mutters with a half-hearted shrug. Kristen doesn't hear her; she's already moved to the front door in search of her shoes.

I move quickly to Melanie's side and pull her into a hug. She melts into me, and I feel her inhale deeply, nuzzling into my chest. She lets out a sigh.

"You don't have to throw your drink in the sink when you see me, you know," I whisper into her ear.

"I know," she says, pulling back to look at me. "I just...want to be respectful."

I hook my index finger under her chin, pulling her gaze up to mine. "You already are."

We settle on the beach ten minutes later, spreading out big blankets for the kids and positioning our chairs in a circle. It's only 8:00. We still have another hour before fireworks start, but I'm told the beach gets crowded, so we stake out our spots. I sit in my chair at the end, watching as Danny, Kristen, Jack, and Steph try to finagle their kids into sunset photos at the shoreline. Most of the kids are grumbling but it still tugs at something deep inside my chest. A longing for family. I remember watching fireworks from the beach with my parents and Cara, adorned in glow necklaces and holding sparklers while we waited for the big show.

"I should call my parents." I don't mean to say it aloud, but it prompts a concerned look from Melanie, who is sitting next to me, looking at Sophie and Liam's little girls with awe.

She cups her hand around my kneecap and squeezes. "Maybe you should."

I don't reply. Instead, I let my mind go back to the last Fourth of July I remember with my parents and Cara. We must've been fourteen or fifteen—before we were too cool to watch the fireworks with our parents. I remember having my guitar down here, my mom and sister sprawled out on a blanket, snacking and making requests. My dad and I leading the sing-along. My chest constricts. I was not prepared for the emotions of being back here. I threw myself into the ocean of memories with no life preserver and now I suddenly feel as if I'm drowning in grief. The beach is starting to fill up and I am lost in thought when Melanie passes me my guitar. "Play us something patriotic," she suggests. The look in her eyes tells me she knows it'll make me feel better—the music always does.

I take the guitar from her and give her a sidelong glance before swallowing hard. "Will you sing along?" I ask, my voice thick with emotion.

"If you want me to." Melanie pats my forearm. She must sense that I went someplace else for a minute.

I unzip my guitar from its case and start strumming "America, the Beautiful." Before I've even realized, Melanie's angelic voice fills the space around us. Our friends stop what they're doing and turn their attention to us. Before long, others start singing along and my whole body fills with warmth. For so long, I've been missing this feeling of home—of comfort.

I don't speak when the song finishes, instead I begin playing "I'm Proud to be an American," and it amps up even more people around us. Even strangers scoot closer to hear us better and join in the sing-along. Liam and Jack light sparklers and pass them around to everyone. The feeling of camaraderie that I have lacked for so long envelops me until a knot of emotions forms in my throat and I have to stop singing. I strum along, my eyes scanning the crowd of strangers and friends alike, singing together, and I realize in this moment—*this* is what it's about. Not playing sold out arenas. There's a place for that, sure, but I came here looking for something life-affirming and dare I say, at this moment on this beach, I've found it.

When I finish the last verse, the crowd erupts into happy cheers that are quickly interrupted by a few test fireworks shooting into the air with a high-pitched whistle. I gently lay my guitar back in its case, and I'm settling into my chair when someone taps my shoulder.

"E-excuse," a young voice says carefully. "Are you—are you Josh Cote?"

I turn to see a boy, not more than ten, shifting from foot to foot like he'd rather the ocean swallow him whole, his hands twisting in the hem of his T-shirt.

"I sure am." I grin. "Would you like a picture?"

The boy shrugs, his eyes darting away before flicking back to mine. "I don't have a phone. I was just wondering if I could ask a question." He pauses, swallowing hard, and I nod.

The boy sucks in a shaky breath. "How did you get your guitar to sound like that on 'Fell Too Far'? I'm learning it now and I can't get it right."

In the song he's referring to, I emulate the sound of a pedal steel guitar by holding down two strings together. I crack a smile. This is *so* not what I expected this kid to say. I expected him to ask me something silly about my personal life. Here he is asking me to show him something. I kneel down and pick up my guitar.

"You mean the pedal steel sound?" I ask, balancing the guitar on my knee.

"Yeah. How do you do that?" The kid cocks his head sideways at me. I take a second to marvel at his courage, approaching me with a technical question simply because he saw his chance.

"Like this." I show him. "I place my index finger on the B string, on the 7$^{th}$ fret and my ring finger on the G string on the 8$^{th}$ fret. Then I pick both strings together, bending the B string up and holding the G string steady."

"So cool," the boy muses.

"Want to try?" I ask, quirking an eyebrow.

"Try? Try your guitar?" The boy can't hide his excited disbelief.

"Sure." I pass my ax to him. "Do what I just did. Index finger on the B on the 7th, good." I watch as the boy moves his ring finger to the 8th fret, G string without direction. He mimics the exact sound I made moments ago.

"Whoa. Cool." His grin is infectious. "Thank you so much!"

I laugh. "Don't mention it, kid. What's your name?"

He passes the guitar back to me. "Carter. I can't believe I just played Josh Cote's guitar."

"Believe it." I chuckle. "And I'm playing at Fin's every Wednesday now. Come play a song with me one of these nights."

"Seriously?" Carter gasps. "I'll ask my mom."

I laugh. "All right. That sounds good." I turn to Melanie. "Mel, can you snap a photo of us?"

"I'd love to." Melanie pulls out her phone.

I hold up my guitar, and Carter and I grin as Melanie snaps the last photo we could probably take before the sky turned dark.

"Look for it on Instagram," I tell him.

Carter thanks us and jogs back to his family. I settle into my chair and find myself smiling. "That was cool," I say, glancing at Melanie.

"It was. You probably just made that kid's life." An easy, proud grin slides across her face. "Did it make *you* feel good?"

"You know what? It really did," I say, holding out my hand to her. She takes it and her palm is warm, fitting into mine like a lost puzzle piece. The first fireworks start, and everyone settles in to watch the show. "I think maybe I'd like that," I say, more to myself than to Melanie.

"Like what?" She turns her eyes from the blaze in the sky to look at me.

"Working with kids. Teaching them music." I shrug, meeting

her gaze. "If the deal doesn't work out."

"You'd be great at it." Melanie turns back to the sky. "But the deal will work out."

"It's just the first time in a long time that I didn't feel like I was pretending. That kid looked at me like I could teach him something, not like I owed him something." I rest my head on the back of the metal beach chair. "It's just something to think about, maybe."

Melanie looks my way again and squeezes my hand. "It's never too late to find a new dream."

# Chapter Twenty-Five

## Melanie

Three days later, I can't get out of bed. Josh's blaring alarm to my left builds irrational rage in my tired body. My eyes burn, even though I haven't opened them yet. My throat is drier than the Sahara Desert, and there's a deep ache under my chin.

"Please," I whine, pulling a pillow over my head. "Will you turn that off?"

A moment later the sound stops, and Josh's strong arm drapes over my hip bone. I squirm out of his embrace, too uncomfortable to be touched.

"Whoa, what's with you this morning?" Josh asks, sitting up on his elbow and pulling the pillow off my face. He lets out a soft gasp. "Do you feel okay? You don't look so hot."

His palm finds my forehead. He feels it for a moment before flipping his hand over and feeling my cheeks. "I think you have a fever."

"I feel like I got run over by a school bus," I moan. "What is happening to me? I never get sick."

"I am pretty sure you *are* sick." Josh hops out of bed and disappears into the kitchen. I close my eyes again and I'm just drifting back into sleep when I feel his touch on my arm. "Here, drink this."

I peer at him through one eye. He's holding a glass of ice water with a twisty straw. "Ugh," I groan. "I can't. I'm nauseous."

"You have to stay hydrated." He pushes the straw toward my lips, and I open for him, taking a small sip. My throat instantly feels relief. He pulls it back when I stop drinking.

"More," I whisper, and seconds later the straw is in my mouth again.

"Do you have a thermometer? Do you want some Advil or anything?" Josh sits on the edge of the bed by my feet.

"In the bathroom drawer," I mumble.

Josh disappears again and returns a moment later with the thermometer. "Open," he tells me, poking my lips with the silver tip.

"I just drank water. It won't even be accurate." I drape my forearm over my forehead.

"Just humor me," Josh says, sitting again and patting my knee. His touch sends a chill through me and not the good kind.

I open my mouth and the thermometer beeps almost instantly. "102.6. Shit." Josh mutters. "Mel, that's really high for an adult. Do you want to go to the doctor? I can take you."

"No," I whine, rolling into the fetal position. "Not moving." My voice is muffled into the pillow.

"Okay," Josh says, even though he doesn't sound sure. He stands and pulls the covers up to my chin. "I'm going to run to the pharmacy and get some things that might help you. Will you be okay for a little bit?"

I don't look at him, my eyes are already closed again. "I'll be fine," I murmur into the pillow. "Just go."

I'm not sure how long I sleep but a while later, I awaken to the faint clatter of pots and pans and the smell of something nostalgic. Soup. I have no appetite and my body aches like I climbed Mount Everest, but appreciation for the man in the next room fills me up. In the past, if I was sick like this, I was on my own. If I called my dad, he'd drop food or medication on my front stoop, but I'd wave him off, never wanting to share my germs.

Josh doesn't think twice about it. He's in my kitchen, moving around like he belongs there, and every small sound from the other room tells me what I must mean to him. Before I can stop it, my eyes fill with self-pity tears and I sniff them quickly away, wiping the fallen ones with the back of my hand.

Josh must hear me because he bolts for my room. He stands in my doorway, leaning into the frame. "You're awake," he rasps.

I shake my head. "Barely," I murmur, wincing. My whole body throbs.

"How about some more liquids?" Josh doesn't wait for me to reply—he darts to the kitchen and returns with a bag with the local pharmacy logo on it and a water bottle. "I got you some electrolyte powder with immune support and some ibuprofen." He strides over to the bed and sits at my feet. "Can you sit up?"

I push to my elbow on one arm and hold out my hand for the water bottle, taking a sip. Ice-cold lime flavor fills my mouth and a knot forms in my stomach. Hunger. It's quickly followed by a wave of nausea.

"I made you soup." Josh rakes a finger through his hair. "I'm not sure it's any good but I tried. Nobody likes that canned shit."

"Thank you," I murmur. "I don't think I'm ready to eat anything."

Josh puts a palm to my forehead. "You're still really hot." Then he cracks a smile, "Literally and figuratively."

My eyes fill with burning tears again, and I rapidly blink them away but fail miserably.

Josh's face falls. "Hey, baby, what's wrong?" He inches closer to me.

"I just feel so awful. And you're taking care of me. You made me soup," I wail, falling back on the pillow.

Josh gets up from his spot at the foot of the bed and kneels down beside me, thumbing away a tear. "Hey, of course I did. I'm here, babe. I'm not going anywhere." He strokes some hair off my forehead that got wet with my tears.

I sniffle and nod. "Thank you. I've never had anyone take care of me before."

Josh pushes his lips into a line, and I can't tell what he's thinking. He quickly changes the subject. "I want you to take some meds and I got..." He pauses, rummaging in the bag. "I got you an at home flu-COVID test. If the results are negative, you need to see a doctor, Mel. It's not normal for an adult to have a fever this high."

"I don't like things in my nose." I shoot him a suspicious look and hug myself, leaning away from him.

"Come on, babe. Don't you want to feel better?" Josh quirks an eyebrow. "Then we can get back to making music?"

"Fine," I grumble. I force myself to sit up and hold out my hand. Josh puts Tylenol Cold and Flu capsules in my palm, and I toss them back.

"When they wear off, you can take some Advil to stay ahead of the body aches." The corner of his mouth quirks. "Now, it's time for the test. Do you want to do it, or shall I help you?"

I furrow my brow and pout.

A playful curve touches Josh's mouth. "Mel, we just talked about this. You can go back to sleep after."

"Fine." I huff out an exasperated breath. "You do it," I mutter sullenly.

"What was that?" Josh leans in, cupping his ear, a teasing glint in his eye. "I didn't hear you."

I relent, sighing. "I would really like it if you could help me with it."

Josh leans forward and kisses my forehead. He is so unafraid to catch whatever this is, and his closeness brings me so much comfort. "Good girl," he murmurs, before moving his mouth from my forehead. "You're still really warm."

He reads the back of the test packaging, ensuring he knows just how to do it and then he opens it. "Rest back on the pillow and close your eyes."

I do as I'm told, settling in, ignoring the ridiculous fact that even with whatever this mysterious illness is and perhaps the highest fever I've ever had, Josh still makes desire pool between my thighs.

"Okay, it only takes a second and then ten minutes to process. It can differentiate between Flu A, B, and COVID," he tells me. I hear him opening the test swab. "Are you ready?"

"As I'll ever be, I guess," I mutter.

"Coming in. Please, do not punch me," he jokes, but he holds down my hands with his opposite hand anyway.

Josh is right, it only takes a second and he is careful as he swirls the swab in each nostril.

"All done," he says.

I peer at him through slitted eyes and watch him swirl the swab in a solution and squeeze a drop into the testing cassette. Gratefulness blooms in my chest once again, and after he sets the cassette on my nightstand, he sets his cellphone timer for ten minutes.

"Thank you," I murmur, letting my fingertips just graze his forearm.

"Don't mention it," Josh says, his lips twitching. "You'd do the same for me."

"Um...I don't really think I would." I let out a pathetic giggle. "I hate germs."

Josh mocks offense. "What? You would leave me in here to suffer?" He frowns, folding his arms across his chest.

"I don't know about suffer." I drop his hand and tug the blanket up higher. "I'd leave stuff at your door."

"Pshh," Josh scoffs. "Some girlfriend you are."

He looks at me then and our gazes lock. *Girlfriend.* Neither of us acknowledges it but there's an emotion written on his face that I can't read. Embarrassment? Hope? Do people call each other boyfriend/girlfriend at our ages? It hangs in the air between us for what feels like an eternity.

Josh clears his throat just as his phone timer goes off, bringing us back to reality and away from topics we haven't discussed yet. "It's time. The moment of truth." He leans over and picks up the test, reading it quickly. “Flu A,” he says, standing. “That’s a relief. Nothing to do but rest and fluids.”

“Okay,” I breathe, suddenly ready to close my eyes.

“Shout for me if you need me, okay?” Josh moves toward the door. If I wasn’t so unwell, I’d be worried about whatever it is he isn’t saying. Josh is the type of man who will stay—who will be there even when things are hard. I can see that now. He had no choice at sixteen, but he does now, and he’s here. But I can’t escape the feeling that there are things he needs to say.

“You mean you didn’t get me a little bell?” I tease, curling onto my side.

“Ha-ha.” Josh turns back. “If you don’t mind...I’m going to sleep on the couch until you’re better.”

At this, a sadness envelops me, and I have the sudden irrational fear that I am losing him. Tears sting my eyes again. I’m just having a regular old pity party over here.

“Really?” I ask, not even bothering to hide the desperation in my voice.

Josh chuckles. “I’ll be right out there. You can sleep with the door open.” He rests his hand on the door handle. “For now, I want you to sleep.”

I don’t reply—I only sniffle and bat at my eyes that are completely betraying me.

Josh sees it because he moves swiftly back toward me until he’s standing next to me. He plants a soft kiss on the crown of my head. “I’ll be right outside,” he whispers. “I’m not going anywhere.”

“Okay,” I say, my voice barely above a whisper. For now, I allow myself to be reassured by that.

“Sleep now,” Josh says, stroking my hair. And then he’s gone.

# Chapter Twenty-Six

For the next few days, Melanie is in and out of sleep. She doesn't move from the bedroom, except to use the bathroom and then she falls back into bed. On day four, her fever breaks. She's so relieved she calls for me.

"I'm so sweaty," she says from the bed.

I'm lingering in the doorway, eyeing her carefully. "That usually means your fever has broken. Did you take any meds yet today?"

Melanie shakes her head. "No, I just woke up in a cold sweat. Maybe I'm on the other side of this thing." The first genuine smile I've seen from her in days slowly spreads across her face, and she pats the bed next to her.

I hesitate but then cautiously move to the other side and sit down.

"I've missed you," she murmurs, reaching for my hand.

I sniff the air. "Maybe we should open some windows in here."

Melanie frowns. "It's like ninety degrees outside this week."

I roll my lips over my teeth thoughtfully. "Okay...would you be...opposed to a shower?" I tread lightly. "Now that your temp has broken?"

Melanie feigns offense. "Are you trying to say I smell?" She lifts her arm and sniffs herself. "I mean, no one smells good when they're sick." She pouts playfully.

My lips twitch upward. "The room...smells like *sick*. And, well, you do too." I reach for her hand, tilting my head at her. "You're still beautiful and perfect, but...you need to shower. You will feel better."

Melanie sighs. "I just feel so weak still."

I hold up my hands. "Okay, okay, you don't have to." I get up and start to move toward the door.

"Josh?" Melanie's voice comes out soft.

I turn back and she's looking at me, worrying her lower lip.

"Will you...maybe help me shower?"

I don't need to be asked twice.

"Stay in bed until the water's warm," I tell her softly. The faucet hisses to life, the water streaming from cold to lukewarm—just enough to keep her fever from spiking again. When the temperature feels right, I go back for her.

Trembling, she reaches for me. I loop an arm around her waist to steady her. I close the door behind me, careful not to let the warmth of the room escape.

God, I've missed her. The couch has been hell these last few nights—too quiet, too cold without the feel of her pressed against me. I've missed falling asleep beside her, trading stories from when we were kids, laughing until our eyes drifted shut. Missed the way our legs tangle, the way her breathing evens out against my chest.

When I don't move, she lifts her arms in silent invitation. My fingers find the hem of her pajama shirt, hesitating for half a second before tugging it over her head. A low gasp escapes me. She's beautiful—always has been—but she's pale and fragile now, warmth still clinging to her skin. I want to touch her, to remind her she's mine, but not like this. Not when she's sick. My teeth catch on my lower lip, holding everything back.

"You got the rest?" I rasp, taking a step backward.

Melanie swallows, tracing her hand along her collarbone, over her breasts, making her nipples peak. She slides her hands sensually down to the waistband of her shorts, dipping her fingers just under it. When she slips them off and steps out of them, my breath catches.

"You better get in before it gets cold," I say, weakly gesturing to the shower behind her.

"Aren't you coming?" Melanie quirks a brow at me.

"Mel..." I let my voice drop.

"I know... I'm probably contagious. We don't have to do anything. I just want to feel close to you." She bites her lower lip and my heart lurches. I can't resist.

I whip my shirt over my head and drop my gym shorts. I can't even hide the beginnings of my arousal. Melanie steps toward me, running her fingers up my six pack and I let out a hiss. I grip her hand in mine.

"Let's get you washed," I step around her and slide open the glass shower door. The water pressure isn't made for two people, but I don't mind. I step in first and take Melanie's hand as she steps in after me, guiding her under the water. I run my fingers through her hair, helping her to get it thoroughly wet. Squirting some of her forbidden—I'm not allowed to use it—shampoo into my palm, I gently lather it through her hair, root to tip, slowing to massage her scalp.

She lets out a moan, and I drag my hands down to the back of her neck and shoulders, applying gentle pressure to her aching limbs. "Josh," she breathes.

"Shhh," I whisper. "Just enjoy it." I gently cup the back of her neck and guide her back under the stream of water, rinsing her hair.

When the water runs clear, she whirls around, placing her hands on my hips and pulling me close. My mouth aches to be on hers, but I'm not aching to get the flu. My dick is rock hard and settles between her legs in this tiny shower.

Melanie leans into me, wrapping her arms around me as the water runs through us. "Conditioner," she murmurs and I chuckle.

I reach above me to the hanging rack over the shower head and pluck out a teal bottle of conditioner that reads "Deep moisture." My mind immediately goes to another type of deep moisture, and my dick moves involuntarily.

"I think he misses me," Melanie giggles, looking down at my throbbing cock.

"He's not the only one," I say. I give her a gentle nudge so she's forced to take a step back, and I squirt the conditioner in my hand. "Spin," I command. Melanie does as she's told.

I gather her hair, smoothing the conditioner through it. Then I reach for the loofah and the body wash and lather it up, gently washing her back. She spins around, her breath catching, as if she's overwhelmed by the tenderness of my touch.

"Josh," Melanie says, and it catches in her throat.

"Hmm?" I ask, taking some suds from the loofah into my hand and rubbing my hands down her arms, over each breast, her nipples pebbling under my touch.

"No one has ever taken care of me like this," Melanie whimpers.

"You don't need to worry about that anymore," I murmur, pulling her close. "I'm here now."

Melanie melts into me and we stay like that, covered in Dove body wash, the water running cooler between us, for several minutes before I realize Melanie is softly crying.

"Hey, hey, that's not supposed to be happening. What's wrong?" I cup her cheek, forcing her to meet my gaze.

Melanie sniffles. "I'm just...I'm just thinking about how this can't last forever. The summer will end, you'll be gone, and I'll be all alone again."

I swallow the knot that forms in my throat, hesitating before I reply. I stroke Melanie's cheek, brushing away a tear that's hotter than the water we're under. We haven't even had the chance to talk about what's next for us. I faltered earlier this week when I called her my girlfriend. I know it's something we need to talk about, but she was so sick, I let it go. Things are getting serious now though. What initially felt impulsive now feels incredibly natural, as if Mel and I were missing from each other's lives for the past couple decades and suddenly, we've picked up right where we left off. Only now, we get to do it for real—as adults.

"Hey," I say, finally. "I know we haven't talked about what comes next, and we will when you're better."

Melanie nods, swallowing more emotion, but she doesn't reply.

"I know one thing, though," I say softly.

"Yeah?" Melanie looks up at me. "What's that?"

"I know I don't want to lose you. I can't go back to the way things were before," I murmur, pulling her close again.

"Me neither." She shivers into my chest.

I kiss the top of her head. "Ugh," I say, wiping my mouth. "Conditioner. Let's get you out of here before you get the chills."

I rinse her hair, our bodies, and I climb out first so she can stay in the warmth. I reach above the toilet and pull down the fluffiest towel, holding it open for her to step into, then I grab one for myself. We dry off in silence before I hurry her back to her room.

"Quick, get under the covers," I tell her. "I'll dig you out clothes."

When Melanie is dressed, I tuck her in and tell her I'll be right back.

I pull on a pair of joggers, forgoing a shirt and reappear a moment later with a bundle of notebooks in my arms. I'd found them a few days earlier while Melanie slept.

"What's that?" Melanie furrows her brow.

"I found our notebooks." I grin. "Want to read some?"

Melanie giggles. "I'd love nothing more."

I pull back the covers and climb in next to her, adjusting my pillows so I'm propped up.

"Okay..." I begin, picking up a blue composition book with our signature "J+M" etched in the corner. We thought we were so inconspicuous. "In no particular order." I clear my throat, flipping to a page.

"Josh, I think Cara knows. She told me if I ever hurt you, she'd hate to have to beat me up. Did you tell her?" I read the note in my girl voice, making Melanie quietly laugh.

"Oh my gosh. I remember that one. That's when I started to feel like we should tell her for real. We were hanging out and doing it in my bedroom literally every day." Melanie turns on her side so she's looking at me. "Read another one."

"Well, my response is, 'She doesn't know, relax.' So, I'd say someone should have told me back then never to tell a girl to relax," I tease, laughing.

"I was absolutely not relaxed," Melanie agrees, pursing her lips.

I flip the page. "You wrote this next one," I say, skimming it quickly. "I didn't sleep last night. My parents hate each other, Josh. They say such horrific things to each other when they're arguing. I don't even know how they got to this point. I can't even remember a time when my family was happy. It didn't used to be like this, I know that, but it was never as happy as yours." I pause and look at Melanie for a sign that she might be upset.

"Keep going," she urges.

"You sure?" I ask, touching her hand that she pulled above the covers.

She nods.

I take in a shaky breath. "I wish I was part of your family, Josh. It would be so easy. We would be so happy. Instead, I worry I'll be alone forever, caught between two parents who can't stand to be in the same room." My voice turns hoarse as I read. "You sure you want me to keep reading?" I ask, squeezing her hand.

Melanie nods.

I let out a sigh and continue. "Sometimes, I wish I could just run away and not look back. I would pack up all my things and make a break for it if I wouldn't lose you in the process. I could never leave you. Thank you for being my safe place. Love, Mel."

Melanie sniffles and I realize her eyes have filled with tears.

"Hey, we don't have to do this," I say gently, closing the book but keeping my index finger on the page. "It was supposed to be fun. Let's put it aside."

Melanie shakes her head. "I want to hear what you said back."

"If you're sure." I flip the book back open and begin to read. "I'm so sorry, Strawberry Girl. One day soon, we can get out of this place together. I've been thinking more about Nashville. I've always planned to go there alone but—what if we go together? I can't imagine not having you with me. Until then, when the world gets too loud, find me here."

And beneath it, my scrappy hand-drawn map of all our favorite places.

God, we really were in love. The realization hits me like a freight train. I can't lose her again.

## THEN

MEL-

IF THESE SUMMER NIGHT BONFIRES WITH CARA AND LIAM TELL ME ANYTHING, IT'S THAT I CAN'T KEEP THIS A SECRET MUCH LONGER.

WE'RE ALREADY A FOURSOME. WE HANG OUT WITH THEM ALL THE TIME. WHAT ARE YOU SO AFRAID OF? SINGING AROUND THE FIRE PIT LAST NIGHT WAS SO MUCH FUN. YOU WERE QUIET THOUGH AND IT'S SCARING ME. IS THERE SOMETHING YOU AREN'T SAYING? ASIDE FROM WORRYING ABOUT CARA? I CAN'T STOP THINKING ABOUT WHAT SHE SAID ABOUT NASHVILLE. MAYBE WE'RE REALLY MEANT TO BE A COUNTRY DUO. WE COULD GIVE IT A REAL TRY?? AS SOON AS I GRADUATE. WHAT DO YOU THINK? I LOVE YOU.

-J

Josh-

I'm fine, like I've told you for the fiftieth time. I'm not mad at you, you didn't do anything wrong. I think I'm coming down with something. I've been feeling queasy off and on. That's all it was last night, I swear. Can you please stop pressuring me now? I'll tell Cara when I'm ready. I'd have to think about Nashville, but maybe. It's possible, I guess. I love you too.

Mel

# Chapter Twenty-Seven

## NOW

I slam the notebook closed and let out a sigh. Ever since Josh dug out our old notebooks when I was sick, I read them any time he isn't around. I'm trying to build up the courage to have the conversation I don't want to have. But when I read through them, instead of feeling empowered, I feel sick. The past should stay buried where it belongs. If I dig it up, the beautiful future we're building now will be in jeopardy. I just don't know if I can go on like this. Building a relationship based on lies. It doesn't sit well with me. Either way, it's a lose-lose.

We're nearing the end of July, and Josh and I have both been so busy. He has picked up two nights a week playing music for the tourists. For the first couple of weeks, I'd go and watch, but as people recognized him, I grew more and more uncomfortable. He told me he wanted to lay low here but now it feels like he's some kind of local celebrity. I've never been fully comfortable in the limelight, and he does it with such ease. It feels like a reminder of why we're fooling ourselves—we could never actually be together. To top it all off, I feel as if we've hardly spent any meaningful time together. It's just as well because the longer this goes on, the harder it gets to face him and the truth.

I sigh, scooping up the notebooks before Josh gets back from the store. Out of the one on top slides a letter in an envelope. It's worn at the edges, and it's still sealed. Nothing is written on the front except *Josh* scribbled quickly in my handwriting. A letter I never gave him and never intend to. He's been so into reading our old letters lately, I know I have to get rid of this before he sees it. I should throw it away, but I can't bring myself to do that either. That would erase the truth for good, and I have a lot of complicated feelings surrounding that too. I put the notebooks back in the corner cabinet of the TV stand, the place they've been in since I moved in.

I let myself finger the envelope for a moment longer, debating where it should go when Josh opens the front door, startling me.

"Hey," he calls.

I quickly shove the narrow envelope into my back pocket.

Josh eyes me suspiciously. "What's that?"

"Oh, just a bill." I wave my hand and dart into my room, shoving it into the drawer of my nightstand.

There's a pause, then I hear the doubt in his reply. "A bill... right." His tone is edged with suspicion. By the time I return to the kitchen, he's already shaking his head and unloading groceries onto the counter.

I told him when he first got here, he doesn't need to pay me any rent but if he wanted to help by keeping our fridge stocked, that would be awesome. He's taken that job very seriously.

"That's...a lot of fruit," I say, my lips quirking.

"I have been feeling like we're eating too much takeout." He pats his flat stomach. "I thought we could start our mornings with fruit smoothies. I might've gotten a little overzealous."

I let out a low whistle as I scan the items on the counter. Josh got oranges, apples, bananas, strawberries, blackberries, blueberries, peaches, and fresh cherries. I walk over and pick a cherry off the bunch, popping it in my mouth and removing the pit with my tongue.

Josh watches, amused.

"I love cherries," I say, my lips seductively curving around the words.

"I remember." Josh's eyes lock with mine.

"I used to be able to—"

"Tie the stem in a knot with your tongue." Josh and I finish the sentence simultaneously, and my neck heats instinctively.

"I was really proud of that," I say wistfully.

"Oh, I know you were." Josh chuckles, stepping closer to me. He tugs my hips closer to his and wraps me in a hug. "Someone has a birthday coming up this weekend," he murmurs in my ear.

I groan. "Don't remind me. I don't want to turn forty-two." I lean into his chest and take a deep breath.

"Why?" Josh pulls back to look at me, concern etched in his features. "You used to love your birthday."

I let out a defeated sigh. "Yeah, but the older I get, the more I'm reminded of everything I don't have—haven't achieved. I'd rather treat it like any other day." I pull away from him and move into the living room, plopping on the couch.

"Hey now," Josh says from his spot in the kitchen. "You have done a lot in your forty-two years. Don't discount yourself."

I shift so I'm lying on the couch and cover my eyes with my forearm. "Whatever."

Josh chuckles as he passes me on his way to the bathroom. "Well, don't make any plans for Saturday night."

By four o'clock on Saturday, I have still not acknowledged my birthday. I ignored my dad's phone call and couldn't bring myself to listen to him singing "Happy Birthday" on my voicemail, instead settling for reading the transcription. I'm sitting on the couch, scrolling TikTok when Josh comes out of the bathroom, a towel around his trim waist and toweling off his honey blond hair with a hand towel.

"You need to get dressed," he tells me, walking into the kitchen and pulling a cold water bottle out of the fridge. "We have plans."

"Josh." I give him a pointed look. "I told you, this is just any other Saturday."

Josh lets out a slow puff of air. "Well, are you going to call all your friends and cancel or am I? Because we've got a very special birthday dinner to attend, and it won't make much sense without the birthday girl."

I groan, standing. "You really didn't have to do this." I fight back the grin that threatens to spill the gratitude I can't quite say out loud.

"I wanted to," Josh says, walking around the couch to meet me. He pulls me close and plants a soft kiss on my lips. Then, turning serious, "You mean so much to me, Mel."

I sigh. "You mean a lot to me too, Josh," I admit, ignoring the nagging in my chest reminding me that we still haven't talked about what happens after August. And since August is tomorrow, I'd really like to have a conversation about it. Yet, in true Melanie fashion, I haven't had the courage to bring it up. "What should I be wearing to this thing?"

Josh grins. "That's my girl. I made reservations at Harpoons. Everyone is coming so... whatever you'd wear there?"

I step on my tiptoes and plant a kiss on his cheek. "I'll go get ready."

Two hours later, we're walking into Harpoons. I settled on a long tie-dye linen maxi dress that matches my pink hibiscus tattoo. I am wearing my copper hair in soft waves around my shoulders and gold hoop earrings. Josh looks incredible in a pair of gray hybrid shorts that hug his ass and a tight-fitting seafoam T-shirt with Cape May sprawled across the front. He grabs my hand as we walk up the steps to find our friends.

Gathered around the bar on the back deck, overlooking the bay with a little beach you can hang out on, are all of my nearest and dearest: Sophie, Liam, Jenna, Miles, Danny, Kristen, Steph, and Jack. Even Ellie and Robert are here. When they spot me, they all shout "Surprise," confusing me and the other patrons around us.

"Why don't you look surprised?" Sophie whines, stomping a foot. "We thought we had you."

Josh laughs, then shoots me a wry look. "I had to tell her, or she wasn't going to come."

"You guys know how I feel about my birthday." I shrug unapologetically. "Let's pretend this is just a regular night out."

"So, I should cancel the cake?" Jenna asks with a mischievous grin.

"Well, I didn't say that." We all laugh.

Hours later, after a delicious dinner, complete with a sentimental toast from Josh that made me cry, we're hanging out in Sophie and Liam's backyard. Liam has taken the guys into his workshop, and they've left us ladies with several bottles of wine around the outdoor table. Remnants of my delicious cake are scattered about, and I start to move to clean up when Sophie grabs my arm.

"No way, birthday girl. Sit down and relax," she scolds with a teasing grin.

"I was just trying to help." I set the pile down in the center of the table as Stephanie, Jack's wife, tops off my glass of rosé.

"Not tonight you're not," Kristen says from her end of the table. "We want the scoop on your man in there before he comes back out here."

Leave it to Kristen to cut right to the chase. I roll my eyes, but I'm smiling as I take a seat next to Jenna. She slings an arm over my shoulder and gives me a squeeze.

"I don't know if I'd call him that," I say with a small, uncertain lift of my shoulders. "We haven't even talked about it."

Steph's eyes go wide. "You wouldn't call him your man? After that toast? After this whole night that *he* planned?"

"Oh my god, the toast," Sophie swoons. "I teared up."

"Me too!" Kristen agrees, vigorously shaking her head.

"It was *so* romantic," Jenna sighs.

"He's a keeper," Steph agrees.

It's true. Josh's toast was extremely sentimental. I close my eyes and take a breath, remembering his words. "To our birthday girl, Melanie. Thank you for showing me that I wasn't really living. For bringing light back into my life and for seeing me exactly as I am. You mean the world to me, baby."

I sniffle, as tears brim in my eyes.

Sophie sees it first and her expression falters. "What's wrong, Mel?"

I shake my head, wiping away a stray tear. "It's the wine," I deflect, waving my hand.

Steph and Kristen look at each other, frowning.

"Are you sure, sweetie?" Jenna puts her hand on mine, squeezing.

I shake my head no but for some reason, I can't find the words.

"Oh, Mel," Sophie whispers, scooting closer to me. "Don't cry, sweetheart." She drapes her arm around my shoulders, pulling me into a hug.

I take in a shuddering breath, leaning into her embrace. "There's just a lot he doesn't know...about that time. That no one knows."

I catch Kristen and Steph exchanging a glance. They're the only ones around this table that have known me that long, but we didn't become close friends until adulthood.

Steph's eyes grow wide. "Do you...want to tell us?" she asks carefully.

"Not before he and I talk," I say, wiping my eyes abruptly, as the door to Liam's workshop opens.

Josh and Miles come striding out, headed straight for the deck. A slight look of concern crosses over Josh's face when our eyes meet but I offer him a smile, and he relaxes.

When he gets to me, he kisses the side of my head. "Ready to head out, birthday girl?" he murmurs in my ear. His breath sends a shiver down my spine. "I still have more to give you."

I give him a sly smile, figuring he wants to carry me to bed. "Oh yeah?"

Josh catches his lip in his teeth. "I'm serious," he says. "I haven't given you your gift yet."

"Josh, don't be silly. This whole night is my gift." I turn to face him, catching his lips in a gentle kiss.

"Are you okay?" he whispers, tangling his fingers in my hair and leaning his forehead into mine.

I force a smile, holding back everything I want—need—to say to him. "I'm better than okay," I say softly. "Let's go home."

Josh shakes his head. "I'm taking you to our beach."

We say our goodbyes, thanking everyone for making the night special, and head out to Higbee Beach. Josh has a carefully wrapped birthday gift in one hand and a beach blanket in the other. He treks down the path, me trailing behind, wondering how the hell I'm going to broach the difficult topics. I've thought an awful lot about what my dad said—about Josh deserving to know everything that happened back then. I think he's right and I want to share it with Josh, but it's still so painful to this day. I'm not sure how I'd even do it. He's so happy and content lately. We've really hit our stride. This will mess everything up.

"For someone who just had a great birthday, you're awfully quiet," Josh says, looking over his shoulder. "You sure you're all right? You're making me nervous."

I don't immediately reply because we reach our spot. Instead, I help Josh spread out the blanket. Kicking off my sandals, I sit down. Josh sits next to me, and his hand naturally finds mine, just like it always does. The ocean is uncharacteristically calm tonight. The sun is beginning to set in the almost-August sky, and the pinks and yellows reflecting ripple like petals floating on glass.

"I'm sorry, I'm good." I look over at him, taking in his honey blond hair and five o'clock shadow, both speckled with gray. It's hard for me to believe that the first boy I ever loved is sitting here next to me, gray peppering his hair, soft creases around his eyes from years of laughter and a life well-lived. "Thank you for tonight," I add.

"It was my pleasure," Josh says, tipping my mouth to his with nothing more than his index finger. He reaches behind him and picks up the gift. It's wrapped in brown paper with a pale pink satin ribbon tied around it. "Mel" is written in the corner in black Sharpie. "I didn't want to give this to you in front of everyone else. This is...this is just for us." He licks his lips. "I hope you love it."

He hands me the box, and I take it, running my fingers over my name in his familiar handwriting. I finger the soft satin ribbon, enjoying the silky feel of it, before gently pulling it off. Instead of tearing the paper, I gently undo the tape, careful not to rip it. Then, I lift the lid on the box and a gasp escapes me.

Blown up and made to look like a piece of art in a black frame is our map. The one Josh drew for me in our crappy little composition book all those years ago—but better. Josh recreated it on tea-stained, cold-pressed paper in black ink. In the middle, it says "When the world gets too loud, find me here" and he replicated his original drawing. My eyes immediately fill with tears.

"As soon as I saw it in the notebook, I knew I had to recreate it for you," he croaks.

I trace my fingers over the glass of the frame to each place he drew, and then I see it. A new place. Josh drew a heart and labeled it "Your Heart." A small sob escapes me, and I turn to meet his gaze. He cups my face, brushing a tear away.

"I know, it's cheesy. But Mel, I need you to know—I'm in this. I am *all* in. I'm not letting you go. I will not make that mistake again. I was young and dumb back then but I know enough now to know, second chances like this don't come around twice. You're it for me, okay?" Josh's voice is husky, thick with emotion.

I nod into his hand, sniffling, not bothering to hold back the tears. "Me too," I whisper.

"Good." Josh tugs me into the crook of his arm. "It's you and me now, baby."

# Chapter Twenty-Eight

## *Josh*

It's been a week since Melanie's birthday, and despite my telling her that I'm all in, I feel like she's pulling back. I'm trying not to read into it too much. She's told me repeatedly that she needs a change, she's tired of tending bar, she wants to do something different. When I ask what's eating at her, she says it's that. But I'm not so sure.

I've been playing at Fin's every Wednesday and Saturday night. It was supposed to just be mid-week but when the owner, Mike, saw the crowd I drew, he asked for standing Saturdays as well. It works out nicely since Melanie is often at work on Saturdays, but it means less time for us to rehearse together. Summer is flying by. Labor Day weekend is only a few weeks away, and it'll be here before we know it. I'm anxious because I worry that we won't have enough songs for the EP. It's not the concert I'm worried about. Melanie knows all my songs. We can play "Every Song" and I'm almost finished with "The Sound of Her Name." I just know I'll be letting Gary and the record company down if I don't follow through.

The crazy part is, I almost don't care anymore. I've spent years chasing fame—the high that comes along with a crowd singing along with your words. And once I got it, it didn't fill the void that seems to exist permanently in my chest the way I thought it would. What do I care about now? Melanie. I want a life with her, and I can't believe how stupid I've been all these years to not come and get her.

Back when we were kids, I used to dream about Nashville, but never once did I picture going without her. In my mind, it was always the two of us—loading up her beat-up old Buick, guitars in the backseat, chasing songs and neon lights together. Somewhere along the way, I let that dream twist into something lonelier. I went, and she stayed. And it never felt right, not once. Maybe that's why it never filled the hole inside me. Because the truth is, Nashville was never the dream. She was.

Today, while Melanie's at work, I'm doing some research, looking for studio space we can rent to get these two songs recorded and over to Gary and Mark. I have been dragging my feet, and I don't know why. Gary's ears must be ringing because just as I click on the website for Rockstar Rehearsal Studios, about an hour and a half away, my phone buzzes.

"Hey, Gary," I say, tapping the speaker phone icon so I can keep my focus on the computer in front of me.

"Why do you sound so glum?" Gary barks into the phone. "Mark said your song is fantastic!"

I let out a defeated sigh. "It is. It's a great song."

"So, what's the problem? This is what you wanted." His optimism annoys me. It shouldn't surprise me though. Gary is not the type of manager who entertains deeper than surface-level emotions. I can't tell him how complicated writing this album has been for me, he'd never get it.

"Nothing. I'm trying to find a studio space to rent so we can record it for you guys." I force positivity into my voice.

"Well, get to it then. I just wanted to check on you. It's been a while since we've talked." Gary sounds like he's holding something back.

"I'm good. Just...keeping busy."

"Okay. Have you gone to any meetings?" Gary asks, and I know he's trying to sound casual.

"AA?" I all but growl. "No, why would I? I'm not an alcoholic."

"I know man, but it can't hurt," Gary says carefully. It's not his usual topic of conversation, and it makes me wonder if Mark put him up to this.

"I'm *fine*," I stress. "I haven't had a drink since I've been back here." That much is true. I've actually felt pretty proud of myself for it, too. It's been tempting, hanging with the guys and staying sober, but it's always worth it when I feel good and remember everything the next day.

"All right," Gary relents. "I'll let you get back to it."

"Thanks," I say, my tone clipped. "I'll let you know when we've got something."

We hang up and the immense pressure to get this song recorded all but pummels me. I immediately dial Rockstar Recording but come up empty—they're booked through the month. I try three more and get that or no answer.

"I guess we'll have to record it here," I mutter, falling back on the couch.

"What was that?" Melanie startles me.

"You scared the shit out of me," I bristle, sitting up.

"Sorry." She smiles. "You were on the phone when I came in."

I turn to look at her. "I've called the five closest studios—which by the way none of them are actually *close*—and no one has any open availability for us to record." I rake a hand through my hair. "I don't know how we're going to get this done."

Melanie moves behind the couch, leans over, wraps her arms around my neck in a hug, and kisses my temple. "It'll be okay. We have a lot of quiet here. We can use your mics and the recording app. And I'm sure we can find another app to mix and layer it. It should be fine for Mark to just hear what we've got."

I gently move out of her grasp and she lets go, perhaps sensing my barriers going up.

"I guess so," I grumble.

"Let's do it on Sunday. I'm off and we can take as long as we need to get it right." Melanie comes to sit next to me, tucking her feet up under her. Just her nearness to me softens my prickly mood.

I reach for her hand, rubbing tiny circles on the top of it with my thumb. "Thanks, babe," I say, leaning in for a kiss.

I'll feel better once it's done.

Saturday morning, Melanie suggests we take a walk around Rotary Park and get a feel for the set up. I haven't been there in years, so I agree. We shower and dress, and we're heading out the door when I pause to grab my guitar.

Melanie gives me a playful smirk. "We're supposed to be taking a walk," she teases. "You are worse than me, dragging that thing around."

"Hey, you never know." I hold up my hands.

Rotary Park is in the center of town. On quiet afternoons during our teen years, Melanie and I often came here to play. The grounds are lush with green grass and beautiful gardens. There is a fountain in the center and various little kids stand around it, throwing in coins and making wishes. The park isn't large, only spanning about a half a block, but there are benches scattered around and lots of green space for lounging. In the center of it all is a large gazebo bandstand, used for concerts in the summertime. It's where Melanie and I will be performing together in a few weeks. We've spent many an afternoon on the steps of the gazebo, strumming away. I pause when I see it, closing my eyes as memories envelop me.

*Melanie's head falling back as a melodic laugh escapes her. Melanie strumming her guitar, a glint in her eyes as she watches me sing my verse. Melanie leaning over to kiss me, not caring who sees.*

"You okay?" She elbows me now, bringing me out of my trance.

I glance her way, a wistful smile pulling on my lip. "Yeah.

Just...nostalgia."

"Lots of memories here," she agrees, nodding. "Come on, let's walk."

She holds an open palm out to me.

I sling the strap of my guitar case higher on my shoulder and grasp her hand. We start slow, walking the beautiful gray brick pavers, silently people watching.

"It's changed so much," I murmur, looking around.

"They've re-done it a couple of times in the last two decades, yeah." Melanie playfully nudges me with her shoulder.

"I can't believe I've been away that long," I mutter.

"I can. You had a dream, and you chased it," Melanie says, looking up at me. "I'd have expected nothing less."

"What about you?" I ask, and my voice comes out more emotional than I expect it to. "What's your dream?"

Melanie pushes her lips together in a tight line. "I'm still figuring that out," she says quietly.

"I know you will." I stop as we near the end of our first lap. Before us is the gazebo. People are sitting scattered on the steps. Others walk around the park, some sit on benches with coffees, others reading in the shade of an oak tree. A group of twenty-something women sit on a picnic blanket in the grass, drinking iced coffees.

"So, this is where we'll play on September sixth," Melanie says, one corner of her mouth turned upward. "It's pretty full circle, isn't it?" Her eyes glisten with wonderment.

I scratch my jaw, looking at the gazebo. "It is pretty crazy. We played here nearly every afternoon that spring." I glance at her. "Now we'll be playing here for real."

Melanie grins. "It feels like serendipity."

I nod, feeling myself relax. "Should we sit and play? For old time's sake?"

Melanie grimaces. "I don't know," she says, looking around. "There are a lot of people out this morning."

My mouth quirks into a crooked smile. "Think of it as

practice, come on." I move to the steps in front of us, sitting on the top one and unzipping my guitar.

Melanie bites her lip, pausing for a moment before finally sitting next to me. "Well, what are we going to play?"

"'Every Song,' of course." I grin, strumming the first few chords. I play through the first verse with no words, waiting for Melanie to get comfortable with the idea of singing in front of a crowd. "Come on," I murmur in her ear. "You have a beautiful voice, and no one is even paying attention."

I strum a little louder as I approach the second verse. The sound of my guitar gets the attention of the twenty-somethings, and a few of them move toward us, lingering on the benches just outside the gazebo.

"Oh my god," Melanie says under her breath, tensing beside me.

I turn and whisper in her ear. "How will you do this in a few weeks if you can't do it now?" I let my breath linger on her ear for a second before I move into the intro again. Melanie's voice catches me by surprise.

As soon as she starts singing, attention turns to us. Several in the group of women, who I've now figured out is a bachelorette party, whip out their phones and start recording. When Melanie notices, she glances at me, but she doesn't falter.

I join her in harmony on the chorus, taking the third verse for myself. By the final chorus, we're grinning at each other, singing together, looking into each other's eyes. I've forgotten everyone around me but Melanie.

We sing the last line in unison. As soon as the note ends, the crowd of onlookers erupts into cheers. Mel and I wave and smile, but we don't move to play anything else.

"See, you did it," I say, giving her a peck on the lips. "It gets easier every time."

We're immediately interrupted by an excited voice. "Oh my gosh, it *is* you. You're Josh Cote."

I slowly turn my gaze from Melanie to find the bachelorette

herself, two friends gathered on either side of her. Their faces could only be described as starstruck.

"In the flesh," I say, grinning. "This is Melanie."

The woman gives Mel the once over before turning her attention back to me. "I'm Maddie and I'm getting married next week. I cannot believe I'm seeing Josh Cote on my bachelorette weekend!"

A chuckle escapes me, and I wave my hand dismissively. "Trust me, I'm nobody."

"He's humble," Melanie chimes in.

"We're huge fans. We're here from Tennessee!" another girl chimes in. "We've seen you play on Broadway a whole bunch."

"This is April," Maddie juts her thumb in the direction of the girl who spoke last. "And this is Olivia." She gestures to her other friend.

"Can we take a selfie?" Olivia asks, eagerly.

I sling my arm over Melanie's shoulder and give her a reassuring smile. "Of course," I say. The girls turn and crouch in front of us, Maddie holding up her arm in an effort to get the shot. It's not lost on me that Mel's face gets cut out.

"So, are you guys a duo now?" Maddie asks eagerly.

"Something like that," I say, planting a kiss on the side of Mel's head. She looks uncomfortable, but she wasn't until these girls showed up.

Maddie and her friends start to move away. "Thanks for the photo. You made my weekend!"

"You're welcome." I grin with a nod.

"Oh, and I was really sorry to hear about you and Keira. I thought you made such a cute couple," she whines. "I saw she's engaged now." Maddie makes a face as if she's trying to poke the bear.

I don't take the bait. "Wasn't meant to be." I shrug, sensing this conversation going in a different direction than I'd like. Standing, I move to put my guitar back in its bag, still feeling the women's eyes on me. I turn back to them. "It was nice meeting you girls—have fun." Then I turn to Melanie who has gone still, caving into herself. "Ready, baby?" I murmur, tipping her chin to meet my gaze. I hope she gets my message: *It's you and me.*

This seems to snap Melanie out of it. "Yeah," she says, standing, wiping her hands on her shorts. "It was nice meeting you girls."

"You good?" I ask Mel on our walk back, concern laced in my voice.

Melanie gives me an almost sad smile. "Yeah, I'm good," she says. "I just...sometimes forget you're Josh Cote. You'll always be just Josh to me."

My chest constricts. "I will always be just Josh," I say, stopping to look at her.

"You don't know that," Mel says, shaking her head. "You have star power."

I suck in a breath and reach to tuck a hair behind her ear. I'm not sure what to say. She's right, I *don't* know that for sure. But all it has taken is half a summer with Melanie for me to realize that fame and fortune may not be what I want anymore.

## THEN

Josh -

I'm sorry I had to bail tonight. I know you're disappointed. An under 21 open mic night doesn't come around often, but I know it'll be successful and they will do it again. I just don't feel well at all and I'm afraid I'd get up on the stage and puke. Please say you aren't mad at me??? I know you'll do great. Tell Cara to take pictures for me. I'm so *sorry again.*

*I love you. I mean it.*

*Mel*

MEL –

IT WAS SO AWESOME. THE ONLY THING MISSING WAS YOU. IT MADE ME REALIZE I DEFINITELY HAVE TO GO TO NASHVILLE. THERE'S NO OTHER WAY AROUND IT. MAYBE I CAN TAKE A GAP YEAR AND TRY TO MAKE IT DOWN THERE BEFORE MY PARENTS FORCE ME TO GO TO COLLEGE. I CAN'T IMAGINE DOING ANYTHING ELSE WITH MY LIFE. THIS IS IT FOR ME.

I'M SORRY YOU WEREN'T THERE. I HOPE YOU'RE FEELING BETTER NOW.

JOSH

# Chapter Twenty-Nine

## *Melanie*

### NOW

Josh didn't turn off his ringer last night and the annoying sound of a phone call wakes us up promptly at eight a.m. Sunday morning. I'm not thrilled since we were both out late last night—Josh playing at Fin's and me closing down the bar. I'm off today, and my only plans are to sleep in and record "Every Song" with Josh.

Josh lets out a muffled groan, reaching behind him for his phone on the nightstand.

"Who is it?" I roll over to find him squinting at his screen.

"It's Gary." Josh frowns, tapping his screen. "Gary, it's eight a.m., this better be good."

"Oh, it's good all right, Joshy," Gary bellows through the phone. He's so loud, if I didn't know better, I'd say Josh had us on speaker.

"What is it?" Josh growls. There's a hint of agitation in his voice telling me that maybe what Gary thinks is good, isn't actually good.

"Are you sitting down?" Gary deflects.

"I'm in bed, Gary, so yes. Spit it out."

"You. Are. Viral." Gary enunciates and then pauses for effect.

At this, I sit up, a sense of panic building and heat racing through my veins. Viral? How would Josh be viral? I wrack my brain. Fin's maybe? Maybe someone filmed him there.

"Viral?" Josh sits up too, gesturing for me to hand him my phone. "Viral where?"

"TikTok, of course, where else?" Gary scoffs, like it should be obvious.

*TikTok.*

I hand Josh my phone. He taps his screen to put Gary on speaker and opens TikTok on mine. He doesn't even have to look for it. The color drains from my face and bile rises in my throat as I see it. The first video on my For You page is *me.* And Josh. Playing our song—our very *personal* song for the world to see. I reach for my water bottle on my nightstand and take a long pull from it.

"Holy shit," Josh mutters.

"Isn't this great? When did you do this? Did you do it on purpose?" Gary is firing questions a mile a minute.

"No..." Josh shakes his head, blinking rapidly. "We didn't *do it* on purpose."

"Well, you stepped in shit that's for sure. Five million views overnight and people are going crazy for Josh and Melanie!" Gary is downright gleeful. My pulse skips. This is too much, too fast.

"How—how did this happen?" I squeak, my voice barely above a whisper. Just as I'm getting comfortable performing publicly, we go viral. Naturally.

"Apparently, the girl who posted it is some kind of lifestyle influencer? You made her whole bachelorette weekend." Gary claps from the other end of the line. "Well done, my friends."

"I'm going to be sick," I mutter, falling back on the pillow.

"Josh, tell her how great this is," Gary urges. "You two make a great team."

Josh glances at me, patting my leg. "It'll be okay," he murmurs, and I'm not sure who he is trying to reassure, me or himself. "Gary, I'll call you later," he says, hanging up before Gary replies.

Josh turns to me, watching me carefully. "So...I've never been viral before." He cracks a grin.

I cover my face with my forearm and moan. "I have never

*wanted* to be viral before."

Josh lays down next to me, propping up on his elbow. "Come on, you mean to tell me my music-loving Mel wouldn't have wanted the world to see and hear her back in 1999?" His lips twitch teasingly. "I don't believe that for a second."

I sigh, knowing he's right. "I've just... retreated into myself the past twenty years or so. This feels foreign." I bite my lip, exhaling as my reluctance slips away. "What are they saying?"

Josh chuckles. "That's my girl." He picks up my phone and starts to scroll through the comments, reading them aloud.

"Wait... Why is this actually a BOP?"

"THE COMEBACK WE DIDN'T KNOW WE NEEDED."

"Not me adding this to my breakup playlist immediately."

"This man took a two-year nap and came back with the hit of the year and a hot girlfriend? Fire duo." He smirks at this. "*Nap*?"

"Hot *girlfriend*? Let me see that." I snatch the phone from Josh's hands, my eyes skimming the comments. "There's so many..." We scroll together, our heads tipped together as we slowly read.

"Bet he was washed-up to y'all...till this hit one million views overnight."

"Country radio better clear a lane...HE'S BACK!"

"Two years off and he comes back with THIS? Music industry take note."

"He really said 'miss me?' and dropped a heater."

"It's giving 'took a step back and found the sound again' and I am HERE FOR IT."

"Y'all were calling him washed but he was just marinating."

Most of the comments are about Josh, rightfully so, but as I scroll through, there are a few that mention me. Instead of sending me into a spiral, something blossoms inside me. Something that may just convince me that this is really within reach. When I get to the first one that mentions me, I read it aloud.

"Okay, but who is *she* and where has she been hiding?" I giggle. "They put a hot emoji."

"That's because you're hot," Josh says, kissing my temple.

I make a *pshh* sound and keep reading. "She's not just harmonizing, she's healing souls."

"I came here for him but I'm staying for HER."

"SOMEONE SIGN HER ALREADY."

"Not the vocals aging like a fine wine."

"She's the reason this man remembered how to write a love song."

I look over at Josh, but he isn't looking at the phone—he's looking at me.

"That one's true," he rasps.

A chill runs up my spine and I suck in a breath, telling myself I'll only read five more comments and then I'll forget about this silly little TikTok.

"I smell a CMA comeback performance," Josh reads with a snort. "I doubt that."

"Okay but this better be on Spotify by Friday or I'll riot (respectfully)." I laugh. "That one's funny."

I scroll down once more. "This is giving, 'we broke up but still did the duet at church' energy."

"Oh my gosh, people are wild." Josh chuckles. "But look at this one..." he points to the comment at the bottom of the screen and reads: "This feels like sitting on a porch swing with someone you love and a secret you're not ready to share yet."

I feel Josh's gaze on me, and I turn to meet it.

I lick my lips. "Well, damn."

The only thing on our agenda today is to get "Every Song" recorded and sent over to Mark. Josh and I spend another hour in bed proving just how well we harmonize *offstage* before we finally decide we'd better get to it. "Got to give the people what they want," he mutters with a sigh, climbing over me to get out of my large bed in this tiny bedroom. "How about I make us a fruit smoothie and we get started?"

I yawn, covering my mouth. "Sure, sounds good." I roll to my side. "I'll just be another minute behind you."

"Take your time." Josh plants a kiss on my lips. I want nothing more than to pull him back into bed with me, but he's motivated, and I can't crush that. A moment later, he's in the kitchen and I hear the blender. I pick up my phone again, my thumb hovering over TikTok. I can see where these comments provide content creators and artists alike with a dopamine hit. I already want to see if there are more—more about me. I have so many complicated emotions running through me. A couple of months ago, Josh showing up here was the last thing I expected. I never thought I'd get to see him again—to love him again. Now, I'll be sharing the stage with him after all these years and that's a dream I'd let go of a *long* time ago.

On top of all that, there are still things I haven't told him. Things he deserves to know. I push them out of my head, day after day, because I'm terrified of wrecking this, of tainting it. This is our second chance. What if I tell him everything and I ruin it all?

"Babe, smoothie!" Josh calls from the kitchen.

I sigh, tossing my phone aside. If I keep looking at the TikTok comments, I'll get my hopes up. And the higher up they go, the less likely I am to tell Josh the truth.

I throw the covers off me and slip into some pants. Josh and I have taken to sleeping in nothing—or next to nothing. Another reminder of how close we're becoming.

I head to the bathroom to freshen up and brush my teeth, and by the time I come out, Josh has set our smoothies on the table and is working to set up some recording equipment.

"This will be pretty grassroots," he says, without looking up from his MacBook. "I've got some mics and GarageBand. And some very basic software. But since it's quiet here, I think we'll be okay to at least get something down for Mark and the guys at SoundShift." He clicks something on his screen and then looks up at me. "You okay?"

I smile, this time not bothering to push my hope aside. Josh is excited. He's excited about going viral, he's excited about his blossoming career, he's excited about making music again—maybe he's even excited about me.

"I'm good," I say, taking a sip of my smoothie. "So good."

Josh moves to me then, pulling me close. "The TikTok thing didn't freak you out?" His voice is soft, lips hovering just over mine.

"Surprisingly, no." I shake my head. "I think I'm really ready to do this with you."

"Woo!" Josh cheers, pulling back to look at me, as if checking my face for seriousness. "It's about damn time!"

We spend the entire morning recording—not because we couldn't get it right the first time, but because we want it to be perfect. Finally, after about seven tries, Josh hits the play back button and our voices fill my apartment. Crisp and clear, hauntingly beautiful as they meld together in harmony. I blink back tears when the song finishes and when I look at Josh, an unidentifiable emotion is clouding his expression too.

"I think we did it," he says, reaching for my hand.

"I think so too." I lick my lips. "It's beautiful."

"You're beautiful," Josh murmurs, pulling me close and kissing me deeply. I open for him, our tongues dancing together in the same way our voices did moments ago. Desire pools low in my gut and I move to his lap. He pulls me into him, and I feel his hardness against my heat. Josh's mouth moves from my lips, down my neck, gently sucking until a soft moan escapes me. He puts his lips to my earlobe, nibbling gently. "Shall we go celebrate?" he teases.

"Definitely," I breathe.

Josh reaches around me and clicks the mouse of the computer. "Just let me send this."

I rake my fingers through his hair, dragging my teeth gently along his jaw, planting soft kisses on his neck. His dick moves against me and I moan.

"Done," he whispers, finding my mouth again. He hoists to

a stand, carrying me into what I now think of as *our* bedroom. I haven't stopped to think about how fast things between us have moved. It's only been about two months, but Josh and I have found our rhythm and I don't want to let it go.

He gently lays me on the edge of the bed, tugging off my shorts to find me bare. "Oh my god, woman." He lets out a chuckle before reaching up to tug off my loose T-shirt. I'm not wearing a bra either. Josh lets out a guttural moan, taking a nipple into his mouth and sucking until I breathe his name. Then he moves to the other and I'm writhing beneath his weight.

He stands, pulling his white T-shirt off and stepping out of his shorts. A sigh falls from my lips as I see his erection pressing against his boxer briefs and I reach to touch him.

"Uh-uh," he says, dropping to his knees. He spreads my legs, planting kisses up my thighs until I'm trembling. "Jesus, Josh. Give it to me," I growl.

Josh's mouth finds my slit then, his tongue sinking into me, sending pleasure to the tips of my toes. He drags his teeth over the bundle of nerves that has the power to unravel me. Before I know what's happening, Josh reaches into my nightstand drawer. He pauses, looking at the contents for a moment. Panic replaces pleasure when I remember the letter I tucked in there the other day, and I pray it's not face up.

"What are you doing?" I breathe. "I need you."

Josh snaps out of it. He rummages through the drawer and seconds later holds up a small silver bullet vibrator—something I haven't needed to use the past two months. "Looking for this." A sultry grin creeps across his face and I relax again, panic leaving my body. "Arms up," Josh commands, standing and pushing my arms over my head. "Grab the headboard, no touching."

"Oooh, you're bossy today," I tease.

Josh powers up the vibrator and a familiar buzzing sound fills the room. He kneels again, slowly dragging the vibrator up my thighs until it hovers just outside my lips. "Is this okay?" he asks, sincerely.

"Uh-huh," I breathe, because I can't make any other sound come out.

Before using it on me, Josh sinks his tongue into my center one more time. Nipping, tasting, and gently sucking until I'm begging for him. Then he does it—glides the vibrator to the little bud of nerves that will send me into oblivion. As soon as it touches my clit, I cry out, but that's only amplified by Josh sliding two fingers into my core, swirling them around and making a come-hither motion. "Josh," I cry out.

"You're so wet, baby," he murmurs, moving the vibrator aside and sinking his mouth into me again. The brashness of his teeth sends a shudder through me and my thighs tremble.

"I won't make it," I hiss. "I'm too close."

"You have to hold on for me baby, not yet." Josh moves away from my opening and brings the vibrator up to my nipples, dragging it across and following it with his mouth, sucking until I beg. Then he takes it back in his hand and cups it over my clit, while simultaneously sucking on each breast. I'm writhing beneath him, begging for release. "I like teasing you," he whispers, moving his lips to mine and kissing me deeply. "Can you taste yourself?"

My response is unintelligible. My whole body is buzzing with desire, I'm dripping with wetness, and all I want to do is come. "Josh, please. Please let me come," I whimper.

At my plea, he's back between my thighs. His fingers find my opening and this time it's three he shoves inside. Using his other hand, he holds the vibrator to my clit and watches as I squirm, my orgasm building. "So fucking beautiful," he whispers.

That does it for me, I scream as a wave of pleasure crashes into me, vibrating every nerve ending in my body as ripples of orgasms send me over the edge.

"That's my girl," Josh says, when my legs stop trembling. Not a moment later, he steps out of his boxers and sinks his dick into me with ease. "So fucking wet for me."

Josh doesn't take long, but I don't mind. My body is depleted, so I let him fuck me like a rag doll, flipping me over and taking me from behind. His thrusts are needy, urgent in a way they haven't been before. He yanks at my hair, sending a jolt through me, only further igniting my pleasure. "Come for me again, baby," Josh growls in my ear. "Come with me."

That's all it takes for my undoing—three more thrusts and we're unraveling together, the sounds erupting from us in shared harmony. Josh collapses on top of me, remaining inside me and rolling on his side so we're spooning. I'm not sure how long we stay that way but neither of us is in a rush to move.

We have had sex many times since his return, but never like this. This was carnal—desperate, almost bordering on make-up sex, but we hadn't fought. I try not to think about what that means because right now, I feel closer to him than ever.

# Chapter Thirty

## Josh

I saw the letter in Melanie's drawer when I was going for her vibrator last week. It looked old—a piece of our past that for some reason, she doesn't want me to see. It's nagging at me, but for the past few days, I've tried to put it out of my mind. If she wanted me to have it, she'd give it to me. But something about it doesn't sit right with me. What the hell could be in that letter that she won't share with me now, twenty-five years later?

But now we're a week out from the concert, and I know I have to put it aside. Something has shifted with us since we recorded our song. Melanie, who's usually hesitant about putting herself out there, has started to let a quiet hope slip through. Several times she's asked me if I think the record company will like our song, if I think she'll be good enough, but there's a light behind her eyes when she asks. It's cautious, like she's afraid to hope too much.

Several times I've had to talk myself off the solo career ledge. The truth is, I'm terrified they will only want me with her. Or worse, *only* her. The viral TikTok video is still gaining traction, and I can't believe the comments. It went from people discussing the song, to discussing my personal life, my accident, my breakup with Keira, and speculation on my relationship with Melanie. I am trying not to let it bother me. I want it to be about my music, and it mostly is, but there's a part of me that wonders if this will all fizzle out. And if it does, if I would even care.

Melanie is on day shift today, so after a morning shower I decide to go visit Cara's grave. I am looking for inspiration to finish my song for her. I've written most of the song with Mel, but I feel like the end of it must come from me. I hop in my car. Remembering how bare Cara's grave looked the last time I was there, I quickly stop at Sunset Blooms for some flowers.

The bell jingles above the door when I walk in and a woman, who I assume is the owner, whirls around. When she sees me, a look of surprise flashes across her face. "Good morning!" she chirps.

I walk up to the counter, leaning on it and perusing her premade bouquets. "Hi, good morning," I say, my voice thick. "I'm looking for a small bouquet to put on my sister's headstone."

"Of course, I can help you with that. I'm Tina." She smiles genuinely, and I let my guard down some.

"Josh," I say, returning her smile.

"I know who you are," Tina says quietly. "I saw your TikTok. I knew who you were before, but, wow." Tina appears momentarily starstruck but quickly recovers. "Anyway, I think it's so great you're back in town and singing with Melanie."

I chuckle. "Thank you, it really has been awesome," I say, scratching my jaw. Suddenly feeling undeserving of such praise, I'm desperate to escape the conversation. I point at a pale pink and white bouquet of carnations, roses, and baby's breath. "How about this one?"

"That's lovely," Tina agrees.

"I'll take it," I say, opening my wallet.

Tina takes the bouquet from the case and hands it to me. "It's on the house," she says with a genuine smile.

"No way," I say, waving my hand.

"Yes way." Tina gives me a pointed look, as if to say don't challenge me.

I ignore it and slide a fifty-dollar bill on the counter anyway. Money feels like such a small thing compared to the welcome I've been given here, the kindness that keeps meeting me at every turn. "Then consider this a thank-you donation." I turn and start walking out the door.

"Josh, that's way too much," Tina calls after me.

But I'm already gone.

I FIND CARA'S gravesite easier this time, parking my car on the dirt trail just off to the side of it. I grab my guitar, the flowers, and the beach towel that I brought, and as an afterthought, the notebook sitting on my seat. My plan is to sit with Cara, talk to her, and then work on her song. I spread the towel out and place the flowers gently on the headstone and then take out my guitar.

"Hey, sis," I croak, talking aloud to her, something that felt strange to me the last time I was here. "I told you I'd be back."

Then I tell her everything I've never said before. I tell her how much I loved Melanie when we were seventeen and that when I lost her, I lost Melanie too. I tell her how we've reconnected, and it seems as though we're getting our second chance, a thought that thrills and terrifies me at the same time. Then I tell her everything I am ashamed of—my drinking, my own accident, my lack of ability to move past it. This time, when I talk to her, a weight lifts off my chest. I'm not sitting here crying and feeling guilty. I feel almost free.

I pick up my guitar and start strumming the chord progression that I've decided fits but I'm still unsure of the lyrics. I don't want the song to be sad; I want it to feel uplifting. I want Cara's spirit to be ingrained in the words.

"The sound of her name, soft in the air. Melody's fading, but she's still there," I sing softly. "She could light up a room just walking through. If you knew her then, you still do." I pause, jotting down those words. "Hmm," I say, putting the pencil between my teeth. I close my eyes and try to picture Cara. I picture her laughing over a spaghetti dinner, telling my parents and me about her day. I picture her fighting with me over the bathroom.

I can see her scoring the winning goal at the state championship.

The second verse comes easier then, as memories flood my mind of times we spent together. Most of my memories are from the summer before she died. Because Melanie and I were close, Cara and I spent more and more time together. She'd stopped thinking of me as her annoying younger brother and began thinking of me as a friend. I will always cherish those summers spent around the fire pit, laughing and talking about our dreams, making music with Mel. I pick up my pencil and begin to write feverishly.

*We keep her alive in the stories we tell*
*Every late-night fire, every found seashell*
*We talk about her like she just stepped out*
*Like she'll walk right in when the sun goes down*

*[Chorus]*
*So here's to the girl with the wildflower soul*
*Gone too soon, but never let go*
*The sound of her name still carries me home*
*Through every high note and every low*
*She's the laugh in the dark, the tear in your eye*
*She's not just a memory—this isn't goodbye*
*No, this isn't goodbye*

*So we raise our glass and we play her song*
*Tell the same old jokes like she's not gone*
*She's the heart of the night when the sun sinks low*
*The reason we dance when the music is slow*

I pause when I get stuck. I need Melanie to help me with the bridge, and I'm sure I've been here long enough. I pack up my things and stand, stretching. Maybe some old photos of Cara would help. I'm sure Mel has some around her house. I drive back quickly, only one thing on my mind. *Finish this song, play it for Melanie, tell her I want to do this thing with her. For real.*

When I get in my car, I do something I haven't done in a long time. I dial my parents.

My mother answers on the first ring. "Josh? Is everything okay?"

A laugh bubbles out of me. What a shame it is that I haven't called my parents in so long that my mom immediately assumes something is wrong when I do.

"Yes, Mom. I just called to say hi. I wanted to hear your voice," I say slowly, cautiously.

"Oh!" my mother chirps. "Well, hang on, your father is here too. Let me put you on speaker." Then I hear her call for him. I take a second to wonder if they'd seen the TikTok but quickly abandon that thought. No way they're looking at social media.

"Josh! How are ya?" my dad barks a moment later.

I chuckle. "I'm good, Dad. How are you?"

"You know, same old, same old. Life in retirement is boring." My dad sounds grumbly, but I recognize it as contentment. He is probably happy to be bored, having spent thirty years doing manual labor.

"What have you been up to, sweetheart?" My mother's voice interjects.

"I'm actually... I'm in Cape May." I pause, waiting for a response.

"Oh...you are?" My mom sounds uneasy.

"I am. Liam and Melanie and I are working on a memorial scholarship concert in Cara's name. It'll be September sixth at Rotary Park. I'd love if you two came." I blurt this out quickly, so I don't chicken out. My parents haven't been back here since Cara died. I'm not sure how they would feel about it.

"Oh, I don't know, son." My dad's voice is quiet, regretful. "It's been so long."

"We'll think about it," my mom interrupts.

"Please. I'd love to see you." I rub the back of my neck, feeling the tension slowly creep up. "It would mean the world to me. And Mel."

"Mel? Are you two seeing each other?" My dad has never been subtle.

I let out an easy laugh, relaxing then. "Yeah, we are."

"I always loved Melanie," my mom chimes in.

"We'll think about it," my dad repeats my mom's earlier words.

"Thanks," I say. "I love you guys."

"Love you, too." Their voices come in unison and then they're gone.

As soon as I've hung up, my phone rings again. Mark's name flashes across the screen on my dash. I tap the green button.

"Mark," I say, easily. "How goes it?"

"How's the latest viral sensation?" Mark barks happily.

I laugh. "I'm...optimistic," I say cautiously. "What's going on?"

"I just wanted to tell you that Gary, Chip, and I *loved* your record, and we will be up for your concert. We can't wait to see you two live!"

A grin spreads across my face. Sometimes Mark comes off like a slimy record producer, but most of the time, his approval means a lot to me.

"That's great. I've got some other things I'm working on too," I say. "Solo." I add after a beat. The truth of the matter is, I haven't discussed the future with Melanie beyond this concert. I have been waiting to hear what SoundShift Records wants from me. Waiting to see if I have a reason to stay, or if it's better that I go.

"Solo? No, no, Josh. You and Melanie have something special here," Mark argues.

"I know..." I tread carefully. "But I don't know if she wants to go on the road with me. If she wants to do this with me."

"Well, you better find out. Because we want both of you." Mark's words come out more demanding than I'm sure he means, but a dull feeling of dread settles in my chest.

I guess it's about time Mel and I have a serious conversation about the future—our future.

I hang up with Mark as I turn onto Melanie's street, determined to go upstairs and finish this song. Or as much of it as I can before she gets home.

When I get to the apartment, Melanie isn't home yet. That's all right. I kick my shoes off at the door, grab a bottle of water from the fridge, stopping to look at the photo of Melanie and Cara held up by a magnet, their faces lit with joy. Cara's eyes are crinkling, like she's laughing at something. I grab my guitar and my notebook and spread everything out on the coffee table. Then I start rummaging through the cabinets we have been keeping our old notebooks in, but there are no photos in there.

I look in Melanie's hall closet, wondering if I missed any photo albums. I'm coming up empty. Finally, I walk into her room. I know she has some photos in here. There are a couple stuck in the mirror on her dresser. But I don't want to take them off—that feels wrong. I gaze at them for a moment. There's one of junior prom, the two girls dressed up, wearing their corsages and smiling big. Melanie looked *so beautiful* that night. A chill runs through me as I remember what happened after prom. That night changed me forever.

I open her small closet and there are a bunch of boxes on the shelves, but it feels intrusive to get them down and go through them. I just need a couple of loose photos to spread out on the table for inspiration while I write. I want to remember specific things about Cara—her big blue eyes, the dimple in her left cheek, the way her eyes crinkled in the corners when she laughed.

Then I remember, there was a packet of 4x6 photos in Mel's nightstand drawer. I remember because it looked old and the One Hour Photo logo was printed on it. I saw it when I was looking for her vibrator. I don't know what they are, but it's worth a shot. I move toward it, opening the drawer and rooting through some miscellaneous birthday cards, lists, and other things in search of the vintage Kodak sleeve that reads, "Share Moments. Share Life."

But then, my eyes catch on something else. An envelope, worn and unopened. A memory from a couple of weeks ago flashes through my mind—Melanie hiding something behind her back that she claimed to be a bill. I didn't buy it, but I certainly didn't think anything of it either. I noticed it last week but all I wanted to do was get her off, so I pushed it out of my mind. But now, there's a nagging feeling in the back of my brain, urging me to turn the envelope over. I can't ignore it.

I reach for it, flipping it over to see who the sender might be, but there's only one thing scrawled on the front of it. In Melanie's familiar curvy handwriting: *Josh.*

I study it for a moment. It's from back then. It has to be. If it were new, there's no way the edges would be tearing and worn. There wouldn't be spotted fingerprints on it. It's a letter for me that clearly Melanie never gave me. Against all my better judgment, I tear it open and begin to read.

Then everything goes black.

## THEN

*Josh,*

*I don't know how I'll ever have the courage to give you this letter but if I don't tell you now, I never will. I tried to talk to you at the funeral but I couldn't bring myself to do it. Everyone looked so sad and I didn't want to make things worse.*

*Josh, I'm pregnant. Or, I was. Remember a month ago how I started bailing on you? Saying I felt sick? Well, I realized that I hadn't gotten my period in a long time. I couldn't remember the last time. I used to always write it in a notebook but I haven't since before prom. So I had no idea how late I really was. I went to the dollar store up the parkway so no one would see me and bought ten tests. They all came back positive. I've been sick over it for weeks–not telling you. Then the nausea started and I was completely terrified that this would ruin everything. Music, Nashville, us. I don't know how it happened. I thought you always pulled out. That you were careful. It doesn't matter now anyway.*

*I was going to tell you about it the night of the accident, after the game. I thought we could decide what to do together. But when I got to the hospital, I was bleeding. I started screaming hysterically, my parents didn't understand, the doctors didn't. They thought it was just my period, maybe brought on by the accident or my broken leg. But I told them I was pregnant. My mom started crying then and my dad held my hand. They took care of my leg first, casted it. Then they wheeled me back for an ultrasound. My dad sat next to me, holding my hand. I cried the whole time. And then there it was. Our baby on the screen in a black bubble. I thought, "Thank God. We can keep it, it'll be okay." It looked like a little gummy bear. At that moment all I wanted was to keep it. To get to hold our baby one day.*

*I thought everything would be okay. But the doctor just shook her head and looked at me sadly. She said there was no heartbeat. The impact of the crash must've triggered a miscarriage.*

*I would have never wished to be seventeen and pregnant but I am devastated. My mom says it's just as well. That no one wants to be a teen mom. I'm so sad without Cara and this baby that I started to picture in my head. I don't even see the point anymore.*

*I don't know how to tell you. I want to see you but I am scared you'll hate me. I've lost Cara and our baby and I feel like life is over. I don't know what to do.*

*I'm so sorry. I love you so much.*

*Mel*

# Chapter Thirty-One

## Melanie

### NOW

I can hardly wait to get home from work and see Josh. Things with us have felt like magic lately—the connection, the music, the intimacy. It feels like a piece of me that has been missing for years has finally found its way back. I'm trying desperately to cling to it, even as the weight of everything I haven't told him presses harder on my chest with each passing day.

I park next to his car in the back alley to my apartment. My neighbor is still out of town, so everything is quiet—too quiet. Most days when I get home, I hear Josh rehearsing from outside through the open windows. Today, there's only silence. Maybe he went out for a walk. Maybe he's napping.

But as soon as I push open the door, I know that something is terribly wrong. The air is too thick, too still. The shades are drawn. And there on the couch sits Josh, staring down a single glass of amber liquor and a bottle of Jack Daniels sitting on the coffee table. Panic surges through me and I immediately feel like I'm going to be sick. That's when I see it. Next to the glass...my note. My stomach drops. I wondered if he had seen it in my drawer that day. I guess he had.

He doesn't look at me. Doesn't even flinch at the sound of the door.

"H-hi," I manage but my voice breaks, and I sound as if I have laryngitis. "Everything okay?"

Josh turns to me then and the moment our eyes meet, I know I've made a terrible mistake. His eyes are rimmed red and puffy—not just tired. Wrecked. My pulse quickens and my heart sinks. Regret settles in my bones.

"You were pregnant?" he asks, his voice hoarse, barely above a whisper.

The knot in my throat rises fast, choking back the words before I can say them. And then I'm back in the hospital, remembering the sterile blue of the hospital walls, the coolness of the sheets, and that fleeting feeling of hope when I saw the ultrasound. And then staring at the doctor's shoes as she said, *"I'm so sorry, there's no heartbeat."*

"Yes, but—"

"And you never told me?" His voice cracks. "How could you?" His eyes look back at the glass of bronze liquid. "How could you keep something like that from me?" Josh's voice is thick with something I've never heard before. Hurt, yes, but also bitterness. Disgust.

My chest tightens.

He's never directed his anger at me before. It startles me.

"Josh...I was—we were so young." I move to sit beside him, but he stands abruptly, shaking me off without even touching me.

"No," he snaps. "That's not an excuse. We were young? So what? You could have told me. Called me. *Anything.*" He moves away from me, emptiness in his eyes.

"You could have called *me,*" I shoot back, my voice rising. "You left me with a letter. A fucking letter. Remember that?" I fold my arms defensively.

"I didn't have a choice!" he yells, pacing now, hands tangled in his hair. "And this—this is something I should have known. God, Melanie."

"What was I supposed to do?" I follow him, even though he keeps pulling away. "Track you down with my broken leg and say, 'I was pregnant but not anymore'? You think that would have *helped* you back then? With everything else you were going through?"

He spins around to face me, chest heaving. "And what about now? All this time you've kept this from me. How am I supposed to—" He swallows hard, then his voice thick, "How am I supposed to trust you now?"

"Trust me?" The accusation hits harder than I expect. I wrap my arms around myself. "Josh, it was a teenage miscarriage. It happened a lifetime ago. It wasn't about trust—I was barely surviving. I was seventeen and broken and *alone*," I croak.

Josh stares at me, eyes glassy. "I'm *trying* to make a life with you, Melanie." His voice is quieter now but somehow that makes it worse. "I let you in. I let you *see* me. But somehow you didn't think I deserved to know this?"

I blink rapidly, trying to keep the tears from falling.

"I don't know," I whisper, barely able to stand under the weight of this pain. "I just—I didn't know how." I reach for his hand, and for a second his fingers twitch, like they might take mine. But then he backs away and the air between us closes like a door.

Josh nods once. The motion is stiff. Final.

He rakes a hand through his hair and settles his gaze on mine. We're at a standoff, neither able to rationally discuss the past without our emotions getting the better of us. His jaw ticks and he sucks in a breath. "I think—I think I need some time."

I can't breathe. It's like the room is closing in on me, and all I can think is, *please don't let this be the moment that ends us.*

He walks into the bedroom, and I don't follow. My legs won't move. A minute later, he returns with his black duffle bag in one hand and guitar slung over his shoulder. His jaw is clenched, his eyes distant. Cold.

"You're leaving?" My voice breaks. "But...you've been drinking." I gesture at the untouched glass.

"I didn't touch it," he says, flatly. Then he moves toward the door.

"What about the concert?" It comes out as a whisper, a final plea.

Josh pauses, his back to me and his hand resting on the knob. Then he turns back to me. His jaw ticks for a beat. "I'll be there."

And then he's gone.

❧

The door clicks shut and the silence that follows is deafening. I stand there, frozen, watching the door as if he might turn around and whisk back through it, apologizing for losing his cool. That doesn't happen though. I wrap my arms around myself as if they might hold me together, keep me from breaking open. But they don't. Not this time.

I sink into the couch, staring at the glass he left behind. The Jack Daniels glows in the dim light, still untouched. Still full of all the things we didn't say.

I reach for the glass, my hands trembling, and bring it to my lips. I smell it and it stings my nose, sharp and warm, and dangerous.

Josh didn't drink it.

But I do.

One sip and the liquid scorches its way down, my throat tightening in protest. My eyes sting and I cough, setting the glass down quickly. And yet, I feel closer to him somehow. I pick it up again and toss the rest of it back in one large gulp.

And then I unravel.

Curling into the corner of the couch, I cry into the silence, sobbing until my chest aches and my whole body feels hot and puffy. Sobbing for Josh. Sobbing for losing him and Cara and our baby all those years ago. Sobbing for losing him now, the weight of it all too heavy to carry. I don't even try to hold it back. There's no one here to see me crack open. That's the worst part of all.

Eventually, I drag myself to my feet, my body feeling like stone. I forgo dinner and move on autopilot to my room, to Josh's drawer. He didn't take *everything* and that somehow gives me hope. I take one of his T-shirts from the drawer, and it smells like him, laundry detergent and sandalwood. I press it to my face for a long moment before slipping out of my work clothes and pulling it on.

Swapping my pillow for Josh's, I climb into bed and clutch the fabric close to me, taking comfort in his scent like a lifeline. Then, after what feels like hours of blinking into the darkness, my tears slow.

Sleep doesn't come easily.

But eventually, it comes.

# Chapter Thirty-Two

## Josh

"Fuck!" I curse as I slam my car door closed. I shouldn't have walked out on Melanie, I know that, but I can't wrap my brain around everything I'm feeling. I haven't felt pain like this in a very long time. I haven't let myself. I let Melanie in, knowing this relationship had the ability to break me but not fearing it actually would. Everything fell neatly into place as it did all those years ago. I should have kept my guard up, not let her in so easily. Now I don't know what to think. Or what to do. I need some space. Time to clear my head.

I slam my fist into my steering wheel, sounding a loud honk.

"Damnit," I mutter.

I pick up my phone, prepared to look for a hotel room. It would be costly at this time of the summer, right before Labor Day Weekend.

My phone buzzes in my hand before I can even open the search engine. Liam.

I suck in a breath, worrying he already knows about the fallout with Mel.

I tap the screen. "Hey, buddy."

"Josh, what's up man? I am calling to see if you want to come hang out with me and the guys over at my place?" Liam sounds jovial, which assures me that he doesn't know anything. "If Melanie will let you out, of course." He laughs at his own joke.

He definitely doesn't know. I force a laugh of my own. "Actually, you called at a good time."

"Yeah?"

"Mel and I are...taking a little bit of space," I say it cautiously. I would never want Liam to feel as if he had to take sides and even if he did, he'd choose Melanie in a heartbeat.

"Oh, man. I'm sorry to hear that." And he does sound genuinely sorry.

"Thanks." I sigh and wait for him to continue.

"Well, where are you staying?" Liam asks.

"That I haven't figured out yet. It just happened." I rake my hand down my face, glancing at myself in the rearview mirror. I look like shit.

"Shit." Liam sounds remorseful. "Well listen, I didn't call anyone else yet. Just come over and have a beer with me. Whatever you need."

"I don't know," I say, unsure if I want to disclose all my shortcomings to Liam.

"Come on, we go way back, man," Liam urges. "I'll see you in a few minutes."

I don't argue. Partly because I don't have the fortitude to argue with Liam and partly because a beer sounds really fucking good right now.

I pull up to Liam's house a few minutes later and kill the engine. He's already waiting for me on the porch, a beer in each hand. He stands when he sees me, then jogs down the steps, handing me a cold Corona.

"Yo."

"Hey." I take the beer, but I don't take a sip. I let myself remember the cool feeling of the bubbles dancing on my tongue, a hint of sour and lime filling my mouth. Instead, I just hold it, running my fingers over the label, wet with condensation.

"Let's head out back," Liam says, already walking toward the side of the house.

"Where are Sophie and the girls?" I ask. "I'm going to block her from pulling in."

"She took the girls to her dads for the weekend, and I have a side project to work on tomorrow, so I stayed behind." Liam jogs up the steps of the deck and drops into an Adirondack chair. His dog, a golden retriever named Maggie, immediately trots up bringing him her beat-up tennis ball.

Liam takes it and launches it across the yard, reminding me that he used to be a pretty serious ball player. "Get it," he says.

I sit down on the other chair. For a moment, both of us watch the dog go for the neon green ball.

"You good?" he finally asks, glancing sideways.

I shrug. "Not really."

"Have a drink, it'll take the edge off." Liam takes a long pull from his own beer.

I shake my head. "Haven't had one in a year."

He turns, eyebrows up. "Shit. Sorry, man—I didn't know." He reaches over and gently takes the beer out of my hand. "Do you mind if I have one?"

"It's fine. Honestly, just holding it was good for me. Like a little reminder."

"Sounds like torture."

I laugh once, short. "Sometimes you need a test of the wills, ya know?"

He huffs a quiet breath. "Yeah... I used to think that too. Then I realized willpower isn't the enemy—silence is." He takes another sip before adding, almost to himself, "I've had my own battle with the bottle. I used to think being numb was better than hurting."

Maggie comes jaunting up the steps and puts her ball in my hand this time. I toss it half as far as Liam. She bolts anyway, tail wagging.

"You wanna talk about it? Or I can throw the game on, and we can pretend it's just another night."

I exhale. "Which part?"

Liam tips his head toward me, lips pulling to one side. "Whatever one's stuck in your chest."

"I guess I'll start by explaining why I quit drinking. Two years ago, I got a DUI. Swerved to avoid hitting a kid on a bike and wrapped my car around a tree."

Liam's quiet, letting it settle. "Shit. But you were okay? The kid?"

I tilt my head back and forth, mulling over his question. "Physically, yes, but I've struggled mentally ever since. The kid was fine." I rake my hands through my hair before resting my elbows on my knees. "I became the same type of asshole that killed Cara. I was so wrapped up in my career and the music industry. I lost sight of what mattered."

Liam's jaw works and he nods. "Booze can make monsters out of decent men if we don't watch it. I drank myself stupid nearly every night after I lost Cara. Thought if I stopped feeling, I'd stop missing her. Stop feeling like it was my fault." His voice goes gruff. "Then I lost Leah too. It was a different pain, but there was still that same instinct to disappear into a bottle."

He looks at me. "Grief's a hell of a drinking buddy. But Josh, you're not that guy. You can't punish yourself forever."

"I know. I've done the work. Therapy. Meetings. All of it." I lean forward, elbows on my knees. "Tonight, I poured a glass of Jack and just stared it down until Melanie got home."

Maggie brings her ball back to me, full of drool. I take it and toss it again. She watches it but then lays down at my feet instead. We laugh and I nudge her with my flip-flop.

"Ahh," Liam says. "So, it's not about the booze." He drains the rest of his beer.

"Nope."

Liam waits, doesn't push. He just looks at me, his gaze steady.

"Can I tell you something and have it stay here?"

"Course."

I scratch my jaw, standing, then pacing a little. "Did you

know that Melanie was pregnant? Back then."

Liam frowns, clearly confused. "No. Wait...what?"

I push my lips together into a tight line and nod.

Liam's jaw falls slack then. "Y-yours?"

"Yeah." I shake my head, still in disbelief.

"Fuck," Liam mutters.

"She lost the baby in the accident. I just found out. I found a letter she never gave me in a drawer. It crushed me."

"You talk to her about it?"

"Kind of. I flipped out. I didn't have it in me to stay calm." I move to the steps now and sit, rubbing my eyes.

Liam takes a sip of the beer he intended for me, hanging on my every word.

Then I tell him everything. How I wrestled with what to say to her but when she came in, I lost my cool and couldn't talk about it rationally. I tell him how I had been planning a life with her, she was it for me, and now I don't know what to think. Liam listens intently the whole time, and I'm brought back to the days we spent together that summer. The girls would wander away on the beach or leave us alone to go to the bathroom together. Liam and I were buds. Not best friends, but we had things to talk about. He listens to me now like a brother would and I'm grateful.

When I finish, I glance at him. "Tell me what to do, man. You're married. You know this shit. What do I do?"

Liam shakes his head. "I wish I could. But this one's for you to figure out."

"You got nothing?" I look at him, confused.

"Nope." Liam sighs. "I'll tell you this, though. After you moved, Melanie and I got close. For many years. She never once mentioned a pregnancy or miscarriage to me. God. She was hurting, and she still showed up for me when I was at my worst."

His words stop me cold and my head jerks up before I can school my reaction. Then I look away, fixing my gaze on the deck. Close? For many years? Jesus. I didn't know. She never told me that either. That hits me harder than anything. "She took care of everyone but herself," I finally manage, my voice rough.

"Yeah," he says softly.

I rub the back of my neck, trying to push down the knot in my chest. It shouldn't matter who she was with back then, not after everything we've shared now, but it stings all the same. Another secret. Another reminder of how much time we lost. I'm starting to feel like I don't know her at all.

"You know, I'm not mad at seventeen-year-old Melanie. She lost me, Cara, and our baby all at once. That's hell." I clear my throat, trying to keep it together. "But why wouldn't she tell me now?"

Liam shakes his head. "I can't answer that for her," he says slowly. "But for what it's worth, I have never seen Melanie so happy. Ever."

I nod, biting the inside of my cheek. "I just need some time to think."

Liam nods. He moves to sit next to me on the step and claps me on the back. "Then take it. But don't wait too long."

I let out a chuckle, eyes still on the yard. "What have you had years of therapy or something?"

Liam takes a sip of his drink with a smirk. "You could say that. Come on, let's find you a bed."

# Chapter Thirty-Three

## Melanie

I wake up Sunday morning with a pain in my head that feels like someone took a jackhammer to it. I reach across the mattress next to me for Josh, but he isn't there. For a moment, I think maybe he's gotten up to make us breakfast. I smell the air for a hint of bacon or coffee. But there's nothing. Just a thick stillness of stale apartment air.

Bile rises in my throat as the memory of the night before comes crashing back to me. I hurl myself out of bed and into the living room. The bottle of Jack Daniels, the empty glass, and my crumpled letter all still sit on the coffee table. The shades are drawn, and the room is dark, summer sunlight desperate to peek through. I move the curtains to the side. Then I open the front door and step into the sunroom porch, gazing down at the alley, hoping I might see Josh's truck. Maybe he slept in it. But it's not there. He really left.

I didn't go after him last night. I should have, but guilt and shame overpowered my fight response, like I already knew we were over. I deserve it. Keeping a secret like that from him. I'm surprised he even said he'd be at the concert. I trudge back to my room and climb back into my bed. It's Sunday so I'm off today, and I have no intention of leaving this room. I reach for my phone but there are no messages from Josh or anyone else. Not even my dad. How could I have hurt Josh like this? I hate myself for selfishly keeping a secret because I knew it would bring up old feelings of hurt and loss for me. I don't deserve him anyway and that's the truth of it all.

I tap on my messages, his name pinned to the top. It's amazing how quickly he fell into place as my number one and now what? I tap on his name and type out a simple text.

I'm sorry.

I want to beg him to please come home, tell him he belongs with me, tell him it was a mistake. But he said he needed time, so instead I roll over and drift back to sleep.

I awake many hours later, but I don't feel better. My heart races when I pick up my phone this time and see several messages, a missed call, and a voicemail. The latter is just my dad. He's taken to doing a Sunday check-in, which I appreciate. His effort makes me feel as if I'm not totally alone. My dad really tries to keep us together, to be a family, but as hard as he tries, there is an emptiness that cannot be filled. It started with his bad marriage to my mom, followed by losing everything senior year, to my mom leaving. I've just never really felt connected that way to anyone. Maybe it's why I never found a partner of my own. No matter which guy I chose, none of them chose me.

I open my texts to see a few from Sophie. She doesn't usually text me, so I am anxious to read them.

Sophie

Melanie, I'm gone until late today but Liam told me Josh is staying at Ellie's. Are you two okay?

Sophie

Mel, I'm here if you need to talk. Liam said Josh was pretty upset. I'm sure whatever it is, you two will work it out. Call me if you need me.

My heart warms at her messages. I wasn't the nicest to Sophie when she moved here a couple of years ago. I didn't know her at all, but I thought I wanted Liam. I thought we belonged together. Sophie never judged me, never treated me any differently. She only looked at me with kindness and empathy. As time went on, we've gotten closer and despite raising two young girls, she always makes time for our friendship. I type out a reply to her.

Thanks, Soph. I am glad he's at Ellie's. Unfortunately, I think I hurt him pretty badly. I'm not sure if he'll forgive me.

Sophie

He will. He loves you. Anyone who looks at you two can see that. Let's have lunch tomorrow. I'll come by your work.

I sigh, texting back a time to meet and suggesting coffee instead, before tossing my phone on the bed. The thought of working tomorrow sends a sickening dread through my body. I thought I saw a future with Josh and in my mind, that was my way out. My way out of a dead-end job, of this town. A chance at a life with the man I first loved. And maybe it doesn't look like I thought it did at seventeen. Maybe we're not going to be rock stars touring the country. Maybe it looks like a quiet life in Tennessee, writing music together, a house full of pets. I just feel as if all of that is ruined now, and I don't know how to get it back when he says he needs time.

I glance at the time on the clock beside me—just before noon. I groan, getting out of bed and padding toward the bathroom. My stomach grumbles and my head pounds. And suddenly my phone is ringing. Hopeful that it might be Josh, I dive for it.

Dad.

I suck in a breath and answer it. "Hey, Dad."

"Hi, sweetheart. I hadn't heard from you. I was starting to get a little worried." His voice is filled with such sincerity I feel my chest tighten.

"I'm fine," I say, my voice wavering. Shit.

"You don't sound fine," my dad says, treading lightly. "Is everything okay with Josh?"

Before I can stop them, tears flood my eyes again. I'm surprised there are any left after the sea I cried last night. I sniffle and I know he'll know I'm crying. "No," I admit with a shudder.

"I'm coming over and bringing you lunch." Dad hangs up before I can argue.

I force myself into the shower, letting the hot water run over me for several minutes before washing, focusing on taking deep, cleansing breaths. But it's not working. I'm crushed and the best thing I've had in years is over. I get washed quickly, towel off, and stare at myself in the mirror for a few long minutes. I look like death run over. My eyelids are pink and so swollen they look as if they've swallowed my blonde eyelashes. My blue eyes are bloodshot, and dark circles cloud my features. My dad is going to think something is terribly wrong.

I pinch my cheeks, hoping to bring some color back to them. I brush my teeth and my hair and then hurry to dress. As soon as my shirt is over my head, my dad is knocking on the door.

Realizing it's still locked, I meet him there, swinging it open.

Dad grins, holding up a brown paper bag and a cup carrier with two frozen coffees from Coffee Tyme. "I brought bagels!"

"Dad, your cholesterol," I mutter, but take the bag from him anyway.

"You look like shit," he says gently, following me into the kitchen.

"Gee, thanks." I roll my eyes, walking to the cabinet to get paper plates and napkins.

"Grab the ketchup, will you?" Dad says as an afterthought.

I spin back around, grabbing the ketchup, and a moment later we're sitting face to face at my tiny café table. I get to work unwrapping my favorite breakfast sandwich—pork roll, egg, and cheese, but Dad just watches me.

"I drove all the way over here, are you going to tell me what happened?" His brows knit with concern. "I can't take it anymore."

I sigh. "Can I eat first?"

"I guess." My dad holds up his hands.

I take a bite, chewing thoughtfully, and look at him still watching me.

"He knows," I say softly. "About the baby."

"Oh," my dad says carefully. "He didn't take it well, I guess?"

"Well, no. Because I didn't get to tell him. He found my old letter snooping through my drawer. We fought. It got ugly. He said he needed time." I shrug, taking another bite. It's amazing how food can make things better, even temporarily.

"He'll come around." My dad pats my hand and picks up his own sandwich.

"That's it? That's all you're going to say?" I scoff. "Aren't you supposed to impart some relationship wisdom on me?"

"Honey, if you haven't noticed, I've been divorced and alone for twenty-five years. Longer than I was married to your mother. I've got wisdom. It's just more of the 'don't marry your high school sweetheart just because she likes your car' variety." My dad takes a large bite, watching me carefully as he chews.

He has a point. I just thought maybe he'd have something a

bit more comforting to say.

"I just feel like everything is ruined," I mutter, looking down at my half-eaten sandwich.

"He's just digesting information, Melly. He'll figure it out and come crawling back." My dad nods. "Like when your mother told me about her affair, I needed time to digest it. But we stuck it out. We stayed together."

I stare blankly at him. "You hated each other. It would've been better if you split up right then."

He tips his head back and forth in thought. "Yeah, I guess that's a bad example." He chuckles, and I marvel at the fact that he can laugh about his failed marriage decades later. "Look, my point is, being with someone is a choice. You choose if you want to love someone for better or for worse, despite all that comes with it. If Josh needs time to mourn or to digest something that happened years ago that he's just finding out about, and he still comes back to you...then you'll know. He's choosing you."

"What if I broke something in him? What if he doesn't come back?" I whimper, like the little girl I used to be.

My dad squeezes my hand. "That boy has been carrying you around in his chest all these years. He wouldn't have come back here otherwise. One little secret isn't going to change that. And if he doesn't come back? Then he wasn't ready for the kind of love you have to give."

My face must fall because my dad pats my arm. "He'll be back."

# Chapter Thirty-Four

## Josh

"Melanie, Mel, stop!" I call uselessly. But Melanie is running away from me, as fast as she can with something bundled in her arms.

I run for my truck, buckling my seatbelt and peeling out of my parking spot after Melanie, but I can't catch her. She's running too fast. Then I see him, a kid on a bike. I try to slam on my brakes, but I can't stop in time. The tires screech as the truck tumbles over an embankment and around a large oak tree. Etched in the tree, inside a heart, are the initials J+M.

"Hey, mister! Mister! Are you okay?" The sound of a boy's voice calls to me from above. My body radiates pain and stiffness.

I can't move out of the truck.

In the distance, a baby cries and I see a white light.

*"Melanie!" I shout but it's no use.*

I jolt awake, drenched in sweat. My breaths come in rapid pants. I sit up, wiping sweat from my brow, trying to figure out where the hell I am. Then it all comes rushing back to me. Melanie. Our argument. The baby. *God, the baby.*

I had never really wanted to be a parent. Not that I even thought about it at sixteen. But as time went on, my focus shifted solely to a music career full of sold out arenas, studio time, autographs, and paparazzi. Living my best life with an entourage. Maybe I'm selfish, but nowhere in that fantasy did a wife and family fit. I always assumed I'd settle down with someone, I guess, but I never once pictured kids. Adult Josh knows that most of us guys don't picture that until we're in it. I just never got in it so deep with someone that I pictured myself as a father.

And yet, learning of the loss of my own unborn child twenty-five years ago is enough to crush me. I managed to keep it together in front of Liam but as soon as I was alone in Ellie's guest cottage for the night, I broke down. Sobs wracked my body for the life that might have been—with me, Mel, and our baby. But more than that, it's the weight of knowing I wasn't there for her when she needed me most. I know I had no control over that. But I should have seen her before we left. I should have called her.

And last night, I stormed out like a fool, letting my shame and fear of saying the wrong thing drive me instead of my heart. Maybe it was irrational, but the truth is, I'm not angry at Melanie. I'm angry at myself—for all the ways I failed her back then, and for the ways I keep failing her now.

I lie back on the pillow, staring across the room at the teal velvet sofa in Ellie's tiny guest house. I close my eyes and remember.

*Our moving truck, packed to the brim, a for sale sign planted on the lawn. I stood on the sidewalk, watching my parents pack the car with whatever didn't fit in the truck, fiddling with an envelope in my hand. "Mel" scribbled on the front of it.*

*"Josh, I thought you were going over to see Melanie?" My mother's terse voice startled me. "We have to get on the road," she had said.*

*"I know." I looked down at the envelope again, fiddled with the bent corner. I knew I should go there, check on her. Bring her some flowers or ice cream. She was my girlfriend after all. But I didn't know how to comfort Melanie when my family was falling apart without my sister. "It's okay, let's just stop there on the way and I'll leave her this." I held up the envelope.*

*My mother nodded, probably not having it in her to argue or insist that I see Melanie before we moved out of state.*

So that's what I did—rolled up to her mailbox and dropped the letter inside. And God do I regret it.

My phone buzzes on the night table text to me. It's Liam.

Liam

You doing okay this morning?

I don't have the energy to answer him or the host of other messages I see as I scroll through. I pause when I reach Melanie's name. It's only one message and it simply reads, "I'm sorry." My chest tightens. I don't know what I was expecting. Maybe some proof she wanted me to stay, a sign she was willing to fight for us—at the very least fight *with* me. But this feels so small, so final. Like she's already let me go. The ache that follows is worse than anger, worse than anything. It feels like we've been erased.

I scroll past, leaving the message unread, even though my eyes keep going back to it. Anxiety flickers when I see five missed messages from Gary, but when I click on them, it's just his flight and hotel itinerary for the concert. He wants to take me and Melanie for a late lunch before the concert. A sickening feeling washes over me.

All of this with Melanie the past few months feels like a lie. We've written music about how much we love one another and all along she's had this secret. I can't help it, I'm fucking mad. But with six days until the concert, I can't afford to be.

I dart out of bed and grab my guitar, sitting on the teal sofa and tuning it. Then I fix it the only way I know how... I play. I work through the whole set list Melanie and I talked about. She'd even written some female harmonies into a few of my originals. The plan was to open with "Every Song," play through my five biggest hits, and close with "The Sound of Her Name." I'd hoped to finish that song with Melanie but now, I selfishly want it only for myself.

When I get to the final song, I start to work. I write the bridge, adjust the chorus, and record myself playing it. Then I send the audio and a photo of the lyrics and the chords written out to Mel, without acknowledging her apology.

I finished the song. Can you please learn it?

Melanie

Okay.

I growl in frustration, but I do feel mildly better having finished the song. At the very least, we'll be fine for the concert. But now there's nothing left to do but be alone with my thoughts.

It's hot as shit on this late August day but I go for a jog anyway. I run all over town, past my old stomping grounds, past the playground I played on for hours as a kid, and finally past my old house. I pause in front of it, staring for a moment too long.

"Can I help you?" an elderly woman's voice calls to me from the porch. I hadn't seen her behind the garden shrubbery.

I shake my head, quickly. "I'm sorry, no. I just—I grew up here."

The woman moves down the front steps to the front gate and offers me a warm smile. "We bought this house in 1999. Your parents must've owned it." She offers me a soft, wistful smile. "Would you like to come in?"

My heart twists in my chest. Would I? Maybe it would help me now, to see the home filled with love. Or it would bring up painful memories of a past I wish I could forget.

"Maybe another time," I say, softly. "It was nice meeting you."

I swipe the sweat off my brow and start walking.

"Take care, now," the woman calls after me.

I turn and give her a wave but the smile on my face is sad, and she can probably see it. Maybe what I need is to go off-grid for a couple of days, shut out the world, and figure my shit out. The truth of the matter is, I'd been using Melanie as a Band-Aid to fix all my gaping wounds—and that's not fair to either of us.

I pick up my pace and sprint hard until my breath runs out and my chest is tight. I nearly crash into Ellie when I get to her house.

"Oh, my!" Ellie steps quickly aside. "Joshua, you nearly took me out." She holds her hand over her chest but she's laughing.

I stop abruptly, breathing heavy with my hands on the back of my head as I pace the sidewalk.

"Sorry, Ellie," I grumble. "I didn't see you."

"You sure didn't." Ellie crooks her mouth upward, cocking her head toward the house. "Come, let's have some iced tea. You look like you need it."

Truthfully, the last thing I need is a life lesson, but Liam says Ellie is everyone's grandma. She means well and who knows, maybe she'll impart some wisdom on me and make me feel better.

I don't reply but follow her up her front steps and through the door to the kitchen at the back of the house. Through the window, I see an older man picking tomatoes from the garden outside the guest house. He's inspecting each one very carefully, tossing the ones that have blemishes.

Ellie notices me watching him. "That's Robert," she says, smiling fondly. "You missed him yesterday."

"Husband?" The last I remembered, Ellie was married to a man named Edward. He'd occasionally pal around with the neighborhood kids, tossing the football back and forth.

Ellie shakes her head and smiles softly. "Partner."

I nod in understanding as she brings over a glass of iced tea with fresh peaches floating near the top.

"Sit, sit, tell me what you've been up to." Ellie gestures to the chair in front of me.

I am self-conscious but I sit anyway. "First, thank you for letting me stay here so last minute. I was sorry to hear about Eddie when Liam told me," I say softly.

"Thank you, sweet boy. And you are always welcome here." Ellie pats my hand. "But tell me all about you and Nashville! I can't wait to see you and Melanie perform."

I pale at the mention of her name and take a sip of the tea, but Ellie doesn't notice.

"It's good... The industry is a rollercoaster. I was happy for a change of scenery," I tell her. I'm hoping if I keep things vague, she won't ask too many questions.

"Get yourself in trouble down there, did you?" Ellie gives me a pointed look.

I let out a smirk. "Are you keeping tabs on me, Ellie?"

Ellie tilts her head, her eyes filled with mischief. "Maybe. But I'm glad you're back, even if it's just for a short while. I sure loved your parents. And Cara."

"I was thinking about hanging around a little longer, but now I don't know," I admit with a sigh.

"Something you want to talk about?" Ellie quirks an eyebrow at me.

I laugh, taking another sip of tea. "Why do I have a feeling this is what you're best at?"

Ellie holds up her hands. "I am who I am."

So I do. Everything comes out in a rush—Nashville, the crash, the breakups. The whole messy spiral. How coming here felt like a chance to find something that'd been missing for a long time, and how it finally felt within reach with Melanie. Then comes the hardest part—the letter, the baby—and a quiet plea for Ellie to keep it between us.

Ellie's face crumples.

"Oh, my heart just aches for both of you. That was a terrible time for all of us but you two—gosh. It would have just been nice if you could grieve together." She reaches for my hand and gives it a squeeze. I don't realize until just this moment how much I have missed my own mother, her comfort, her nurturing. But so much of that disappeared with Cara's passing. My mother became stoic—hardened by life's heartbreak.

Before I can stop it, a sob bursts through my tough exterior and Ellie moves closer, putting an arm around me, patting my back.

"There, there, my dear boy," she soothes. "Everything will be all right."

And at this moment, for some reason, I believe her.

# Chapter Thirty-Five

## Melanie

By the time Monday rolls around, I've resigned myself to the fact that after the concert, Josh and I may just go our separate ways. He sent me the finished song for Cara yesterday and with nothing else to do once my dad left, I worked on it all day. I asked him what he wanted the set list to be and the only thing he replied was a photo of the song list in his scribbled handwriting. A total of seven songs. Once I got Cara's song down, I worked through the others, rehearsing the harmonies I'd written until my voice was scratchy and my fingers bled.

I thought about calling out of work today and letting myself be consumed by the weight of it all, but as I've learned many times throughout these forty-two years, falling apart does nothing to help anyone. Instead, I take a shower, blow dry my hair and carefully apply my makeup—my armor for the day. There will be time to fall apart later, but before work or at work is not the time. Besides, I'm used to life alone. I've been alone way more than not, and I know that this sadness, this heaviness, will pass.

But then, there is a small, optimistic part of me that thinks, maybe Josh will come around. That he might realize what we have. After all, I've had twenty-five years to heal from the loss of our baby. He's had two days. I have to give him time. I don't text him, no matter how much I want to beg that he talk to me. No matter how much waking up in my empty bed hurts. He's only been gone for two nights, and I can't believe I ever lived without him. But the ball is in his court. I can't make him forgive me, so I steel myself for a future without him.

I walk to work, despite the heat, smiling politely at people as I pass by. Other store owners are opening up, writing on chalkboard signs, and cleaning windows. They wave at me, big smiles on their faces, completely unaware of the turmoil swirling inside me.

"Hey, Melanie!" Joyce, the coffee shop owner, calls to me. "I can't wait to see you sing this weekend!"

My chest tightens, and I have to swallow the lump that rises in my throat. I wave back, forcing cheerfulness into my voice. "Thanks, Joyce," I say, picking up my pace before she can carry the conversation any further.

When I walk through the door, the restaurant is quiet. We don't open for another twenty minutes. Andrew is at the host stand, assigning server stations.

"Morning," I say, hoping to breeze past.

"How's our favorite singing bartender?" Andrew teases, looking up from the board.

I shoot him a stare that I hope lets him know I don't love the hallmark.

He meets my eyes then, raising a brow at me. "You all right?"

I sigh, "I'm *fine.*"

"You look...well, you don't look great." Andrew treads carefully.

"Josh moved out," I admit, catching the tremble in my voice. "If you don't mind, I *really* don't want to talk about it."

"Oh shit. I'm sorry, Mel." Andrew's mouth pulls in with a frown, sympathy in his eyes but no surprise, like this was something he half-expected. I try not to take that personally. "You know how these musicians are."

"No," I interrupt. "It's not the musician. It's me. And that's all I can say right now because I'm really, *really* trying to keep it together today." It's the most candid I've ever been with Andrew, but the guy is used to my stolid demeanor—and if I don't let him know how I'm feeling, he'll go on and on about how it wasn't meant to be.

"Okay," he says, holding up his hands. "I'm sorry."

"Thank you." I peer over the host stand at the white board he was writing on moments ago. "Who is on the day shift?"

"Lexi, Kaylee, Jordan, and Finn. Wes behind the bar." Andrew crosses off a section of tables in the back where we usually set up the open mic night stage. "I have no one to cover here so I'm just going to close the section until dinner."

"Sounds good." I worry at my lip, looking around the restaurant, praying for a busy shift. The busier the better because when it's slow, all I do is worry about Josh and everything that went wrong.

"Mel?" Andrew nudges me. I get the impression it's not the first time he's said my name.

"Hmm? Sorry." I shake my head.

"The concert is still on, right?" Andrew frowns.

"Yes." I sigh. "The concert is still on."

"For what it's worth, I think the town will love it," Andrew says, squeezing my shoulder.

"Hope so."

The lunch crowd comes and just as I'd hoped, it's super busy. Around two o'clock, I get a text from Sophie that she's on her way down for that cup of coffee we talked about. I almost want to bail and tell her I'm too busy to get away. But I'm due for my break and Sophie has never been anything but an amazing friend to me.

I poke my head into the office and Andrew looks up.

"I'm going to take my break and grab a coffee. Do you want anything?"

"Why don't you call it a day?" Andrew offers, ignoring my question. "Marcus is coming in an hour anyway."

Marcus is a new guy that Andrew hired to co-manage with

us. We've both felt as if we can't get our heads above water this summer and there needs to be a manager on every shift. I didn't even have to try to convince Andrew when I brought it up. He was all for it. So now there will be someone else picking up the slack around here. I haven't met him yet, but it doesn't matter. Andrew is offering me a chance to leave early when my world is crumbling around me. I'm taking it.

"You sure?"

"Definitely. Go do some self-care spa or whatever it is you women do." He waves me off.

I grin, raising my eyebrows. "Self-care spa?"

"You know, Lauren is always going on and on about how important her self-care is." He shrugs. "Just get out of here, will you?"

"You don't have to tell me twice."

I burst through the front door and find Sophie waiting for me on a bench under a tree. Her eyes light up when she sees me and she meets me halfway, immediately wrapping me in a hug.

"Mel," she murmurs, squeezing me tight. "Are you all right?" she asks, pulling back to get a look at me.

"Not really," I confess, my voice cracking. "But I will be."

"Have you talked to him?" Sophie starts walking toward Coffee Tyme and I fall in step beside her.

I shake my head. "He's only sent over the finished song for Cara and told me to learn it. That's it."

"Wow." Sophie looks perplexed. "It's just, Liam said he was really upset. I can't believe he wouldn't want to talk it through with you."

"Me neither. Everything fell into place with us. I mean, it was like magic. Things just clicked. It sounds totally cliché but it's true. I've never felt anything like it. I can't believe he'd just walk away from it." We reach the coffee shop and peer at the line for a moment before falling into the back of it. This place has a line outside the door, no matter the time.

"Maybe he's not. Maybe he's just...sad?" Sophie suggests gently.

"Then talk to me about it, you know? I'm sad too."

"He told Liam he was planning a life with you. I don't think he'll just walk away from that."

My heart pulls tight. *Planning a life with me? News to me.* "That's interesting. We hadn't talked about anything beyond the concert."

"Really?" Sophie frowns. "Maybe he wanted to and then he found the letter."

"Maybe."

The line picks up a bit and before we know it, we're at the door to the shop. It's sweltering and I'm sweating through my jeans and black polo shirt.

"Days like this, I wish I had a giant pool to jump into," I moan.

Sophie giggles. "You do. It's called the Atlantic Ocean."

That sparks an idea.

"Andrew told me to go home. The new manager is coming in and he doesn't need me. Want to go to the beach for a little bit?" I'm going out on a limb. Sophie has two little girls she probably has to get home to, but I ask her anyway. I haven't been to the beach for a swim in ages.

"You know what? Liam's got the girls. Why not?"

# Chapter Thirty-Six

## Josh

After talking with Ellie, I feel lighter—but not steady. I still don't know what I'm going to say to Melanie, but time is ticking. The concert will be here, and Mark has made it clear he wants to see more from me *and* Melanie.

The thing is, I don't know if I can move past this. Or if I even should.

But God I want to.

And underneath the anger I keep directing at Melanie, there's a voice I can't quiet—the one reminding me I left her first. That I've made my share of mistakes. Maybe I'm furious at her for keeping secrets, but mostly I'm furious at myself for not being there when it counted.

I have nothing to eat in Ellie's guest house, so I hit the grocery store late Monday afternoon. The kitchen is barely big enough to boil water, but I can't keep eating takeout and pretending I'm fine. I'm just pulling in when I hear something through my cracked window that stops me cold.

Laughter.

Hers.

Melanie.

I know it like I know the sound of my own name. I don't move from my truck, unsure if I want her to see me. But I watch.

She's in Sophie and Liam's front yard, rinsing her feet off

from the beach. She's wearing a swimsuit, her skin sun-kissed and glowing. Melanie lifts the hose to her chest, and then her hair, the rose gold strands darkening as the water runs down her back. It's so familiar yet so far away. She looks radiant, happy. Carefree. Like she's doing just fine without me.

And that wrecks me.

Not that I want her to be hurting—I don't.

But it's because I asked for time and she's actually giving it to me. She hasn't reached out once to talk about things.

I grip the steering wheel until my knuckles turn white. My instinct is to get out and go to her. Have it out, once and for all. But I still have so much I'm wrestling with. I don't know what she wants. What I want. If I'm even capable of giving it to her.

I'm gutted over what she lost, what we lost, but it's the secret of it all that keeps cutting me open. That she carried the pain alone. She kept it from me all this time. And maybe that's because I left without saying goodbye—because I made it easy for her to shut me out. The guilt of that crushes me. But what twists the knife even deeper is that she's had these last few months, and she still hasn't told me. If she could keep something this big from me, what else is she holding back?

Still, my gaze is pulled to her like a magnet. She hands the hose to Sophie and wraps herself in a towel, jogging up the front steps to say hello to Liam and his youngest daughter. I ache for Melanie, watching as the toddler giggles when Melanie tickles her. I could be on her in three long strides if I wanted to. But I don't move.

And then, as if she can feel my eyes on her. She looks toward my truck and our eyes lock through the windshield.

Everything stills.

She gives me a small, wistful smile, like we're strangers who used to know each other inside and out. And then she looks away.

She says something to Liam, and he chuckles. A mix of emotions swirl through me, envy and grief and this deep guttural need to go to her and fix everything that is broken between us.

I reach for my door handle, ready to swing open my door and close the distance between us when Melanie jogs back down the steps and rummages through her beach bag, picking up her phone. She answers it and her face immediately pales.

I lower my window a bit more, desperate to know who she's talking to and what they want but I can't quite make out the words. I just know something is wrong. She ends the call, a look of panic etched across her beautiful face.

"Mel, you good?" Liam frowns at her from the porch.

I open my door then, my feet moving involuntarily until I'm three feet from her. I want to reach for her, but I don't. Not yet.

"It's my dad," she says, her voice barely above a whisper. "He had a heart attack."

"Where is he?" Liam asks, jogging down the steps, already passing the baby to Sophie. "Is he okay?"

"Cape Memorial Hospital. I—I don't know."

"I'll drive you," Liam offers.

"No," I say, my voice louder than I intended. "I will."

Melanie turns to me and then she just breaks.

No hesitation, no words. She walks straight into my arms. Sobs wrack her small frame as she falls apart.

But I catch her.

Her cries tear through me. I wrap my arms tighter around her, feeling the water from her suit soak through to my shirt. My hand finds the back of her head, and I pull her into my chest, anchoring her to me. Anchoring myself to *this*. There we stand, on the sidewalk, the weight of twenty-five years crashing over us. The heartbreak, the first love—and then the *silence*, the songs that never got written. I don't know how long we stay like that; I just know one thing is crystal clear—I can't let her go.

Not now. Not ever.

Sophie runs inside and returns before Melanie has even pulled away. “I brought you some dry clothes, Mel.” She holds out a tank top and a pair of women’s gym shorts. “You should change before you go.”

Melanie pulls back from me then but doesn’t look away. My thumbs swipe at the tears on her cheeks. “Sophie’s right,” I say, glancing toward her. “Maybe we should pack a small bag, you might be there for a while.”

Melanie nods, looking between the three of us. “Okay, yeah. Thanks.” She takes the clothes from Sophie and rushes toward the house, pausing to look at me. “I’ll just be a minute.”

“Okay, I’ll be here.” I give her a grim smile. While she’s inside, I move toward the guest cottage, stripping off my wet T-shirt on my way. I find a dry one and throw it on. I grab my backpack, my phone charger, and a couple of water bottles. Then I remember my groceries. I jog back to the truck, throwing my backpack inside and grabbing the bags. I hurry, putting the cold stuff away before spotting Melanie waiting for me at my truck. Leaving the rest of the groceries, I move toward her, like she’s my lifeline.

Opening the passenger door, I help her inside and hurry around to my side.

“Do you want to stop at home?” I ask, glancing at her as I start the engine.

She shakes her head. “No. Just...let’s go. I don’t know how bad it is.”

I reach across and squeeze her knee cap. She doesn’t pull back, but she looks uncomfortable. “It’ll be okay,” I say, pulling my hand away.

Melanie is quiet for the short drive up the parkway to the hospital. There is so much I want—need—to say, but it’s not the right time. I pull in the emergency room parking lot and she’s unbuckling her seatbelt before I’ve found a spot.

“You can just let me out here.” She doesn’t look at me, only out the window, desperate to get inside the building.

“No way. I’m going with you,” I say, pulling into the closet spot.

"Josh." Melanie looks at me, her gaze watery.

"Mel, I'm not leaving you."

She swallows hard and nods. "Okay. Thank you."

Melanie is out of the truck before I have even picked up my backpack, racing to the crosswalk. I jog to catch up with her. All I want is to pull her close to me and I know this isn't the time, but I selfishly can't stop myself. I grip her hand while we wait for the *walk* signal.

We clamor up the front steps and the automatic door opens for us. The ER is surprisingly quiet and Melanie bolts toward the check-in desk. "Frank Glick?" she asks, urgency clinging to her voice.

"Are you family?" the receptionist asks without looking up.

"I'm his daughter." Melanie looks at me, panic in her blue eyes.

"And you?" the woman peers up at me now.

"Him too. He's family," Melanie answers for me and my heart pulls.

"He's just through those doors." She points to her right. "Bay thirteen."

Melanie rushes to the doors, pressing the button to open them.

"Thank you," I say to the receptionist, tapping the counter, before hurrying to catch up.

She reaches Bay thirteen first and ducks inside. I follow behind slower, and when I pull back the curtain, I find Melanie already at his bedside, holding his hand.

"Daddy," she whispers.

Frank Glick, a man I probably haven't seen since the night of prom in 1999, looks small and frail in the hospital bed. He is propped up and alert, but he looks pale and tired, the skin around his eyes loose and tinged with shadows. His gray hair is flattened on one side and the hospital gown falls off his shoulder slightly, revealing lines to his heart monitor. A blood pressure cuff is on his arm and beeps periodically. His other arm rests above the blanket, an IV taped to the back.

When he sees Melanie, he turns his head gently and offers her a tired smile, but it's more in his eyes than his mouth.

"Melly," he murmurs, his voice gravelly. Then he looks up at me. "Hey, Josh."

"Frank." I nod. I hang back, feeling as if I don't deserve to be here.

Melanie threads her fingers through her dad's and pulls his hand to her lips, kissing it. "How did you get here? I don't know who it was that called me."

"My friend Joan brought me here," Frank says, looking between us. "She's still around here somewhere."

"Who is Joan?" Melanie asks. It's not accusatory, just curious.

If I'm not mistaken, Frank's cheeks pinken before he answers.

"We've been seeing each other, casually." Frank stifles a cough.

Melanie's expression is unreadable, but we're interrupted by a doctor, stepping in and pulling the curtain closed.

"Mr. Glick." He nods at Frank and Melanie. "I'm Dr. Ramos, the attending cardiologist."

"Doc, this is my daughter Melanie and her..." He looks to me.

"Partner. Josh."

"Nice to meet you," Dr. Ramos says, nodding at each of us. He pulls the stool from the wall and sits. "Frank, based on your EKG and bloodwork, we're seeing signs that part of your heart isn't getting enough blood. The good news is, you're stable, but there's likely a blockage that needs to be looked at more closely."

"So what does that mean?" Melanie asks, reaching for her dad's hand again.

I keep a wide berth, standing just inside the curtain, but I don't take my eyes off Frank and Melanie.

"It means you'll need a procedure called a cardiac catheterization. It's a minimally invasive procedure where they look at the arteries around your heart by inserting a small tube through your groin. If they find a blockage while they're in there, they will fix it right then with a stent."

"Can they do that here?" Frank asks, fear etched in his features.

Dr. Ramos pushes his lips together. "I'm afraid we don't have a cardiac catheterization lab here. We're going to transfer you to Cooper University Hospital by ambulance, non-emergency transport, unless something changes. You'll have the procedure first thing tomorrow morning."

"Is it safe to wait that long?" I pipe up from my spot near the door.

Melanie jerks her eyes to mine, appreciation behind her watery gaze.

"It is. Frank is stable, his vitals look great. We've already started the medications to protect his heart. The team at Cooper will take great care of him." Dr. Ramos stands. "I'm going to put the transfer orders in and call the cath lab to let them know you're on your way. It shouldn't be too long."

"Thank you, doctor," Melanie says softly.

Dr. Ramos gives her a reassuring look before shifting his attention to me, taking me by surprise. "If you have any questions in the meantime, let the nurses know. I'll check back in with you before you go." Then he turns back to Frank. "Don't worry. We'll get this taken care of."

When he leaves, Melanie sighs. "How do you feel?"

Frank tilts his head at her, a resigned smile twitching on his lips. "You told me to watch my cholesterol."

"I did." Melanie smiles softly. "I'm scared."

"I'm not," Frank says, patting her arm. "I trust the doctors."

"Okay," Melanie whispers. "I'll be scared for both of us."

We're interrupted by a joyful, "Yoohoo!" as a woman dressed like the tropics pulls back the curtain.

"Melly, Josh, I'd like you to meet Joan."

# Chapter Thirty-Seven

## *Melanie*

My eyes go wide at the sight of the woman who is apparently my father's girlfriend. Joan has a brunette, cropped pixie cut with chunky caramel highlights. Large hoop earrings and an abundance of daytime makeup let me know she does not want to be mistaken for a man. She's wearing white capri pants and a tropical-patterned floral blouse. She looks as if they were out on a day-date when this happened. Maybe they were.

"Joan, this is my daughter, Melanie, and her partner, Josh." My dad's gravelly voice startles me. He's clearly trying to break the ice.

I shake my daze away. "Hi," I say, offering Joan a smile. "Thank you so much for taking care of my dad. We've got it from here."

Josh makes a throaty noise from his place by the edge of the room, his jaw slack with surprise at my candor.

"Oh, no, Melly, Joan isn't going anywhere," my dad corrects me. "We are an item."

"An...item?" My brows raise. I look to Josh, with his arms folded over his chest. He's looking at his feet and he may be stifling a smile.

"I was going to tell you on Sunday, but you were so upset," my dad says softly, looking between Josh and me. "Which by the way, I'm happy to see you two here together."

"We're not." The words are out of my mouth before I realize. "I mean, we haven't—"

My dad holds up his hand. "That's not a conversation for here." He rests his head back and closes his eyes for a moment. Joan moves to the other side of his bed and takes his other hand. A mix of envy and gratefulness surges through me. On the one hand, my dad has been alone for *so* long. It's nice to see he found someone. On the other hand, this is *my* dad. *Go away, Joan.*

Josh breaks the silence. "So, how did you two meet?"

I start to shoot him a glare but when I see the twinkling of amusement in his eyes, I soften. He's *actually* here with me, despite how badly I hurt him. That's something.

"Oh, we met on Silver Singles dot com." Joan grins and her eyes crinkle. "Frank just swept me right off my old feet."

We laugh and I catch Josh's eye. Our gazes hold for a split second before my dad turns our attention back to him.

"So, we should probably talk about how to navigate this." He looks between the three of us.

Josh moves from his place by the exit and pulls up a spare chair. "Melanie and I will grab a hotel by the hospital. I've already found a couple that look decent. Mel, you ride in the ambulance with your dad if they'll let you. I'll go home and pack us some clothes. Joan, you're welcome to drive up to Cooper with me." Josh takes charge, and my heart swells. I never said I needed him to, but God, I wanted him to. It's like he knows just what I need.

Before I realize it, tears have brimmed in my eyes, and a sniffle escapes. All eyes turn to me as I swipe a loose tear away.

"Melly, don't cry." My dad reaches for my hand. "This is going to be fine." He looks at Josh, a fondness in his eyes. "Thank you for taking care of that."

Josh gives him a tight-lipped smile and a nod.

"Well, I have to get home to take care of the pups tonight," Joan says apologetically. "But I'll be up to see you first thing tomorrow."

My dad smiles tenderly at Joan. "I know you do, babe. I'll be okay here with Melly and Josh." He kisses her hand.

"You two seem pretty serious," I say, my voice soft. I cough to clear it.

"We are." My dad doesn't beat around the bush, and I appreciate that. I'm a grown woman and he's my senior citizen father. He does not need my permission, no matter how much it surprises me.

"We were both seeking companionship, and we fell in love along the way," Joan says, smiling at me. "I know I'm not your mom, Melanie, but I hope we can be friends."

A laugh bubbles out of me. "I don't know what he's told you but it's a *damn* good thing you aren't my mom. Those two couldn't have been worse for each other."

This time everyone laughs softly.

"I'm happy for you," I add, looking directly at my dad.

"Thank you, sweetheart."

A knock sounds from just outside the curtain and Dr. Ramos appears with a nurse at his side.

"Okay, Mr. Glick, we've got an ambulance transfer en route. Is there someone you'd like to ride with you?" Dr. Ramos asks.

"My daughter, Melanie, please." Dad coughs.

I stand and move toward Josh at the curtain. He puts his hand on my shoulder and gives it a comforting squeeze. I don't turn to look at him because if I do, I'll break.

"Okay, Melanie, you'll need to ride in the front seat and stay buckled. Since this is a medical transport, they will need space to work in case your father's condition changes," Dr. Ramos says.

I nod. "Okay."

"Don't worry, kid. If we hit a pothole, I'll bounce—I'm tougher than I look," Dad says from his bed while the nurse, Maria, gets him ready to be moved.

Maria flushes Dad's IV and tapes it off. She checks the monitor for changes in blood pressure before removing the cuff. "They will put this back on in the ambulance," she says, just as three paramedics enter the room.

"Hey, Frank. I'm Mike, this is Jimmy, and Nick. We're going to get you moved onto the gurney, okay? Just let us do the work. If anything feels off, let us know." The two other paramedics stand on either side of Dad, while Mike takes a position near the head of the gurney.

He lowers the bedrail and raises the gurney to match the height of the bed and locks the wheels. Josh, Joan, and I watch while they check the heart monitor lines, IV, and oxygen tubing.

Then, before I realize, the two on either side of Dad roll the edges of his bed sheet and Mike gives the command.

"Okay, on three—one, two, three, slide."

Then Dad is moved, and Mike busies himself propping his pillow up and adjusting the wires. Maria brings over a couple of blankets and layers them on Dad, tucking his feet in.

"Are you comfortable, Mr. Frank?" Maria asks, grinning.

Dad gives a thumbs up as they pull the curtain open and prepare to move.

Joan moves to Dad's side. "Call me when you get settled in a room, okay? Or have Melanie call me." She plants a kiss on his cheek, and I look away.

My gaze catches Josh's for the first time. He's been quiet for the past couple of minutes, looking at his phone.

Josh licks his lips and steps toward me, raking a hand through his hair. "So, uh, if you're okay with it, I'll stop by your place and grab some clothes for us. I left some things there." Josh's voice is thick, raspy with emotion.

"I noticed." My eyes move from his to his lips and then back again. I fight the urge to caress his cheek. "Josh," I whisper, unable to hold back the emotions flooding me.

"I got the hotel room. I'll drive up, check in, and then come to the hospital." He looks like he wants to reach for me but puts his hand in his pocket instead.

Oh, how I want to reach for him. Hold him, and kiss him, apologize to him for all the words left unspoken.

"Melanie, we're going." My dad's voice carries from the hall.

"I'll see you." I back away slowly and turn.

"Call me if you think of anything," Josh calls after me.

But I don't reply. I have to jog to catch up to my dad.

I climb into the passenger seat in the front of the ambulance and buckle my seatbelt, turning around to watch as they get Dad settled.

"You okay, Daddy?" I ask, trying desperately to steady my wavering voice.

"I'm as okay as I can be, sweetheart," he croaks. "Mike, we get the sirens? Or are we taking the scenic route?"

Mike chuckles as he slides in next to me. "Scenic route, big guy. You're stable, and we want to keep it that way."

"Got it." Dad's voice sounds far away now.

"Just try to relax," one of the other men says.

"Listen to them, Daddy. Close your eyes," I murmur.

"Melly?"

"Yeah, Dad?"

"I told you he would be back."

# Chapter Thirty-Eight

## *Josh*

I don't waste any time going back to Melanie's apartment. On the way over, I call Liam and Sophie and fill them in. Then I call The Ugly Mug and ask to speak to Andrew. I fill him in too, letting him know that Melanie would probably need a few days off from work. He sounds surprised to hear from me and guilt burns hot under my skin. He probably knows about our split. If you could even call it that.

This has got to be one of the hardest things Melanie has ever been through, seeing her dad like that. I hate hospitals—always have since Cara—but today? There is nowhere else I'd have rather been then by Melanie's side, taking care of things for her. I'm still angry and sad, but I can't leave her to carry this alone. I won't do it.

I hurry into her apartment and head straight for the bedroom. The sight of the unmade bed hits me in the gut. When we first started sleeping together, Melanie made me promise to make the bed if I was the last one here—said she couldn't start her day without it. How bad must things be if she's stopped? The mattress dips under my weight as I sit on the edge. I hold her pillow to my chest, the faint scent of her shampoo still clinging to it. For a moment, everything inside me aches. Then I spring into action.

The phone charger goes in first, then the pajamas she always wears. Denim shorts. A few T-shirts. Leggings. A hoodie in case the hospital's cold. Bra. Underwear. Deodorant. The body spray she likes. My gaze sweeps the room, searching for anything else she might need, but nothing comes. Just silence—and the ghost of her everywhere.

I move to the single drawer she gave me and yank it open. All that's inside are a couple of pairs of underwear, black gym shorts, and my white undershirts. I frown. I know I left more than that. I look around the room thinking maybe she thought I wasn't coming back and put my stuff in a bag or a box. My eyes land on her hamper and on top of it are at least three of my T-shirts. I walk over and pick one up, holding it to my face. Her. It smells like her. *Melanie has been sleeping in my shirts.* I laugh, not because it's funny, but because she misses me as much as I miss her and it's fucking great.

I drop the shirt back in the hamper and settle for my gym shorts, some underwear, and the white tees. It's a good thing I grabbed a couple items at the cottage.

After one last sweep of the place, I flick off the lights and head for the kitchen, grabbing a few waters and snacks for the road. The sight of untouched fruit on the counter makes me pause, so a couple of bananas, apples, and oranges go into the bag too. Then I lock the door behind me, and I'm gone.

I have a lot of time to reflect on my drive to the hospital. It's over an hour away, and I really wish Melanie and I shared our locations so I could see if they made it yet. I'll admit that since Saturday, I worried that starting things up with her was a mistake. That I could have just protected myself from all this pain if I just never revisited the relationship to begin with. But today? Seeing Mel break the way she did, I know there are no mistakes. There are wounds, yes. Secrets that gutted me when I found out too late, grief for a child we'll never meet, guilt for leaving her alone in it. And there's anger, too, at her for not trusting me enough to tell me, and at myself for giving her a reason not to.

But none of that changes the truth that's clearer now than ever—I still want her. All of her. Even the parts that hurt. We have a lot to talk about, a concert to perform, and things to work through, but for the first time in days, I know it'll be okay.

Just as I'm pulling in the hotel parking lot, Melanie texts me.

Melanie

We're here. They've assigned Dad a room but he hasn't made it up here yet. I'm waiting in the hallway.

I quickly reply, not wanting to keep her waiting.

Good. I'm just checking into the hotel. I'll be there soon. What's the room number?

Melanie

364B

I'll see you soon.

Thankfully, there aren't a lot of people checking into the hotel at this time of night, so the process is quick, and the room is ready. I head upstairs, drop the bags of clothes, and grab only the things I'll need if we're there for a long time. I also bring the fruit, knowing Melanie must be starved. We're well past dinner time now. I head for the elevator, opening my Maps app as I walk, so I can get to her faster.

By the time I'm pulling into the parking garage, it's dark out. This is a much larger hospital than the one Frank was at before. I can park in the garage and walk across the bridge to his floor. This place isn't in the best area, and I'm glad I didn't let Mel come alone.

I reach Frank's hospital room quickly, knocking as I open the door. It's a two-person room but thankfully, he doesn't have a roommate tonight. Frank is reclined in the bed with his eyes closed while two nurses get him situated, checking his vitals and replacing his IV. Melanie sits in the chair across from the foot of the bed, looking forlorn and exhausted.

"Hey, baby," I murmur in her ear when I walk in. I drop in the chair next to her and peck a kiss on the side of her temple. She looks caught off guard, like she wasn't expecting any affection from me. I don't want to make her uncomfortable, so I pull back. "What's going on?"

"The nurses are getting him all set up so they can monitor him tonight and then they said he can order some food but that he should rest soon." Melanie answers me but looks at her dad.

I pick up the hospital room service menu on the small table next to me, slowly looking it over. There's a section that specifically says Heart Healthy. "What do you want to eat, Frank?" I ask. "You can have some grilled chicken and steamed broccoli...or—"

"I don't want that garbage," Frank waves me off. "Let me see that."

I laugh and step closer, handing him the menu. My own stomach grumbles just from reading the words.

The nurse finishes with his IV and turns to us, a little amused at Frank's surliness. "How about a nice Turkey sandwich, Frank? A little fruit salad on the side? Crackers and hummus too."

He tosses the menu back at her. "Fine," he grumbles.

The nurse pats his arm and says, "I'll order it." She taps into an iPad. Then to Mel and me, "The doctor on call should be stopping in shortly."

Shortly comes before she even leaves the room with a knock on the door. A tall man with neatly styled dark hair steps in, his crisp white coat embroidered with his name: Dr. Sharif. His presence is calm, assured, the kind that fills the room without effort.

"Hello, Mr. Glick, my name is Dr. Sharif. How are you?" He reaches for the hand sanitizer on the wall and pumps some into his palms before putting gloves on.

"I've had better days," Frank admits, resting his head back on the pillows.

I glance at Melanie, but she looks as if she's fading fast, so I make sure I tune in to the doctor.

Dr. Sharif cracks a smile. "I'm the hospitalist on tonight. I've reviewed your chart, and I just want to take a quick listen to make sure everything looks good while you settle in." He moves toward Frank and starts listening with his stethoscope, murmuring for Frank to take breaths.

"Okay, this sounds good for now. I want you to try and get some rest. If you have any pain or discomfort, let your nurses know and they will page me. Cardiology will be by in the morning." Dr. Sharif says.

He steps back from Frank just as his food is wheeled in by an orderly. Turning to us, he says, "Did you two have any questions for me tonight?"

Melanie shakes her head.

"I think we're okay for now, Doc, thanks," I say, looking back and forth from Melanie to Frank, who is already munching on a piece of watermelon.

"Good. You folks have a good night."

We sit in silence, watching Frank eat. Melanie's stomach rumbles next to me and I tilt my head at her. "You're hungry. Get the banana out of my bookbag."

"You brought food?"

"Well, we had all that fruit..." I shrug.

Melanie doesn't reply, but her eyes fill with gratitude. She reaches for my bag and sifts through, pulling out an apple and a banana.

She's peeling the banana when the nurse pops her head back in.

"You'll have to leave in just a couple of minutes, you two. You can come back in the morning." She offers us an apologetic smile.

"Go on, you guys," Frank says, waving us off. "Let your old man get some rest."

Melanie passes me her banana and stands, moving to her dad's bedside. She picks up his hand and squeezes it, planting a soft kiss on his cheek. "You sure you'll be okay?"

"I'm going to sleep like the dead." Frank barks out a laugh.

Melanie stares blankly at him.

"Too soon, Frank," I mutter.

"Okay, I'm sorry, I'm sorry." He looks at Melanie. "I love you, my girl. Thank you for taking care of your dear old dad."

Melanie sniffles, shaking her head. "I didn't do anything."

"Hey, you being here is doing something." Frank reaches up and strokes her face. "Go get some rest."

"Okay," Melanie whispers. She steps back and I stand, picking up our things.

"Take it easy, Frank," I say, putting my hand on the small of Mel's back. "We'll be back in the morning."

"Thanks, Josh," Frank says. "And thanks for taking care of Melly."

"You got it." I wink at him.

"Bye, Daddy." Melanie sniffles.

I drape my arm around her, and she leans into me, and we walk out the door, just like that.

Melanie breaks away once we step into the hallway, and I immediately miss the contact. I get it. We just left her dad lying in a hospital bed, now isn't the time to talk about us. But standing this close to her and not knowing where we stand is a special kind of torture. I press the button on the elevator and Melanie leans against the wall like she needs it to hold her up from the weight of the day.

"How are you holding up?" I ask, watching her carefully.

"I'm exhausted, and starving, and so sad." Her voice is flat, and her sigh is so heavy, it makes my chest ache.

She does look sad, dark circles rim her blue eyes in exhaustion, grief turning them a steel gray. Her expression is hollow, like her body is here but her mind is somewhere else. The flush is gone from her cheeks, and she looks so weary, I almost offer to carry her to the car.

The elevator dings and we step onto it. I'm grateful it's just us.

"I'm not sure what's open around here at nine p.m.," I say, trying to keep the conversation normal. "I think I saw a McDonald's."

"McDonald's is fine." Melanie's voice is weak, like all ability to fight has left her.

I don't reply, and we ride in the type of silence that's filled with everything and nothing at the same time. I want to say something—God, there is so much I want to say. That I'm gutted for what she went through. That I hate myself for not being there, for leaving her to carry it all alone. That I'm angry she didn't tell me, and that I don't know how to make peace with that. That I love her, still, maybe more than I ever have. But one look at her and I know it's not the time. She's already carrying enough. So, I swallow it down, let it press hard against my ribs, and instead just reach for her hand when the elevator doors slide open.

She slides her hand into mine without hesitation, and her touch is a small relief. I lead her out to my truck, open the door for her and help her in.

We're in the drive-thru within five minutes. Melanie orders a quarter-pounder with cheese and a large fry with a Dr. Pepper.

"That sounds good," I say, and I order the same.

Melanie shoots me a wry look. "Copycat."

"Couldn't resist," I say, giving her a playful smile.

We pull around and pick up our food, and I pull into a parking spot.

"Car picnic?" I ask.

The first glimpse of a smile I've seen since we got to the

hospital. "Okay."

I hand her the food, and she takes hers out of the bag before passing it back to me. We eat in silence, both of us too hungry and drained to say much. When I finish, I shove the trash in the bag and start the truck.

Her voice is soft when it breaks the quiet. "Hey. I don't think I said thank you—for today."

My breath hitches and I glance at her. "You don't have to."

"I know." She pauses. "Josh, I know we have a lot to talk about—"

"Not tonight." I shake my head, shifting into drive. "Not like this."

Melanie settles back in the seat, folding her arms across her chest. She looks out the window and doesn't say another word for the rest of the ride. She stays silent the whole way up to the room.

Inside, I stride over to the duffel bag that I packed, sitting on one of the queen beds. I pull out Melanie's pajamas, the ones I know she loves, and toss them to her. "I hope these are okay."

"Thank you," she murmurs. Then she pulls off her shirt unceremoniously.

My heart stumbles. I turn away quickly, jaw clenched. I can't look at her—not like this. Not when everything in me wants to forget the hurt and fall back into the very thing that feels like home.

"I'll be back," I say, grabbing my clothes and heading for the bathroom. I splash water on my face, giving myself a pep talk. When I come out, Melanie is tucked in the opposite bed, facing away. I move toward mine.

"Josh." Her voice catches me off guard.

I stop, my heart lurching. "Yeah?"

"Will you sleep here? With me?"

I hesitate, searching her eyes. "You want me to?" I croak.

Melanie nods. "Please."

I exhale. "Okay. Move over."

She pulls back the covers and I slide into bed, flicking off the lamp. Then I gently pull her into me, her back against my chest. Our bodies meld together like they always have. We just fit.

"Thank you," she whispers.

I only squeeze her tighter.

# Chapter Thirty-Nine

## Melanie

I wake in a satisfied, sleepy haze. Warmth spreads through me, and I feel more content than I have in days. I try to move but an arm is wrapped tightly around my hip, a hardness pressing into me. Then everything comes back to me. My dad. Josh. The hospital. McDonald's. Hotel room. Surgery today. I move Josh's arm off my hip and slip out of bed.

A sigh escapes him, and I turn back, studying him carefully. His forehead is creased, like he's dreaming about something concerning. His long lashes flutter and he smacks his lips in his sleep before rolling to his back. Every part of me aches to crawl back in bed and curl into the crook of his arm. I would whisper I'm sorry in his ear and show him how much he means to me. But visiting hours start at eight a.m. and I need to get back to my dad.

I move quickly to the bathroom, stripping down and turning on the shower. I never showered after the beach yesterday, and the warm water cascading down my body feels heavenly. I close my eyes and moan as the warmth runs through, soothing my tired bones. A memory of when I had the flu a few weeks ago and Josh showered me floods my mind, and heat pools in the apex of my thighs. What I wouldn't give for him to come wash my hair for me now.

I love Josh. I know that. The way he stepped up for me yesterday softened something inside me. No one has ever done anything like this for me before. I've never had someone see me, see my pain, and carry it for me. Josh does that. He must love me, too. Right?

I tried to broach the subject last night, but he said it wasn't the time. And now I'm terrified he hasn't forgiven me. I need to talk to him before the concert. I can't go into that without clearing the air between us.

I finish washing and turn off the shower and that's when I hear Josh talking on the phone. I dry off quickly, wrapping the towel around me. I crack open the door and listen.

"I don't know, Gary, we need to see how things are with her Dad." Josh's voice sounds strained. "It might just be me."

I frown, fighting the urge to storm out of the bathroom in protest.

"I mean the concert is still on, of course it is," Josh is saying. "I just have to see what Mel will be up for. We haven't talked about it yet."

At this, I swing open the door all the way and stomp over to him, frustration bubbling beneath me.

At the sight of my tiny hotel towel, Josh's mouth falls open. I stare at him incredulously.

"What do you mean, it might just be you?" I mouth to him.

He furrows his brow, confused. "What?" He mouths back.

I stomp my foot, crossing my arms.

"Okay, okay, hold on Gary." Josh covers the mouthpiece. "What's wrong?"

"Why did you say it might just be you? Are you kicking me out of the concert?" I sit down on the edge of the bed opposite him.

"What? No, of course not." Josh shakes his head.

"Then what?"

"Hang on, Gary," Josh says into his phone. "Gary wants to take us to dinner before the concert or after. I just said... I just said we have to see how your dad is."

"Oh."

"I'm not kicking you out of anywhere," Josh murmurs. His

gaze turns fiery for a moment, and it takes everything in me not to climb into his lap. "Okay, Gar." He turns his attention back to the call. "I'll let you know later today how we make out. Okay. Thanks." Then to me, "Gary says he'll say some prayers for your dad."

My frustration softens. "Thanks, Gary," I say, hoping he catches it.

"I'll call you later. Bye." Josh ends the call.

He meets my gaze then, amusement flickering in his eyes.

"What?" I frown.

"You were spying on me." His lips twitch.

"I was not. I heard you on the phone and I was worried it might be about Dad." I fold my arms across my chest.

"So, you stormed out in your...towel...to get to the bottom of it?" Josh swallows, raking his gaze up the length of my body. A shiver runs through me.

My jaw falls slack. How could just his gaze turn me on like this? "Y-yes."

"Okay." Josh grins.

He stands, letting his eyes linger a moment longer before moving toward the bathroom.

"Are you done in here?" he calls, but he's already inside.

"Sure. Yes." I face palm myself. "You're good."

Josh pokes his head outside the door once more. "I'll hurry."

It turns out that by the time we get to the hospital, they're already preparing Dad for his cardiac catheterization. I only get to see him for a moment before they take him back. Just before they do, I lean down, squeezing his hand. "You've carried me my whole life, Dad. Now it's my turn. So, you fight, okay? Because I still need you. More than I ever say. I'll be right here waiting to carry you when you get back."

His lips twitch into the faintest smile, and he gives my hand a weak squeeze back. "Then I guess I'd better stick around, huh? Can't have my girl needing me and not show up."

I sniffle as they wheel him away. I'm grateful that they're moving quickly, but now anxiety has hit me like a tidal wave. I sit in the same chair I was in last night, twiddling my thumbs.

"Come on, Mel. They said it could be four hours before he's finished. Let's go get some coffee." Josh says, putting his hand on my shoulder.

I startle. "What?"

"Let's go get some coffee. It's going to be a while." Josh repeats himself. He tucks his hand under my arm and gently pulls me out of the chair. His patience with me is astounding, and I know I owe him more than a thank you and an apology. I owe him an explanation. I should be begging him for forgiveness.

Yet I marvel at him. Despite how much he's hurting, despite what I've put him through, he is here. He is acting as if he's my partner and supporting me through this. I don't know what I did to deserve this—him. Certainly not keep a decades-old secret from him.

The concert is in four days. We have to clear the air.

Josh leads me to the hospital cafeteria, through a breakfast buffet line and the coffee station. I'm quiet, letting him fix two identical plates, giving simple yes or no answers when he asks if I'd like something.

We find a small two-person table near a window overlooking the city. Across the Delaware River, we can see the Philadelphia skyline, the tops of the skyscrapers still covered in dense fog from summer's haze. I stare at them, worrying the corner of my lip.

"Mel," Josh says carefully.

I shake my head, clearing the daze. "Sorry."

"What's on your mind?"

"Truthfully?" I roll my lips together. "The concert being four days away. Not knowing how Dad will be."

Josh pushes his lips together and nods. "Your Dad will be okay. He'd want you to do the concert."

Melanie nods. "I know. I know that. I just feel guilty."

"He can hang out with Joan for a few hours." Josh cracks a smile and nudges me with his foot.

"Gross." I crinkle my nose, but I can't stop the smile from spreading across my face. "Truthfully, I'm happy he has someone."

"They seem happy."

"Yeah, well I'm sure at their ages, relationships are a lot easier...less complicated. You have fun together? Great. No pressure about the future or whatever." I shrug, not bothering to hide the frustration in my voice.

"Relationships don't have to be complicated." Josh's words sting, even though I'm sure he doesn't mean for them to.

I take a sip of my coffee and change the subject. "Did you fix this for me? You remembered how I take it?"

Josh chuckles. "Of course I do. Three creams, two sugars. Light and sweet."

"Yeah..."

He clears his throat. "So, they have both of our cell phone numbers. They'll call us when Frank is in recovery. What should we do to pass the time?"

I chew on my lower lip and lock my eyes to his. "Did you bring your guitar?"

# Chapter Forty

## Josh

I nearly burst out laughing when Melanie asks if I have my guitar. Of course I do, in the cab of my truck. We find a quiet spot in the hospital atrium and play, drawing the attention of a few others in the area. It is good practice, and I can't help but notice how much more relaxed Melanie is playing in public now. We spend most of the time waiting for Frank, playing through Saturday's setlist. As soon as she starts singing, several heads turn. My voice is momentarily gone—I'm captivated by the angelic sound coming from Melanie. If I thought I was sure about us before, it's hearing her sing our words now that solidifies it for me. I still need all my questions answered, but I love her. I'm not leaving her.

When we hear from the doctor right around the three-hour mark, I think I see the tension in Mel's shoulders physically melt away. Frank is in recovery and did great. He is resting comfortably and had a stent placed for the small blockage in his arteries.

Melanie is desperate to see him, so we walk back to the cardiac floor and plan to wait in the waiting room until they call us to come back. As soon as we walk through the entryway, we find Joan sitting in a chair and quietly knitting.

She must sense us because she looks up.

"Oh, hello, you two." She offers us a shaky smile. "I just thought I would come here and wait. I should have gotten your phone number yesterday."

Melanie takes the seat next to Joan and gives her hand a quick squeeze. "It's okay. Dad's recovering. They said we can see him soon."

Relief moves across Joan's features, which leads me to wonder just how serious the two of them are.

"Oh, good." She sighs. "I was so worried."

"The doctor said he'd explain more when they come up but that he had a stent placed and he'll need some cardiac rehab," I explain further.

"Well, good. We can help him with all of that, right dear?" She turns to Melanie and Mel's face softens.

"I think he would like that very much." She puts her hand on top of Joan's, and the two women smile at each other.

"Is there family of Frank Glick here?" A voice interrupts.

We all turn to find two doctors standing in the entryway. One of them is a tall, lean man with light brown hair and kind eyes. The other is a slight young woman, with dark eyes and a surgical cap.

"That's us," Melanie says, rising quickly to meet them.

"I'm Dr. Comfort," the man says. I almost laugh at the irony of his name—a cardiac surgeon with a name like Comfort. But I stop myself when it's clear that actually is his name.

The doctor continues, "This is Dr. Stowe, one of our cardiac residents. She assisted with the catheterization today."

"Hi. I'm Melanie, Frank's daughter. This is Josh and Joan." Mel gestures toward us.

"Good to meet you. So, the procedure went very well. We found a significant blockage that was blocking about eighty percent of the blood flow to one of his coronary arteries. We were able to place a stent and blood flow was restored immediately." He pauses, letting that sink in. "He was awake the entire time and is doing great. We're going to monitor him closely for a few hours, but everything looks really good."

"Is that permanent? The stent?" Joan asks, surprising me.

"I was going to ask the same thing," Melanie says, glancing

at me.

"Yes, the stent is a tiny mesh tube that stays in place permanently to help the blood flow. He'll need to be on blood thinners to prevent clotting around it. That's all very normal."

"When can we see him?" Melanie asks, not bothering to hide the urgency in her voice.

"He'll be in recovery for about an hour and then we'll move him up to his room. He's tired, but his spirits are good. He's already asking when he can eat." Dr. Comfort chuckles.

"How long does he have to stay?" I ask.

"He'll stay tonight for observation, and then, provided there are no further complications or bleeding issues, he'll be able to go home in 24 to 48 hours," Dr. Stowe chimes in.

"And then, once he's home?" Melanie quirks her eyebrows in concern. "What will that look like?"

"Well, we'd like him to enroll in cardiac rehab, which offers exercise, diet and lifestyle, and emotional support," Dr. Comfort says. "He won't be able to drive or lift anything more than ten pounds for a week or so. We'd love for him to start slow walks daily. And he'll be on some new medications that we'll go over with his discharge. Make sure you ask all the questions, so you know how to best support him."

"Thank you so much, doctor," I say, offering my hand.

"Of course, absolutely. I'll let the nurses know to come get you when they're moving him to his room." The doctors turn to go, and Melanie lets out an audible exhale.

"He's okay," she whimpers.

I pull her close to me and kiss her temple. "He's okay."

Mel and I decide to stay one more night in the hotel. The plan is to come back tomorrow and hopefully take Frank home. After spending all day watching the rise and fall of his chest, we let him and Joan have some quiet alone time.

"Try to rest, Daddy," Melanie says, kissing his forehead.

"Joan, are you sure you're okay to drive back to Cape May tonight?" I ask, watching her closely.

"I'll be just fine, Josh, thank you." Joan pats my arm, like I'm not a foot taller than her.

"Okay, well call me if you need anything," I say, meaning it.

I offer Frank a fist bump. "Frank, my man. You are a warrior."

Frank huffs a tired laugh. "Hardly. I wouldn't have gotten through it without you all."

"We wouldn't have been anywhere else." Melanie squeezes his hand. "Josh and I will be back tomorrow to take you home."

We say our goodbyes, and then Mel and I are on our way back to the hotel and suddenly the air between us is thicker.

"I am DoorDashing us dinner," Melanie says, clicking her seatbelt into place.

"You don't have to do that."

"I want to..." She pauses, then quietly continues, "to say thank you for everything."

I glance at her and her eyes glisten. "God, Josh, I don't know what I would have done without you here."

"You would have figured it out," I tell her, because I believe it. "You're stronger than you think."

"No, I'm not." Melanie shakes her head.

"You *are.*" I press. "Liam told me how you held him up all those years ago."

"For other people maybe. I'm never strong for myself." Her hands are in her lap, twisting together.

I don't argue, I pull into the hotel lot and cut the engine. The silence between us shifts. Heavy, but not cold. Just full of everything left unspoken.

We sit for a minute, neither of us eager to get out of the truck.

Then we're speaking at the same time.

"I'm sorry—" we both say.

Mel lets out a soft laugh. "You first."

I clear my throat. "I was just going to say, I'm sorry I stormed out the other night. I should have stayed. Should have talked it through."

Melanie sucks in a shuddering breath. "I'm the one who should be sorry, Josh, not you. I'm so sorry I have kept this from you all these years."

Her voice cracks. Mine almost does too.

"We were young," I say, choosing the same words Melanie used the other night.

"I was also terrified and heartbroken and so...*lost*. A little part of me died that day. I lost Cara and our baby and then...you."

Something inside me breaks.

"You never should have lost me," I say, my voice low.

Melanie sniffles and I realize silent tears are falling from her eyes. I unbuckle my seatbelt and turn to face her.

She turns toward me, wiping her eyes. "I had just gotten used to the idea of having a baby. I know that sounds crazy, but I thought we'd make it work. I'd be pregnant all senior year and then take care of the baby while you finished high school. And then we could get married."

Melanie looks at me through her long, wet eyelashes.

"I thought before we told Liam and Cara about us, I'd tell you. I'd made up this whole vision in my mind that you'd be so happy. But really? You'd probably have been terrified." Melanie shakes her head. "Then, in the hospital, when I saw the bleeding, my whole world just came crashing down. But I still thought I'd tell you when things were better. And then one day, you were just gone. My dad found your letter in the mailbox."

My throat tightens, the weight of regret hitting like a punch. "I'm so sorry," I say, reaching for her hand. "I would've been there, Mel. I would've done anything. You know that, don't you?"

Melanie nods but she can't stop the flow of tears now. I feel tears of my own pricking the back of my eyes so I reach for her hand like she might slip away again. She breaks all the way then and I do too. I pull her into me, and we come undone. We cry for what we lost. For the kids we were. For the life that never had the chance to happen.

When Melanie's sobs quiet, she pulls back just enough to look at me.

Her palm finds my cheek, and she brushes the wetness away. "I never thought I'd have another shot with you. Honestly, I wasn't even sure I meant that much to you back then."

I meet her eyes, no hesitation. "You meant *everything* to me, Melanie. You still do."

And then my mouth is on hers and it's like coming up for air after being underwater too long. It's her. It's always been her.

# Chapter Forty-One

## Melanie

Josh kisses me deeply and it's like a fuse igniting—heat surges through me, electric and instant. His mouth moves with urgency, all tongue and teeth, a mess of grief and longing and something that feels like home. We don't kiss like people reuniting. We kiss like two people mourning all the things we never got to say.

His mouth moves down my neck, stubble scraping as he plants a trail of kisses down to the base of my neck. I let out a hiss and reach for him, tugging for his shirt, fumbling with my seatbelt until I can slide into his lap. I feel him hard beneath me and the warmth between us quickly turns molten. Josh finds my mouth again, taking my lower lip in his teeth.

I lace my fingers through his hair, and a groan escapes him. I answer it with a soft moan of my own, rolling my hips over his slow and deliberate.

His hands find my hips, and our breaths come quick and shallow. Wetness pools between my thighs and suddenly the desire turns to more—a burning need. Every nerve in my body is awake. Needing this connection, this reminder that I'm not alone in my pain.

"Upstairs," I whisper into his mouth. "I need you."

Josh doesn't reply. He never breaks contact as he feels for the door handle and flings the driver's side door open. He slides out of the truck, gripping my ass and hoisting me up. He kicks the door shut but before anything else, leans me against the truck, his grip possessive and steady.

His hips push forward in a slow, hard thrust. I cry out at the feel of him, already spiraling.

"Baby," he murmurs, his voice low and rough. "I can't stop long enough to go upstairs."

"Josh." His name falls from my lips. "Please. You're going to make me come right here."

He lets out a quiet laugh, but there's hunger in it. "I might like that."

"Please." I hear the desperation in my own voice.

Josh pulls back and sets me down. I sway, knees shaky, thighs aching with desire. He wraps an arm around my waist to steady me.

"Your wish is my command," he rasps, and takes my hand.

He never lets go of my hand as he leads me quickly to the elevator. As soon as the doors open and we see we're alone, he's on me again, hoisting me up like I weigh nothing and pushing me against the mirrored wall. His mouth finds mine again and this time his kiss is slower—deeper. A reclaiming. Every part of me that he touches ignites a fire on my skin.

"I love feeling you against me like this," he growls in my ear, before gently sucking on the lobe.

"Uh-huh." A breathless sound escapes me. I'm unable to formulate words.

It's a long fucking ride to fourteen, tension coiling tighter in me with every floor. My breath comes faster, my heart pounding in rhythm with his. I want to lose myself in him.

His hand skims up the side of my thigh, fingers slipping beneath my shorts and drawing a straight line up my center. He groans when he feels how wet I am already.

"So fucking ready for me," Josh growls.

He kisses me again, softer this time, like he's trying to memorize the shape of my mouth. We're a mess of heat and desperation and I don't care who sees.

The elevator dings and without any hesitation, Josh carries me off, down the long hallway, straight to our room. I cling to him, dizzy from the closeness. As if I'm afraid I'm somehow imagining this.

He stops at our room, balancing me as he reaches for the room key in his pocket. Unlocking the door, he kicks it wide enough that we can step through without breaking contact. And then he gently lays me on the bed.

"You're so fucking beautiful, Melanie." His voice is raw, trembling with emotion I haven't heard from him in decades.

I don't reply. Instead, I sit up, stripping away my T-shirt and unhooking my bra in one swift movement.

Josh's breath hitches audibly, and he pulls his shirt over his head. Then he's crawling toward me, his breath hot and hungry as his mouth folds around one nipple. I gasp, arching into him, my hands threading through his hair. He moves to the other nipple, sucking and nibbling until my body thrums with need. His palm presses gently over my sternum, easing me back onto the bed. Using one arm, he pins my hands above my head, tethering us together. His other hand glides up the inside of my thigh until he's at the hem of my shorts again.

"Let me feel you," he murmurs, sliding two fingers inside, slow at first and then curling with just the right amount of pressure.

I cry out, lifting my hips to meet his hand. My eyes flutter close. He knows exactly how to touch me—it's like he's remembering a language we used to speak fluently.

He pulls his hand back and I open my eyes to see him licking his fingers clean, a moan escaping him.

"You're so sweet." Then, his eyes lock on me and his hand finds my lips. "Want a taste?"

I nod, dazed, as his fingers slide into my mouth. I suck gently, savoring the taste and the way his pupils dilate as he watches.

"Fuck baby," he whispers. "You undo me."

Then his mouth is on mine again, kissing me like he's trying to kiss away all the years we lost. Everything collapses—grief, guilt, love, longing. Like he's trying to devour all the pain, all the years between us. It's rough and desperate and unlike any other time before.

I free a hand and reach for the waistband of his shorts, yanking them and his boxers down in one tug.

A gasp falls from my mouth and into his. I wrap my hands around him, stroking feverishly until he's growling into my mouth and urgently tugging at my own shorts.

"Two can play at this game," I murmur into our kiss.

Josh pushes my shorts down and immediately settles between my legs, sinking into me. I cry out at the skin-to-skin sensation. He pulls out agonizingly slow before quickly sinking back in. With each thrust, my walls grow slicker. I wrap my legs around him, and his lips find mine again. Suddenly, it's not so desperate—it's achingly beautiful.

Our eyes lock, breath tangled between us, hearts beating in sync.

Josh presses his forehead to mine. "God, Mel," he breathes. "You feel like home."

He shifts, freeing one of my hands to lace our fingers together. He pushes sweaty strands of hair from my forehead, and our noses brush together. I close my eyes and allow my body to meld with his completely.

His lips are on mine then, kissing me softer this time. His hand presses against mine, anchoring us. I open my eyes to find him gazing at me. He brushes hair out of my eyes, tucking it behind my ear, moving slowly in and out of me like we have all the time in the world.

"You're shaking," he whispers.

"I don't want this to end," I confess.

He kisses me softer, then deeply, like he's making a vow. "It won't."

Our bodies fall into a slow, savory rhythm, chests flushed and slick with sweat. Every thrust, every sigh, every kiss feels like a conversation we've never had until now.

A tear slides down my cheek, and Josh sees it, brushing it away with his mouth, tender and aching.

"I am so in love with you," he whispers.

A sob catches in my throat. "I love you too."

At my admission, the urgency returns but gentler. He slides a hand under my back and flips us over without sliding out of me, as I settle into his lap. I rise and sink with the rhythm of his thrusts, and his name falls from my lips like a prayer.

Josh reaches up, thumbs grazing my nipples simultaneously, and I cry out. Sitting up, he settles me in his lap, so we're face to face. He brings his mouth down to each nipple and his thumb finds the button of nerves that is sure to put me over the edge. My breaths become faster as the various sensations send my entire body coiling with pleasure. I tremble and clutch his shoulders, unable to move as he thrusts beneath me.

"I'm—Josh—I'm coming," I cry, clinging to him as waves of release crash into me.

"Come for me," he growls. At last, my legs tremble around him and he shakes beneath me, his face buried in my neck as his own release follows hard after mine.

We collapse together, breaths tangled, hearts pounding as one. Josh's fingertips trace up and down my spine.

"Mel," he whispers.

I tilt my head just enough to see his eyes. They're clear and open in a way I haven't seen since we were kids. Stripped bare.

"I love you so fucking much," he says, his voice raw. Like he's stunned by the weight of it.

I nod, pressing a kiss to his heart. "I know. I feel it."

A single tear slips down my cheek and Josh catches it with his thumb.

"I never stopped." His voice is barely above a whisper.

"Me neither," I admit softly. "But I'm scared."

Josh rakes his fingers through my tangled hair, damp with sweat. He kisses the top of my head.

"Me too, kind of. But I'm not going anywhere. Not this time."

His arms wrap tighter around me as if we could somehow get closer than we already are.

I swallow the knot in my throat and close my eyes, breathing him in. Salt. Sweat. Sandalwood. Josh.

"I think we're going to be okay this time," I murmur.

He pulls the blanket over us and snuggles into me. "Me too."

# Chapter Forty-Two

## *Josh*

Melanie and I take our time the next morning. I think she feels better now that she knows her dad is through the worst of it. I'm up well before her and I quietly shower, letting her rest. Then I find her phone and text her dad to let him know we'll be over soon but that I was letting Mel rest. Then I slip out to get us coffees—forgetting of course to leave her a note.

When I return, coffees and bagels in hand, Mel is awake, sitting on the edge of the bed, looking unnerved.

"I thought you left." Her voice is barely above a whisper. She looks up at me, eyes shining.

I set down everything in my hands and rush to kneel before her. "Hey, I told you last night I'm not going anywhere. Didn't I?"

Melanie nods, sniffling.

"And if you would have looked at your phone, you'd have seen that I texted your dad letting him know our plans."

Melanie pushes off the bed and grabs her phone from the nightstand. I watch as she scrolls through the text, her lips moving as she reads it.

"I'm sorry," she says, looking back at me. "I am just so terrified to lose you again."

I stand then, moving to her in one quick motion. "I'm here to stay, baby." I pull her close to me and cradle the back of her head. "Now, let's go bust out your dad."

An hour later, we're sitting in Frank's room, waiting for him to take a shower—for that I'm grateful. The doctors are making their rounds and are due to see Frank shortly to go over everything he'll need to know.

Frank emerges after just a few minutes and climbs back into the bed. Melanie rushes to help him get settled. Once she's next to me again, Frank gestures to my guitar leaning against the wall. We didn't want to leave it in the truck in a rough area of town so I carried it up with us.

Frank quirks his brows, the corner of his mouth turning up. "You guys have a big show this weekend."

"Yep. Sure do," Melanie says with a tight smile, but her voice is uneasy.

"I'm not sure I'll make it," Frank says, casting his eyes to his lap. "I'd like to, if Joan could help me get there."

"It's okay, Daddy. I don't want you to worry about that. Not one bit," Melanie reassures him.

"Can you play me something right now?" Frank's expression shifts from guilt to hope, and I know Melanie can't resist.

I cock my head at her, lips twitching. "What do you say?"

"'Every Song'?" she suggests. "But not too loud, people are resting."

I take my guitar out of its case, and Melanie stands to close the door. I strum the first chord without thinking, my fingers remembering just where to go. It's instinct, muscle memory. And then Melanie starts to sing. The sound is low at first, just a few soft notes under the guitar. But then she gains her confidence, and it's strong and steady like it never left.

I glance at Frank's face—he doesn't take his eyes off his daughter and neither do I. My chest tightens, remembering how amazing it is to sing with her. This was the first song we'd ever written together, just three chords and half of a chorus we'd thrown together one late spring night on my front porch. It wasn't complicated—it was honest. It was us.

Back then we didn't know anything except what it was like to be reckless teens, counting dreams. We were completely wrapped up in each other. The first time we sang that song together, I knew I was falling in love with her. We fit. Now, all these years later, we still do. Even with the history, even with the heartbreak. It's always been us.

Her voice catches at the bridge, and she looks away, like if she catches my eye, she'll fall apart. But I can see it on her face, she feels it too. I let the last chord ring out, filling the silence between us.

It's broken by Dr. Comfort and Frank's nurse, Gwen, clapping in the doorway. We hadn't heard them come in. I peer over their shoulders and see even more staff in the hall. They'd all been listening. Melanie's cheeks flush and her palms find them. She lets out an embarrassed laugh.

"That was beautiful," Frank murmurs, keeping his eyes locked on Melanie. He swipes a finger under his eye. "I'm so glad you're singing again."

"I *knew* it!" another nurse interrupts. "Yesterday I saw you two in here and I told Gwen, I think I saw them on TikTok. Holy crap. You guys are like *famous*."

Melanie shakes her head, jutting her thumb in my direction. "He is, not me."

"Yet," I say, squeezing her knee.

"These two are performing on Saturday in Cape May at Rotary Park. You guys should go." Frank grins proudly, looking back and forth between us.

Dr. Comfort laughs. "Maybe we will. But you, sir, need to take care of yourself. What do you say we get you out of here?"

"Yes!" Frank throws a fist into the air. "Let's blow this pop stand."

And we all laugh.

WE MAKE IT back to Cape May by the afternoon and Joan is already there, waiting for us. I pull slowly into Frank's driveway and hop out quickly. Melanie climbs down and then we open Frank's door, helping him down together. To my surprise, he doesn't wave us off. Melanie loops an arm around his waist and leads him to the front door. I follow closely behind.

"A wreath?" Melanie gives her dad a sideways glance. "Just how serious is it with Joan? Because I know you didn't put a wreath on your door."

Frank laughs but it turns into a dry cough. "Pretty serious." His voice cracks.

Melanie nods, smiling softly. "If I didn't know any better, I'd say it was pretty hard for you to choke out the word serious."

"Yeah, yeah. Your old man needs some company, okay?" Frank pulls Melanie closer. "You're still my number one girl though."

Melanie tilts her head into Frank's and before she pulls away, I snap a picture of the two of them. Their backs, but they're standing close, leaning into each other. It's a Kodak moment.

The front door swings open before we can get to it, and Joan greets us with a bright smile.

"You're home!" Two little curly-haired dogs yip at Joan's feet. She holds open her arms and Frank steps into them.

Mel and I exchange a look. It's definitely serious with them.

"I made soup and chicken salad in case anyone is hungry," Joan says, leading Frank inside by his elbow. She has his recliner set up with a blanket and pillow. Next to it is a snack tray with a remote.

Silence hangs in the air before I clear my throat. "These are Frank's meds," I say, setting the paper bag down on the snack tray. Desperate to fill the silence. "There are instructions on each bottle for time of day... Well, you know how prescriptions work." I scratch the back of my neck and look away.

"Great!" Joan claps her hands together. "Frankie, why don't you sit, and I'll fix you some food?"

Frank does as he's told, and Mel and I exchange another amused look.

Joan fixes her eyes on us, a soft, hopeful smile on her face. "Did you kids want to eat?"

Melanie feigns a yawn, shaking her head. "Oh, no. I'm really tired. You know, hotel beds."

She glances at me, and I desperately fight the twitch of my lips.

"Thank you, though," she adds quickly.

I look to Joan, wondering exactly how this is going to work. "Will you be staying here, Joan?"

Frank glances between the two women. "Joan's going to stay as long as I need her."

A small noise escapes Melanie, and we all look at her.

"I just don't want to put you two out any more than I already have," Frank says gently, looking at Melanie.

"Dad. You're my *dad*." Her voice comes out small.

Joan slowly backs out of the living area, and I hear her bustling around the kitchen. I step closer to Mel, putting an arm around her.

"I know, honey, but you and Josh are doing your thing. I don't want you to have to worry about me." Frank looks between us. "You have a concert to play."

Melanie lets out a relenting sigh. "Okay. That's fair. But I'll be back every day to check on you."

"I'd expect nothing less."

We say our goodbyes and head right to Ellie's to get my stuff. I'm coming home.

# Chapter Forty-Three

## Melanie

The days leading up to the concert blur by faster than I expect. It feels like just yesterday that Josh showed up here, upending my life and somehow putting it back together at the same time. Ever since the night in the hotel, things have been downright blissful. Josh moved back in and it's as if he never left. We've easily slipped back into our rhythm—work, write, rehearse, fall into bed together, repeat—and I still catch myself wondering how I got this lucky.

We still haven't talked about what happens next. About Tennessee. I think he's really waiting to see what Mark and the label people have to say after the show. I'd be lying if I said I'm not anxious. But one thing feels solid: we're together. And I want to believe that's enough. I *hope* it's enough.

Friday morning, I stop by my dad's house. Joan is out and I'm quietly grateful. I fix us two glasses of ice water and a bowl of fruit salad. Dad's moving around a bit more than he was when we brought him home from the hospital, slow but steady. For the first time in days, he actually looks comfortable—less pale, more himself.

"How are you feeling?" I ask, spooning some fruit into a bowl and setting it in front of him.

"I'm okay. Better. The real question is, how are *you* feeling? Tomorrow is the big show." His grin is wide and proud as he pats my hand. "I'm so proud of you, baby."

I feel my cheeks flush and a smile tugs at my mouth. "Thanks, Dad. Josh and I are ready."

"And the record company?"

"They fly in tomorrow morning. We're supposed to have dinner with them after the show but... I don't know. I might let Josh handle that."

"What? Why?" He looks at me like I've lost my marbles. "They're interested in *both* of you."

"You know how I am," I say, with a weary sigh. "The limelight is hard for me. Besides, I'll want to get back here and check on you."

"I'll be just fine. Sophie is going to FaceTime me while you're onstage." Dad chuckles. "It'll be like I'm there, just with air conditioning."

I smile softly. "You're right. And I know Josh wants me by his side. I just... I haven't thought about what I'll do if they make us an offer that takes me away from here." I study my dad's face for any hesitation, any flicker of fear. But I come up empty.

"You'll do it," he says simply. "Because it's your dream."

"What about you though?" I press. "I can't leave you."

"You can. And you will. *If* it comes to that."

Dad takes a sip of his water and clears his throat. "Joan and I are talking about making things a bit more permanent around here."

The subject change makes the back of my neck prickle.

"You mean...marriage? I thought you said you'd never get married again." My jaw falls slack with surprise.

Dad barks out a laugh, waving his hand. "No, no. But I might ask her to move in."

I blink, momentarily speechless before feeling a smile spread across my face. "That's great, Dad. I'm really glad you found each other."

"Yeah?" His voice is almost shy.

"Yeah." I smile warmly, reaching over to pull him into a hug.

"I was a little nervous to tell you," Dad admits, sipping his water. "Didn't know how you'd react."

"Yeah, I kind of picked up on that when I didn't know she existed until you were in the hospital." I give him a teasing glance.

Pink creeps into Dad's cheeks. "Sorry about that. I've just been on my own for so long, I didn't know how to explain it."

Before I can reply, a timer sounds, its soft beep interrupting us.

"Time for my meds," he says, standing up. "Joan set me a timer for when she's not here." Dad moves slowly around the peninsula to get his prescription bottles.

I watch him closely, something loosening in my chest. Yeah. I think we're both going to be okay.

---

Saturday morning hits me hard, thanks to the sound of Josh's excruciating alarm. I'll never understand why he picked the most offensive sound in the iPhone alarm library, but every time it goes off, I'm convinced I'm waking up in crisis. My nervous system thanks him.

I pull the pillow over my head and groan. We're lying back-to-back but I feel the tap of his knuckles on my hip.

"Come on," he says, his voice rough with sleep but amused. "You have to get up."

I keep the pillow over my head but roll over, peering at him as he sits up and turns off the alarm.

"Why?" I mumble.

"Because, I thought you could use a little pampering."

I chuckle. "Sex doesn't count as pampering."

Josh barks out a laugh. "I wouldn't *set an alarm* for that."

He reaches over and peeks at me beneath the pillow, revealing my squinty, skeptical face. "I made you an appointment for a mani-pedi *and* you're getting your hair done. I thought you would want to relax before tonight. You deserve to feel your best."

I blink at him. His words land with more weight than he probably realizes. "Are you serious?"

Josh nods, a proud grin climbing his face.

"But I am picky about who I let touch my hair and nails." I frown instinctively.

"Already handled. Sophie gave me a full list for the future and booked everything for you."

Josh leans back against the headboard, folding his arms across his chest, clearly pleased with himself.

"Wow." I sit up, scooting close, my fingers finding the waves at the nape of his neck. "You really thought of everything."

Josh looks at me, tucking a strand of hair behind my ear. "This is your chance at your dream, babe. I want you to walk into that show tonight feeling unstoppable."

My heart squeezes and I can't speak, so I nod, leaning in to kiss his cheek before slipping out of bed.

"Okay," I say, grinning now. "I'm going."

The ocean breeze is light when I arrive at the nail salon, and there's Sophie, leaning against the brick building, holding two iced coffees.

"What are you doing here?" I ask, a smile already blooming on my face.

"I figured if I was booking an appointment for you, I should treat myself, too." She hands me a drink.

I laugh, touched that she thought of me. "What is it?"

"I hope you like it. I asked Liam what you like, and he wasn't sure, so I took a guess."

"I'm sure it's great," I say, taking a sip. "Shall we?"

We spend the next two hours getting pampered in the best kind of way—hot towels, scrubs, perfectly polished nails, and the easy rhythm of conversation. My hair salon is a short walk away and I'm so looking forward to the scalp massage and blowout in my future.

"Tell your dad I'll FaceTime him a little before six," Sophie says, pulling off the toe separators as we walk toward the door.

"I will. Thank you so much for doing that for him. He's going to love it."

I lean in for a hug and Sophie squeezes me tight, lingering a little before pulling back.

"You know, Mel, I don't think I've ever seen you this happy. Your dad sees it too."

I look down, swallowing the knot that forms in my throat. "Thanks. I...I am happy. It's all felt like a dream."

Sophie places a hand on my shoulder, firm and grounding. "So, keep going. Don't stop here. Trust me when I say, it's never too late to go after what you want. You have spent a long time watching other people be happy, supporting them. It's your turn, Mel."

At this something pulls loose inside me, quiet and sure. For so long, I've been afraid to go after what I really want. I've played it safe, kept myself in the background. But Sophie's right. Maybe it's time I believe that I deserve more out of life than simply surviving it.

By the time six p.m. rolls around, the confidence I felt earlier is dwindling. I am not sure what I expected, but I did not expect every ounce of green space in this park to be taken up by bodies. I did not expect people to be holding up "We Love Josh & Melanie" signs or cheering and calling out to us while we set up. This was supposed to be a friendly neighborhood concert. A small acoustic set. Instead, it feels like we're playing for a sold-out stadium.

Sweat beads at my temples, and I feel the color drain from my face as I move my stool in front of the microphone. I've reapplied my lip gloss twice and if I keep messing with my hair, it might fall out. I step into the wings, away from the crowd, to take out my second guitar—my original seafoam green acoustic from our teen years. For old time's sake.

"You good?" Josh asks, startling me as he steps behind me. His voice is low and calm, steady in a way I'm not.

"Honestly? No. I think I might throw up." I turn and meet his eyes, and he pulls me close.

"That's how you know it matters," he murmurs. "We've got this."

I exhale a laugh. "But I've never played my music for a crowd like this. And there are record execs out there."

He leans in, brushing his lips against the shell of my ear. "They're lucky to be here."

I close my eyes, grounding myself to this moment—to this man. The feeling of his hands, the warmth of his body behind mine. All of it is something I never thought I'd get again.

"We've got this," he whispers, and a shiver runs up my spine from the feel of his breath on my ear. He whirls me around to face him, cupping my cheek. "I know it's been a long road to get here, Mel. But this is only the beginning."

He kisses me then, slow and reassuring. I feel the beat of his heart against mine, anchoring me to him.

"Ladies and gentlemen." Councilman Corbin's voice comes over the loudspeaker. "I'd like to welcome you to Rotary Park for a very special Labor Day Weekend concert..."

Josh tips my chin to his, meeting my eyes. "You ready?" he whispers.

I nod, my breath catching. "With you? Yeah."

He nods, lacing his fingers through mine as we wait to be announced.

"Please welcome, Cape May's own Josh Cote and Melanie Glick!"

The crowd cheers, beckoning us. But just before we walk on stage, Josh turns to me.

"Let them see what I see when they look at you," he murmurs.

Just like that, my nerves settle. I smile at him, squeezing his hand, and we walk on stage—together.

# Chapter Forty-Four

## Josh

"Hey everybody," I say into the microphone.

The crowd goes wild. I laugh, scanning the audience, waiting for them to quiet. Mark, Chip, and Gary are in the reserved seats in the front row. And next to them...my parents, who shocked the hell out of me when they called me this morning to say they are in town. Behind them are all the guys from the old neighborhood and their wives. Sophie is sitting down in front on a blanket in the grass, holding up a cellphone, no doubt facetiming Frank.

The crowd stretches before us like a patchwork quilt of people spread out on folding chairs, lawn chairs, and beach blankets. It's not a sold-out tour stop under stadium lights, but I've played enough shows to know, this is better—this is home. It's the kind of crowd I grew up playing for, where people show up early, with coolers, some people know every word, some just wander up to see what's going on. Some may have seen us on TikTok, some may have seen me open for someone bigger. But tonight, I'm back. This is our town and they're here for us, for Cara.

But it's my first time back on stage in a while, Melanie's first time—maybe ever. It's not just a show—it's *our* shot. To show the world what she and I are capable of together. For the first time in a long time, I'm not nervous. I'm proud of what they're about to hear. Melanie sits down next to me on her stool, but I remain standing.

"Thank you all for being here," I murmur into the mic. "If you don't know me, my name is Josh." A few wolf whistles erupt through the crowd. A husky laugh escapes me. "Many of you probably know this already, but twenty-five years ago, my sister Cara was killed in a car crash. She was just entering her senior year of high school, and she was going to be the captain of the girls' soccer team." I pause, letting that sink in. "I know when someone dies, everyone says they lit up a room, that everyone loved them. But Cara really *did* light up the room. She made everyone feel like they were her best friend."

A hush follows, a ripple of "awws" through the crowd that people make when their chests tighten a little. Like the sound of their hearts quietly cracking open. I glance at my mom, already holding a tissue to her nose.

"But this beautiful woman," I say, gesturing to Melanie, "she was *actually* Cara's best friend. And then she became mine."

Another chorus of "aww" and I'm pretty sure I see Melanie's cheeks flush.

"Melanie and I started playing music together when we were sixteen and seventeen, and we fell in love. That kind of first love that makes you think you're invincible, nothing can touch you, and all that matters is each other. Well, we wrote a song about that, and it's called 'Every Song.' We're going to sing it for you now."

The crowd erupts and I grin into the mic, glancing over at my girl. "Take it away, baby."

The crowd quiets. People lean in, nudging each other, eyes glued to the stage. Some of them take out their phones to record, like it's something they want to remember.

And then Melanie's voice fills the air.

Just the first few notes, hanging in the warm summer air. The sound is pure and clear, but her voice has a tremble in it too, like she's holding back.

Goose bumps rise on my arms as my fingers find the chords. Performing publicly may be unnerving to her, but she glows as if she belongs here. She looks at me as she sings the first verse of our song, and the rest of the world falls away.

I sing the song like I always have, watching couples holding hands, my mom in the front row wiping her eyes, and a little girl in a sundress twirling around. I watch them, watching her.

But none of them see what I see.

I see the girl I fell in love with at sixteen, wearing my hoodie, playing guitar on the front porch with nothing but a flashlight to see. I see the strength it took her to get back here. The fear and sadness she had to push through to get to this moment. The way she almost quit, but didn't.

Our voices meld together on the second verse like they were never meant to stand alone. We alternate verses, harmonizing on the chorus, seamless and strong, picking up where the other leaves off. The crowd is silent, reverent even, waiting for the last note to fall.

I strum the final chord, giving the last line to Mel, and she sings it softly:

*"But our love lives on in every song."*

The moment the last note fades, the crowd goes wild.

Cheers roll across the lawn like a wave, loud and joyful. Someone lets out a long whistle. Phones rise up and the applause is deafening. I glance at Melanie and her eyes are lit with something I've never seen in her before.

Belief.

She looks at me for just a beat, a grin plastered across her gorgeous face.

*You did it,* I mouth at her.

And we keep going.

We roll through the rest of the set list with ease, like we've been doing this every night for years. The crowd knows most of the lyrics and sings along—in it with us fully. That gives us momentum. Mark never takes his eyes off us, a good sign for sure.

As the final song fades out, we get a standing ovation. People shout our names, waving their hands in the air. Somewhere in the chaos, I glimpse Sophie, tears in her eyes, holding up the phone so Frank can watch.

"Thank you, everyone," Melanie murmurs into the mic.

I marvel at how comfortable she is after eight songs.

"Thank you all. Cara would have loved this," I add, stepping back and holding my hand out to Melanie.

I squeeze her hand as we take our bow, the crowd still roaring, and all I can think is *why did I ever want to be a solo act?* This moment right here with her? It's everything.

❧

It takes forever to leave the park. As soon as we step off stage, the world shifts—we're flooded with hugs, photos, and congratulations from people we didn't even know were watching.

But then I see them. My parents.

They make a beeline for us and for a moment, I brace myself. It's been so long since we were close but when my mom's arms wrap around me, it feels as if no time has passed at all.

"I'm so proud of you, Joshy," my mother says, her voice thick with emotion as she presses her cheek into my shirt. The nickname makes something sharp and sweet twist in my chest.

My dad claps me on the back. "Me too, kid."

I laugh, blinking back the heat behind my eyes. "Thanks, guys. That means a lot."

"Hi, you two." Melanie creeps up behind me, giving a shy wave, almost like she's unsure if she fits in this part of my life.

My mom doesn't hesitate. She pulls her into a hug so tight it makes her squeak. "Oh, Melanie. We've missed you both so much."

"Where are you guys staying?" I ask.

They whirl around, practically in sync and wave at her across the lawn. "With Ellie," they chorus together.

Melanie lets out a real laugh, open and bright. "I'd expect nothing less."

"Let's get dinner tomorrow?" I say, meaning it in a way I haven't in so long.

"Call us in the morning," my dad says, pulling me in for a hug. It feels good. Like a piece that was missing all these years has finally been found.

We say our goodbyes, and I turn back to help with the breakdown. People are still milling about, buzzing with the afterglow of a great show. Every few minutes someone is brave enough to ask for a selfie or an autograph.

I'm signing a poster for a teenage girl while Melanie takes apart the mic stand.

"Melanie, can I have yours too?" the girl asks.

Melanie can't hide the shock that crosses her features. "Me?" she squeaks.

"Of course," the girl says, nodding eagerly.

"Are you sure?"

"Of course!" the girl says again. "I want to say I met you before you were a huge star."

A blush creeps into Melanie's cheeks, caught somewhere between disbelief and awe. She signs with a shaky hand, and the girl skips off like she just met Taylor Swift herself. I watch as Melanie's eyes follow her—as if she still can't believe this is happening.

We're interrupted again by a throat clearing.

Mark. And with him is Gary, and a new guy in a crisp button-down and expensive-looking boots.

They'd been off to the side talking in hushed tones while Melanie and I busied ourselves breaking down the set and battling interruptions. Now it's here. The moment of truth.

"We *need* to talk," Mark says, grinning bigger than I've ever seen.

"Josh, Melanie—fabulous set," Gary agrees.

"I don't know that you've ever met Chip Michaels. He's our new VP of Artists & Repertoire. Chip, meet Josh Cote and Melanie Glick."

I hold out my hand to Chip and give him a firm shake. Melanie does the same.

"Josh, Melanie, it's a pleasure." Chip's smile is friendly but assessing. He's sizing us up. I know the type.

"Thank you all for being here," I say. "Really."

Mark says, draping an arm around my shoulder. "Let's cut right to the chase. We'd like to sit down and talk about a future at SoundShift. For *both* of you."

Melanie stiffens beside me. "I...um, need to get back to my dad," Melanie says, voice careful.

I place my hand on her lower back, glancing at her.

"Go," I say quietly. "I'll stay. I'll fill you in later."

Melanie hesitates for just a second, then nods, sucking in a breath. "Yeah, okay."

"We'll sit down and talk in detail tomorrow sometime if you're on board," Mark says, patting Melanie's shoulder.

"Thank you," she says sincerely. "I'm sorry to duck out."

"You're fine," Gary says. "We'll see you soon."

I kiss her softly on the lips before she goes, hoping it sends a *we've got this* message. "I'll see you at home," I whisper.

When she's gone, Gary clears his throat. "Josh, Mark and Chip have an offer—for both of you."

"Why don't we find someplace to get something to eat?" Chip suggests. "Talk real numbers."

❧

It's after midnight when I slip into bed next to Melanie. At first, I think she's asleep, but when I slip my arm around her, she shifts, molding into me.

"I'm so proud of you," I whisper, pressing a kiss to the top of her head.

She yawns. "What did they say?"

I grin, wide and uncontrollable. "They want us. Three albums. Full promo. A tour if we want to."

Melanie turns over, facing me, cupping my jaw. She kisses me slowly, tired, but full of something that feels like wonder. "That's incredible."

I hesitate, the last part caught in my throat.

"We'll have to..." I stop and swallow. I know the next thing I say will make or break the decision for us. "They want us to move to Nashville."

Melanie stares at me for a beat and when she speaks, her voice is soft and faraway.

"Oh."

# Chapter Forty-Five

## Melanie

I toss and turn all night. I don't think Josh is sleeping much either, but I don't say a word. Only one thing runs through my mind. Nashville. My dream that I'd tucked away, far in the back of my heart and mind when I lost everything all those years ago. And now, I'm here, lying next to Josh, the world at my fingertips, and I'm petrified.

What about my dad?

I suppose I didn't really think it would come to this. I had no idea the concert would turn out the way it did. I had no idea people would show *up* the way they did. It probably has everything to do with the TikTok video. But nonetheless, the concert was probably the best night of my life. For the first time, maybe ever, I feel like I know where I belong.

Only now that it's close enough for me to reach out and grab, I don't know if I can. I slip out of bed, just after dawn.

Josh reaches for me in his sleep. "Where are you going?" he grumbles.

"Just for a walk," I whisper. "Go back to sleep."

He's snoring again a moment later. I watch him from the doorway; his face is peaceful and boyish in sleep. Memories of his words last night echo in my mind: *they want us to move to Nashville.*

I pull on a hoodie and carry my shoes to the front door, being careful not to wake him. The morning air is cool, everything slicked with dew, still touched by night. Everything is quiet, as if the town is holding its breath before the day begins. I walk aimlessly, no destination in mind.

Cape May is different at this hour. No noise, no tourists. Just the soft call of a seagull in the distance. I pass by the bakery on Washington Street, still dark, but with the smell of bread rising. I pass by the coffee shop, open for the earliest risers. A bike leans against the side of The Ugly Mug, the place itself looking like it's sleeping off the busy Saturday night.

Each familiar corner tugs at my heart.

This town raised me as much as my own parents. It's the place where I learned to stand on my own two feet amidst heartache and loss. It's the town where my childhood friends became family. How am I supposed to leave it all behind?

*You can. And you will. If it comes to that.* My dad's words repeat in my brain like a highlight reel.

The thought of actually doing it fills me with a feeling of panic and possibility.

I walk past my old home, now a vacation rental. Sadness tugs at me, so I don't linger. I walk up to Rotary Park, remembering all the times Josh and I played music there after school. Remembering how that music came alive again last night.

I've spent so much of my life doing the expected, because it felt safe and familiar. Too afraid to chase what I really wanted. But last night, his hand in mine, or that stage. It was everything. I plop onto a cold bench just inside the park's entrance, my eyes glued to the now-empty stage that held so much light and life only twelve hours ago. Promise.

I think about my dad, building something new with Joan, despite his age and his health concerns. I think about Sophie's words to me yesterday: *it's your turn, Mel.*

I take a breath, the kind that reaches all the way to the top of your ribs, and I let it out slowly.

Maybe Nashville isn't goodbye. Maybe it's the start of

something new.

I sit on that park bench for what feels like hours before I rise, my joints stiff, and head toward home. I stop at Coffee Tyme and pick up two iced lattes and a couple of muffins before heading back toward my apartment. I find Josh, sitting on the couch, elbows to his knees, looking over some papers—a contract, no doubt.

He looks up the second he hears the door, eyes flicking toward me like he's trying to read my thoughts.

"I thought maybe you got spooked," he says, a half-laugh caught in his throat. "Took off."

I sigh, avoiding his eyes for a moment before sitting down. "I just went for a walk. Needed some air." I chew the inside of my cheek. "I was thinking of going down to our beach, having a picnic before it gets too hot." I watch him closely. "Will you come with me?"

A slow, relieved smile spreads across Josh's face. "I'd love to."

Fifteen minutes later, Josh pulls his truck into the crushed seashell parking lot and puts it in park. We've been quiet—pensive—the whole ride over. Like we've both got things we want to say and are figuring out how to say them.

Josh grabs his coffee and then reaches into the cab behind him for a flannel blanket. I carry the muffins and my own coffee, and we walk slowly up the path to the spot that's always felt like ours.

The beach is nearly empty, the morning sun glinting off the water. It smells of fresh salt air. Josh spreads out the blanket and we sit, kicking off our flip-flops. I curl my toes through the cool sand, grounding myself. We sit for a long moment, letting the wind move through us. We watch the waves lapping at the shore, an egret diving for its breakfast.

Then we both speak at once.

"Listen," Josh starts.

"I think we should—"

Josh lets out a husky laugh, running a hand through his hair. I smile sheepishly, waiting for him to go first.

He exhales. "I was just going to say, if this isn't what you want, we don't have to do it. I can call Gary. We can tell them no."

The way he looks at me is steady and sure. Like he'd give it all up for me in an instant.

"But this is your dream," I whisper, feeling my eyes fill with tears. "You've worked so hard to get here."

He shakes his head. "It *was* my dream. But dreams can change." Josh tips my face toward his, forcing me to meet his gaze. "You're my dream now, Mel. And if you're not in it, I don't want it."

My chest tightens then, and for a moment I can't speak. The wind rustles through my hair, and I watch the way his gaze lingers on my face, open and patient.

I bite back the smile threatening to give me away. "I want to go," I say finally.

Josh's lips twitch. "You... You want to go?"

I nod. "To Nashville. With you."

He stills. For a long breath, he just looks at me, like he's memorizing this exact moment. Finally, his palm finds my cheek, fingers tangling through my windblown hair.

"You want to *move* to Nashville with me?" he repeats, his voice raspy.

His lips hover over mine.

"Uh-huh," I breathe.

He kisses me deeply then, letting his hands tangle in my hair like he never wants to let go. His mouth is warm, and our breaths mingle as his tongue dances over mine. It's slow and savory, filled with relief. Filled with a promise of the future.

He pulls back, his forehead pressing to mine, and sucks in a deep breath. Then he pulls back to look at me, studying me, tracing his fingers along my jaw, around my lower lip.

"Are you sure this is what you want?" he asks, his voice low and cautious.

I nod, placing my hand over his beating heart. "I'd go anywhere with you," I whisper. "You feel like home."

The smile that blooms across his face then is one I've never seen—so full of hope it steals my breath away. It says, *we found our way home.*

"Okay," he says, his voice hoarse. He pulls me close again and then we're the only people in the world. I lean into his embrace, listening to the crashing of the waves, and inhaling the salty sea air.

And I savor it. All of it.

"Okay."

## THEN

"Okay, fine." I huffed, folding my arms across my chest. "*Only* if Josh wants to."

"Only if Josh wants to what?" Josh asked, poking his head out the back door.

I sighed, rolling my eyes, working hard to hide my feelings for Josh from his sister.

"Cara wants to hear what we've been working on every day," I said through clenched teeth.

Josh laughed, his eyes lit up. The truth is, the song had been perfected a long time ago. Josh and I had been figuring out everything else...like which parts of each other's bodies drove each other crazy. But Cara couldn't know that. Our relationship was still a secret, and I intended to keep it that way for as long as possible.

"Let me get my guitar," he said, disappearing inside.

It was one of those late summer evenings where the sun lingered too long and everyone was desperate for nightfall just to cool things off.

Cara sat crossed-legged on the porch swing, sipping lemonade and swatting mosquitoes, completely unaware that the song she was about to hear wasn't just any song. It was *our* song.

I waited as Josh fiddled with his guitar, tuning it. I watched him carefully, desperately wanting to tell him that my period was late and that I was so unbelievably in love with him but also terrified.

"This one is new," he said, looking up. "Still rough."

Cara laughed, rolling her eyes. "You two always say that."

I moved next to him on the steps, our knees almost touching. But I didn't dare look at him as he strummed the first notes. I kept my voice steady and then he joined in, his harmony wrapping around mine like it always did. But we still didn't make eye contact because every word of this song was a confession we couldn't give.

Cara swayed, captivated by every line. When the song ended, she gaped at us. "That was like...a love song."

My face heated and a wave of nausea surged through me.

Josh coughed. "Yeah. It was."

"It's like you lived it," Cara said, clutching her glass of lemonade.

"It's just a song," I said tersely, desperate to hide my feelings for Josh.

Cara eyed me curiously, but she grinned. "Okay, okay. But how cool would it be if you two really did make it to Nashville one day? You'd be stars, I just know it. Your voices belong together."

I smirked. "Okay, Cara."

"Whatever. Thanks for playing it." She hopped off the swing. "I'm going to go call Liam."

She didn't wait for a reply, just bounded inside, leaving Josh and me feeling all the things we didn't dare say out loud.

"I'd do it, you know?" Josh murmured, brushing his knee against mine.

"Do what?" I frowned.

"Go to Nashville. With you. I bet we'd make it." He grinned, something like hope dancing in his eyes.

I smiled faintly. "Maybe someday."

# Chapter Forty-Six

## Josh

### THIRTEEN MONTHS LATER

I don't know too many people who get to say they have everything they ever wanted in life, but I really think I do. It's a cool autumn morning and I am standing on the back deck of my custom log cabin in Franklin, Tennessee that Melanie and I share. The sun is rising over the rolling hills, casting shades of pink and yellow on the Harpeth River. I've taken to waking up earlier these days. I wake up, go for a long run, lift some weight in our home gym, and then sip my coffee out here in the solace of nature. Most days, Melanie joins me, but today she's sleeping in.

One of Mel's stipulations about moving to Tennessee was that she needed to be near a body of water. She couldn't feel landlocked. I understood that so I searched high and low for the perfect riverside home for us. When I didn't find it, I had it built. It's our dream house, but we still plan to spend our summers in Cape May.

I hear the door open and a bark sounds behind me as our black lab, Duke, bolts past Melanie. I whirl around and take her in. Melanie is always stunning, but the sight of her fresh out of bed in the morning, sleepy eyes and mussed up hair—that's my favorite. She cradles a mug of hot coffee and steps beside me.

"Big day," she murmurs, glancing sideways at me.

"Yep." I sip my coffee and let out a hiss from the heat of it.

"You ready?"

I look sideways at her, my lips quirking upward. "Are you?"

"I'm ready for any adventure I get to have with you."

"Me too." I set my mug on the railing and pull her close. "Thanks for always going along with my whims."

"I wouldn't do it for anyone else," Melanie says, a wry smile crossing her beautiful lips.

Two hours later, we're dressed and out the door, headed down to East Nashville, to an area called The Gulch for a ribbon-cutting ceremony. Not long after Mel and I started working with SoundShift, we decided that touring the country playing sold out shows wasn't for us. We negotiated our contract to be three albums and songwriting for other artists working with SoundShift Records. We lived the dream for a year, writing music all day, popping into the studio to record, falling in love with the music and each other all over again.

But something was still missing for me and when I did some soul searching, I remembered how it felt to help that kid on the beach last Fourth of July. So, I asked Mel if she'd be up for a new adventure. She said yes, and Common Chord Music School was born.

Melanie and I started Common Chord because we both know what it's like to have music shape your life. For us, it has always been more than a passion. It's a path to healing. It's how we first found each other, how we got through some of the hardest things we've ever had to face, and how we eventually found our way back to each other.

The air is cool for Tennessee in October, but it feels fitting. We're early, but I knew we would be. I wanted a few moments alone here with Mel. The opportunity to soak in what we've built—what we're *building* here together. I pull my truck into the driveway in the back and suck in a breath.

I turn to her, and she meets my gaze. "Thanks for doing life with me," I murmur, tucking a hair behind her ear.

"There's no one else I'd want to do it with," she says with an easy shrug.

"Let's go inside." I swing open my door and before I've made my way to the other side, Melanie's closing her door too, waiting for me.

I unlock the back door to the studio and jar it open. It sticks and probably needs to be replaced but it's ours.

I flick on the lights and move down the hall, passing two empty soundproof music rooms. Then we're in the big open space—filled with eclectic seating, bean bag chairs, various guitars hanging on the wall, a baby grand piano in the corner, and music stands scattered about. A jam space for all. For a moment, Mel and I walk around, each marveling at what we've created here. A safe place for children to learn music, no matter their background or family income. They can come here and sing their hearts out, rock out, and discover what they're capable of.

"Wow," Melanie says, spinning around the room, a proud grin spread across her face. Her blue eyes glisten.

It's now or never.

I step closer, taking her hands and clearing my throat.

"Mel." My voice comes out serious and suddenly she's paying attention.

"Yeah..." She meets my gaze expectantly.

I lick my lips. "You doing this with me, it means everything to me. I thought just making music with you was special, but this? This is freaking incredible. I've never been happier in my life."

A gentle, unassuming smile spreads across her face. "I'm happy too."

"I know you don't love the limelight, so I wanted this moment, just for us." My heart pounds in my chest so hard, I'm sure she can hear it.

"Okay..."

"Make me even happier than I already am? Be my business partner, my band mate, *and* my wife?" I reach in my pocket for the navy-blue ring box I've been carrying around for weeks until I finally decided today was the day.

"Oh, Josh..." Melanie's voice is breathless. "Of course I'll be your wife."

Then a laugh bubbles out of her, and she pulls my face toward hers, kissing me deeply.

"Of *course*!" she says again.

I slip the oval diamond on a simple rose gold band on her ring finger. It's understated, elegant, so perfectly Mel. I must have sent Sophie a thousand photos of ring options. As soon as I sent this one, she replied with two words: That's it.

I pull Mel into a tight hug, lifting her off the ground and pressing a kiss to her mouth.

"Thank you," I murmur.

Our private celebration is interrupted by a knock on the glass window. Outside, a crowd has gathered—the mayor and councilmen, people from the chamber of commerce. And of course, everyone we know and love made the trip from Cape May. Mel and I step outside and the crowd cheers. In the sea of faces, we find Frank and Joan, Liam, Sophie, Miles, Jenna, Jack, Stephanie, Danny, and Kristen. Even Ellie and Robert, and next to them, my parents who recently decided they wanted to come home to Cape May.

"Thank you all so much for coming," I say to the small crowd.

The mayor turns and shakes my hand, then Melanie's, before addressing the crowd.

"Good morning, everyone," he says, nodding hello to the people before him. "As mayor, I get to be a witness to a lot of exciting things here in Nashville. I get to see a lot of projects come to life. But this one is special. It's more than a music school; it's a statement about the kind of city we want to be." He looks at the crowd, smiling and nodding in agreement. Then he continues.

"Josh and Melanie, you didn't just build a program, you built a bridge. Between access and opportunity, between community and creativity. You reminded us that music isn't a luxury; it's a language shared between all of us, especially our kids. Thank you for using your platform and passion to give back. Nashville is proud to call you our own."

The crowd applauds, some of our friends let out long whistles. Melanie wipes her eyes.

"Before we cut this ribbon, did either of you want to say a few words?" the mayor asks.

I step up. "I'd like to, yes. First off, I'd like to thank you all for being here, especially our friends and family who traveled quite a distance to celebrate with us. Common Chord has been a dream in the making for a while now. Music is what brought us together all those years ago, and we wanted to build a safe place for kids to walk through the door, no matter their zip code, and know they belong. And so many of you helped us with that. Thank you to all of you for believing in us and our mission, long before the sign was even up on the door. Thank you for opening your hearts to us."

I pause as the crowd applauds, looping an arm around Melanie's waist and tugging her close.

"And as long as we're talking about open hearts, there's one more thing I want to share before we cut this ribbon." I take a deep breath and plant a kiss on Melanie's head.

"You all know Melanie. She's the heart and soul of our duo, the melody to my rhythm, the reason I believe in second chances. But what most of you don't know is that just moments ago, I asked her to marry me."

I pause just as Sophie, Jenna, Steph, and Kristen let out various shrieks of excitement.

"And she said yes." I grin before pulling Melanie to me and kissing her softly. "So not only are we building a music school, we're building a beautiful life together. One filled with joy and purpose, and hopefully a whole lot of off-key beginner singing in these halls. Thank you for being part of our beginning. Let's get this party started!"

The mayor hands us the pair of jumbo scissors, and we each take a side.

"On three," I say, looking at Mel.

"One, two, three," the mayor says, slowly drawing out each number.

We snip and the red ribbon falls away. The small audience before us cheers, embracing us. There's laughter, there's tears, there's us.

And I know, life is about to begin.

# Epilogue

## *Melanie*

### SIX MONTHS LATER

The golden glow of the morning sun gleans through Common Chod's floor-to-ceiling windows, highlighting the dust motes floating in the air like little, tiny fairies. We have an open house here today where some of our students will perform for prospective students. I'm here early—too early. But I love this time of day, walking around the big empty room, marveling at everything Josh and I have built—are *still* building—together.

I flip on the lights and walk slowly down the hallway, past the new rows of student photos we have hung on the wall. Some of the kids posed like rock stars, holding instruments that are bigger than them. I pause, smiling at one of my favorite students, seven-year-old Ava. A spunky little piano prodigy. Against all my better judgment, I let her lie across the back of the baby grand for her photo. In it, she lies on her side, propped up by her elbow, in a red and white polka dot dress, grinning from ear to ear.

Now, I walk into the main room and sit at that same piano, lightly playing our newest tune, "Home Again." Josh and I co-wrote it, and we intend to perform it today for our open house guests. It's fitting since that's exactly how I feel, like I'm home.

I hear the bell chime on the front door, and I know it's him before I even look.

He strides inside, holding two coffees from the shop down the street. I turn to him, smiling, inhaling his sandalwood cologne. His hair is still wet from his shower, and his jeans are slung low on his hips. And he's looking at me like he always does, like he can't believe he gets to.

"Morning, Mrs. Cote," he says, handing me my coffee.

I roll my eyes. "That's still weird." I move to make room for him on the bench.

"You'll get used to it." He grins, sitting next to me and planting a soft kiss on my lips.

After he proposed, Josh and I decided we wanted a quiet, private wedding, so we did it at home, outside, overlooking the Harpeth River. Josh strung twinkle lights across the large deck and we said our vows at sunset in front of only our parents, Liam, and Sophie. I cried. He did too. It was perfect.

And now we're here, building something that matters for kids who may not otherwise get a chance to learn music. Some families donate what they can, others pay tuition, but every week we get to watch shy kids walk out of here standing a little bit taller. It's never been about money for us, anyway. When we're not here, we're still writing and producing music for SoundShift Records.

I take a sip of my coffee and lean my head on his shoulder. "You nervous for the open house?"

"Petrified." He laughs softly. "You?"

I nod. "A little. Excited, too."

He pats my knee, and we stay like that, sitting in the safe, comfortable silence that comes with loving someone for so long.

"Oh, I had the strangest dream last night," Josh says, after a beat. "I was holding a red-headed baby, chewing on a guitar pick."

I flick my gaze to him in surprise. "You've been dreaming about babies?"

His cheeks flush. "Maybe." He pauses, watching me for a moment. "Do you ever think about it?"

I look at my hands, fiddling with my wedding rings. "Sometimes," I admit.

"Me too. Sometimes."

We're interrupted by voices echoing coming in the front door, children arriving early for lessons, carrying tiny guitar cases, their parents trailing behind them.

Josh has taken to high-fiving every kid that walks through the door and now is no exception. He stands by the door, greeting them all as they come in, and my heart bursts for the man I love. Whether or not there is another baby in our future, I know we've got each other. And we've got all this.

I watch him from my place at the bench. I used to think leaving Cape May meant leaving everything I knew and loved behind. But sitting here in this space, filled with music and light, the laughter of children bouncing off the walls, I realize, I didn't leave any of it behind. I brought it with me. The grief, the love, the years of figuring out who I am and what I want, are all the things that have made me, me. This place, the music, and the way Josh looks at me like I've always been his. It's all ours. Whatever comes next—be it more albums, babies, quiet nights, or chaos—I know we'll be okay. Because I finally feel like I'm home again.

THE END

To listen to "Every Song" scan the QR code below.

# Acknowledgements

Two years ago (plus ten days, if you want to be specific), I sat down to write my first novel. I had always wanted to write a book, but after becoming a teacher and then ten years spent losing myself in motherhood, that dream got lost, too. I shouldn't say it got lost but it got quieter. It sat in the back of my mind, waiting for me to find it again.

Then, in early 2024, I reached a point in my life where I'd begun asking myself, "What's left of me when my children no longer need me as much?" I couldn't answer that. So, after a few weeks of soul searching, I sat down and started the Cape May Series. It began with *Changing Tides, Chasing Stars* followed that, and now here we are, closing this chapter with *Choosing You.*

Writing this series has been a journey of love, growth, and resilience—both for me and for the characters who've lived in my head for two years. When I started this series, I never imagined it would change my life in so many ways. This journey has been a whirlwind filled with late nights, early mornings, and more coffee than is probably healthy. But it's also been one of the most rewarding seasons of my life. This series began as a quiet story about healing and second chances, and it grew into something so much bigger, something I get to share with all of you.

To my incredible team at Page & Vine, my steadfast agent, Katie Monson, and all my wonderful friends in this industry, thank you. Thank you for believing in my stories and helping me to get them out in the world. You make all this possible.

To Lindsey Lara, for being up to the challenge of writing "Every Song" with me. Not only that, but performing and recording it. I never imagined my words would create a melody. I'm so grateful to the production team, Dean, Frank and James. To my father-in-law, Brian, who jumped right in when we needed to record, and everyone else who had a hand in making this beautiful song come to life. I can't wait for you all to hear it.

To my critique partner, Christine Drummond, I'm convinced that you're the reason this book needed less edits than the others! Thank you for helping me brainstorm and thank you for helping me perfect this story. I'm so grateful for your friendship and I can't wait to see what's to come.

To the booksellers, bloggers, and bookstagrammers who've shared, reviewed, and championed the Cape May Series—you helped this small coastal town find its way into the hearts of so many. To my Street Team—lovingly dubbed the Mack Pack—I am eternally grateful for each and every one of you. Kate and Jess, for all you have done to help me. You've kept me from losing my mind on more than one occasion! I don't know where I would be without your support.

To my husband and children, thank you for always putting up with me and my "book stuff." Kevin, you are the reason I'm able to write stories like this—even after seventeen years, you make me believe in the kind of love that moves mountains.

To my parents, friends, and the amazingly supportive local community I live in, I'm so grateful to you. It's a wild feeling to be out somewhere and have someone say, "You write the Cape May books, right?" I still can't believe this is my life. I'm so grateful for the love.

And to my readers—you've been the heartbeat of this series. Every message, every photo, every word of encouragement has carried me through the long days and made the work worthwhile.

Writing and publishing three books in ten months has been a wild, beautiful blur—one that stretched me, changed me, and reminded me again and again why I love telling stories. What started as a single idea about healing and second chances grew into a world that feels as real to me as the one outside my window. Cape May became a home I wasn't ready to leave, and somehow, you made it feel like yours too.

This past year has been proof that dreams rarely unfold the

way we expect, but always exactly when we're ready for them. Thank you for being part of mine.

# About the Author

Linny Mack grew up a voracious reader and writer. She spent her days of adolescence up in her room writing her own stories and cutting her characters out of the Delia's catalog. Now, Linny is a debut author of contemporary romance. When she isn't writing your next book boyfriend, she is spending time with her real-life romantic hero and their three children in New Jersey.

To learn more, visit: www.linnymack.com

PAGE
&
VINE